Rave reviews for

DICK FRANCIS AND FELIX FRANCIS

"Francis aficionados will hope that Felix chooses to carry on the family tradition on his own." —*Publishers Weekly*

"Francis knows how to control this wild run of a plot and also knows how to create a conflicted character in the midst of crisis. A stunning addition to the family line."

—*Booklist* (starred review)

"Felix Francis shows that the apple hasn't fallen far from the tree . . . The story unfolds with the suspense and insistent pace readers expect from their annual Francis fix."

—*The Washington Times*

"With wit and an expert's understanding of both horses and homicide, the Francises will keep you riveted."

—*People*

"Swiftly paced . . . excellent . . . action-packed."

—*Los Angeles Times*

"A blissfully satisfying blend of suspense, revenge, and horse-racing info in a multilayered mystery."

—*Kirkus Reviews*

"This dynamic writing team has hit the big money yet again with their latest quick-paced read."

—Bookreporter.com

"A taut crime thriller." —*Publishers Weekly*

BY FELIX FRANCIS

Dick Francis's Damage
Dick Francis's Gamble
Dick Francis's Bloodline
Dick Francis's Refusal

BY DICK FRANCIS AND FELIX FRANCIS

Dead Heat
Silks
Even Money
Crossfire

BY DICK FRANCIS

Dead Cert
Nerve
For Kicks
Odds Against
Flying Finish
Blood Sport
Forfeit
Enquiry
Rat Race
Bonecrack
Smokescreen
Slay Ride
Knockdown
High Stakes
In the Frame
Risk
Trial Run
Whip Hand
Reflex
Twice Shy
Banker
The Danger
Proof
Break In
Bolt
Hot Money
The Edge
Straight
Longshot
Comeback
Driving Force
Decider
Wild Horses
Come to Grief
To the Hilt
10 Lb. Penalty
Field of Thirteen
Second Wind
Shattered
Under Orders

NONFICTION

The Sport of Queens
(Autobiography)
A Jockey's Life: The
Biography of Lester Piggott

DICK FRANCIS'S

DAMAGE

FELIX FRANCIS

BERKLEY BOOKS
NEW YORK

BERKLEY
An imprint of Penguin Random House LLC
375 Hudson Street, New York, New York 10014

DICK FRANCIS'S DAMAGE

A Berkley Book / published by arrangement with the author

ISBN: 978-0-425-27624-2

PUBLISHING HISTORY
G. P. Putnam's Sons hardcover edition / October 2014
Berkley premium edition / July 2015

PRINTED IN THE UNITED STATES OF AMERICA

10 9 8 7 6 5 4 3 2 1

Cover photo: *Jockeys Riding Horses* © John Kelly / Getty Images Sport / Getty Images.
Cover design by Andrea Ho.

With my special thanks to
Brian Greenan,
former member of
Metropolitan Police Special Operations,
SO11—Criminal Intelligence Branch

And, as always, to
Debbie

1

"I've had the test results and the news isn't good."

I couldn't get the words out of my head.

I was sitting in the shadows at the back of a race-program kiosk near the north entrance to Cheltenham racetrack, scanning the faces of the crowd as they flooded through the turnstiles.

I was looking out for any one of the fifty or so individuals who were banned from British racetracks, but my mind kept drifting back to the telephone conversation I'd had that morning with my sister.

"I've had the test results and the news isn't good."

"In what way?" I asked with rising dread.

"It's cancer," she said quietly.

I'd feared so but had hoped desperately that I was wrong.

I waited silently. She'd go on if she wanted to.

"It's all a bit of a bugger." She sighed audibly down the line. "I've got to have surgery next Monday and then some chemo."

"What's the surgery for?"

"To remove my gallbladder. That's where the cancer is."

"Can you live without it?"

She laughed. "The gallbladder or the cancer?"

"Both."

"I hope so." The laughter evaporated from her voice. "Time will tell. Things don't appear very rosy at the moment. I may have only a few months left."

Oh God, I thought. What does one do when given that scenario? Do you try to carry on as normal or attempt to cram as much into the remaining time as possible? In reality, I suspected that treatment and feeling ill would take over everything. Not very rosy indeed.

I realized that I hadn't been paying attention to the flow of humanity passing by in front of me.

Concentrate, I said to myself, and went back to studying faces.

It was Champion Hurdle Day, the first of the annual Cheltenham Steeplechasing Festival, and, in spite of the inclement weather, a crowd of over fifty thousand was expected to cram into the Gloucestershire racetrack. Everyone had an umbrella or a rain hat of some kind—ideal conditions for the unwelcome few to hide among the masses.

I knew by sight all those who had racetrack-banning orders, but I was on the lookout for one particular individual that our intelligence branch had suggested might come to Cheltenham that day.

A large man walked up to the kiosk to buy a race program, standing there while he hunted for change in his pockets. I shifted my position to see past him, looking over the head of the program seller who sat directly in front of me.

It was a role I was used to.

My name is Jeff Hinkley and I was an investigator for the British Horseracing Authority. Hence, I spent much of my time half hidden, scanning faces, watching out for those who had no place in racing. Not that being banned from entering racetracks ever stopped them trying.

Cancer of the gallbladder.

How could Faye, my big sister, have cancer of the gallbladder?

Faye was forty-two, twelve years my senior, and she had acted like a mother to me after our real mom had died when I was eight.

I wondered if cancer was hereditary.

Our mom had died of it but I didn't know where the cancer had been in her body. It was something that wasn't talked about either before or after her death.

I spotted a face in the crowd.

Nick Ledder, an ex-jock, banned from all racetracks for three years for attempting to bribe another young jockey to lose. I watched as he scanned his ticket and hurried through the turnstile with his coat collar turned up against the icy wind and a tweed cap pulled down over his forehead. It was his eyes that I spotted. It was always the eyes.

But his was not the face I was really looking for.

Nick Ledder was a small-time crook of limited intelligence who hadn't been able to resist taking a handful of readies to try to fix a race and he had paid a heavy price for his folly. He was hopeful of getting his riding license back early, but he'd hardly endear himself to the stewards by sneaking into Cheltenham while he was still banned.

I let him go by, I could always find him later, and went back to scanning other faces.

I thought about gallbladders. What did they do if you could live without one?

"Jeff, are you there?" said a voice in my earpiece.

"Here, Nigel," I replied via the microphone I wore on my left wrist.

"Any sign?"

"No," I said. "Nick Ledder's here. I saw him. I'll deal with him later."

"Bloody fool."

"How about you?"

"Nothing yet."

Nigel Green was a colleague of mine in the BHA Integrity Service. He was watching the south entrance. Two other BHA staff were covering the remaining ways in, but Nigel and I reckoned that our target would most likely use either the north or south entrance where the crowds were bigger—that is, if he came at all.

I continued to study faces and tried to keep my mind

off gallbladders and chemotherapy. How could she have cancer?

My task would have been easier if I had known none of the people funneling through the turnstiles. Then I would just have had to look for someone familiar. As it was, I knew about a quarter of those passing in front of me: owners, trainers, jockeys, as well as other regular racegoers that I had seen many times before. One of the reasons I had a job with the Integrity Service was because I had an uncanny knack of remembering faces and of putting names to them.

I watched as Duncan Johnson, a top steeplechase trainer, made his way into the racetrack followed closely, and rather indiscreetly, by a young woman twenty years his junior with whom he was currently having an affair. Mrs. Johnson, meanwhile, was nowhere to be seen. She would probably be at home in Lambourn waiting expectantly for James Sutton, a young groom from the village, who would come and spend the afternoon in bed with her, enjoying the racing on Channel 4 and other things, just as they did on most Saturdays.

It was amazing what one could discover simply by frequenting the Lambourn pubs and keeping one's eyes and ears open. Snooping was a major part of my job, but I'd learned to be discreet and inconspicuous, asking very few questions myself whilst encouraging others to ask for me.

Duncan Johnson drifted away out of my sight with his high-heeled concubine clicking away on the tarmac five paces behind him, fooling nobody.

What sort of gall did a gallbladder store?

I hadn't had time to search on the Internet as Faye had called me just as I was leaving my hotel for the racetrack. I'd look it up later.

The human swarm was beginning to thin out as the first race approached, most people having arrived early to grab a bite and a beer before the start of proceedings, with time to make their selections and place their bets. Those held up in the race-day traffic now hurried through the turnstiles, making a beeline for the betting ring and the grandstand.

"They're off!" The public address announced the start of the first race of the Festival, greeted as always with a huge roar from the excited crowd.

Perhaps the cancer has been caught early.

I knew Faye had been for tests after having pains in her abdomen over Christmas, but she'd assumed it was kidney stones, something she'd had once before.

What had she said that morning? *I may have only a few months left.* But Faye always tended to look on the darker side of life.

As she had also said, time would tell.

My mind was drifting again and I almost missed him.

Just as the race was coming towards an exhilarating finale with the crowd cheering, the target came through the end turnstile in a rush, hurrying on as if he wanted to catch the finish, a red scarf wound around his neck and mouth and with a battered and damp trilby pulled down hard over his ears. Again, it was the eyes that gave him away.

"Bingo," I said into my microphone. "He's here. Following now."

I slipped out of the race-program kiosk and scurried along behind him, keeping about ten yards back.

He went past the shops of the tented village then turned right towards the concourse between the parade ring and the grandstand. There was purpose in his progress as if he had a specific agenda rather than merely wandering around. Perhaps, as we suspected, he was on his way to meet someone. But why here when it would be safer to do so elsewhere in private?

Suddenly he stopped completely and turned around to face me.

Bugger.

I went past him without breaking step and without a glance in his direction, instead looking down at the iPhone in my hand.

I knew he wouldn't know me.

I'd hardly recognized myself that morning as I looked in the hotel bathroom mirror. I was constantly being ribbed by my colleagues, but I believed that I was most effective if none of those I was pursuing knew what I really looked like. Hence, I used disguises, frequently changing the color of my own curls, or using wigs and various degrees of facial hair, glued in place with a latex-based adhesive.

A good disguise was all about distracting people's attention away from the eyes. Give them something else to stare at and they might remember that feature but would not recognize the man beneath.

On that particular day I sported a well-trimmed goatee with collar-length dark hair under a brown woolen beanie, as well as a faded green anorak over a gray shirt and navy sweater, plus blue chinos. I purposely didn't want to look like one of the "establishment," but equally I needed to blend into the background.

I went on twenty strides and then stopped, half turning back. I put my cell to my ear as if making a call and, using my thumb on the touchscreen, I silently took two photos back towards the target.

He was moving again and I stood quite still, talking to no one on my phone, as he walked right past me. I waited for a moment, letting him get ten or fifteen yards away, before following him up past the bookshop and the confectionary kiosk and then on towards the Centaur Centre and the Tattersall end of the grandstand.

We were moving against the human traffic that was spilling out of the grandstand towards the winners' enclosure now that the race was over.

The target pressed on into the stream, forcing his way through, as I struggled to keep up behind him.

I almost lost him altogether as a group of six well-built and inebriated punters insisted on walking in line abreast, jostling me to and fro with guffaws as I tried to get past.

"What's the 'urry, mate?" said one as he pushed me back. "Got a date, 'ave you?"

He laughed enthusiastically at his own weak joke and took another swig from his beer while I ducked under his raised arm. How could anyone, I wondered, be drunk after only the first race?

I scanned the mass of heads in front of me, searching for a battered trilby.

Where had he gone?

I rushed forward in desperation and almost ran straight into the back of the target as he himself was slowed by the congestion in the pinch point beneath the Hall of Fame.

Calm down, I told myself.

"Have you still got him, Jeff?" Nigel asked into my ear.

"Yes," I said quietly into my left sleeve.

"Need any help?"

"Yes," I said.

"Where?"

"Under the Hall of Fame bridge."

"On my way," Nigel replied.

The target was on the move again, ducking into one of the bars beneath the grandstand.

"Going into the Winged Ox bar," I said into my sleeve.

"OK," came the reply. "One minute away."

The bar was packed with long queues at every counter, but the target was clearly not here to get a drink. Instead, he weaved his way right through the throng and out onto the now almost empty viewing steps beyond.

I'd been close to him as he crossed the teeming bar, but now I hung back so as not to alert him to my presence.

I watched as he stood for a moment, moving his head from side to side as if searching for something, before setting off again down the steps.

What was he doing here? I asked myself again. Surely he must know that meeting someone at a racetrack was likely to provoke a reaction from the racing authorities.

I went out onto the viewing steps and looked down.

The target moved swiftly towards where the lines of bookmakers were sheltering from the rain under their multicolored and name-branded umbrellas.

Had he come to speak to a bookmaker?

Nigel Green joined me.

"That's our man," I said, pointing, "with the red scarf."

The target was about twenty yards away and, as we watched, he took his right hand out of his coat pocket. His hand was not empty.

"Knife! Knife!" I shouted loudly, rushing down the steps.

My shouts were swept away by the wind and there was nothing I could do but watch as the target went straight up to one of the bookmakers and slashed at his throat. There was no warning, no words at all, just a clean swipe of the blade across the bookie's unprotected skin, which turned instantly from pink to bright red.

It had occurred so fast that even those standing close by seemed not to realize what had happened until the bookmaker in question toppled face-first onto the wet tarmac, blood gushing from the wound in his neck like a scarlet fountain.

Meanwhile, the target moved away, walking fast along the line of bookmakers, dodging other racegoers, some of whom were running towards the spot behind him where a woman had begun screaming loudly.

I went on following the target while Nigel went to tend to the victim.

So that was why he'd come. Not to meet or to talk but to kill.

I followed him along to the end of the grandstand, where the food stalls were doing brisk business. He turned right and started up the slope towards the south exit. I hurried after him, the need for stealth now ended.

He glanced back over his shoulder, noticed me pushing my way through the hamburger queue, and began to run.

I ran after him, towards the entrance, where late arrivals were still streaming through the turnstiles.

The official at the exit gate alongside the turnstiles wouldn't let the target out. He kept asking for his ticket so it could be scanned for reentry.

I was by now just a few feet away. The target looked up and saw me watching him.

He panicked and reached into his coat pocket for the knife, its blade still showing red.

"Get back," he shouted, waving the knife in front of him. "Get back, all of you."

I stepped back a pace or two while others moved much farther away.

"Give it up," I said to him. "There's no escape."

He looked around with wide eyes and grabbed hold of the gateman, who had been cornered next to his gate.

"Open the gate," the target ordered, ignoring the two large policemen in bright yellow jackets who had appeared on its far side, one of whom was talking urgently into his radio. "Open the bloody gate!" He was desperate.

The gateman tried to comply, but in his haste and nervousness he couldn't get the latch to open.

"Give yourself up," I shouted, but the target simply waved his knife more vigorously, slashing it towards me.

I retreated a few more steps.

More police arrived and a standoff ensued, with the target holding the unfortunate gateman in his left hand, with the knife in his right.

"Open the gate or I'll kill him." The knife was close to the gateman's neck.

"Let him go and then we'll open the gate," shouted one of the policemen on the far side.

"No," yelled the target in escalating distress. "Open the gate first."

The impasse continued and was finally broken only when one of the newly arrived police officers stepped forward and shot him with a Taser stun gun.

The target instantly dropped to the ground, his body writhing around uncontrollably from the multithousand-volt electric shocks delivered by the Taser. Two more policemen came forward, carefully removing the knife before bending the target's arms behind his back and applying a pair of sturdy handcuffs to his wrists.

Satisfied, they stood up, leaving the target lying face-down on the cold, wet tarmac.

"Who is he?" one of them asked me.

"Matthew Unwin," I said. "He's a banned ex-racehorse trainer."

"Banned?" he said. "Banned from what?"

"All racetracks and racing stables."

"So what's he doing here, then?" the policeman asked.

Murdering a bookmaker.

2

You're a pair of complete idiots."

Nigel and I were sitting on a bed in our hotel getting a roasting from our immediate boss, Paul Maldini, head of operations at the BHA Integrity Service.

"You have Unwin under close surveillance and yet you allow him to just walk up and murder someone in broad daylight while you two stand by and watch!" Paul's voice went up in both tone and volume, and he waved his arms around in the manner of his Italian ancestors.

Nigel and I knew better than to interrupt.

It would not have been helpful to point out that neither of us was actually standing still when Matthew Unwin had sliced right through the jugular vein of the hapless bookmaker, Jordan Furness. Or that it happened so fast that we couldn't have stopped it even if we'd been standing right next to him. Or that it was only due to my continuing to follow Unwin after the event that he had been so rapidly detained by the police.

Nigel and I both knew that Paul needed to "blow his top," as he did occasionally when operations did not pan out as planned.

"And whose stupid idea was it not to apprehend him at the racetrack entrance when he arrived?"

Nigel and I looked at each other. As far as we could remember, it had been Paul himself who had ultimately given the go-ahead to allow Unwin access to the racetrack so that we could see who he was there to meet. But now was clearly not the time nor the place to point that out.

And who was to say he wouldn't then have used his knife on us?

As Paul Maldini droned on above my head, I thought back to the previous day. I had spent much of the afternoon and evening with Detective Sergeant Galley of Gloucestershire Police, going over again and again every detail of Matthew Unwin's brief appearance at the racetrack.

In particular, he had wanted to know why Nigel and I had thought Unwin would be there.

"One of our intelligence analysts received a tip-off from a CHIS."

"A CHIS?"

"Covert human intelligence source."

"And who exactly was this CHIS?"

"I'm sorry, I don't have that information." I was sure he hadn't believed me even though I'd been telling him the truth.

However, I did know that the source was considered to be very reliable.

All intelligence was graded as to the nature of the informant, from A to D, and the quality of the information, from 1 to 5. Something rated as A1 was pretty much considered as a fact, while anything below C3 was ignored completely as merely malicious rumor and gossip. B2 was fairly average, but, in this case, the analyst had given the info an A2 rating. Well worth acting on.

"Mr. Hinkley, can you tell me why Mr. Unwin was banned from Cheltenham racetrack?" the DS had asked.

"From all racetracks, not just Cheltenham. In January he was banned for eight years from all licensed racing premises."

"Why?"

"He used to be a racehorse trainer and horses in his stable were found to have been given banned substances. They'd been doped."

"Eight years seems rather harsh."

"Not really. He could have been banned for up to twenty-five. Many in racing thought he'd got off rather lightly."

"It won't make much difference now," the policeman had said. "He'll be in prison for far more than eight years anyway after today's little performance. Have you any idea why he would attack Mr. Furness?"

"None at all," I'd said, "but I do know it was a deliberate choice. I watched as he searched with his eyes for the right man."

Paul Maldini moaned on for another half an hour about our incompetence, but I wasn't really listening. I'd heard it before and knew that he'd calm down in a day or two. Most of the time he really was pretty good at his job, although, in my opinion, he needed to learn to control his rages.

But at least he didn't fire us.

Instead, he sent Nigel and me back to the racetrack for the second day of the Festival.

ALL THE TALK was about the murder of the bookmaker, but it was more because of the delay it caused to racing and the postponement of the last race due to failing light rather than any altruistic concerns for the man himself.

"I'm glad it wasn't today," I overheard one man say, laughing. "Their loss is our gain." The postponed race had been rescheduled to be run before the official first race of day two.

Sympathy for the murdered bookmaker was in short supply in spite of the violent manner of his passing.

"He probably deserved it," said a tweed-suited woman in the Arkle Bar, who received nodding agreement from those around her.

There was less talk but certainly more compassion for Matthew Unwin, the perpetrator of the crime.

"Obviously, driven to it, poor man," said one of the stallholders in the tented village.

"Must have been desperate," agreed his customer, pursing her lips and shaking her head.

I drifted around the enclosures, listening and watching. I was dressed and appeared as myself, not least because, as a result of Paul Maldini's diatribe, I hadn't had enough time to "make up."

I had an official right of entry to everywhere on each of the fifty-eight currently operated British racetracks including, if I'd wanted, the jockeys' changing rooms and the Royal Boxes. However, rather than putting on my *BHA Access All Areas* lanyard, which made me stand out as "an authority," I usually arranged to wear a cardboard *Owner* badge that let me wander wherever I wanted in anonymity. On the rare occasions I had been asked which horse I owned I simply said that I was a member of a syndicate, an answer guaranteed to cause the inquisitor to instantly lose interest.

I watched the rescheduled race from the stand reserved for owners and trainers, my ears tuned for any tidbits of gossip.

"Did you hear about Peter and Marianne?" a lady said behind me to her companion. "A trial separation, they call it, but I know for a fact he's screwing one of his stable girls. I hope Marianne takes him to the cleaners."

"I see Lorne Taylor is pregnant again," said a male voice on my right. "That'll be their sixth. How many kids do they want, for goodness' sake?"

"I heard from Trevor that Hot Target is to be gelded

and sent to Lawrence Ford as a hurdler. Such a shame he's been firing blanks."

I absorbed it all like a sponge. One never knew if, when, or what information might be useful.

"Do you think we'll win?" an excited lady owner asked the man on her far side, a middle-ability Lambourn-based trainer.

"He has a fair chance," the trainer replied without any great enthusiasm. "Depends on how well he jumps."

The horse in question jumped well enough but ran out of gas in the run up the hill to the line, finishing a creditable fifth out of twelve.

"Maybe next time," the trainer said in comfort to his clearly disappointed owner as they departed to unsaddle their charge.

I wandered up to the lines of bookmakers in the betting ring.

Someone had been busy with a high-pressure hose and there was no sign of the blood that had been spilled there only twenty-four hours before. The only thing different was that there was no *Jordan Furness*–emblazoned umbrella in the line. Not that a respectful space had been left empty. All the other bookmakers had simply moved along one place to fill in the gap.

The detective sergeant had asked me over and over again if I had any inkling of why Matthew Unwin might have murdered Furness.

"Why don't you ask him?" I'd said. "Perhaps he owed money."

But murder was rather a drastic measure to get out of paying a debt.

I thought back to the case that had resulted in Unwin being disqualified and excluded from racing. Several of the horses in his stables had tested positive for banned performance-enhancing drugs after an anonymous telephone tip-off to the BHA.

Had that been a reason? Was it revenge?

But surely a bookmaker wouldn't have been the one to make the call?

The ringing of my cell phone interrupted my thoughts.

"Hello?"

"Jeff? It's Quentin."

Quentin was my brother-in-law, Faye's husband.

"Hi," I said. "I am so sorry to hear the news about Faye."

"Yes," he said. "It's not looking too good, but she's a fighter and determined to see this thing off."

"Good."

"I actually rang you about something else. I need your help."

"Yes, of course. How?"

"I need something investigated and you're an investigator."

"But I only investigate horseracing," I said.

"Look, I can't tell you everything over the phone. Can you pop over and see me at home?"

"I can't. I'm at Cheltenham until Friday night."

"Saturday morning would be perfect." Quentin could be very persistent.

"All right," I said. "It will be good to see Faye."

"Don't mention any of this to Faye," he said sharply. "She has enough troubles of her own at the moment. I don't want her bothered by this."

"OK," I said somewhat uneasily. "How about eleven o'clock?"

"Make it nine," he said decisively. "I have a conference call at ten-thirty."

Bang went my hoped-for lie-in. But how could I say no? I had decided that I would go see Faye over the weekend as it was.

"OK," I said again without enthusiasm. "I'll be there at nine for our meeting, then I'll spend some time after with Faye."

"Don't tell Faye about your investigation," he snapped again.

"Look, Quentin," I said, equally abruptly. "I haven't even agreed to investigate anything for you yet and I'm not sure I will. But I will see you at nine o'clock on Saturday."

I hung up.

Why, I thought, did my brother-in-law always manage to bring out the worst in me? Or maybe I brought out the worst in him. Either way, we had never really got on.

He was some ten years older than my sister and he had been married twice previously when, one summer's day, he swept Faye off her feet in a whirlwind romance just as she was beginning to resign herself to the fact that at thirty-two and with no boyfriend, she would never get married.

Quentin Calderfield was an eminent barrister, known universally by his fellow advocates simply as QC, and Faye had been one of the junior clerks in his chambers. He was a man of immense self-confidence, used to getting his own way, and someone not to argue with unless you wanted to lose.

Quentin had risen rapidly up the legal ranks to become Quentin's Counsel and was therefore now more accurately known as QC,QC. His father had been a distinguished judge and a justice of the UK Supreme Court, having previously sat as a senior Law Lord in the House of Lords. Quentin was expected, at least by himself, to take a similar path to the pinnacle of the legal profession, and not many doubted that he'd get there.

I meandered up and down the lines of bookmakers, but my mind was preoccupied with Quentin and what he wanted investigated.

He surely knows masses of investigators, I thought. The courts must be full of them. So why did he need me? No doubt, I'd find out on Saturday.

THE REST OF THE WEEK at Cheltenham was uneventful in comparison, and I crammed myself onto the London-bound train on Friday evening, having seen Electrode, a Duncan Johnson–trained horse, win the Gold Cup for the second time.

Matthew Unwin had appeared at the town's magistrates' court on Thursday morning, charged with the murder of Jordan Furness, and had been remanded in custody.

There had been some speculation at the racetrack as to Unwin's mental state, but the police seemed to be treating it as an open-and-shut murder case. A detective had called me to say that I wouldn't be needed at the magistrates' hearing but, in the light of my signed statement, I would certainly be required as a witness for the prosecution at the trial unless, of course, Unwin pleaded guilty first.

The train rolled into Paddington Station a little after eight o'clock and I caught the Bakerloo Line tube to Willesden Junction, before walking the last few hundred yards to my home in Spezia Road.

"I'm back," I shouted as I turned the key.

"In the kitchen," came the reply.

Lydia Swiffin, my girlfriend of four years, was standing in front of the stove, wearing a striped apron, stirring the contents of a saucepan.

"Good journey?" she asked, turning around for a peck.

"Not really. Too many drunk punters singing out of tune."

"Not much chance of a snooze, then?"

"None. How about you? Good day?"

"Yeah, pretty much. I had two purchase offers accepted by vendors." She smiled. "But that means nothing these days. I never count commissions until the contracts are exchanged and deposits paid."

"Well done anyway. I'll go and unpack."

"Your supper will be ready in five minutes. I'm afraid I've had mine."

I took my bag along to our bedroom.

In the run-up to our second Christmas as a couple we had jointly bought this ground-floor flat in a house that had once been a single-family home but now accommodated two, with an Italian couple and a baby upstairs.

It had been a day of great joy when I had carried Lydia over the threshold and into our first home together, but, lately, I had begun to feel slightly trapped.

Our relationship was still pretty sound, but I knew there was a great expectation from Lydia, and from both our families, that we would soon get married. I had even found a sheet of paper on which Lydia had been practicing her signature, *Lydia Hinkley.*

But the prospect of marriage rather frightened me. It was too long-term, too permanent. I was reminded of the joke about the three stages of sex. Initially, there is house sex, when you have sex all over the house. Then there is bedroom sex, when you have sex only in the bedroom. And finally there is hall sex, when the only sexual encounter you have with your partner is to pass in the hall and say, "Fuck you."

Lydia and I seemed to have moved on to stage two already. Gone were the spontaneous and uninhibited encounters on the kitchen table or the sitting-room floor. Even our outdoor bonking under the stars had waned with the moon into nothingness.

Maybe that's what happens as one moves into one's thirties.

I went back along the hall and sat down at that kitchen table.

"What have you been up to while I was away?" I asked.

"Not much," Lydia replied. "Work every day and TV every night."

She put a plate of penne pasta with a pesto sauce down in front of me.

I had thought, on the train, of us going out to our local Indian restaurant on Harrow Road, but Lydia was on a seemingly never-ending diet and curries were definitely not one of her allowable foods.

Somehow we didn't do things like that very often anymore.

"There's a drama on the box in half an hour that I want to see," Lydia said as she washed up the saucepan. "The first half was on last night and it's really good."

I desperately wanted to say that sitting at home on a Friday evening in front of the television was not really my idea of a fun time. I longed to tell her to get her glad rags on because we were going out clubbing in the West End, where we would drink far too much, dance until the early hours, and then make passionate love on the backseat of a taxi on the way home. All things we had done before.

"Who's in it?" I asked.

"Some new chap called Jack Sherwood. He's good, and very sexy."

I wondered if she still found me sexy.

"Do you fancy a drink?" I asked. "I've got some wine in the cupboard."

"Not for me, thanks, not allowed. But you have one."

Why not? I thought. Maybe I'd get drunk. Not that it ever made anything better, or easier, in the long run.

"I'm going to see Faye tomorrow," I said.

"So you said on the phone. How is she?"

"Not looking forward to Monday."

"No, I bet she's not. Any further news?"

"No. I looked up gallbladder cancer and it wasn't very encouraging. It's not got a particularly great survival rate."

"Oh dear," Lydia said. "I'm so sorry."

I sighed. "Let's hope they've caught it early enough. I expect I'll find out tomorrow."

"Do you want me to come with you?"

"I'd love you to, but Quentin wants to discuss something else with me. He wants me there by nine. He apparently has something else at ten-thirty."

She made a face. Both of us liked our weekend lie-ins. Nowadays, it was our preferred "sex time."

"You go for nine. I'll come along later, after you've spoken to Quentin."

Lydia also didn't really get on with Quentin. I'm not sure anyone did. I suppose if you spend your life working in the fiercely adversarial system that we have in the English courts, then you become used to continuously trying to score points off everyone. Undoubtedly, it wins him cases but, I suspected, not many friends.

If he hadn't been married to my ailing sister, there's no way I'd have forgone a bit of nooky to go talk to him about some investigating that I had absolutely no intention of carrying out.

3

Lydia watched her television drama while I spent the time working in my study, as I had started calling our second bedroom. Lydia, meanwhile, always referred to it as the nursery.

For about the tenth time I looked up gallbladder cancer on the Internet.

Depending on which website one looked at, there were either four or five stages, but none of them sounded very promising. The one mildly encouraging fact was that only those whose cancer was detected in the early stages were considered suitable for surgery to remove the gallbladder. But, even so, half of the patients diagnosed with just stage one cancer did not survive for five years, and most of those with stage two were dead within six months.

It was depressing.

I tried to look on the bright side and told myself that

the other half of the patients did survive, and, after listening to Faye's doom and gloom on the telephone, I'd happily take odds of even money.

Next I looked up the details of Matthew Unwin's case by remotely logging in to the BHA main computer and studying the file.

Six horses in his stable had tested positive for the stimulant Dexedrine.

He had denied any knowledge of how the drug had been administered and stated to the BHA disciplinary panel that someone else must have given it to the horses because he had refused to pay them. However, Unwin had been unable to provide the panel with the name of the person responsible or a single piece of evidence to back up his claim.

In spite of repeated and insistent declarations of his innocence, he had been found guilty of administering a banned stimulant and had been disqualified and excluded from racing for eight years.

Detective Sergeant Galley, the Cheltenham detective, had thought that an eight-year ban had been rather harsh, and, looking at the minute trace quantities of Dexedrine that had been detected in the six horses, one might tend to agree.

However, it wasn't Matthew Unwin's first doping offense. Three years previously a horse of his had tested positive for Lasix, a banned diuretic, and he had been reprimanded and warned about his future conduct after pleading guilty.

Stupid man, I thought. He'd been given a second

chance and he'd thrown it all away. Now he would rot in jail. But for how long? Life imprisonment almost never meant that. For him it would probably be at least twelve years. Fifteen maybe. Either way, he was finished in racing.

But he'd been finished even before he went on the rampage with the knife.

Training racehorses was not like any other job.

British racing had become a seven-day-a-week activity, while the horses at home needed constant care.

Typical early mornings on the training gallops would be followed by afternoons at the races and then late nights at a desk, going through the race entries and doing all the other paperwork, not to mention the hours of driving to and from the racetracks. One trainer's wife told me that she always went with her husband to the races not because she particularly wanted to be there every day but because the journey was the only opportunity she had to talk to him during the entire week. And now cell phones had put paid to that too.

A trainer was also an employer and "the boss" to an army of grooms, work riders, and other stable staff, while at the same time being the deferential and courteous individual to whom owners of horses might turn to look after their precious darlings.

Even after his ban was served, Matthew Unwin would never have again earned the trust of potential owners. In reality, an eight-year ban from racing was a life sentence.

I went through the Unwin computer file right to the end.

Way down at the bottom of page twenty-two of his

disciplinary hearing report was a note of mitigation stating that Unwin's fifteen-year-old son had learning difficulties from having contracted meningitis as a baby, his marriage had recently broken down, and, without an income from training, he would likely have his house and stables repossessed by the bank. None of which had prevented the disciplinary panel from removing his training license.

Maybe he simply believed that he had nothing left to lose.

I searched through the BHA files for any mention of Jordan Furness.

Unlike horses, owners, trainers, jockeys, agents, valets, grooms, racing stables, racetracks, and equine swimming pools, all of which are regulated by the BHA, bookmakers are registered and licensed by the Gambling Commission. Hence, there was nothing to find about the victim of Unwin's attack. However, there was a record of a Lee Furness, formerly registered as a member of the stable staff in Matthew Unwin's yard.

Now, was that a coincidence or what?

I TOOK the London Overground train to Richmond-on-Thames and Quentin was waiting for me outside the station.

"I'd rather not talk at home," he said. "Let's go and have a coffee."

We went to a café in Brewers Lane, close to Quentin and Faye's house, and sat far back, well away from the window.

"Now," said Quentin when we had been served our coffee, "I need you to investigate something for me, something very hush-hush. You must understand it needs to be very discreet."

"Just hold on a minute," I said, slightly irritated. "I work for the BHA. I only investigate racing matters."

It was like Canute trying to hold back the tide.

"Yes, I know all that," he said dismissively, "but you're family and I really need you to do this for me. And for Faye," he added, just a fraction too late. "Especially now."

"What is it?" I asked.

"It's to do with Kenneth," he said, looking around him to ensure no one else was listening to our conversation. "Silly boy seems to have got himself into a spot of trouble."

Kenneth was Quentin's twenty-three-year-old son. Not by Faye but from an earlier union. My stepnephew. I'd met him once or twice over the years at family gatherings, but I hardly knew him very well.

"What sort of trouble?" I asked.

"He was arrested."

"For what?"

"He hasn't been convicted—not yet anyway." Quentin was quite agitated, something that I hadn't expected to see in my ultra-in-control brother-in-law.

"For what?" I asked again.

He looked around once more to make sure the waitress wasn't hovering nearby and finally spoke softly. "Possession with intent to supply a Class A drug."

"Oh," I said. It sounded to me like rather a lot more than just a spot of trouble. "Is he guilty?"

"No, of course not," Quentin said quickly. "Kenneth swears to me that he's been set up. The drugs were planted in his flat and one of his so-called friends is telling porkies to the police." He made it sound as if that alone was shocking, but, in my experience, almost everybody lies to the police at some stage in their lives, particularly if it helps them escape a conviction, and Quentin should know that better than most.

"Which drug?" I asked.

"Crystal meth. The friend is saying Kenneth agreed to sell him some."

"And you expect Kenneth to be convicted?" I said.

He sighed. "If the jury believes the friend, then yes I do. We need to show that the drugs were planted or the friend is lying."

"Can't the police establish that?"

"The man has gone walkabout, disappeared completely. Moved out of his flat, changed his cell phone number, and bloody vanished. And, anyway, the police believe that Kenneth is bang to rights over this. They're not even looking. They're convinced he's guilty."

Maybe that's because he was.

"Couldn't Kenneth just plead guilty in the magistrates' court and pay a fine? Surely it's not such a big deal these days."

Quentin looked at me with a degree of contempt and not a little anger.

"I can see that asking you was a waste of time. You clearly don't understand the situation."

"Tell me, then."

"For a start, it won't be just a fine. The case has been sent to the Crown Court and Kenneth will definitely go to jail if convicted. But that's not even the worst of it. He is currently doing his pupilage in chambers to become a barrister. A conviction of this sort would end all that, he'd lose his career completely. He would never be called to the Bar, having been to prison."

"Haven't you got some contacts in the police that you can use to get the investigation restarted?"

"Don't you think I've been trying, for God's sake? But I spend most of my time defending at the Old Bailey, so I've hardly endeared myself to the police, and I've been privately warned off by the head of the Crown Prosecution Service for sticking my nose in where it's not wanted." I wondered with astonishment if those were tears I saw in his eyes. "It's a complete disaster," he said with passion. "And it will probably prevent me from ever being a judge, certainly not an Appeal Court judge or higher."

Ah, I thought. The nub.

"Can you imagine how the press would describe me: *Mr. Justice Calderfield, whose own son went to jail for intent to supply a Class A drug, was sitting today in the case of a drug dealer.* They'd have a bloody field day."

"Does Faye know about all this?" I asked.

"No. Thank God. So far, Kenneth has managed to keep everything quiet. He thought it would all go away, that the case would be dropped. But, last week, at the plea and case management hearing, the CPS gave their decision that thanks to the bloody friend's statement, they believe there is enough evidence for a conviction and are proceeding to trial. A date has been set in June."

Quentin looked wretched. He could clearly see that the meteoric rise of QC,QC was about to hit the buffers, and the next generation was not even going to get onto the main line.

"So what exactly do you want me to do?" I asked.

He looked at me afresh.

"Find the bastard friend who gave the police the statement and prove he's lying."

"What if he's not lying?"

Quentin looked at me again. "Then buy him off. Offer him a few hundred quid to retract his evidence."

It all sounded so easy.

I HAD another cappuccino at the café while Quentin went home alone.

"It wouldn't do to turn up together," he'd explained needlessly.

I called Lydia.

"I'm just leaving," she said.

"Then I'll wait for you. I'm in a café in Brewers Lane—you know, the lane we sometimes take from the station to Faye's house."

"I know it."

"Right. See you in a bit."

I left my coffee to cool while I nipped down to the corner to buy a copy of the *Racing Post.* I usually read it on my tablet computer, but I'd carelessly left it at home.

The Saturday after the Cheltenham Festival always seemed to me to be a bit of an anticlimax, all the best horses having run in the preceding four days, but there were still five race meetings in Great Britain and another two in Ireland. And with over twenty-five thousand racehorses in training in both countries, there were plenty of horses available.

The British racing industry moved on relentlessly.

On all but a handful of days in a year, there were at least two race meetings scheduled somewhere in the UK, and on Boxing Day there could be as many as ten in England alone.

Much of the newspaper, however, looked back at the previous four days' racing, with a front-page color picture of Electrode jumping the last fence on his way to victory in the Gold Cup. There were more pictures inside, one of Duncan Johnson standing with his wife, both all smiles, in the winner's enclosure after the race. The horse was already being quoted at just six-to-one by the bookmakers to complete the hat trick the following year.

I wondered if the current Mrs. Johnson would still be around to see it.

While I waited, I read through the racing news section as well as the gossip columns. It was an essential part of my job to be "up-to-date" with all things happening on or around a racetrack.

Lydia arrived at ten o'clock and the two of us walked together around the corner to Faye and Quentin's magnificent three-story Georgian town house overlooking Richmond Green. Being a top barrister, QC,QC wasn't short of the odd bob or two.

"We'd better not stay too long," Lydia said as we walked down the path to their front door. "We don't want to tire Faye."

"I agree. We'll stay just half an hour or so."

Faye answered the door looking nothing like someone who was battling with a life-threatening illness. She was bright and cheerful, with immaculate makeup beneath her neatly styled brown curls, and she wore a smart navy blue dress with white belt and shoes.

"Hello, my darlings," she squealed, throwing her arms out wide. "Come on in. Q said you might be coming."

She gave both of us hugs and kisses and then ushered us through the hall into her expansive kitchen.

"Coffee?" she asked. "Or something stronger?"

It was ten past ten in the morning.

"Coffee," Lydia said and I nodded.

"Lovely."

We watched as Faye set to work with her fancy black-and-chrome coffee machine, producing three steaming cups, each topped with frothy white milk.

"I can't stand instant coffee," she said. "There's nothing like the real thing."

We sat at the kitchen breakfast bar sipping our drinks, not talking about the one topic that filled our minds.

"So how are you feeling?" Lydia asked eventually.

"Fine," said Faye. "That's what's so damn annoying. Most of the time I'm absolutely fine. I can't really believe there's anything wrong with me, but the wretched doctors say otherwise. And I'm not looking forward to Monday, I can tell you."

"No," I said inadequately. "Which hospital?"

"The Royal Marsden."

"How long will you be in?"

"Two, three, or four nights, maybe even five. It depends."

"On what?"

"The surgeon, I suppose."

"What exactly will he do?" Lydia asked.

"Take out some bits," she said with a forced smile. "Maybe it'll help me lose some weight."

We didn't laugh.

"If I'm lucky," she went on, "he'll just remove my gallbladder. That's if the cancer hasn't broken through the wall. Otherwise, he might have to take out some more. I really don't want to think about it." She breathed deeply. "But I can't think of anything else."

"Why didn't you have the surgery last week as soon as you knew?" I asked.

"I've been waiting for the right man to do it. He's been away at some conference or other in the United States. Apparently, he gets back on Sunday, so Monday is the earliest he could do it. The hospital told me it was worth the wait to get the top guy, so I did. I just hope it was the right thing."

Faye lost all her composure. Her shoulders drooped and she was close to tears.

"I'm sorry," she said unnecessarily.

Lydia stood up and went to put her arms around Faye as a series of sobs shuddered through her body.

I felt helpless and distraught.

Faye had always been my rock. She had been the one to wipe away my tears, right from when our dear mother had *Gone off to see God*, as our father had always put it.

I desperately didn't want Faye to go off to see God, not yet, not ever, but what could I do? Nothing. Only pray that the surgeon would do his work and save her.

I stood up and went and put my arms around them both.

"What's this?" said Quentin loudly, coming into the kitchen. "Group hug?"

The moment passed and Faye pulled herself away, dabbing at her eyes with a tissue and smudging her mascara.

"Oh God, what a mess," she said, trying to laugh. "I'll just go and fix this."

"I'll come with you," said Lydia, and the two girls went off to make repairs upstairs.

"It's very difficult for her," I said to Quentin.

"She'll be fine," he said with confidence. "She's a tough old bird."

I wasn't sure if he really thought that she would be fine or if he was just putting on a brave front. I couldn't believe that he didn't know the odds. Either way, I thought that he should be more consoling towards his wife, but I suppose that wasn't Quentin's style.

"Is there anything you need from me to start your investigation?" he asked.

"The so-called friend's name," I said.

"Daniel something," he said. "Foreign name. It's in the CPS bundle. I'll get it for you on Monday."

"Can I see the whole file?" I asked.

"I'll try, but I really shouldn't be having anything to do with it."

"Then don't. Tell me who to talk to and I'll get it from them."

"You'll have to approach Kenneth's solicitor. It's a woman." He said it as if he didn't fully approve of female lawyers. "I have her card somewhere. I'll give it to you before you go."

"Where is Kenneth?" I asked.

"He sits in his flat most days just feeling sorry for himself. He's been suspended from his pupilage pending the outcome of the case."

"Why doesn't he spend his time looking for the missing friend?"

"It's a condition of his bail that he can have no contact with the Crown's witnesses."

"*Witnesses* plural?" I asked. "Who are the others?"

"The police mostly. Arrest officers, search officers, and so on. And then there's also the drug analysis company."

"Is it legal for me to have any contact with the friend?"

"Probably not."

"What could be the consequences?" I asked.

"If you found him and then the friend complained that you'd been in contact, Kenneth would probably lose his bail. So be careful. It's also possible that you might be arrested for attempting to pervert the course of justice, although that's unlikely."

"How unlikely?"

"Very unlikely, I'd say. Unless, of course, you offered him money or threatened him in order to get him to change his story."

I might need to do both.

Faye and Lydia came back downstairs.

Quentin looked at his watch. "I have a client conference call in five minutes," he said. "Don't leave until after I'm finished." It was more of a directive than a request.

"We mustn't be too long," I said hesitantly.

"But you will stay to lunch, won't you?" Faye asked anxiously. "I've got a whole fridge full of food that needs eating before Monday. Q will eat at his club all week."

I looked at Lydia.

"Yes, we'd love to," she said. "I'll help you."

WE DIDN'T LEAVE until well after two, by which time Faye was exhausted. So much for us not making her tired.

"I'm sorry," she said, again unnecessarily, as Lydia and I stood on her doorstep to say good-bye. "It's not the cancer or any treatment that makes me so tired, it's more because I'm not sleeping very well at the moment."

"Darling Faye," I said, "you don't have to apologize. It is all our fault for staying so long."

She gave me a big hug while whispering ever so quietly into my ear, "Now, Jeff, get along and marry Lydia, won't you. I want to still be round for my little brother's wedding."

She pulled back and smiled at me.

Oh God, I thought. Now what do I do?

4

On Monday morning I took the Tube from Willesden to the British Horseracing Authority offices in High Holborn, to my desk in the Integrity, Licensing and Compliance Department, more commonly referred to as the racing security service.

I sat for an hour and tried to reply to the multitude of e-mails that had accumulated unanswered in my in-box during my week away in Cheltenham, but I wasn't really concentrating. My mind kept wandering off to what was happening three and a half miles away at the Royal Marsden Hospital.

Faye had been admitted at six that morning and was scheduled to go to surgery as the second patient of the day for the surgeon.

I wondered what time that would be. How long would his first operation last? How long for Faye's?

I had asked Quentin to please keep me informed, but I had little faith that phoning his brother-in-law would be high on his priority list unless it was to ask about progress in finding Kenneth's erstwhile friend.

How long should I wait before I called the hospital? Perhaps I shouldn't call before noon. Or maybe at eleven-thirty. Or eleven.

I looked up at the clock on the office wall for the umpteenth time. Ten past ten. The hands seemed to move so slowly. Had it stopped? I stared at the minute hand for a full minute, timing it against my wristwatch, until it clicked over to eleven minutes past ten. No, it was still working.

I stood up and walked down the corridor to the little kitchen area to make myself a cup of coffee. Pacing up and back helped my nervousness, but the clock had grudgingly moved on just five minutes to ten-sixteen when I sat down again.

Come on, I told myself. Do something useful. Take your mind off it.

I forced myself back to the e-mails.

Most were update reports from my colleagues. There were five out-and-out investigators in the department, of which I was one, three of the others being ex–police officers, and the fifth a financial expert who had recently joined our ranks, reflecting the increasing financial complexity of many of the dubious practices we spent our time investigating.

In addition, there were eight equine integrity officers

who were responsible, among other things, for checking that the runners in all races were indeed the horses that everyone expected them to be. The penalty for knowingly substituting a different horse or "running a ringer," as it was called, was one of the harshest in the rule book, with an expected twenty years' disqualification and exclusion from the sport even for a first offense.

And then there were the stable inspectors who spent their days making unannounced visits to licensed training facilities to check on the suitability of the premises and the welfare of the horses, and also arranging the random drug testing of the sport's participants, both equine and human.

We all regularly updated one another with progress and irregularities as we had found that it was not unusual for our investigations to overlap. An investigation into person A might throw up a connection to persons X and Y, while a completely separate inquiry into person B might show that he is also connected to one of or both X and Y and hence possibly to A.

I scanned through the reports looking out for names that were familiar.

Currently, I personally had three open cases, one of which concerned the continuing fallout from the Matthew Unwin affair. I was trying to ascertain if any other individuals had profited from the doping of the horses. In particular, did the betting records show any unusual patterns during the running of those horses? It was painstaking work searching through the race results and cross-referencing them against computer betting data. So far, it had not turned up any discrepancies and I was beginning to think that it wouldn't.

But the case was the reason Nigel and I had been on the lookout at Cheltenham on the previous Tuesday. One of our covert sources had provided information to the intelligence branch that had led us to believe Unwin might be at the races that day to meet someone who had benefited from the doping.

Little had I realized he was there to commit murder.

Had Jordan Furness been more than just the victim of a vicious knife attack? Had he also been profiting from Unwin's doped horses?

Racehorse trainers, typically, have little contact with bookmakers and vice versa, other than the placing of bets, one with the other. Social contact, although not prohibited, was discouraged by the authorities. It would be all too easy to pass on privileged information, and doing so for financial gain was strictly against the Rules of Racing.

So had there been any previous contact between Matthew Unwin and Jordan Furness? And had Unwin's former stable employee, Lee Furness, been related to Jordan?

These would be my next lines of inquiry into the matter.

As well as the e-mails, there was a thin, translucent blue pocket folder that had been left on my desk by Crispin Larson, chief analyst in the intelligence section. There was a short, handwritten note paper-clipped to the front:

Jeff, Enclosed came via RaceStraight. Worth a look, methinks. Use your customary dark methods to scour the land. Toodle-pip, Crispin.

A blue folder indicated that the intelligence section believed it to be a matter worth pursuing but that it was not particularly urgent; those came in red folders and needed dealing with immediately.

Crispin Larson was, in my view, totally obsessed with security. He started out with the assumption that every phone and every computer connected to the Internet was hacked and nothing should be sent by external e-mail unless you were prepared to have it read by others. Hence, he persisted in delivering the blue and red folders to investigators' desks personally.

I glanced up at the clock. The hands had miraculously moved on to eight minutes to eleven without me having watched them once since ten-twenty.

Could I call the hospital yet?

I dialed the number and, after being put through to the correct department, was informed by a firm but polite voice that Mrs. Calderfield had not yet gone down for the surgery. She was still waiting in her room.

Poor Faye.

The waiting must feel interminable. I now wished I'd gone to be with her, but she had insisted she would be fine with just Quentin.

I watched as the clock's hands moved reluctantly to eleven o'clock.

Thinking about Quentin reminded me of Kenneth's

missing ex-friend. I dug the solicitor's business card out of my pant pocket and dialed her direct number.

"Diane Shorrocks," said a female voice briskly.

"Hello, Mrs. Shorrocks," I said. "You don't know me, but my name is Jeff Hinkley. I'm Kenneth Calderfield's uncle."

"Yes, Mr. Hinkley," she said slowly. "How can I help you?"

"I'd like to look at the Crown's evidence bundle for Kenneth's case."

"I'm sorry, Mr. Hinkley, but that would be impossible without Mr. Calderfield's written authority."

"I only want to find out the name of the person who provided a statement to the police. Could you look for me?"

"I'm sorry, Mr. Hinkley," she said again without sounding it. "I am unable to discuss anything about the case with you, or with anyone else for that matter, without Mr. Calderfield's express permission. It would constitute a breach of client/solicitor privilege."

"Oh," I said. "Well, I'd better get a written authority, then."

"Yes," she said, "although my client has his own copy of the Crown's case. He would be at liberty to show it to you, if he so wished."

"Right," I said. "I'll ask him. Thank you."

I hung up and rang Kenneth's cell instead.

He answered at the sixth ring just as I was beginning to think he wouldn't.

"Hello," he said in a bored-sounding monotone.

"Hello, Kenneth, this is Jeff Hinkley, your uncle, Faye's brother."

"I know who you are," he replied without any enthusiasm.

"Your father has asked me to try and help you out of your present predicament."

"I can't think how." He sounded as if he had already given up hope and was resigned to his fate.

"Kenneth," I said sharply, "are you guilty?"

"Call me Ken," he said. "Only my father calls me Kenneth. And, no, I'm not guilty."

"Then please stop sounding like you are. Do you want my help or not?"

"Yes I do," he said, "but I can't see how you can."

"Let me be the judge of that. Now, what is the name of the man who gave the statement to the police?"

"Daniel Jubowski."

"Is he English?" I asked.

"As far as I know," Ken replied. "I think his grandfather was Polish. Came over to fight in the Second World War and never went back."

"Where does this Daniel Jubowski live?" I asked.

"He had a place near King's Cross overlooking the canal."

"But now he's gone?"

"According to someone he shared with. I went to find him and was told he'd moved out."

"What does he do for a living?"

"I'm not really sure," Ken said. "Something in the City, I think."

"How did you meet him?"

"Oh, you know, at a party."

"I'd like to have a look at the complete prosecution bundle of evidence. I'm told you have a copy. Where do you live?"

"I have a flat in Tower Hamlets, off Bethnal Green Road."

"Right," I said. "I'll see you at five o'clock at your flat." He gave me the address and directions from Bethnal Green tube station.

I looked up at the clock. It was eleven-twenty.

I called the Royal Marsden again and was informed that Mrs. Calderfield had just gone down. She wasn't expected back for at least a couple of hours.

I fretted.

It was a good job that Paul Maldini wasn't looking over my shoulder. The head of operations would not have considered me good value for money on that particular day. I had probably spent only half an hour on BHA business so far.

Perhaps if I did some work it would take my mind off what awfulness was being performed on Faye.

I opened the blue folder from Crispin Larson to find a single sheet of paper inside:

A male caller to the RaceStraight anonymous tip-off line has claimed that the trainer Graham Perry is using performance-enhancing substances on some or all of his horses.

When pressed for evidence to support such a damning allegation, the caller said "he just knew" before hanging up.

About an hour later the same or a second caller to RaceStraight made the same accusation but again gave no details.

The last routine inspection of Graham Perry's yard was in February this year, when all was found to be in order. In addition, an unannounced team carried out tests on a random selection of twelve of his horses three years ago and all were found to be negative.

This is an unsubstantiated claim of a suspect nature (rated C/D3) and any investigation must be performed with utmost tact so as to protect the hitherto good name and reputation of Mr. Perry, who is currently unaware of these allegations.

I wondered why Crispin had given it to me. I was considered to be the department's specialist in undercover work, but surely this should be dealt with in an upfront and open manner. The usual practice would be to send a testing team back to Perry's yard, with the bells ringing and the lights flashing, to do blood tests on all his horses, and to hell with any secrecy. The tests would either be positive, in which case he'd lose his training license forever, or negative, in which case his good name and reputation would not only remain intact but be enhanced.

I took the blue folder down the stairs to the intelligence section and knocked on Crispin Larson's door.

"Come in," he shouted from within. I opened the door. "Ah, Jeff, dear boy, our resident genius and champion of the dark arts. Come in and sit down."

I did both.

"Now," said Crispin, "what brings you down to the murky shadows of intelligence?"

"It's about this file you left on my desk."

"Ah," he said again expansively. "The Perry file."

"Yes," I said. "Why have you given it to me and not to one of the testing teams? Is it really a matter for utmost tact? Don't we just send in the scientists to find out if the horses are high on amphetamines?"

"Well. We could do just that. But wait! What if our caller is merely a mischief-maker? Analyses are expensive, you know. Would the substantial outlay be prudent?"

It would be prudent, I thought, if not doing so endangered the good name of racing. "Surely we don't have to worry about the cost if the sport's integrity is at stake."

"I have my reasons," Crispin said. "I want you, our shadowy, silent sleuth, to have a quiet look first."

"So what is it you want me to do, exactly?" I asked.

"Do your usual business, dear boy. Ask quiet questions, look under stones, discover if there's any substance to the accusation. Or is it some vengeful malcontent spreading unsubstantiated tittle-tattle? Report back to me asap."

Crispin tended to speak in a manner that was as cryptic as the crossword puzzles he was renowned for completing in double-quick time.

"When by?"

"There is a requirement for prompt results. If it is true, then we must be seen to react. Say, next week?"

"OK. I'll have a look and ask the questions."

"Quietly, now, dear boy. Quietly. We don't need the proverbial scrambled on our faces, now do we? Aye, aye."

I wondered why Crispin couldn't speak normally like everyone else. Particularly as he had a brain that was so sharp.

Even though he always jokingly referred to me as the BHA resident genius, and I was pretty good at understanding complicated situations, Crispin outdid me with ease. He would recognize issues that everyone else would miss. All intelligence is information, he would often say, but not all information is intelligence. The real trick was distinguishing which was and which wasn't, and Crispin was the real genius at doing that.

He had been the chief intelligence officer for the BHA since its creation, having been a secret agent in either MI5 or MI6 before that. No one really knew which, as he wouldn't say. Since his arrival, many a disgruntled racing miscreant had received his just desserts because Crispin Larson could decode the intelligence.

If he said that quiet questions should be asked first rather than a full-frontal approach with the testing team, then I was not the one to argue. He must have good reasons, and maybe I'd find out what they were or maybe I wouldn't. Crispin could be so secretive that I wondered if his wife knew what he did for a living, if indeed he even had a wife. That was something else he was secretive about.

Once, as we had been leaving the offices together at the end of the day, I'd casually asked him, by way of conversation, where he lived and how he got home. He'd looked at me keenly and asked, dear boy, why I needed to know. Clearly, such information was issued only on a need-to-know basis and, as I obviously hadn't needed to know, he didn't tell me.

BACK AT MY DESK, the hands on the clock had crept around to twelve twenty-three.

Surely by now the top-guy surgeon would be hard at work in Faye's innards. I tried to visualize what he might be doing but decided not to linger too long on the image. I was always a bit squeamish about abdominal operations when they were shown on the television, thankful that the patient was fast asleep and unaware of all the pushing and pulling, the cutting and the burning, that was going on inside them.

God, I hoped she would be all right.

Health issues, especially those of a life-threatening nature, put everything else into perspective. There was little point in worrying about how the nation's economy might perform over the next few years if simply being alive after six months was going to be a toss-up.

And did it really matter, in the big picture, if Graham Perry was or was not dosing his horses with amphetamines when Faye's very existence lay literally in the hands of a jet-lagged surgeon on some operating table in southwest London?

Well, of course it did.

As they say, life has to go on.

Using the internal computer network, I looked up Graham Perry's BHA file.

He was forty-one and he had held a trainer's license for the past seven years, having previously been the assistant trainer to Matthew Unwin.

That alone made me sit up straight and pay attention.

5

According to the nurse I spoke to on the telephone, Faye was brought back to her room at three o'clock, having spent the preceding hour gradually waking from the anesthetic in the recovery ward. All I was told was that she was back and that the operation had been a success, whatever that might mean. Probably that she was still alive.

I was also informed that there would be no word on what had actually been done to my sister's insides until the following day. It seemed that the top-guy surgeon was currently busy poking his fingers into someone else's guts.

But thankfully Faye was awake and *comfortable*, although that must be a relative term after having had bits of her removed.

"No visitors today," said the nurse with authority, "other than immediate family."

I thought brothers were pretty immediate, but, in this case, it apparently meant spouses only or, failing that, the parents or children of the patient.

Quentin, as expected, did not call to tell me how things had gone. Maybe he didn't know either, but a call to confirm that the operation was over and successful would have been nice.

I went back to studying the Perry file.

Graham James Perry had come into racing as an eighteen-year-old conditional jockey, a trainee, under the stewardship of a young Duncan Johnson. According to the records, he'd had fifteen rides under rules in his first season, twenty-seven in his second, and just twelve in his third, at which point he had given up his jockey's license.

He won only two of the fifty-four races in which he rode, so jockeyship was clearly not his strong suit. However, he had remained on the staff at the Johnson stable for the next six years before disappearing off the BHA radar. Perhaps he had gone to work abroad for a while because, five years later, he resurfaced as Matthew Unwin's assistant, before taking on a trainer's license himself, at age thirty-four, when he took over a yard near the village of Tilston in Cheshire.

His progress since then had been steady rather than spectacular. He had built his string from just ten horses in his first season up to a recent figure of twenty-eight, and he'd had some moderate success in races at the smaller tracks, in particular at his local track, Bangor-on-Dee, where he was the second leading trainer in the current season.

It was ages since I'd been racing at Bangor-on-Dee.

I consulted the fixture list and discovered there was a meeting the coming weekend. I decided to go north by train on Friday morning, spend the evening at the local pub in Tilston, before attending the racing on Saturday afternoon.

I used my computer to look up the train times from Euston. Then I fixed a room at the Queen Hotel in Chester, opposite the railway station, and arranged for a rental car—something fairly small and inconspicuous.

I TOOK the Central Line from Holborn to Bethnal Green and followed Kenneth's directions to his front door. I pushed the bell button marked *K. Calderfield* and was rewarded by a metallic-sounding voice emanating from the grille alongside.

"Hello?"

"It's Jeff Hinkley," I said, leaning forward.

"Third floor," came the reply, accompanied by a buzzing as he released the door lock.

I went in and climbed the stairs. Ken was waiting for me on the third-floor landing.

"Come in," he said, leading me into his sitting room. "Do you want some tea?"

"I'd rather have a beer. It's been a long day at the office."

He disappeared and returned with two green bottles, tops removed.

"Thanks," I said as he gave me one and I took a welcome mouthful.

I walked over to the picture window and looked out at the view over Bethnal Green Gardens and on towards the high-rises of the City of London, visible in the distance against the brightness of the western sky.

"Nice flat," I said. "Do you own it?"

"Dad does," he said. "I couldn't afford this on my pay. Pupilage is like legalized slavery. Dad pays the mortgage. He says it's cheap compared to paying rent."

Cheap was a word that no one could associate with this flat.

"How many bedrooms?" I asked.

"Two," he said. "But I use one of them as my study. I'm very lucky."

I thought back to when I was Ken's age. I'd been living in an army barracks block in Bedfordshire with just four toilets and three showers for fifty soldiers. Either that or I'd been away on operations overseas, snatching sleep whenever I could either in some dusty army tent or, more likely, out in the open in the middle of some godforsaken Middle Eastern desert, baking hot by day and freezing cold by night.

Ken had indeed been very lucky in the accommodation stakes. Going to prison from this would be more than just a mere wake-up call.

"Where were the drugs found?" I asked.

Ken seemed slightly taken aback by my sudden change of tack.

"In my bedroom."

"Show me."

He led me down the corridor past the kitchen and study.

"In my bedside cabinet," he said, pointing.

"How much?"

"A couple of grams."

"Of crystal meth?" He nodded. "A couple of grams is not much."

"It was ground up to a powder in eight individual wraps of two hundred and fifty milligrams each."

"And you claim they were planted?"

"Yes," he said, getting rather agitated. "I had a party here and someone must have put them in the drawer. I'd never seen them before."

I took two quick strides forward and pulled open the drawer in question. I could tell that Ken didn't like it. He stood on the balls of his feet, clenching and unclenching his fists.

The drawer was full of the usual accumulation one might expect in a bedside drawer: batteries, bubble packs of painkillers, scraps of paper, some dog-eared business cards, a couple of pens, some assorted creams and lotions, a half-eaten tube of mints, a cigarette lighter, and a packet of condoms.

I closed the drawer again and turned around.

"I'm scared stiff," Kenneth said.

"Of going to jail?"

"Yeah, I suppose," he said. "But more of what my dad will say."

"I know he's not pleased," I said.

"So he keeps telling me," Kenneth said with a sigh. "But he knows only the half of it."

"Half of what?"

"Oh, nothing." He waved a hand dismissively.

"Kenneth," I said firmly. "If you want my help, you need to be completely honest and open. What does your father only know the half of?"

"The details of the party."

"What details?"

"If I tell you something, do you promise not to tell my father?" he asked with a glimmer of desperation in his eyes.

"That depends on what it is," I said.

He looked at me for a long while without saying anything, as if deciding.

"I'm gay," he said eventually.

"So?" I said. "What's the problem?"

"My dad doesn't know and I'm absolutely terrified that he'll find out at the trial."

"Then tell him yourself before the trial starts. It's nothing to be worried about."

"You don't understand," Kenneth said miserably. "Dad absolutely hates gays. He's always saying they should all be castrated."

That was another reason, I thought, why Quentin should never be a judge.

"Let's have that cup of tea, shall we?" I said.

WE SAT at his small kitchen table, drinking tea, while he told me his sorry tale.

He lived constantly in awe of his father, trying his best to please him and afraid that he couldn't.

Kenneth's whole life had been mapped out almost from birth with the parental expectation that he would take his rightful place at the Bar and progress from there up the ladder of justice. His father even called him Kenneth in the sure belief that in due course Quentin Calderfield, Queen's Counsel—QC,QC—would be followed logically by Kenneth Calderfield, King's Counsel—KC,KC.

"It's not that I don't enjoy the law," he said, "just that any question of me doing anything else for a career had been stifled and dismissed out of hand. I feel I'm living my life in a straitjacket." He swallowed noisily. "I suppose I should be grateful that Dad has helped me so much, like with this flat and fixing my pupilage and such, and he's always been interested in everything I do, but I feel trapped."

I knew a little of how he was feeling, yet I'd had no parent directing my route in life, only my big sister.

We drank our tea in silence for a bit, with Kenneth keenly studying the tabletop.

"*Please* don't tell my dad about me being gay," Kenneth said finally.

"I won't," I said. "I promise. But you must."

Ken looked horrified. "I can't."

"Yes you can, and you'll have to. It's much better that you tell him than he finds out in court, as he surely will. Even if the prosecution doesn't know for sure, they are bound to ask you during cross-examination. What will you do then? Lie because your dad might hear? I think not. It would instantly destroy any credibility you might still have with the jury."

"Oh God!" he said. "It's all such a bloody disaster."

It certainly was.

"This Daniel Jubowski, was he your boyfriend?"

"No," he said sharply. Rather too sharply.

"Who was he, then?"

"Someone I met at a gym."

"Which gym?"

He hesitated, again looking down at the table.

"Come on, Ken," I said, "I need the full truth if I'm to help you."

"The Fit Man gym in Soho. It has a huge sauna."

"Did you end up back here?" I asked.

"No," he said. "Not that time. I went with him to his place."

"Near King's Cross?"

"Yes. In Tiber Gardens."

"But he came here on other occasions?"

"Yes," Ken replied sheepishly. "He came a couple of times."

"So he was your boyfriend."

"No, not really. He was just someone I met. A short fling, that's all. Nothing serious. In fact, I went off him."

"Was that before or after your party?" I asked.

"Before," he said. "I'd met a couple of other guys at the gym. The three of us . . . Well, it was rather fun." He smiled for the first time since I'd arrived.

Quentin, I thought, was in for rather a shock.

"But Daniel was *at* your party?"

"Yes," he said. "He helped to organize it."

"Do you think it was him who planted the drugs?"

"I don't know."

"How did the police find them? Why did they come here in the first place?"

"We were raided."

He made it sound like something out of *CSI: Miami.*

"But the police don't just raid people's houses without any reason."

"The party was rather noisy and it disturbed the neighbors. The police turned up to shut us down and found most of the guests were stoned. That's when they searched the flat."

"When was this?" I asked.

"Just before Christmas."

"Who else was at the party?"

"Friends. You know, people I'd met at the gym. About ten of us altogether."

"All men?" I asked.

"Yeah." His tone indicated that of course they were all men.

"So when was it, exactly?"

"December twentieth," he said. "But, to be accurate, the raid was on the twenty-first at about three in the morning." He smiled. "It was a great party. At least it was until the police arrived." He laughed. "In fact, they seemed rather shocked. We were mostly down to our boxers, and some had even discarded those. It was that sort of party." He blushed slightly. "But we were all consenting adults."

Maybe so, I thought, but it was no surprise the police had raided the place. How Ken had hoped to keep his sexuality a secret from his father was beyond me. It was bound to get out and it would probably not be to his advantage. I couldn't imagine a jury being particularly sympathetic towards the host of a drug-fueled orgy that had disturbed the neighbors at three o'clock in the morning.

Quentin had been right. If it went to trial, Ken was almost sure to be convicted of possession, and I wasn't at all certain that finding Daniel Jubowski would make any difference even if I could prove he was lying about the dealing.

"Did the police arrest anyone else?" I asked.

"They arrested us all, but the others were never charged. Only me, because they found the drugs in my drawer. Even then, the case probably wouldn't have gone anywhere as I claimed I had no knowledge and the cops took the view that any one of us could have placed them there and they wouldn't be able to prove which one. It was only when that bastard Daniel told them it was definitely mine and I'd agreed to sell him some that they decided to proceed."

"And had you agreed to sell him some?" I asked.

"No. I swear to you, I didn't."

"So why did he say that?" I asked.

"I've no idea."

Perhaps Daniel's statement would give me some clue.

"Where's your copy of the Crown case bundle?" I asked. "I'll need to go through everything."

He stood up and collected a stapled stack of papers that had been lying on the kitchen counter and tossed it onto the table in front of me.

"It's all in there," he said. "But half of it's a load of rubbish."

I skimmed through the pages. There were certified copies of statements from the arresting officers, the search team, the custody sergeant, and the drug-testing laboratories, together with the damning one from Daniel Jubowski. There were also typed transcripts of two police interviews with Ken but no statements or interview records for any of the other men arrested at the same time.

"Do you have the names of all the men who were here that night?"

"Don't be stupid," Ken said. "Other than Daniel, there were a couple of Johns and a Mike among them, but I've no idea of their surnames. They didn't sign a visitors' book or wear badges. And they were all so high on Tina that half of them didn't know who they were anyway."

"Did you also do some?" I asked, but I reckoned his use of the slang name *Tina* for crystal meth had already given me the answer.

"Only a bit," he said.

"And you were aware that it was illegal?"

He nodded.

Of course he knew it was illegal, he had a law degree from Oxford and he'd taken the Bar final.

"How often?" I asked.

"That was the only time. I swear it. I was talked into it. Bullied, even."

"Who by?" I asked.

"Daniel," he said, "and some of the others. They were all taking it. They said it gave them increased sexual performance. Just like Viagra, only more so. I didn't want to be the odd one out. It was only a bit of fun."

His "bit of fun" would probably cost him his career. And quite possibly destroy his father's as well.

6

I caught the train from Euston Station to Chester at nine-thirty on Friday morning after a busy week at my desk.

I had managed to close two of my outstanding cases. One concerned a registered owner who had been suspected of contacting an excluded person and supplying insider information. The owner had submitted cell telephone records that indicated that no such contact existed. I had been asked to carry out some surveillance of the owner, during which I had discovered—simply by looking into the said owner's Jaguar when it was parked at a racetrack—that he had a second pay-as-you-go cell that he had failed to declare to the authorities. The records for the second phone had arrived on my desk, proving that the suspected contact had indeed occurred. I had now written my report and passed the whole file to the relevant section so that a Disciplinary Panel inquiry could be convened.

The second case was of a jockey whose routine urine test had proved to be positive for benzodiazepine—or *benzo,* as it is also known—a notifiable substance under the Rules of Racing. The jockey had claimed that he had taken one of his girlfriend's sleeping pills to help him sleep after a bad fall and he had been unaware that it contained a banned substance. An inquiry, however, had dismissed this excuse due to a sizable amount of benzo in his system and had found him guilty. He had been suspended from riding for three months.

I had subsequently been asked to conduct a covert investigation to ensure that the jockey in question did not have a prescription drug problem prior to him being relicensed to ride again.

In the week before Cheltenham I had acted like his shadow, following him everywhere he went and watching everything he did. I was certain he hadn't known I was there. I'd photographed everyone he'd met or talked to, and I'd even been through his rubbish to look for thrown-away prescription pill containers.

More than ten years previously, when I'd been a trainee in the British Army Intelligence Corps, for our final test in surveillance, three of us, wearing civilian clothes, had been taken to Victoria Station during the morning rush hour. Our examiner had selected three individuals at random, each of them hurrying from their trains. He had instructed us to use the rest of the day to determine as much as we could about them without speaking to them directly and without their knowledge.

I'd been allocated a smartly dressed woman. By midnight I had discovered not only her name but also her address, her job, her date of birth, her Social Security number, her tax code, her bank details, her bank card PIN, her husband's name and those of her two children and her parents. I found out what she'd had for lunch and dinner, that she secretly smoked Marlboro Light cigarettes, was taking the pill, and even the balance in her checking account. I also knew that she'd met a man called Charlie for a drink after work at a wine bar in Grosvenor Gardens and that they had held hands under the table so that no one would see. Except, of course, I had.

And all of that was simply from watching, listening, a little rummaging in her trash bin, plus a touch of subterfuge on the telephone.

I had first followed her to work on the Tube and read her name from an airline frequent-flier tag attached to the handle of her briefcase. Once I had her name and the company she worked for, a call to their payroll department, supposedly from the tax authorities, had produced the tax code, the SSN, and her date of birth. The PIN came from careful observation of her obtaining cash from an ATM at lunchtime. Most of the rest came from observing her purchases at a city convenience store and from what I found at her home in the garbage, including an empty plastic pill strip, some of her husband's old birthday cards, and a discarded bank statement.

It never ceased to amaze me what information people put in their trash that should have been kept confidential.

Of course, if I'd used any of the information for gain or reward, I would have been breaking the law, and maybe the telephone call had sailed rather close to the mark. But watching, listening, and even an inspection of what people throw away was not illegal, provided you didn't remove anything. It was just good surveillance, and I had passed the test.

My shadowing of the suspect jockey had produced not a shred of evidence to suggest that he had an ongoing drug problem, prescription or otherwise, and I had reported so to the BHA licensing department. He would soon be back riding and earning his living again.

I sat on the speeding train gazing out at the northern suburbs of London as they passed by in a blur.

My week had not only been busy on the work front. Family matters had also been prominent.

Faye had come home from the hospital the previous day. Lydia and I had been to visit her on Tuesday evening and had been much encouraged by both her condition and the news. The surgeon had removed only her gallbladder, rather than anything further, and he had been confident that the cancer had not grown through the wall. It didn't mean she was out of danger—far from it—but she had much brighter prospects than we had all originally feared. She would be starting chemotherapy just as soon as she had recovered from the operation, maybe even as soon as the following week.

On the Kenneth Calderfield front, I had also made some pleasing headway.

First, I had searched for anyone called Jubowski on Facebook.

Fortunately, people called Jubowski were rare, with only a total of six of them having Facebook pages and only one of those was a Daniel, who appeared to live in London, which was promising. I went through Daniel's page, looking at all his posted photographs and noting down the names of those who had made any comments about them. I read through his profile and made a list of those people he was following. His status was given as *Single*, but there was no clear indication that he was gay other than the fact that none of his photos showed anyone who was female.

But was this the right Daniel Jubowski?

The clincher was tucked away in his *Likes*.

Way down at the bottom was the Fit Man gym in Greek Street, Soho, which, according to its website, had the biggest men's sauna in London.

Facebook gave me not only what Daniel looked like but also where he worked. He had posted that he was a market analyst at the City of London office of an international finance company called Hawthorn Pearce.

Quentin had told me in Richmond that Daniel had disappeared, gone walkabout and moved out of his flat, but he was still at work. I'd called Hawthorn Pearce at half past twelve on Wednesday and asked to be put through to him. A colleague had answered and confirmed that Daniel Jubowski was in the office that day.

"He's nipped out to buy his lunch," the colleague had explained.

"Will he be long?" I'd asked.

"I doubt it," said the colleague. "He's most likely in the deli round the corner. Do you want to leave a message?"

"No thanks. I'll try again later."

I had no particular wish to talk with Daniel directly. Not yet.

Instead, I'd been waiting close to the front door of Hawthorn Pearce in King Street when he appeared at five-twenty, turning left and hurrying towards Bank tube station.

He was in his late twenties or early thirties, slim, clean-shaven, with short brown hair, appearing just as he did in his Facebook profile photo. He was wearing a business suit, white shirt and striped tie, and he carried a black briefcase with his right hand, as he hurried down the steps from street level.

It is always simpler to follow someone covertly when there are lots of people around and I was easily able to track him down the crowded escalators and onto a Northern Line tube train. We were in the same car only about three or four yards apart, but I was certain he had no idea that I was interested in him.

Tube passengers in general live in their own little bubble, thinking their own thoughts, neither communicating with, nor even noticing, their fellow travelers. It made my life so much easier.

I was able to watch his reflection in the train window,

making sure that as I couldn't actually see his face, he couldn't see mine.

He alighted at King's Cross, and I was the third person behind him as we both rode the escalator to the mainline station. But he was not catching a train. He walked straight across the crowded concourse and out of the station, heading north on York Way.

Here, following unobserved was much more difficult as there were not as many other people to hide among. I crossed over the road to walk parallel to him but on the far side. He didn't once glance over towards me as he hurried along, but then he too crossed over and turned right into Wharfdale Road. I hung back a little before continuing.

I tailed him to the far end of New Wharf Road, where he used a key to enter a smart new block of flats at number 17. I scanned through the names next to the bell buttons. There was no Daniel Jubowski listed, but half of the buttons had no names alongside them or perhaps he was sharing. Short of pushing each bell in turn, there was no way of telling which flat he had entered.

He may have moved out of the flat that Kenneth had visited in Tiber Gardens, but he hadn't gone far. Just across the Grand Union Canal, in fact. And he seemed to have moved up in the world. Flats hereabouts were hardly cheap, especially in a smart new apartment block overlooking the canal.

Hawthorn Pearce must pay well.

Offering him a few hundred quid to retract his statement might not be enough.

The train arrived into Chester Station on time at twenty-five minutes to twelve and the man from the rental car company was waiting for me at the station exit, holding a white board with *Jefferson* written across it in black letters.

"That's me," I said.

And it was.

The name in my passport was Jefferson Roosevelt Hinkley. I often thought my parents must have been going through an "American presidents" phase when I was born. But things could have been worse. I might have been called Madison McKinley. Or even Eisenhower Coolidge.

As it was, I was known universally by my colleagues, my friends, and family as Jeff, but that didn't stop me using my full first name when it was convenient, like when I didn't particularly want the name Hinkley on public view.

I completed the rental paperwork for a Toyota and then walked across to the Queen Hotel, resplendent with its statue of Queen Victoria balanced high on a portico above the front door.

When I walked out of the hotel later, the young woman behind the reception desk didn't recognize me as the guest she had checked in just an hour earlier.

My short bright-blond hair was hidden beneath a somewhat-tousled mousy brown wig that covered my ears, and my previously clean-shaven chin now sported a matching beard and mustache. The black-rimmed spectacles I had been wearing earlier had been consigned to the suitcase in my room, and the blazer, gray pants and tie had been swapped for a black roll-neck sweater, dark-blue jeans and a brown leather bomber jacket.

There was a time when I had avoided wearing jeans as they might prevent me following a target into a smart location, like some five-star London hotels, where a top-hatted doorman would try to bar the way. However, even these grand establishments were having to admit defeat in the sartorial stakes, with the likes of millionaire Hollywood film stars, multimillionaire computer software entrepreneurs and even some billionaire Russian oligarchs, all wearing jeans as their standard dress code, sometimes with a business suit jacket and tie.

For me, hoping to pass the evening unobtrusively in the local Tilston pub with the grooms from Graham Perry's yard, blue jeans and a bomber jacket were perfect.

Next for a makeover was the rental car.

I always booked the most basic model and asked for silver or gray as they were the least conspicuous or memorable colors. Invariably, however, the cars were always delivered sparkling clean all over, which, to my mind, marked them as being rented. Most people drove cars that were slightly dirty, and even those that had been through an automated car wash had grubby bits in the recesses of their wheels.

I drove the brand-new Toyota Yaris out of Chester south on the A41. As soon as I was clear of the town, I turned down a farm track and spent some minutes splashing muddy water into the wheel wells and over the silver bodywork until the new-car look had gone forever. With apologies to the rental company, I also wiped my muddy feet all over the pristine carpets, scattered a few candy wrappers over the backseat and placed some crumbled-up old leaves into the driver and passenger footwells.

It may have all been unnecessary, but those were the sorts of things I would have looked out for if I suspected someone of not being who they claimed to be. And if I would check, so might somebody else. It was all about not standing out and thus remaining unnoticed. For good measure, I wiped my muddy hands on the seat of my jeans.

Satisfied, I drove on towards Tilston.

ACCORDING TO the Ordnance Survey map I'd studied on the train, Graham Perry's yard was off the beaten track at the end of a half-mile lane. Driving down there would have surely courted attention, so I decided to make an initial inspection on foot, approaching from the hill behind via a public path through the woods.

All was quiet as I stood close to the tree line and studied the layout of the place through high-powered binoculars. I hadn't expected to see much movement, not at half past two on a Friday afternoon, but I wanted to be aware of the physical setup of the house and stables in case the information might be useful later.

The stables themselves appeared to be two U-shaped

blocks, both with traditional facing rows of separate stalls, with the horses' heads poking out through the open top halves of the stall doors.

There were two separate residential buildings, one a substantial box-shaped house with large Georgian-style windows on the far side of the stable yards, the other a smaller red-brick bungalow set to the right-hand side as I looked. There also was a two-story building between the two stable blocks, with what seemed to be garages below and six dormer-style windows above. I wondered if it might be accommodation for stable staff.

Running around the left side was a railed all-weather training gallop, which started at the lane beyond the house, curved around the buildings and ran up the hill to near where I sat at the edge of the woods. The gallop was about half a mile in total length and would be where the horses were exercised in the mornings.

I sat down on the damp grass and ate the cheese-and-pickle sandwich that Lydia had made for me the previous evening.

I was used to doing nothing for long periods, simply watching and waiting, but I did wonder about the purpose of this current surveillance. I could hardly tell from here if Graham Perry was or was not doping his horses with amphetamines. If it were up to me, I'd have sent in the testing teams. But Crispin must have his motives for asking me to watch, so watch I did.

After some time, a woman in a blue coat came out of the big house and began placing bedding plants into some window boxes.

Mrs. Perry, I assumed.

She moved from window to window, filling each box in turn with compost from a wheelbarrow before pricking out the seedlings from plastic trays. Finally, she used a dainty white watering can to give her new brood a drenching, no doubt in the hope that nighttime frosts were finally over for the winter.

I sat and daydreamed for a while, watching Mrs. Perry and wondering if she and Mr. Perry were happy in their marriage.

Would marrying Lydia be the sensible thing to do? Was I simply hanging back in the vain hope that things might change for the better? Perhaps this was as good as it gets and I'd be a fool to let such happiness I had slip through my fingers.

It was not as if Lydia and I argued at all. We didn't. It just seemed to me that we had lost the passion and excitement from our relationship, and I grieved for it. Sex had become routine rather than spontaneous and less satisfying as a result.

Maybe, I thought, I was having a midlife crisis. But, at thirty, surely I was too young for that.

But what was the alternative? Force the relationship to a close, along with all its inherent problems, both emotional and financial, and then start the long process of finding a new mate?

I'd always wanted children; I suppose almost everyone did. To re-create the next generation in one's own image is a powerful human instinct, to perpetuate the species. But if I had to start all over again, might I be too old to be the active young father I always thought I'd be. Body clock ticking and all that. True for dads as well as moms.

What, I wondered, would happen if and when the scientists found the magic potion to prevent aging so human beings could live for much longer, maybe even forever? What would happen to fertility? The world is very nearly full of people now, with hardly enough productive land available to feed us all here already. If we continued in the future to procreate at the present rate and nobody died, the human species would very quickly be in deep trouble.

My thoughts of impending doom were interrupted by a small car that drove along the lane towards the house. I raised my binoculars and watched as Mrs. Perry waved at the driver. I couldn't see if the wave was returned, but I watched as the car pulled into the courtyard between the house and the stables. Two men got out and then disappeared from view into the two-story building. Perhaps some of the stable staff returning to their digs above the garages.

I waited a while longer, again checking the layout of the stables and the house to ensure that I had it correctly logged in to my memory. Mrs. Perry completed her window boxes and went back inside, and all was quiet.

I looked at my watch. It was nearly four o'clock.

Like every other racing yard in the country, the one below me would soon be coming to life for "evening stables," when the grooms would come back on duty to brush the horses, give them food and water, muck out the stalls and finally rug up the horses for the night. It is also when the trainer would generally do his daily round, examining each horse in turn, feeling for any unusual heat in its legs, and arranging for any special feeds or medications.

According to the BHA register, Graham Perry currently employed ten staff, all of whom had also been issued a Racehorse Attendant's Identity Card to allow access to the secure areas at British racetracks. Over the past couple of days, I had learned the names of all ten by heart and had even searched the files to study the photographs on their identity card applications. I was confident that I'd know them if any came into the pub that evening.

Not one of the ten was Lee Furness, former employee of Matthew Unwin and possible relation to Jordan Furness, the murdered bookmaker.

7

I walked into the Tilston local at ten past seven, having parked the rental car a couple of streets away. I didn't want anyone who might have seen the car parked off the road earlier near the woods spotting it again outside the pub and asking difficult questions.

I had remained at my vantage point up the hill until evening stables were well under way, with the lights in the stalls beginning to shine brightly in the gloom of the March afternoon. I had departed only when the daylight began to fade to such an extent that waiting any longer would have left me unlikely to find my way back to the car through the trees.

Graham Perry had emerged from his house at twenty minutes to five, and I had watched him intently through the binoculars as he had moved from stall to stall to inspect the horses within. There appeared nothing unusual about his actions, but, without night vision goggles, I had no idea if he'd again crossed the courtyard to the stables after the other staff had left with mischief on his mind and a loaded syringe in his hand.

THE PUB was busy, with Friday-evening drinkers raiding their weekly pay packets for a few pints with their mates.

A large circle of ten men stood in front of the bar loudly discussing soccer, especially the match between Liverpool and Manchester United scheduled for the following afternoon.

"That new boy—you know, the Czech with the unpronounceable name—he'll make all the difference for United," one said. "Can't see them losing with him on the team."

"Nonsense," said another. "Liverpool at home—no contest."

I bought myself a nonalcoholic beer at the bar and stood on the periphery of the circle, scrutinizing my fellow drinkers, as the banter continued back and forth.

"Your goalie's no good anyway. He couldn't catch a cold."

"He saved that penalty last week against Chelsea—kept us in the game."

None of them were grooms from Graham Perry's stable. I was sure of it.

"Are you a Liverpool or United fan?" asked the man standing on my right.

"Neither," I said with a smile. "Can't stand either of them. I want them to draw so they both lose ground." I was using my best Newcastle accent.

"Bloody Geordie," said one of the others, a big man who'd had a few pints in his time if his protruding beer gut was anything to go by.

"And proud of it," I replied with a laugh. They all laughed with me. I was now an accepted member of the circle. "I'm more of a horseracing man myself. I'm off to Bangor-on-Dee tomorrow."

"Me too," said the tall young man on my left.

"And me," piped up another. "I reckon Perry will win the big race. He always does well at Bangor."

"Perry?" I queried.

"Graham Perry," said the big man. "His place is just down the road."

I nodded in understanding. "So do you get any local tips? Any insider info?"

"His grooms are usually down here on a Friday. They'll put you right."

As if on cue, the door of the bar opened and four of Graham Perry's stable staff came in.

"Speak of the devil," said the big man with a huge guffaw. "Evening, lads. Want a drink? Who's going to win tomorrow?"

"Ah. That would be telling," one of the four replied, placing a finger alongside his nose.

I knew him from his BHA photo. His name was Sean Caddick, and he'd been at Perry's yard for at least the last five years.

"Come on, lads," said the big man, not giving up so easily. "You must know what's going to win. It's only fair you let us locals in on the deal."

"If only we knew," Sean replied. "We're forever losing because we think ours will win and then they don't."

The talk was all in good humor with plenty of smiles

"Surely you use go-faster juice?" I said it with a laugh.

I watched him closely for any reaction. A tightening of the muscles in the face, a widening of the pupils of the eyes—both involuntary consequences of increased adrenaline, both giveaways of stress and fear.

"You must be joking," Sean said. "You can't even give a horse a piece of chocolate these days without it failing a dope test."

"Chocolate?" said the big man. "How the hell does chocolate make a horse go faster?"

"I've no idea," Sean replied. "But I do know that it will make it fail a dope test. It once happened to a horse I looked after. The bloody owner gave it a Mars bar as a treat on the morning of a race. Stupid woman. The horse was disqualified and we all nearly lost our jobs."

I decided not to tell them that it was the theobromine in chocolate that was the prohibited substance, along with the caffeine. Both were banned stimulants.

Paradoxically, eating chocolates could make you run faster, provided you didn't spend all day sitting on the sofa watching television while you ate it.

"How many runners have you got at Bangor?" asked the tall young man on my left.

"Three," said one of the other grooms, a man I

recognized as Tom Lindsay. "One in the first, and two in the Wrexham."

The Wrexham Handicap Chase would be the big race of the day.

"Will they win?" asked the big man.

"If they're fast enough," came the ironic reply.

"You're no bloody help."

"Tribute Lunch has a great chance," Sean Caddick said, "but don't blame me if you lose your shirt."

That seemed to end the conversation, and the four grooms collected beers from the bar before moving over to sit together at a table by the window. The circle broke up into smaller groups, and I found myself talking to the tall man who was going to Bangor races the following day.

"You're a long way from home," he said. "Don't get many Geordies round here."

"Visiting my aunt," I said. "And for the races."

"Where does she live?" he asked.

Damn it, I thought, I really didn't need an inquisitive local.

"Fancy a game of darts?" I asked him, ignoring his question.

"No thanks, I'm rubbish." He turned away to talk to the man on the other side.

Meanwhile, I took a set of darts from behind the bar and practiced on my own. Not that I really liked throwing darts, but the board was on the same side of the room as the grooms now sitting at a table.

All the better for hearing what they were talking about.

That is, if they'd been saying anything interesting, or at least something interesting about racing. Instead, they were discussing the relative merits of girls—in particular, the four members of a popular band who were all the rage.

"God, I'd like to give that Justine one," said Tom Lindsay. "I wouldn't chuck her out of bed for eating biscuits."

"Much too snobbish, if you ask me," said one of the others. "But Gillian—now, she's just my sort. Nice and cuddly, with gorgeous tits."

It was not great conversation and of little use to me. Not for the first time, I wondered why I was here. These lads were like all other grooms the world over, spending their time drinking beer and chatting about girls. And I was sure that listening to them wouldn't give me any insight into whether their boss was or was not doping his horses.

Sean Caddick's face and eyes had remained steadfast and completely unaffected by my comment concerning go-faster juice. If Graham Perry was indeed dosing his horses with amphetamine, then one of his long-serving stable staff didn't know about it. Of that I was certain.

I went on throwing darts.

"Fancy a game?" I turned around. Tom Lindsay was on his feet.

"Sure," I said. "Loser buys the beers?"

"OK," he said. "But it'll be you."

"How are you so sure?"

"I'm the local champion."

"Now you tell me."

I was good at darts, the result of having had a board on the back of my bedroom door during my early teens, but I was no match for Tom Lindsay.

I bought the beers, mine again nonalcoholic, and we played a second game with him giving me a 200-point start.

"Are you going to Bangor races tomorrow?" I asked as I finally managed to hit a treble twenty.

"Yeah," he replied. "We all go to Bangor on race days. The gaffer lets us do evening stables late."

"Good to work for, then, is he?"

"He's OK," Tom said. "I've worked for worse."

He beat me again. Easily.

"Thanks," he said, drifting back to the table to rejoin his mates. I was clearly not a sufficient challenge for his skills.

"Yeah," I said. "Thanks."

I returned the darts to the barman, drained my glass, and decided it was time to leave. There was nothing else to gain by staying any longer.

I WAS BACK at my vantage point in the woods above Graham Perry's yard by eight in the morning.

Some of the horses were exercising up the gallop when I arrived. Hence, I stayed well back behind the tree line so as not to be visible.

I was now dressed and appeared as myself. The beard and tousled mousy brown wig of yesterday were neatly packed away in my overnight bag along with the jeans and the leather bomber jacket. Today I was clean-shaven, short-haired, with gray pants and a navy blue sweater.

I watched as the eight horses walked back down to the start of the all-weather gallop before once again moving fluently up in pairs, galloping upsides under the careful watch of Mr. Perry, who leaned against the front of his Land Rover.

I studied the horses and riders through my binoculars and could clearly distinguish the features of Sean Caddick riding one of the leading pair.

Thirty or more years ago, trainers, especially steeplechase trainers like Graham Perry, would have galloped their horses over a much greater distance than the half mile or so of this all-weather track, perhaps over a mile or even a mile and a half as a single exercise.

All that had changed, not least due to the influence of the trainer Martin Pipe, who had had such phenomenal success either side of the millennium being champion jump trainer a total of fifteen times in seventeen years.

Martin trained his horses in a manner far more akin to how a coach would train a human athlete. Instead of a single long exercise run, he used shorter, interval training gallops. And everyone else soon followed suit.

Graham Perry's horses were blowing hard by the time they reached the top of the rise, their nostrils rhythmically flaring and contracting as the air rushed in and out, the expelled moisture condensing into a fine mist in the morning chill like steam from a two-spout kettle.

They were then walked around in a large circle until their breathing rates had returned to normal.

When all eight horses had recovered from the exertion, the pairs moved off in turn, walking down to the start of the track, from where the whole procedure was repeated.

After the horses had galloped past the Land Rover for a third time, I watched as Graham Perry drove himself back to the yard, the horses following a few minutes later, led home by Sean Caddick.

I REMAINED in the woods all morning, keeping watch as events unfolded beneath me.

Another eight horses were taken through the same exercise regime, with the trainer again watching from in front of his vehicle. And there was considerable movement in the training yard as well.

At eleven o'clock a horse trailer was driven into the loading area close to the stable blocks and I watched as three horses were loaded aboard.

The runners for Bangor-on-Dee, I assumed.

Boxes of tack and other kit were also lifted aboard, and the trailer departed down the lane at twenty past eleven.

It was only about ten miles from Perry's yard to Bangor-on-Dee racetrack, but, sensibly, the horses would be there early, with time to calm down after the journey and relax in the stables until their race times.

There was plenty of other activity as the whole team rushed through their duties, getting ready to depart for the races.

I had checked that the first race at Bangor started at half past two, and, as two o'clock approached, there was a final mad rush, with several people running out to cars and disappearing down the lane with their wheels spinning.

I didn't follow them to Bangor. In fact, I never did get to the races.

I waited on the hill for another half hour to see if there were any lategoers, then I walked back to the rented Toyota and drove around to Graham Perry's stable, pulling up in the middle of the courtyard and sounding the horn with three long loud bursts.

No one came out to greet me.

For good measure, I went over to the house and rang the doorbell.

No reply.

I stood outside the two-story accommodation block and shouted for attention.

I got none.

In my hand I held my BHA credentials and a letter indicating that I had the right to enter any BHA-licensed premises, including this stable yard.

No one emerged to read either.

It appeared that, as Tom Lindsay had told me in the Tilston pub, the whole workforce had decamped to Bangor-on-Dee races, and Mrs. Perry had gone with them.

In fairness, in spite of the place being deserted, security had not been completely compromised. Each lower stall door was padlocked shut, and the feed and tack rooms were locked as well. I tried them.

Fortunately, as far as I could see, there were no CCTV cameras recording my visit.

As my credentials made clear, I had every right to be there, but I didn't really have the right to pick the three-lever lock on the door of the feed store, something I managed with ease.

It was much like any other racing stable's feed store. There were unopened bags of horse pellets stacked in one corner, and a feed bin containing more loose pellets in another. Some trainers with big yards had their own special mixtures made up by the feed companies with added cod liver oil or cider vinegar, others had added garlic or Cortaflex for joints, others still even had Guinness included in the recipe.

It appeared that Graham Perry used the standard mixture, but even he would probably add some vitamin supplement or special potions to the feed. Gone, however, were the days when trainers created their own feed mashes, concoctions of boiled barley, linseed oil, and bran, all mixed hot in an old bathtub. The modern nutritional horse pellet had consigned these mashes to history and no one had complained, not least the poor groom who'd had to stir them.

As a general rule of thumb, racehorses eat one pound in weight of mixed feed for every hand high they stand at their withers. Most Thoroughbreds are around sixteen to seventeen hands high, so they eat sixteen to seventeen pounds of feed a day, plus some hay.

If Graham Perry was dosing his horses with powdered

amphetamine, then there would likely be traces of it in the feed store.

I took some swabs from the floor and also from the bowls that were used to measure out the feed, placing them into sealed plastic bags. I also put a handful of the horse nuts into my pocket, but I was pretty sure they would be all legal and aboveboard.

I checked around for anything unusual without finding it, then used my skeleton keys to relock the feed store.

I walked through an arch into the stable blocks. The lower doors may have been padlocked shut but the upper ones were wide open, and half a dozen horses put their heads out through the opening to see who had arrived.

I went over to each of them in turn, holding a couple of the horse nuts from my pocket flat on my left palm. As they leaned down to take the nuts, I reached up with my right hand to pluck out a few hairs from between their ears. These too went into plastic bags.

Hair could be a splendid source of information. It provided a history of what a horse has consumed, and recent advances in analytical techniques had shown great promise in the detection of even the smallest traces of illicit drugs.

Phar Lap, the New Zealand/Australian hero horse of the Great Depression years, was widely believed to have been deliberately poisoned by gangsters while racing in the United States. Seventy-six years later, in 2008, six mane hairs were taken from his hide, which is still on display in Melbourne Museum, and they confirmed that he had been given a huge dose of arsenic some thirty to forty hours prior to death.

In all, I removed hairs from twelve of Graham Perry's horses, each carefully placed in separate bags.

Enough, I thought. Probably more than enough.

It was time to return to my own troubles in London.

8

By nine o'clock on Monday morning, all hell had broken loose in the BHA office.

"What's going on?" I asked Nigel Green, my co-watcher from Cheltenham, who was standing guard at the main door as I arrived.

"I've no idea," he said. "All I've been told is that there's been a communications embargo put in place. All the phone lines are down and the Internet's been disconnected, internal and external. No one is allowed to use cells or leave the building."

He put out his hand for my phone.

"Is that legal?" I asked. "What about false imprisonment?"

"No one's making you come in," Nigel said rather formally. "But if you do, you have to stay until you're told you can go."

"Who by?" I asked.

"The BHA Board will make the decision. Paul told me they're having an emergency meeting. They've apparently all been here since seven o'clock."

Emergency Board meetings of the BHA were unheard of, especially not at seven on a Monday morning.

"What's it all about?"

"I told you, I don't know. But I'm sure we'll find out soon enough. Poor Crispin's running round like a headless chicken."

It must be bad, I thought, if our ultra-calm chief intelligence analyst was in a panic.

Nigel was still holding his hand out for my phone. I handed it over and he placed it in a box that already contained many others.

I'd never heard of anything like it—not outside the military anyway.

But it was similar to what had happened in Afghanistan whenever a soldier was killed in action. All personal communications with the outside world were shut down so that the details of the incident could not be inadvertently released to the public before the Ministry of Defence had informed the dead soldier's family.

Had anyone died here? Surely not. There would be paramedics and police all over the place.

So what was it?

I walked to my office, trying to imagine a credible scenario that could cause such alarm in the organization.

As Nigel had said, we would find out soon enough, but that didn't stop the gossip. With no access to e-mail and no phone calls, either in or out, the morning was not very productive at BHA headquarters, with most of the staff eventually gathering together to whisper in the corridors or in the office kitchen, where we normally made tea and coffee.

"If you ask me, the boss has had a brainstorm," said one junior assistant. "Thinks he's back in the army."

"Perhaps he's been murdered," said another with relish.

It all sounded so improbable, but nothing else we came up with sounded any less so.

The staff banter was interrupted by Paul Maldini, head of operations, who put his head through the kitchen doorway at half past eleven.

"Jeff," he said, pointing at me. "They want you in the boardroom. Straightaway."

Everyone looked in my direction.

"Me?" I said, surprised. "Do I need to take anything?"

"Just yourself," he said. "And pronto." He jerked his thumb for me to follow.

I just had time to tidy my hair with my fingers before opening the boardroom door and walking in.

There were seven nonexecutive directors of the British Horseracing Authority and they were all present, a further indication that something massive was occurring. I knew them all by name and reputation but had actually met only two of them previously. In addition, there was Howard Lever, the BHA chief executive, and Stephen Kohli, director of Integrity, Legal and Risk.

"Ah, Mr. Hinkley," said Roger Vincent, the chairman. "Please, come and sit down." He pointed to an empty chair on his right. "Gentlemen, this is Jeff Hinkley. He's the investigator in our Integrity Service that we've been talking about."

"He's very young," declared a man sitting at the far end of the table. It wasn't said as a compliment.

"He's also very good," said Neil Wallinger. He was the director responsible for integrity matters and also one of the two I had met before. I looked across at him and smiled. "Jeff Hinkley has a remarkable photographic memory and probably knows more about racing, and racing people, than anyone else alive."

"I'm not so sure." The man at the far end spoke loudly and rather dismissively, drawing supportive signals from a few of his colleagues. "Are you sure he's up to it? I've never even heard of him."

"Maybe not," replied Neil Wallinger, "but I bet he's heard of you."

All the faces swung back to me.

Neil Wallinger nodded at me in encouragement.

"Your name is Ian Tulloch," I said, looking straight at the man. "You are fifty-four years old and have been a director on this Board for the past two years. You are nominated to the position by the Racegoers Association. You were educated at Harrow, where you were Head of House of West Acre. You gained a First Class degree in mathematics from Balliol College, Oxford, before qualifying as a chartered accountant with the firm Tweedale and Vaughan, where you are now the chief operating officer. You are a trustee of two small charities, the Peter Walsh Cancer Fund, named after the son of a friend who died of lymphoma four years ago at age sixteen, and the Surrey Pony Club Trust, based in Dorking, near where you live with your wife, Rebecca, and two teenage daughters, Siân and Valerie. Your interest in racing was initially encouraged by your uncle, Albert Tulloch, who took you as a child to Fontwell Park, where he later became managing director. You currently own five horses in training, three with Duncan Johnson in Lambourn and two with Richard Young in Nether Wallop. Their names are Highlighter, Cruise Reception, Paperclip, Nobis and Annual Return. You have had two winners this year, one at Newbury, where Nobis won a novice hurdle in January, and again last week at Warwick, where Highlighter cruised home by ten lengths in the two-mile novice chase at a price of twelve-to-one."

I stopped.

The nine pairs of eyes stared at me as if I was an alien.

I decided against telling them that I also knew Mr. Tulloch was occasionally unfaithful to his wife with a certain *lady of the night* with whom he sporadically did business while staying in London during the week.

"Does he know as much about all of us?" asked Roger Vincent with a nervous laugh.

"Oh, I expect so," said Howard Lever. "Maybe more. Some of which we probably wouldn't want revealed here."

Some of them mumbled to one another and shifted uneasily in their chairs. And well they might, I thought. Few of us were entirely without a skeleton in a closet somewhere, and that was certainly true of this bunch. I'd been unofficially tasked with carrying out background checks on some of them before they were appointed, including Ian Tulloch.

"Gentlemen," said Roger Vincent, bringing the meeting back to order, "are we in agreement?"

There were determined nods from all around the table, even from Ian Tulloch.

"Right." The chairman turned to me. "Jeff, what we are about to discuss is highly confidential. You may not speak of it to anyone. Do you understand?"

"Yes," I replied.

"The future of racing could depend on it," Howard Lever said. It all sounded rather melodramatic, but he was deadly serious. "Someone is attempting to undermine the authority of the BHA and they are also trying to extort money from us."

"Have you called in the police?" I asked.

"No police," Roger Vincent said sharply. "We have been instructed not to inform the police."

"But surely we must," I said. "Extortion is a serious crime."

"Mr. Hinkley," said the director sitting on Ian Tulloch's left, "it is the Board that makes the decisions on such matters. You are here merely to carry them out."

Bill Ripley was in his early forties and supposedly an independent member of the BHA Board, although it was universally acknowledged that he unofficially represented the Jockey Club.

His grandfather had been a Scottish Earl and also senior steward of the Jockey Club, as his father had been before him. Indeed, Bill Ripley came from a long line of eminent Jockey Club members and he could trace his ancestry back to its very founding by the "Noblemen and Gentlemen" of 1750.

His *Who's Who* biography claimed he was an insurance broker, but, in the family tradition, he appeared to have done little actual work, spending the majority of his time, and his inheritance, being the owner of a substantial string of racehorses, mostly running on the flat.

I looked along the table at him and he stared back at me through his tortoiseshell glasses.

"Not if it involves breaking the law," I said.

"The BHA exercises control over racing by consensus rather than by legal statute," Howard Lever said quickly, trying to defuse the situation. "If the racing public loses confidence in our ability, then the whole fabric of racing will begin to unravel."

"So what is it that's happened that has caused all this furor?" I asked.

Roger Vincent sighed. "Every horse dope-tested during the Cheltenham Festival has returned a positive result for a banned substance."

"What!" I said. "All of them?"

He nodded. "Almost all of them. Forty-nine horses were tested over the four days and forty-six of them have returned a positive result for something called methylphenidate, a banned stimulant, including the first two home in the Gold Cup."

No wonder Crispin Larson had been running around all morning like a headless chicken.

"There must be something wrong with the testing," I said.

"There isn't," replied Stephen Kohli. "I've been at the testing laboratory over the weekend, ever since they called us in on Friday with their initial findings. We all thought it must be a mistake, but it isn't. All the samples were properly collected, properly handled and free from contamination. Every B sample analysis matched the A sample result. There was nothing wrong with the testing. The only conclusion we can draw is that the forty-six horses were all doped."

"But that's incredible," I said.

"Yes, it is, but that's not all," Roger Vincent said. "We have also received a letter."

He handed over a piece of paper.

To Roger Vincent, Chairman of the BHA:

By now you should have found out about my little game at Cheltenham. Be assured that I can do it whenever I like—perhaps I'll play it again at Ascot this coming weekend. I could play it whenever I want and destroy your attempts to keep British racing clear of drugs.

I will stop playing my game and will disappear forever, but only for a fee. Five million pounds would be enough. Not much, really. Racing can afford it. According to your own figures, the racing industry is worth three and a half billion a year.

You will not contact the police or I will destroy all confidence in racing. The betting public will desert you in droves and British Racing will go out of business. So remember, NO POLICE.

Send your acceptance via the personal column in The Times. *Place the following announcement in the paper and you will then be sent further details:* Van Gogh accepts Leonardo's generous offer of marriage.

"Don't tell me this is the original letter," I said with a degree of exasperation.

He looked at me guiltily.

"And you've passed it round this table?"

He nodded

"You're mad," I said. "You will have destroyed any chance of getting any useful fingerprints from it. Where's the envelope? Can we test that?"

"We are not involving the police." Roger Vincent was adamant. "We can't take the risk."

"They may have to be involved eventually," I said. And as far as I was concerned, the sooner the better.

"As may be, but we want you to carry out an investigation first, quietly and effectively, to ascertain who wrote this letter and how he doped so many horses at Cheltenham. In the meantime, we will place the announcement in *The Times.*"

"But surely you're not going to pay this man." I looked around the table at the glum faces. Most of the eyes avoided meeting mine. "There's no guarantee that he won't ask for more money next year, next month or even next week. What will you do then?"

"We feel we have no alternative," Howard Lever said with a sigh.

"Of course you have," I said forcibly. "Ignore him or tell him to take a jump. You must call in the police so they can find out who it is and throw him in jail."

"But what about racing?" Howard Lever said. "Things are financially precarious enough with all the Internet gambling sites now basing themselves offshore to avoid the betting levy. The Board feels that a scandal of this magnitude could bring us down permanently like a house of cards in a wind."

Everyone knew that things weren't great money-wise in racing, but I had no idea they were that bad.

"So you're going to try and keep this all hush-hush?"

"That's the plan," said Ian Tulloch from the far end.

"Well, I think you're all crazy," I said, taking a liberty way beyond my station. "For a start, shutting down all communications and removing every cell phone at the office front door was as good as broadcasting long and loud that something was seriously wrong. Out there in the office it's like speculation city. What are you going to tell the staff?" I looked around at the other members of the Board. "Mr. Pottinger," I went on. "You're a public relations man. Surely this could all blow up in our faces."

Piers Pottinger was a PR heavyweight with a special connection with the media, gaming and horseracing industries. He was a past and present owner of racehorses and had the distinction of owning the oldest horse ever to win a race at Royal Ascot when Caracciola came home to win the Queen Alexandra Stakes at age twelve.

"The PR position is very delicate," he said. "Confidence is everything in this industry. As I see it, as long as the public has confidence in us, there is no problem. But when that confidence drains away . . . well, so would racing's betting revenue. And pretty quickly too." He paused for effect. "Either course of action clearly has some risk. If we say nothing to the police, and provided the matter is resolved without any media coverage, all remains fine in the eyes of the public. However, if the story leaks, then even if we resolve the matter successfully, confidence may have been eroded permanently."

Typical PR, I thought. Sitting on the fence.

"What if we do not resolve the matter successfully?" I said. "If the whole thing goes horribly wrong and the public discovers that we did not inform the police, then surely that would be more of a PR disaster. Public confidence would be severely shaken."

There was a sea of worried faces in front of me.

"And are we sure we can keep it out of the media anyway?" I asked. "What about the labs? Can you be sure no one there will call the papers or the TV stations?"

"Security at the labs is fine," Stephen Kohli said. "The samples are just coded with a number. The name of the horse and the race are not shown. All the lab knows is that there were a large number of positives, not where they came from."

"It won't take rocket science for them to work it out, not with Cheltenham just over."

"Mr. Hinkley," said Bill Ripley abruptly, pointing at me with the arm of his tortoiseshell glasses, "we have discussed this problem at great length throughout the morning and we have agreed to investigate the matter in house, without informing the police, at least for the time being. We have asked you to be present here because Mr. Lever and Mr. Wallinger both insist that you are the best-placed individual in our organization to carry out such an investigation. Are they wrong?"

All nine of them looked at me again.

"No, sir," I said. "They are not wrong." I paused. "However, I can't promise you any results. I may not be able to discover who is doing this or how it is done. But, yes, I believe I am the best person to try, especially if you want it done so that no one outside this room even knows that an investigation is under way."

"Good," Roger Vincent said. "It's settled, then. We will not involve the police at this stage. Jeff will investigate this matter and report back to us. We have a scheduled meeting of the Board a week from Wednesday." He turned to me. "Is nine days long enough for you?"

"More than enough," I said. "If I don't have the results in nine days, I don't think I'll ever get them."

"You don't sound very confident," said George Searle, a former racehorse trainer and the Thoroughbred Owners and Trainers representative on the Board.

"I'm not particularly. Whoever is doing this will have made meticulous plans, probably over many months, if not years. He will probably be expecting us to call in the police, yet he must remain convinced he won't get caught or he wouldn't have started all this in the first place. The police would have had a team of men and all the resources of the forensic services. I am just a single investigator with little or no backup. Would you be confident?"

There were some murmurings around the table. Clearly, the decision not to call in the police had not been a unanimous one and now there were some grumbles from the dissenters.

"But I'll have a go," I said. "I should at least be able to find out how it was done and maybe that will allow us to stop it from happening again."

That seemed to cheer them up somewhat.

"In the meantime," I went on, "by all means place an announcement in *The Times,* but don't agree to everything."

"In what way?" asked Roger Vincent.

"Only agree to a bit at a time. Negotiate. I don't imagine that he will expect to get five million pounds. I'd offer him twenty thousand. Or even less."

"How would we do that?"

"Put an announcement in *The Times* that says that Van Gogh accepts Leonardo's offer of marriage with a proposed dowry of twenty thousand pounds."

"Would twenty thousand be enough?" asked Ian Tulloch. "It's not much compared to five million."

"Twenty thousand pounds is still a lot of money," I said. At least it was for me. Twenty thousand pounds, all of it tax-free, was more than many people earned in a year, but for the likes of Ian Tulloch it might just be petty cash.

"The man might go to the newspapers," said Charles Payne, another of the independent directors.

"He won't," I said decisively, but I looked around at skeptical faces in front of me. "Not if he's in this for the money. As I said before, he'll have spent months planning every single detail—it's not easy, or cheap, to dope every horse at Cheltenham—and he'll want a decent return for his trouble. There's no way he would give up his trump card so easily." They still didn't look convinced. "He probably wants half a million. If he asks you for five million and you end up paying him half a million, then you'll probably all believe you have a bargain, but he, in fact, will have gained everything that he'd hoped for in the first place. I'd maybe offer him less than twenty grand, perhaps only ten."

"How do you know all this?" asked Bill Ripley in a tone that implied he didn't really believe me.

"I've completed several tours of Afghanistan as an army intelligence specialist. Much of my time was spent dealing with kidnapping in Helmand Province—mostly among the Afghan people. A child of one of the few remaining middle-class Afghans would be snatched either by the Taliban or, more often, by the corrupt police. The ransom demanded would always be for millions of dollars, a sum way beyond the means of even the richest parents. Offers and threats would pass back and forth until an amount was agreed upon that was acceptable to both sides. Sometimes it was only a few hundred dollars or maybe a few thousand. I was involved in many of those negotiations, sometimes face-to-face with the kidnappers. They were a source of essential intelligence, especially in learning who were our real friends, rather than those who would happily shoot us in the back as soon as we turned round."

"Why did you leave the army?" It was Bill Ripley again.

"I didn't want to get killed," I said. "I did three six-month tours inside four years and I didn't fancy going back—too many of the bad guys knew me by then."

In truth, I'd been fortunate to get out alive from one particularly hairy situation in an Afghan house when hostage negotiations had rapidly gone tits up and guns had been drawn by both sides, most of them pointing at me. On top of that, a good mate of mine hadn't been so lucky in a similar circumstance and he'd come home in a box.

No one now questioned my assessment of the current situation.

"Tell us what to do," said Roger Vincent.

"Personally, I'd probably call in the police. But if you won't do that and I accept that position, then let's place a notice in the paper and wait for a response. Meanwhile, I'll try to find out how he did it and stop it happening again at Ascot."

"What do you need from us?"

"I assume from his demeanor that Crispin Larson is aware of the situation."

"He's aware of the test results," said Roger Vincent, "but not the letter."

"I'll need his help to find out how the doping was done. And he should be made aware of the letter. He has one of the best analytical minds I know. We could all do with his help."

Roger Vincent looked around the table and received a series of nods.

"That's agreed," he said. "But no one else."

"What shall we tell the staff?" Howard Lever asked no one in particular.

"Tell them that you were concerned about a leak of confidential material to a newspaper," I said, "and you are now happy that the source of the leak has been identified and the individual concerned has been disciplined."

"Which individual?"

"Me, of course," I said. "All the staff in this building will know by now I've been summoned to the boardroom. Most will probably have walked past to have a look." I waved at the glass wall, through which we could see people in the office. "We simply let it be known that I've lost my job for passing unauthorized information to the press. That way, I can work without anyone else knowing what I'm doing. As long as I have remote access to the BHA data files, I can work from home. I will need to keep my credentials, of course, to get into the racetracks and so on. Crispin Larson can be my contact here at headquarters. He'll need to know that I am actually still employed and working totally undercover."

"Isn't that all a bit melodramatic?" Howard Lever asked.

That's rich, I thought, coming from him.

"How would you ever be able to come back to work for the BHA?" Bill Ripley asked.

"You're a member of the Jockey Club," I said to him. "They've never made public any reasons for their decisions for more than two hundred years. I'm sure the BHA can take a page out of their book just for once."

And anyway, I thought, an undercover man not openly acknowledged by the BHA might be very useful.

I'd often stretched the boundaries of legality in my surveillance work, but now I felt a greater freedom, released from the necessity to write reports for my fellow investigators to pore over and tut-tut my actions.

Just as long as the BHA didn't completely hang me out to dry if I got caught on the wrong side.

9

Nigel Green was furious on my behalf.

"They can't just sack you," he screamed. "It's outrageous."

"They didn't sack me," I said rather more quietly as I filled an old shoebox with the personal items from my desk. "I was invited to resign."

"That's tantamount to the same thing. It's a disgrace, and I don't care who hears me say it." He was almost shouting in defiance.

"Nigel," I said, "let it go. I'm quite happy to move on, and this way I get a decent reference. If we make too much of a fuss, I may lose that. That was the deal. So, thank you for your concern, but please drop it."

I hated lying to him.

Nigel had become my closest friend at the BHA, not

that any of my colleagues were really that close. I tended to keep my own company.

Soon after I'd started the job, Nigel and his wife had asked Lydia and me to join them for supper and, shortly thereafter, we had returned their hospitality, but that had been nearly three years ago now and neither of us had seemed that keen to do it again.

I suppose it was something to do with our line of work. We may not be as bad as Crispin Larson, but we were all believers in security and the need-to-know principle. It tended to make us rather reserved on a social level.

"What will you do?" Nigel asked.

"I'm not sure," I said. "Something will turn up. I negotiated three months' pay in lieu of notice, so I have time to look."

"It's a damn shame," he said. "The job has been more interesting with you round. I'm really sorry to see you go."

"You never know," I said. "I might come back, when I've served my time in exile and they've forgotten and forgiven."

"I hope so."

It seemed mean, somehow, putting him through his sorrow, but it wasn't as if I'd died. And he'd soon forget me when I passed through the front door.

THE FIRST TASK was to find out how the horses had been doped and it was the three negative test results that were the key. Why were they negative when all the others had been positive? If I could find out what was different about those three, then I was sure I'd find the method.

Crispin Larson had been apprised of the situation by Howard Lever and he was keen as mustard to assist, meeting me for a drink about an hour after I'd left the building.

"Clandestine operations are my forte," he claimed. "God, if only I was able to turn my body clock back a few years, I'd be out there with you, dear boy. It would be just like old times."

We were speaking together at a table in the back room at El Vino, the famous wine bar in Fleet Street, once the haunt of journalists and newspaper editors but now frequented mostly by those from the legal profession, although the place was almost empty at two-thirty in the afternoon.

Most important, it was not a regular drinking hole for staff from the BHA, who usually walked no farther than the Red Lion pub situated right next door to the offices.

"What exactly did you do in the old times?" I asked him.

He didn't answer. In fact, he said nothing. I wondered if he was internally berating himself for having said too much already.

"I need some information," I said. "For a start, I need the names of all the horses that were tested and especially the three that were not found to be positive."

"I have it all here, dear boy," he said, pulling one of his red folders from his briefcase. He handed it over.

"Thanks," I said. I flicked through the folder, glancing at page after page of positive results for something called methylphenidate.

"What is methylphenidate anyway?"

"It's a central nervous system stimulant, similar in chemical makeup to amphetamine. Methylphenidate hydrochloride is marketed as the drug called Ritalin. Rather conversely, even though it's a stimulant, it is often prescribed for the treatment of hyperactivity in children."

"But does it make horses run faster?"

"It certainly could with the right dosage. The positive tests at Cheltenham were all of fairly low concentrations and probably wouldn't have affected the results, but they were well over the NET."

"The NET?"

"The no-effect threshold," Crispin said. "It's the level below which the drug has no significant pharmacological action. It is effectively the level above which the BHA would take action and disqualify the horse. For some drugs, like anabolic steroids, the NET is zero."

"But we're not disqualifying the horses this time?"

"How can we? It would mean we would disqualify all the winners at the Festival. British racing would be ridiculed and would be laughed at all round the world."

He was right.

And who was to say that the man had doped only the forty-six that had tested positive? In total, four hundred and sixty-two horses had run in twenty-seven races during the four days of the Festival. Only the race winners, beaten favorites and a few other randomly selected horses would have been drug-tested. That added up to just forty-nine. How many of the other four hundred and thirteen had also been dosed with methylphenidate?

If we disqualified the winners, could we be sure that those that finished second, and would hence be promoted to victors, weren't also high on the same stuff? We knew that both the winner and the second horse in the Gold Cup had tested positive, so did we award that race to the well-beaten, and untested, third?

I had some sympathy with the BHA Board and their insistence on secrecy. There would be a god-awful row if this ever became public, with lawsuits galore and everyone trying to get their grubby hands on the gold.

"Is that all?" said Crispin. "I'd better get back."

He started to stand up, but I put my hand on his arm to stop him.

"Crispin," I said. "There's something else I need to ask."

He sat down again. "Fire away, dear boy."

"I want to know why you sent me to have a quiet look at Graham Perry's setup rather than sending in the drug-testing team straightaway."

He was slightly taken unawares.

"Why?" he asked.

"Because of something I read concerning Matthew Unwin. He claimed in his disciplinary hearing that someone had doped his horses without his knowledge because he'd refused to pay them. Was it anything like that with Graham Perry?"

"I don't know what you mean, dear boy."

Crispin was ever so slightly flustered, a state he usually created in others.

"Come on, Crispin," I said, "tell me. You must have had good reasons."

He looked at me as if weighing the pros and cons.

"It was a hunch," he said quietly, then laughed. "And I am the first to scoff at people with hunches."

"So what was this hunch?" I asked.

Crispin looked at me again for some long seconds as if calculating in his ultra-fast brain whether he should disclose such information under his need-to-know criteria. The calculations came down in my favor.

"I have been concerned for some weeks, don't you know. It started with the Unwin case. His claims were summarily dismissed at the inquiry as a pathetic attempt to pass the blame from himself to some mysterious, unnamed individual. But"—he paused as if still debating with his inner self if it was all right to go on—"some of the intel I have received since his case in January may appear to back up his position."

He paused again, looking around him as if for eavesdroppers in the same manner that Quentin had done in the Richmond café.

I waited patiently for him to continue.

"Two other trainers have come forward claiming to have been similarly approached by someone demanding money not to dope their horses."

I didn't ask him which trainers. Crispin would tell me if I needed to know.

"So your hunch in the Perry case was that whoever

had made the anonymous call to RaceStraight was doing so because Perry wouldn't pay, just as may have happened with Unwin?"

"Yes. I wanted you to find out quietly, dear boy. I could have simply sent in the hit squad, but any positive tests would have inevitably ended in Perry losing his license, perhaps unfairly, because far too many people would have been aware of the tests for the results to be kept under wraps. I'd rather hoped you might have discreetly discovered if something was afoot that might indicate a third-party involvement."

"Why didn't you tell me all that beforehand?" I said with a degree of irritation. "I would have approached the situation differently. I'd have tried to spot if someone else was watching the setup rather than concentrating on Perry himself."

Crispin sat in silence. If I wanted an apology, I'd be disappointed.

"Did you send the swabs and hairs for analysis?" I asked, slightly changing the subject.

"Yes indeed. Thank you. They went this morning by courier. I've requested a rush job. Results should be back by the end of the week. I also arranged for all three of Perry's runners to be tested at Bangor. Again, initial results later this week."

"So," I said, leaning forward, "do we think that there are two people trying to extort money from racing or has a small-scale operation targeting individual trainers graduated to demanding cash from the racing authorities as a whole?"

"A good question, dear boy," Crispin said without giving an answer. He would have made a perfect politician. "What will you do first?"

"Go to Cheltenham to determine how he did it," I said. "And then try and stop him from doing it again at Ascot. We ought to organize added security there this weekend."

"I hope I've dealt with that," Crispin said. "I arranged to let it slip accidentally on purpose to the Ascot management that the BHA might be conducting an inspection of racetrack security, with particular reference to the security of the horses. I expect the whole place to be swarming with extra guards."

"How did you let it slip?" I asked.

"I instructed my PA to give Ascot a call and ask for extra parking spaces as we had a racetrack security inspection team coming. They took the bait and called her back for clarification. She then told them she'd made a big mistake in asking for the parking spaces in the first place. It was all meant to be a secret and to please forget she'd ever called, otherwise she could be in serious trouble with her boss."

He chuckled to himself and clearly thought the whole thing was a great joke.

I wasn't at all sure that I agreed with him.

"I'M HOME," I shouted as I walked through the front door at half past four.

I had expected Lydia to be there, as she worked from

home on Mondays, but there was no sign of her. I was not particularly surprised, or worried, as she was probably at a viewing. She worked for a local realtor in Willesden Green and the property market in northwest London was amazingly buoyant, considering the extortionate prices being asked for even the smallest of flats.

I often wondered if we should put ours up for sale, as we could make a huge profit over what we had paid for it only three years ago, but, of course, we would then have had to pay just as high a price for somewhere else to live. Property values weren't like real money except for first-time buyers, who really struggled to find their initial deposits.

I took the box of my possessions along to the study/nursery and stood there emptying it. After three years at the BHA, I realized I had gathered remarkably little in the way of desk clutter. No family pictures in smart frames or fancy paperweights, just a few pens, a stapler, a pair of nail clippers, a stack of hotel notepads and a red-and-white mug with *Keep Calm and Carry on Racing* printed on its side that Lydia had given me at Christmas.

I wondered if the stapler and some of the pens technically still belonged to the BHA, but, since I did too, no one was likely to come looking for them.

It felt rather strange that I no longer had a desk at BHA headquarters. I hoped this was a good idea. I had no one else to blame but myself if it wasn't.

I went back to the kitchen and made myself a cup of tea in the *Keep Calm* mug and looked out the window, thinking while I drank and watching as the shadows lengthened in the late-afternoon sun.

Part of what I'd said to Nigel had been true—I would be happy to move on from the BHA and maybe I would do just that after this particular crisis was over.

On operations in the army I had regularly made decisions on which my life, and those of others, depended. Of course I had known that things would be very different in Civvy Street, but maybe after three years away from it I longed once more for the excitement and adrenaline rush that came with such life-or-death choices.

But I could also remember the fear and the bowel-twisting panic that had gripped my body when things had started to go badly wrong in that Afghan house. I broke out in a cold sweat just thinking about it. Thankfully, working for the BHA had been far less eventful on that front.

So far anyway.

LYDIA CAME HOME just after six, hurrying through the front door.

"Jenny says you've been fired."

Amazing, I thought, how bad news travels so much faster than good.

"Who's Jenny?" I asked.

"Jenny Green," she said. "Nigel's wife. She sent a text to warn me."

"I didn't know you were still in touch."

"We're not, but she must have kept my number. Is it true? Have you been fired? Why? How are we going to pay the mortgage?" She was almost in tears.

What did I say? Was this a need-to-know situation? Probably.

"Yes and no," I said.

"It must be either yes *or* no," said Lydia with ill-disguised impatience. "It can't be both."

"It can," I replied. "Yes, because everyone was told, including Nigel, that I had indeed been fired. And no, because I wasn't really. I'm still working for the BHA on a particular case but I'm doing so undercover."

"Is it safe?" Lydia asked with concern. When we'd first met, she'd had to deal with the mental fallout from my experiences in Afghanistan that had haunted my sleep for ages. Neither of us wanted to go back to those days.

"Perfectly safe," I said. "But don't tell anyone. And especially not Jenny."

"You surely don't think Nigel is involved in anything illegal."

"No, nothing like that."

"What, then?"

I shook my head.

"You're always so bloody secretive. Tell me what you're doing."

"I'm working on a problem that is very hush-hush. So secret, in fact, that hardly anyone at BHA even knows it exists."

"What is it?" she asked.

Need to know?

"Darling," I said, "I'm afraid I can't tell you that."

I could see she didn't like it.

"Don't you trust me?" she asked somewhat indignantly.

"Of course I trust you," I said, "but I still can't tell you."

The only way to keep a secret really secret was to tell nobody.

To my knowledge, apart from me, there were eleven others who knew about the doping and attempted extortion. They were the seven nonexecutive BHA Board members, Howard Lever, the chief executive, Stephen Kohli, director of integrity, Crispin Larson, senior intelligence analyst, plus, of course, the extortionist himself.

In my opinion, eleven was ten too many, and I was worried that some members of the Board may not have fully appreciated the need for complete confidentiality in spite of my plea to them for absolute silence about the matter.

I had insisted that they should tell no one, not even their wives. If each of them told only one person, that person would then tell two others, who would each tell two or three more, and so on. Within a week, the details would be common knowledge among the racing community, if not the whole country.

"I'm sorry," I said to Lydia. "Everyone has been sworn to secrecy and that includes me."

"So what are you going to do?" she asked.

"Work from home, mostly," I said. "I still have remote access to the BHA files. But I'll be going to Cheltenham tomorrow."

She opened her mouth as if she was going to ask why but then shut it again. If there was one thing she must have learned about me by now, it was that I wouldn't say something if I didn't want to.

And that included the words *Will you marry me?*

10

I sat in my study until nearly midnight studying the contents of Crispin Larson's red file, looking for a common denominator that would indicate how the doping of forty-six horses had been done, or, more accurately, I was searching for the difference that had resulted in the three that had tested negative.

Those three, Tail End Charlie, Targetman and Barometer, were all trained in England rather than in Ireland, Wales or Scotland, but so were twenty-seven other horses that had tested positive. Each of the three had a different trainer, one in Lambourn, one in Northamptonshire and the third in the village of Prestbury, close to the racetrack. The only interesting thing they had in common was that all three had run in races on the Friday, the fourth and final day of the Festival, but nine others who had run only on that afternoon had returned positive tests.

How could a single man dope so many horses?

Carrying a bagful of methylphenidate-charged syringes around, ready to stab a needle into any passing horseflesh, was clearly impossible.

Horses are not left on their own at any time except when in the racetrack stables and those were mostly covered by closed-circuit television. The CCTV footage was one of the things I was definitely going to ask to see the following day.

So, if the methylphenidate was not injected, it must have been ingested with food. But more than half the horses arrived at the track in the morning and then went home again in the late afternoon without having eaten anything in between.

Again I wondered about the CCTV footage. Would it show someone wandering around the racetrack stables dishing out drug-laced morsels to those waiting to perform on the track?

I CAUGHT a train from Paddington Station to Swindon at five to eight and changed there for the line to Cheltenham.

Lydia and I had owned our own car, but we had decided two years ago that it was an unnecessary expense and more trouble than it was worth. I always used public transport to get to my office in central London, and on two occasions the car had been broken into and vandalized during the day while parked on the road outside our flat.

The realtor company provided Lydia with a brand-painted Mini that she drove for her work. She was allowed to use it for short, private trips, but I wasn't insured to drive it.

Hence, I was used to going to racetracks by train and taxi. Occasionally I hired a car when I really needed one, but I was generally happy to let the train take the strain.

I usually passed the journey catching up on my e-mails, although I was frustrated that so few of the rail companies provided a reliable Internet service on board their trains.

It always seemed strange to me that phone companies spent so much time and money providing a good cell service on the freeways—where drivers were not allowed to use them—whilst seemingly neglecting the rail network entirely.

I looked out the window at the rolling Gloucestershire hills that completely blocked any hope of making a call. In particular, I was keen to speak to Faye, who had just started her chemotherapy. Quentin had phoned the previous evening, but more to ask how my investigation into Kenneth's problem was proceeding than to report on his wife's condition.

"Have you found the bloody friend yet?" he had said as soon as I'd answered.

"As a matter of fact, I have. But I haven't had a chance to speak to him."

"Offer him five grand to retract his statement."

Quentin, I'd thought, was getting desperate. His initial "few hundred quid" had abruptly risen tenfold.

"Are you sure that's wise?" I'd asked. "Might it not be regarded as perverting the course of justice?"

"Bugger that," Quentin had said. "Just get rid of him."

I wondered if it was going to be quite as easy to "get rid of him" as Quentin had anticipated.

The train made its sedate way through Kemble, Stroud and Gloucester, before arriving at Cheltenham a little after ten o'clock.

The last time I'd been here, just eleven days ago on Gold Cup Day, sixty thousand race fans had been making their way to the racetrack on the northern edge of the town, many of them from the railway station on the specially arranged fleet of double-decker busses. Now the situation was completely different, with only a handful of passengers alighting onto the platform and a line of snoozing taxi drivers waiting outside on the road.

Not that the racetrack itself had returned to the same sleepy existence as the town. There were contractors' trucks all over the place, with a horde of workers taking down the temporary stands, the chalet restaurants and the tented village that two weeks ago had been swarming with eager punters.

Was it really just two weeks since I had watched Matthew Unwin commit murder right here in front of the grandstand? It felt like much longer.

I went to the reception to present my BHA credentials and to inform them that I would be carrying out an inspection of the stables. I asked to speak to the racetrack manager.

"He's away," the woman behind the desk informed me.

"When is he back?" I asked, cross with myself for not checking before I came all this way.

"He only went yesterday," she said. "He's gone skiing in Austria."

"Then can I speak to the head of security?"

"I'm afraid he's away as well. In fact, nearly everyone's away this week. There are only a few of us left in the office, plus the Clerk of Works, of course. He's out and about somewhere, overseeing the removal of everything. Lots of people take time off once the Festival is over." She sounded rather indignant that she wasn't one of them.

"Who has access to the CCTV from the stables? I'd like to view the footage."

"Hold on." She disappeared for a moment but soon reappeared with a young man even I thought looked too young to be out of school. "I'm sure young Freddie can help you," said the woman. "He's our resident boffin."

Young Freddie led me to one of the back rooms that was almost full to the ceiling with banks of black electronic boxes.

"We have over sixty fixed cameras," he said with obvious pride, "as well as several temporary ones we set up just for the Festival. Everything is recorded in here on these." He waved a hand towards the black boxes.

"I'm particularly interested in those covering the racetrack stables," I said.

"Twelve cameras cover the stable area. When are you interested in?"

"Gold Cup Day," I said.

He sat down at a computer console. "You're lucky. Up until last year, we kept the recordings only for seven days. Now, with this new kit, it's twenty-eight. Then they're overwritten. If we need to keep anything longer, it has to be specially downloaded prior to that. Like the stuff showing the murder of that bookie on Champion Hurdle Day. The cops took a permanent record of that."

He typed some instructions into the computer.

"There," he said. "These are the camera recordings for Gold Cup Day." Images of the stable appeared on the monitor, views from four different cameras shown at once. "What time?"

"In the morning," I said. "I'm not really sure when. How about eleven o'clock?"

The images flickered as young Freddie used a tracker ball to move the recordings forward until the readout at the top of the screen showed *11.00.* Then he set the footage running at ×6.

"Saves time," he explained. "You don't miss anything at times six. Not like at times twelve or thirty, where it jumps."

I watched as horses were led in and out of the stables, their movements appearing comically unnatural at six times their normal speed. Grooms rushed in and out of frame like something from the Keystone Kops.

"What are you looking for, exactly?" he asked.

"Anything out of the ordinary."

He glanced up at me. “These images would have been playing on the day in real time in the stable security office. All the cameras’ feeds are shown at once. The staff would surely have noticed if there was anything out of the ordinary going on.”

That depended, I thought, on how vigilant they were. But I decided not to say so.

I could tell it was a hopeless task. With twelve separate cameras covering the stables, each of them recording nonstop for four days, I calculated that it would take me forty-eight hours’ continuous viewing to see it all, even with four images shown at once, and at ×6. I’d require an army of watchers and I didn’t have one.

I needed to narrow down the search.

“Do you have a record of which horse was stabled in which stall?”

“Not here. That’ll be with Mr. Hunter. He’s the stables manager.”

“Can we find him?” I asked. “Or is he away on holiday as well?”

“I know he’s about somewhere,” Freddie said. “I saw him earlier in reception. His office is down at the stables, but I don’t know if he’s there. They’re not open except when we’re racing. But I can try him, if you like.”

He lifted a phone from the desk and dialed, but there was clearly no answer.

“Can I still get in?”

“Sure,” Freddie said. “I’ll fetch the keys.”

We walked down to the stables with the young boffin pointing out to me the CCTV cameras as we passed by.

"How long have you worked here?" I asked.

"Nearly two years now," he said, smiling broadly. "I absolutely love it. Started straight from school. I'm also doing a B.Tech. course in electronics in college. Two days a week."

His enthusiasm was infectious, and I found myself greatly enjoying his company as we made our way down the hill, past the Centaur Centre, to the red-brick complex that housed not only the racetrack stables but also the grooms' canteen and accommodation.

Freddie unlocked the gates under the entrance archway.

About a quarter of the horses running at the Festival were trained in Ireland and they would come over a few days early in order to recover from the journey, especially the crossing of the Irish Sea, which could be notoriously rough in March. And those from the north of England and Scotland also required overnight stops before they ran. And sometimes afterwards as well.

Even the more local trainers were keen to get their horses to Cheltenham early on Festival mornings to avoid the long race-day traffic jams that could build up later around the track.

There were two hundred individual stalls but, with more than one hundred and twenty regularly competing on each day of the Festival, plus the long-stay Irish, space was at a premium and trainers were encouraged to remove their horses quickly after racing.

While some trainers liked their horses to arrive a full eight hours before the race, others were happy to have them there just two or three hours in advance. In any event, all horses had to be checked into the racetrack stables at least forty-five minutes before they were due to race so that their identity could be confirmed using the microchip embedded in their necks.

Hence, the stables were always busy, both in the run-up and throughout the Festival, with a continuous stream of horses entering and leaving, each of them having to be checked in and out by the stable security staff. How they were expected to have time to watch the CCTV screens as well was a mystery.

On this day, however, the place was deserted, with row upon row of closed stable doors and not even the smell of a horse evident.

"It all feels rather sterile," I said to Freddie.

"The stalls are washed out and disinfected after each horse departs, and the whole place is done again before each meeting."

We wandered up and down the rows of stalls, past the place set aside for the washing down of the horses after they'd raced. It was all spotlessly clean. Any evidence of methylphenidate would have surely been washed away by now.

"That's the Irish yard," Freddie said, pointing through an archway into a semi-separate section. "There are fifty-two stalls in there. It's where the Irish trainers like to have their horses at the Festival."

"Is there any way we could find out which horse was in a particular stall on Gold Cup Day?" I asked.

"We could try the stable manager's office," Freddie said, jangling the bunch of keys.

We found a list of sorts pinned to a notice board at the back of the office. It had originally been printed on a computer but now it had multiple crossings-out and additions made in black ink, with arrows all over the place indicating changes that had occurred. It was the sort of plan only fully decipherable by whoever had done the changes.

However, the list did show that Barometer had been housed in stall number 62. His name had not been crossed out or written over in ink, it was still the original print, and there were no arrows to or from it.

Barometer had been one of the three horses that hadn't tested positive.

"I'd like to see number 62, please."

I unpinned the list from the notice board and took it with me.

Stall 62 was on the right of the central block, about two-thirds of the way down from the entrance. It didn't appear any different to any of the others. Why would it?

I donned some thin white latex gloves and took some swab samples from the floor, and also from the manger in the corner.

"What are you doing?" Freddie asked.

"Checking for equine flu," I said. "Just to be sure."

"They've all been disinfected," he replied in a tone that implied he thought I was a complete idiot. "You should have been here when the horses still were. It's a bit late to be doing it now, if you ask me."

I wasn't asking him, but he was right nevertheless. I was far too late.

"Only doing my job as instructed," I said.

I checked the list again. Stall 63 next door had been occupied by a horse called Graduate, the winner of the Triumph Hurdle. Graduate was one of nine horses to have tested positive on the Friday.

I took more swabs from the floor and from the manger, placing them as before into separate plastic bags.

Freddie stood and watched, swaying slightly from foot to foot as if bored.

"You don't have to stay," I said to him. "Leave me the keys. I'll lock up and hand them into reception when I'm done."

He hesitated.

"I do have the authority, you know," I said, "and I could be here some time."

"OK," he said, handing me the keys. "I've got plenty of other things to do."

"Good," I said. "You get on."

He hesitated again, but I turned away and walked up the line of stalls looking for number 86. When I glanced back, he'd gone.

Somehow I felt more comfortable not being watched, except, of course, there were those twelve over-seeing cameras and young Freddie was probably already back in the control room studying my every move.

Stall 86 was the one that had been occupied by the horse that had finished second in the Gold Cup, another of the nine that had tested positive. It was identical to the others and spotlessly clean. I collected more samples anyway, but without much enthusiasm or expectation.

"Can I help you?" said a voice loudly behind me, making me jump.

I turned around to find a man standing in the doorway, hands on hips, his body language screaming out that he wasn't happy.

"Hello," I said, stripping off a latex glove and holding out a hand, "I'm Jeff Hinkley from the BHA."

The information didn't exactly placate him. If anything, it made things worse. He reluctantly shook my hand.

"Fergus Hunter," he said. "Stables manager."

"Ah," I said. "We tried to call you but there was no reply."

"We?"

"Young Freddie from the office. He gave me the keys." I held up the bunch.

I had a suspicion that young Freddie was going to get a bit of an earful later, but it wasn't actually his fault. I did have a right of entry to these stables at any time and Fergus Hunter must have known that.

"What is it that you're after?" he asked in a broad northern accent.

"I'm just doing an inspection," I replied.

"You won't find owt wrong here."

"I'm sure," I said, smiling. "These stables appear to be well maintained and very clean."

"Aye," Fergus said, slightly pacified. "Best racetrack stables in country. You won't find owt wrong here." He repeated the line just in case I'd missed it the first time.

"Do you have a central feed store?" I asked.

"Nah," he said. "They bring their own feeds, if needed. Store them in these." He pointed at one of the cupboards that were spaced around the place. "Each trainer has his own tack box. We have seventy-five in all. That's where they keep the feed, along with bridles, head collars, buckets, rugs and so on. Everything they need."

"Are they secure?"

He laughed. "You bet they are. Stuff walks otherwise. People are always complaining that their good stuff has been switched for bad. Traveling head grooms get a key from me. They have to give a deposit, mind, or I'd never get them back neither."

"So do you provide anything?" I said.

"We supply bedding. Mostly wood shavings these days, but we do offer paper strips as well. It used to be straw, but some horses tended to eat it, then they couldn't race from being so full." He laughed. "They won't touch the shavings."

So it couldn't have been contaminated bedding that was the source.

"How about water?" I asked.

"What about it? It comes out of them taps." He pointed at one of the taps positioned at intervals every three or four stalls.

"How about the supply?" I asked. "Where does it come from?"

Now it was his turn to look at me as if he thought me an idiot.

"Through the bloody pipes, man," he said. "Where else do you think it comes from?"

"What I meant was, do you have storage tanks or is it direct from the mains?"

"From the mains," he said. "We just turn on the tap and out it comes. We don't have any tankers delivering water or anything like that."

That also wasn't what I'd meant.

"Is the mains connected directly to the taps or is there a tank somewhere?"

"I know there's some sort of tank in the space above my office ceiling. I can hear it filling when it's quiet."

"I'll need to take some samples," I said.

He watched as I filled three small glass vials, one from a tap in the main yard, one from the Irish and, for good measure, one from the drain in the horse-washing area.

"I'll need another sample from the tank above your office."

I could tell from Fergus's expression that he thought I was wasting my time as we walked back towards the entrance.

Access to the space was via a trapdoor set in the overhang in front of and above his office window. I used a stepladder. And, sure enough, there was a large tank in the space immediately above the desk. I smiled to myself and hoped that the rafters were strong enough.

I collected a sample of the water from the tank and carefully added the glass vial to the three others in my bag.

"Is that all?" Fergus asked somewhat impatiently.

"Not quite," I said. "I can't see on this list a stable allocated to Tail End Charlie."

"That's because he didn't have one."

"I thought all the horses had to use the stables."

"Technically, they do," Fergus said, "but Simon Booker's runners are a law unto themselves." Simon Booker trained at Prestbury, on the far side of the track. "They get walked over from home, already bridled. Booker would rather not bring them into the stables at all. He claims they pick up viruses, but he has to. That's what the rules say, but somehow Booker manages to get round them."

"Are you saying that Tail End Charlie didn't enter the racetrack stables on Gold Cup Day?"

"Yeah, I am. I remember it well because he, Mr. Booker, was having a bit of a panic because the horse was late. Gave his groom a right telling-off for ambling over so slowly. It was bang on the forty-five minutes before the race. I watched the vet scan the chip through my office window and then the horse went straight to the pre-parade. Went straight home again after too. He never once set foot inside the stables."

But he had been tested, with negative results. Was that significant?

"Look, I'm not trying to get Mr. Booker into any sort of trouble or anything," Fergus said, suddenly becoming worried. "He complied with the rules about identification OK. I could have made Tail End Charlie come into the stables for ten minutes or so if I'd wanted, but it seemed easier to send him straight to the pre-parade ring, especially as we were so full."

"It's all right, Mr. Hunter," I said calmingly. "I'll not

be reporting you or Simon Booker for failing to comply with the regulations. What you did was eminently sensible."

He relaxed a little.

"What can you tell me about Barometer or Targetman?" I said. "They both ran on Gold Cup afternoon. Targetman won the last."

"Bonkers trainer," Fergus said, almost under his breath.

"Which one?" I asked, intrigued.

"Targetman's," he said. "Chap called Matheson, Rupert Matheson. Trains in Lambourn."

"Why is he bonkers?"

"Insists on still using peat for bedding. Brings his own with him. No one else uses peat anymore, it's far too dusty, and it's a bugger for us to clean out afterwards, but he maintains that his horses like it. And he always brings his own water from home in plastic containers. Claims his horses prefer the taste of Lambourn water. Stupid man."

Maybe he was not so stupid after all.

I reckoned the methylphenidate had to have been in the stables' water supply.

11

"He's bloody done it again." It was Crispin Larson. He called me on my cell phone very early on Wednesday morning. So early that Lydia and I were still asleep in bed.

"Who has?" I asked sleepily. "And what's he done again?"

"Our friend, this Leonardo. He didn't wait for Ascot. He did it again at Newbury last Saturday. Preliminary results on the A samples show that all six winners there tested positive for low-dose methylphenidate. The guys at the testing labs are having kittens. They're worried about it being due to contamination at their end. I'm not sure that Stephen Kohli can keep a lid on things there for much longer. How did you get on at Cheltenham?"

"I'm pretty sure it was in the stables' water supply. I've

got some samples for you, along with some swabs. Can you meet me at El Vino later?"

"Lunch?" Crispin asked.

"No. Earlier or later. I have to do something from noon until two."

"Three o'clock, then?"

"Fine," I said. "And in the meantime hire a water truck at Ascot for this weekend. Tell everyone the stable supply is contaminated. Horses should only drink water taken from the truck."

"How do you know it was in the water?"

"It had to be. It's the only common denominator. The three that didn't test positive didn't drink the stables' water. One came straight from his home stable in Prestbury, one has his own water brought with him from Lambourn and the third wasn't allowed any water at the racetrack before racing as he tends to overdrink and that slows him down."

I had telephoned the trainer of Barometer the previous evening and asked him straight out about the water. He'd been a bit wary as he thought I was asking about horse welfare, but he had agreed eventually that the horse had been purposely denied anything to drink once he'd left home early on the Friday morning.

"Right," Crispin said. "I'll arrange a water truck."

"And get some samples of the Newbury stables' water."

"Right," he said again. "I will."

"What has happened about the announcement?" I asked.

"It should be in today's *Times.*"

That's a shame, I thought. If we had found out how the doping took place and were able to stop it happening again, then maybe there was no reason to entertain any demands from "our friend," as Crispin insisted on calling him.

"OK," I said to Crispin. "See you later."

I hung up and lay back on the pillow.

"What was in the water supply?" Lydia asked without turning over.

Did she need to know?

Probably not, but my insistence not to say anything was putting a huge strain on our relationship. She'd hardly said a word to me when I'd got home from Cheltenham the previous evening as she clearly hadn't wanted to ask a question that I wouldn't answer. We had watched the television for a while in frosty silence and then she had taken herself off to bed in a huff at ten o'clock. And I'd been sure that she had been feigning sleep when I'd joined her about an hour later.

"Something called methylphenidate hydrochloride," I said. "It's sold as a drug called Ritalin and it stimulates the central nervous system. Someone has been doping horses indiscriminately by putting it in the water supply at the racetrack stables."

"Is that what is so frightfully hush-hush?"

"Yes," I said. "The BHA Board believe that if the betting public knew they would lose all confidence in racing."

"But is that really likely?"

"It could be," I said. "There's not much confidence in professional cycling at the moment due to all their drug-taking revelations. Some of the sport's superheroes have turned out to be nothing more than lying cheats. And cycle racing doesn't depend on betting revenue in the same way that horseracing does."

"What are you going to do about it, then?" Lydia asked, turning over and snuggling up to me under the bedcovers, her hands seeking me out and sending shivers of excitement down my legs. The aphrodisiac effect of being included in a secret was in full evidence.

"Nothing, just at the moment," I said with a spreading smile.

"Oh, goodie."

Did she need to know?

Definitely.

AT TWELVE NOON, I was waiting across the road from the offices of Hawthorn Pearce, hoping that Daniel Jubowski would soon emerge to purchase his lunch from the deli around the corner.

I really could have done without this distraction—I had enough to do for the BHA—but I had promised Quentin. However, I wasn't entirely sure of the best way to proceed.

The last thing I wanted to do was to jeopardize Kenneth's bail and have the two of us thrown into jail.

Daniel Jubowski came out through the front door and turned left down King Street towards Cheapside. I gave him about ten yards' start and followed.

Lunchtime in the City was a busy time, with thousands heading away from their desks to find some food, and it was easy to disappear among the throng as they all hurried along to their favorite sandwich bar or delicatessen. I was wearing my best business suit, white shirt and tie and carrying a small black backpack, just like many of those around me, and I was certain that Daniel Jubowski had no idea that I was particularly interested in him as I stood right behind him in the queue to order.

"Hot pasta of the day with a side salad," Daniel said to the female server behind the counter.

"Eat in or take away?" she asked.

"Eat in."

She took a plate from the pile on the counter and went down to the far end to fetch the pasta.

"Who's next?" another of the servers called out.

"That's me," I said. "Ham-and-cheese panini, please."

"Toasted?"

"No thanks, just as it is."

The server wrapped the panini in a paper napkin and placed it in a small paper carrier. "Drink?"

"Sparkling water. Small."

The plastic bottle joined the panini in the bag.

"Four pounds ten."

I handed over a fiver and received my change. Meanwhile, Daniel was also paying for his pasta.

We turned away from the counter at almost the same time, but I allowed him to move ahead of me looking for a free table.

He chose one near the window with two chairs and I followed him over to it.

"Mind if we share?" I said.

He said nothing but waved a hand in reluctant agreement.

We sat down facing each other, but Daniel only had eyes for his pasta and salad. I removed my panini from the paper bag and started eating.

"Food's good here," I said with my mouth full.

"Yes," he said, not looking up. He loaded another spoonful of penne and popped it into his mouth. All his body language said that he didn't want to talk.

That was a shame because I did.

"Do you work round here?" I asked.

He looked up at me but without any smile in his eyes. I put on my most I'm-coming-on-to-you face and hoped it might stir an interest.

"In King Street," he said. "Hawthorn and Pearce. And you?"

"In the Bank of England," I said.

I took another bite of my lunch.

"That must be interesting," he said.

"Not really. I'm responsible for recording and cancelling serial numbers of banknotes destined for destruction due to age or damage. It's boring."

"Don't you sometimes feel like stuffing them into your pockets?"

"All the time." We laughed, and I laid my hand upon his arm, giving it a gentle squeeze. "But there are too many bloody security checks."

He stared deep into my eyes. "I'm Daniel," he said, holding out his hand.

"Tony," I said, shaking it and looking right back at him. "Tony Jefferson."

We ate in silence for a moment.

"I must get back," I said, looking at my watch and standing up. "I'll have to walk and eat. Good to meet you. Can we do it again sometime?"

"Do you fancy a drink later?" he said. "After work? A group of us meet every Wednesday."

"Sure," I said. "Where?"

"Do you know The William Ball in Gresham Street? Meet you there after five-thirty?"

Everyone who worked in the City of London was aware that The William Ball was a pub where gay men tended to gather. Daniel was making sure I knew the lay of the land.

"Great idea," I said, picking up my bag. "I'll see you later."

He watched me through the window as I left the deli and walked off jauntily down the street in the direction of the Bank of England, my backpack slung over my shoulder.

The next meeting would be at his request and at his choice of venue.

I hoped I might find him off guard, with his mind on other matters.

CRISPIN DIDN'T recognize me when he arrived at El Vino at three o'clock. I was sitting at the bar and he walked right past looking beyond me towards the room at the back. I smiled inwardly to myself as he sat down at a table facing the door.

I stood up and walked over to him, pulling out the chair opposite.

"Sorry," he said, "I'm waiting for . . ." He tailed off. "Good God, Jeff."

I sat down, laughing.

"What's all this for?" He waved his hand in a circular motion in front of my face, a face that was hidden again behind a full beard and a pair of black, thick-rimmed spectacles, my naturally fair hair stained a dark brown color.

"I've been meeting with someone who I don't particularly want to recognize me if he ever sees me again as myself. I've come straight here."

I'd been working on and off with Crispin for two years. If he hadn't recognized me until I was standing right next to him, I was pretty sure Daniel Jubowski wouldn't know the real me if I ever had need to follow him again.

"Howard Lever is in a blind panic," Crispin said, bringing our attention back to the BHA matter in hand.

"More than usual?" I asked.

"Much more," he said. "After this Newbury business, he's desperately worried that something will leak at the testing lab and then the BHA in general, and he in particular, will have egg all over their faces for not saying anything after Cheltenham."

"But we didn't know about the results from Cheltenham until after the racing at Newbury."

"Well, it seems that we did. The first reports from the lab were on Stephen Kohli's desk as early as Tuesday of last week, a full six days before they were shown to the Board last Monday and four days before the Newbury races. But Stephen simply didn't believe them, not until after the B samples were tested."

"So what's the problem?" I said. "We need Howard Lever to remain calm. Panic leads to poor decisions. Did you tell him my theory about the water?"

"Yes, and he's immediately ordered that no horses in any of the racetrack stables in the country are to drink water except from specially filled trucks."

"That's good," I said, "but it might produce some awkward questions from the trainers." Especially from the "bonkers" trainer Rupert Matheson, I thought, with his plastic containers of Lambourn water.

"Do you have the samples?"

I opened my backpack and gave him the four vials of water and the swabs.

"I don't suppose the swabs will be any good. The stables have been disinfected since the horses were in there."

"I'll get them tested anyway."

"How about those I took at Graham Perry's yard? Are they back yet?"

"Should be tomorrow. I'll call you. What are you going to do now?"

"You don't want to know," I said with a smile.

"Howard has brought forward the meeting of the Board to this Friday. He told me to tell you. And it won't be in the office. He's arranged for it to be at his club, Scrutton's. Do you know it?"

"In St. James's," I said, nodding. "But I'm surprised they allow business to be done there."

"Apparently, they rent out rooms for meetings."

"What time?"

"Nine."

"I'll be there. Have you seen the announcement in the paper?" I'd bought a copy of *The Times* on my way to our meeting and I passed it over to him, open at the correct page.

Van Gogh accepts Leonardo's offer of marriage with a proposed dowry of twenty thousand pounds.

"I suggested they make it ten thousand," I said. "But I see that fell on stony ground."

"Howard thinks twenty thousand is far too little. He wanted to make it a quarter of a million."

"I can't think why we're contemplating paying this man anything at all. Especially now we know how the doping is done and can stop it."

"Are you sure we can stop it?" Crispin said. "Surely our friend will have realized what we would discover and will have made plans to circumvent our interventions."

I couldn't see how.

More the fool me.

THE WILLIAM BALL was fairly quiet when I arrived at a quarter to six.

"I thought you weren't coming," Daniel said. He was standing at the bar with two other men. "John, Mike, this is Tony."

I shook their offered hands. Both were smartly dressed in business suits, as Daniel and I were—still the ubiquitous uniform of City folk. We were all about the same age. Mike had short, dark curly hair, while John had no hair on his head at all, his shaved and shiny pate reflecting the glow from the lights over the bar.

I remembered that Ken had told me there were a couple of Johns and a Mike among the guests at his ill-fated party. Were these two the Mike and one of the Johns?

John looked at me closely, casting his eyes from my feet to my head and back again. "He's not as young as I'm used to," he said.

Daniel ignored him. "Drink?"

"Half a Veltins. Thanks."

The barman handed me the beer and I clinked glasses with the other three.

"Been pocketing any old notes?" Daniel asked.

"Sadly not," I said to him. "I mostly sit at a desk recording numbers."

The other two looked on quizzically.

"Tony here has a job in the Bank of England tearing up money that's got too old."

I smiled. "Something like that. I don't actually tear it up. I help bundle it into packages to be sent to a furnace for destruction."

"It must really save on the Bank's fuel bill to burn banknotes to heat the place," said Mike with a grimace. "Talk about burning government money."

"Can't you swap a bundle of newspaper for a stack of fifties?" said John. "No one would know, surely."

"They would when the fifties turned up again at the bank with numbers that should have already been destroyed."

I needed to change the subject. I'd only made up the Bank of England story so that Daniel couldn't have been able to phone me at work.

"What do you guys do?" I asked.

"I work with Daniel at Hawthorn's," John said. "I'm a broker." He made it sound seductive.

"And I'm at Lloyd's," said Mike, "as a managing agent for syndicates." He took a business card from his breast pocket and handed it over in a manner that suggested he had done the same thing many times before. I looked down at it. *Lloyd's of London, Michael Kennedy, Managing Agent*, complete with his office address and cell number. Convenient, I thought. One thing less I needed to find out.

"Sounds interesting," I said.

The conversation continued for a while about jobs, and I bought Daniel another drink.

"What are you doing this evening?" Daniel asked. "We go to the gym every Wednesday. Do you fancy joining us?"

I remembered back to Daniel's Facebook page. One of his *Likes* had been the Fit Man gym in Soho, the one with the big sauna.

"Oh, do come," John said. "It's great fun. And we might get to see that lovely body of yours." He reached down and ran his fingers up the inside of my thigh.

I wondered just how far I was expected to go to save the judicial career of my cantankerous brother-in-law.

12

On Thursday morning I took the Tube to Bethnal Green to see Ken Calderfield. I wanted to show him some video footage.

The previous evening I'd managed to avoid a visit to the gym in Soho, but not without a struggle.

Daniel, Mike and especially John had been very insistent that I should join them.

"I have things to do," I said. "And my mother will have my dinner ready."

As an excuse, it wasn't the best, but it was all I could come up with on the spur of the moment.

They all laughed at me.

"Still living at home, are you? At your age?"

They laughed again, but it simply increased John's determination to help me "break free" from my mother's apron strings.

"Come with us," he said, putting his arm around my waist inside my jacket. "We'll show you a good time. Make you into a real man."

He slid his hand down and squeezed my bottom, looking into my eyes and smiling at me all the while.

At that point, the phone rang in my pocket. I had been waiting for it to do so. I had had a fake-call app installed and I'd set it to make my phone ring ten minutes after I'd entered the pub. I used it often in such circumstances just in case I needed an excuse to leave or, as in this case, a reason to get my smartphone out.

I pulled myself away from John's wandering hands and answered the fake call, putting the phone to my ear while, at the same time, switching on the phone's built-in camera to record my surroundings.

I turned away from the others as if making the call more private but actually to ensure that all three of them featured large in the video I was taking.

I spoke into the phone to my nonexistent and long-dead mother. "Yes, mom. I'm just having a quick drink with some friends, but I'll be home by seven. Yes, mom, I will. I promise. See you soon. Yes, mom, I love you too. Bye for now."

The three of them laughed at me again, but I kept the phone in my hand. And perhaps they wouldn't have been laughing so much if they'd known I was still recording their faces in high-definition close-up.

"Sorry, guys," I said. "I've got to go."

"That's a real shame," said John. "I'd rather fancied getting my hands properly on that bottom of yours."

"Daniel's got some ice, if you'd like it," Mike said.

"Ice? In my beer?"

"Not that sort of ice," Daniel said, laughing. "Proper ice. One hundred percent pure Tina. You can have your first wrap for just a tenner if you come with us."

"Sorry," I said again. "Not this time. My mom will be waiting."

I downed the last of my beer, picked up my backpack and dragged myself out of John's reach.

"See you again sometime." Daniel said it without much hope or expectation in his voice.

But he could count on it.

I switched off the camera as I walked out into the street.

"THAT'S DANIEL!" Ken said excitedly as I showed him the video. "How did you find him?"

"What about the other two?" I asked. "Do you recognize either of them?"

He looked closely at the screen.

"Yes," he said. "That one's called John." He pointed at the shaven-headed man. "And I recognize the other one too but I'm not sure of his name."

"It's Mike," I said. "Mike Kennedy. He works at Lloyd's of London. Were these two of the men you met at the Fit Man gym?'

"Yes." Ken said it uneasily as if embarrassed. "How did you find them?"

"I traced Daniel to where he works and met the others with him."

I played another video to him.

He stared at the screen of my phone with his eyes almost popping out of his head in disbelief.

The images showed the front of the gym in Greek Street with a brightly lit sign above the door together with several pictures of muscular young men wearing nothing but small white towels around their waists.

"Is this the place?" I asked.

"Y-yes?" Ken stammered, clearly shocked. "Oh God. Please don't show my dad."

"Are you sure you met those men in this gym, or did they take you there?"

"Does it matter?" he mumbled, clearly not wanting to talk about it.

"It might," I said. "I actually met them in a pub."

He nodded. "I did too. Then they took me to the gym. Almost dragged me there. It was John mainly—he couldn't keep his bloody hands off me." He'd nearly done the same to me and I was older, more street-smart, and emotionally stronger than Ken.

"But you've been back since then, haven't you?" I said.

He looked down as if unwilling to answer.

"Ken," I said. "I'm not judging you. You're a grown man who can make his own decisions about what you do. I'm just trying to find out the facts so I can help you."

"I went back several times before all this blew up," he

said finally. "I enjoyed going. It was the only place where I felt I could be myself, be free."

"And did you ever see Daniel or Mike or John on those visits?"

"Daniel was there sometimes. I don't remember about the others. Tell me what Daniel said about his statement to the police."

"I haven't asked him about that yet. But I will."

I would maybe also talk to shaven-headed John to ask why he thought it reasonable to proposition young men in pubs for sex.

Shaven-headed John's full name was Jonathan George McClure and he lived not that far away from me in a flat on Uxbridge Road overlooking Shepherd's Bush Green. I knew because I'd followed him home the previous evening.

I'd left The William Ball pub soon after six o'clock, but the three men didn't arrive at the gym until nearly nine.

I had spent some of the intervening time in the gents of the St. Paul's Hotel, removing my stuck-on facial hair and exchanging my jacket and tie for a black roll-neck sweater and a baseball cap from my backpack.

Fortunately, it was a mild evening, so I sat outside a Greek Street café drinking endless coffee while I waited.

I chose a table directly under an overhanging streetlight so that the peak of the baseball cap would throw my eyes into darker shadow. It was similar to observing someone from inside a stationary car—it was always better to park immediately beneath a light. Its brightness on the exterior of the car somehow made the darkness of the interior deeper and any occupant more difficult to see.

In this case it was my eyes that I wanted to be invisible. It was always the eyes that gave people away, in terms of both recognition and emotion.

Eyes were the picture windows to the soul.

The three men arrived at the gym at eight-fifty, chatting and joking, almost hyper in their excitement, and they were not alone. They had another, much younger man with them, and John was guiding the seemingly reluctant individual eagerly towards the door. Not one of them was paying any attention to the customers at the café across the road.

I settled in for a long night, moving at one point from the café to the bar next door, where I could sit in the window and watch the gym entrance.

Shaven-headed John appeared first, at twenty minutes past ten, exiting the gym and walking briskly away without a backwards glance. I followed him across Soho Square, right into Oxford Street and along to Tottenham Court Road tube station, where he caught a Central Line train heading westwards.

He never once looked behind him, and, even though we were in the same car on the train, he didn't once glance in my direction as I observed him via his reflection in the window of the interconnecting door.

As we traveled out from the city center the number of passengers decreased as more people left the train than got on, but there were still enough to blend into as we approached Shepherd's Bush Station, where John stood up and alighted.

I pulled the baseball cap farther down over my eyes as I followed him up the escalator to street level, but, again, he never looked around. I tailed him out of the station and along Uxbridge Road to a point where he stopped and used a key to open a front door squeezed between an optician and a fast-food outlet.

I watched from across the road as the lights went on in the first floor and John appeared at the window to close the curtains. I walked over to the front door. There were two bell buttons, presumably for two flats. One had no name displayed in the space provided next to it, but the other did—*McClure.*

Like an unruly schoolboy, I pressed the McClure button for two seconds and then ran away across the road onto Shepherd's Bush Green and the dark shadows. I stood behind a tree and watched as shaven-headed John opened the door and looked around. He stepped out onto the sidewalk and peered both ways along Uxbridge Road before retreating inside again and closing the door.

John McClure.

When I'd finally arrived home, I used the Internet to look him up on the electoral register and also on Facebook and Twitter.

John McClure was not only brazen in pubs, he was also somewhat indiscreet on social media.

There were a mass of photographs of him in various states of undress and also numerous posts about his "conquests," with graphic descriptions of his sexual encounters. Why would anyone want to make such information public? Clearly, it was his way of bragging.

At least Kenneth Calderfield was a little more discreet about his private life.

"*Please* don't tell my dad about the gym," he pleaded once more. "I'm so ashamed."

"Don't be ashamed for being gay," I said.

"I'm not. But I am ashamed for going to that place. I'd never done anything like that before."

But he had done it several times since.

"How was it, then," I asked, "that you had a party here in your flat for the men you met at the gym?"

"It was all Daniel's idea. He wouldn't stop talking about it. He organized it and asked his friends to come. I couldn't stop him." His shoulders slumped. "What a fucking mess. I feel so bloody stupid. I didn't want the party in the first place, but Daniel absolutely insisted. I wish I'd never given in to him." He was almost in tears again. "My dad will kill me."

"Don't worry, Ken," I said, "I'm sure it won't be that bad."

I ARRIVED at Scrutton's Club in St. James's at five to nine on Friday morning in time for the BHA meeting.

The Board members were sitting around a large conference table when Crispin Larson and I came into the room and, by the look of the empty coffee cups, they had been there for a while.

The chairman, Roger Vincent, called the meeting back to order by tapping his knuckles on the table. I looked around at the familiar faces. Ian Tulloch again sat next to Bill Ripley, with my champion Neil Wallinger on his other side and Piers Pottinger beyond him next to George Searle. Howard Lever, Stephen Kohli, Crispin Larson and I—"the home team," as it were—were together in a row facing the chairman and Charles Payne.

"So what have you discovered?" asked Ian Tulloch, his tone of voice indicating that he didn't expect it to be very much.

"The methylphenidate was given to the horses via the water supply in the racetrack stables. Analysis has shown that all of the water samples I collected from the Cheltenham stables had a concentration high enough to provide the positive dope tests in horses that had drunk only a small quantity. None of the three horses that tested negative at Cheltenham had been given any of the stable water to drink."

Crispin had given me the results outside in the hall just seconds before we came in. He'd also confirmed that initial tests had shown that Graham Perry's horses had distinct traces of methylphenidate in their hair samples.

Was that another coincidence or were we dealing with the same man?

"How easy is it to obtain this methyl stuff?" Howard Lever asked.

"Pretty easy," I said. "It is controlled, which means you should require a doctor's prescription to get it, but it is widely available on the Internet without one. And it is readily soluble in water. I believe it was added to the water storage tank above the stable manager's office at Cheltenham. I assume a similar situation occurred at Newbury, but I haven't yet checked."

"On Wednesday," Howard Lever added, "I instructed that until further notice, all horses in all the British racetrack stables are to be given water to drink only from special trucks that are filled at secret locations well away from the racetracks."

There were nods of agreement around the table.

"Does that mean we've defeated this man?" asked Charles Payne. "And we don't need to pay him anything?"

"It may not be as easy as that," Crispin said. "We are aware—that is, Jeff and I are aware—that methylphenidate has also been administered to other horses at their home stables, and we are of the opinion that it's likely to have been done by the same man."

"Whose stables?" Stephen Kohli demanded, leaning forward to look down the table at Crispin and me.

Crispin was about to speak again when I cut him off.

"We would prefer not to say at present."

"But you must," spluttered Stephen in disbelief. "I insist. I should have been informed so that the appropriate action could be initiated."

By "appropriate action," I assumed, he meant the setting up of a disciplinary panel and the subsequent disqualification of the trainer. Stephen was apt to assume that all participants in the sport were trying to break the rules at all times. Certainly the current BHA Rules of Racing handbook, produced under his stewardship, seemed to me to be largely a list of penalties that would be handed out for even the slightest misdemeanor, intentional or otherwise.

"I obtained the test results only this morning," Crispin said. "And the trainer in question is unaware that samples have been taken from his horses."

I thought Roger Vincent was about to ask how the samples were taken, but, at the last moment, he obviously opted out, perhaps deciding that he didn't really want to know.

"What makes you think it was done by the same man?" Ian Tulloch asked.

Crispin continued in his usual protracted manner. "An anonymous telephone caller left a voice mail on the whistle-blowing RaceStraight reporting line, claiming that the trainer in question was administering amphetamine to his horses. I instructed Jeff here to take a quick peek at the trainer's setup to establish the veracity of the claim." Crispin paused.

"Yes," Ian Tulloch said impatiently, "but why did you come to the conclusion that this was done by the same man who doped the water at Cheltenham?"

"And why," Stephen Kohli asked, jumping in with two feet, "didn't you immediately send in a BHA testing team rather than relying on a rogue investigator?"

"I am not a rogue investigator," I said sharply. "Please don't confuse being clandestine with being illegal. I work completely within the law."

At least I tried to, although I didn't always tell the truth—except in court under oath.

"Mr. Larson, please answer my question," Ian Tulloch said rather forcefully. "Why do you believe it is the same man?"

Everyone's eyes turned back to Crispin.

"It is a complicated situation, and maybe, dare I say, there is a touch of guesswork involved. In all, three different trainers have claimed they were approached by an individual who demanded money or he would dope their horses and they would lose their livelihood. In the light of that intelligence, I was of the opinion that the call to RaceStraight could be a malicious attempt to bring disgrace to an individual who had refused to pay. Hence, the unorthodox approach."

Stephen Kohli looked apoplectic.

"Who are these trainers?" he demanded. "Why wasn't I informed of this before?"

Crispin tried valiantly to explain that things were often said to him in strictest confidence and that without the trust of those in the sport, he would have been unable to gather the intelligence he was famed for. Any loss of anonymity would instantly cause his network of covert human intelligence sources to evaporate in the wind.

But Stephen Kohli didn't seem to understand that. To him, things were always black or white, never gray. And he was seething.

"Gentlemen," said Roger Vincent, trying to restore some sort of order by banging his palm on the table, "what is important here is the matter at hand and what we do about it."

"Have you had any reply to the notice in *The Times*?" I asked.

"Yes," Howard Lever said, "we have. Our offer was rejected out of hand. I said that twenty thousand wouldn't be enough."

"What was the response, exactly?" I asked.

Roger Vincent handed over a piece of paper. "This is a copy," he said.

I looked down and read the single paragraph.

Don't mess with me. Your offer is not enough. Five million in cash by next week or I will bring down your beloved racing for good. Agree in the Times on Saturday—or else.

"How was this delivered?" I asked.

"Addressed to me personally in the regular mail," said Roger Vincent. "Same as last time."

The paper was passed around the table amid considerable murmurings.

"We couldn't possibly acquire five million pounds in cash even if we wanted to," said Neil Wallinger. "Money-laundering restrictions would prevent it for a start."

"Why don't we ignore him?" I said. All the eyes swung around to face me. "He's being totally unreasonable, so call his bluff. Use the trucks for drinking water, especially at Ascot this Saturday and Sunday, and make sure they're clean. Keep them guarded to prevent contamination. What then can he do?"

There were some nods around the table.

"What if he goes to the newspapers?" asked Piers Pottinger, always acutely aware of the public relations angle.

"Let him," I said. "What can he say that won't incriminate him?"

"He could anonymously say that he had doped all the horses that ran at Cheltenham."

"So what?" I said. "Would any of the newspapers believe him if he refused to give his name?" Now there were shakes of various heads. "And why *would* he go to the newspapers, not when there's still a chance of getting money out of us. He would surely only do that if and when all negotiations are over. And, even if he did, we could still argue that it doesn't invalidate the race results, not if all the horses were equally doped." I conveniently ignored the fact that at least three of the horses at Cheltenham had not ingested any methylphenidate. "We are not going to pay this man five million pounds, that's for sure, so we should pay him absolutely nothing. Let's ignore him. Or, better still, let's call in the police."

Crispin and I were told to wait outside while the others discussed matters and made their decision.

"That didn't go very well," I said to Crispin. "Stephen seems rather angry."

"Stephen is always angry," Crispin replied. "I've always found the best policy is to pay no attention to him."

"But he's your boss."

"So? Paul Maldini is your boss, but I hear you and Nigel Green take little or no notice of him most of the time."

"Who told you that?" I asked, but he just smiled at

me. Clearly, he believed that I didn't need to know, so he didn't tell me.

There wasn't much Crispin didn't know about racing and obviously that included everything going on within the BHA itself.

"What are they going to do, then?" I asked, jerking my thumb towards the conference room behind me.

"Your guess is as good as mine. This lot are totally unpredictable."

The meeting broke up with a decision to do nothing, other than to continue with the water trucks. We were to wait and see what happened over the weekend. No notice would be placed in *The Times* on Saturday, but, equally, no report was to be made to the police either.

"They bottled it," Crispin said to me as we were leaving Scrutton's Club. "They hope by doing nothing it will all go away, but I'm not sure your plan to ignore him is actually the best policy. With our heads stuck in the sand, we may not see the juggernaut coming that will run us all over."

"You really think it's that bad?"

"Don't you?"

13

I caught the District Line from St. James's Park to Richmond and went to see Faye.

"How lovely," she said, opening the front door to their Georgian mansion and giving me a kiss. "Come on in."

"You should be resting in bed," I said with mock admonishment.

"Nonsense," she replied with a laugh. "Coffee, tea or wine?"

"I'd love a coffee." Actually, I would have loved a glass of wine, but I didn't think Faye would be able to join me so I opted for the coffee instead.

I sat on a stool at the breakfast bar while she set to work at her fancy coffee machine.

"What brings you to Richmond on a Friday afternoon?"

"I came to see you."

She beamed with pleasure. "I'd have thought you'd be at your office."

"I'm working away from the office for a while. I tell you, I could get used to not having a supervisor looking over my shoulder all the time."

She went on smiling and passed over a steaming cup of cappuccino.

"How are you anyway?" I asked. "You look amazing."

"Oh, I'm OK," she said. "But I don't like this chemo much. I had to go to the Royal Marsden most of the day on Tuesday. God, it makes me feel sick."

"I'm surprised they started chemo so soon after the surgery. I'd have expected you to have more recovery time."

"The operation was the easy part," Faye said. "The surgeon used some fancy new robot system that only required a few small incisions. It's really clever. The robot's arms and hands did the operation inside me as if they were the surgeon's own, but, of course, they're much thinner. The cuts were a bit sore for a few days, but I'm fine now. At least I would be if I didn't feel so sick all the time."

"How long do you have to have the chemo for?"

"Three or four cycles, according to my oncologist. Each cycle is three weeks long. That's bloody months of feeling like this."

"Poor you," I said, trying to be supportive. "But I'm sure it will be worth it."

"I do hope so," she said. "And, thankfully, they tell me that with Gem/Cis I shouldn't lose my hair."

"Gem/Cis?"

"It's the combination of drugs I'm getting, Gem-something and Cisplatin. Can't quite remember. I had to lie there on a bed for hours with my arm sticking out sideways while they poured the stuff into me through a cannula tube." She laughed. "It reminds me of one of those executions by lethal injection. Any last requests?"

I smiled at her, but I found it all too serious for actual laughter.

"Tell me about you," she said, changing the subject. "What have you been up to?"

"Not much," I said. "Just the usual stuff of chasing cheats and fraudsters."

"Have you caught any?"

"Not yet, but I'm working on it."

Faye knew better than to probe too deeply into what I did for a living. It was a situation that had first occurred when I'd been in the army. Then she hadn't really wanted to know what I'd been up to because she knew she wouldn't like it. Not much had changed since I'd joined the BHA.

"How's Lydia?" she asked.

"She's fine."

Faye knew me too well and must have detected something in the tone of my voice.

"What's wrong?" she asked, full of concern.

"Nothing's wrong," I said.

"Now, don't lie to your big sister."

It was what she'd said to me almost every day throughout my childhood, from age eight onwards, whenever I'd been caught doing something naughty and I'd tried to wriggle out of the punishment.

"I'm not," I said.

"There you are doing it again," she said with mock anger. "I can always tell when you're lying and you know it. Tell me what's wrong."

"I don't want to trouble you, sis, especially when you're not well."

"I will be far more troubled if you don't tell me."

I sighed. This hadn't exactly been on my agenda for this visit. I'd come here intending to support Faye, not the other way around.

"Are you and Lydia having problems? Is that it?"

"Faye, my darling, don't worry yourself. Lydia and I are fine. I just feel a little trapped in our relationship, that's all. I'm sure it will work out."

"Is that why you haven't asked her to marry you?"

"Yes," I said, finally admitting that fact to someone else.

"Oh, Jeff, I'm so sorry," Faye said. "And what I whispered to you last time you were here wouldn't have helped."

"No," I agreed, "not great."

"So what are you going to do?"

"I don't know," I said. "I love Lydia, but I feel life is somehow passing us by. The excitement is less than it was."

"Jeff, it's bound to diminish a bit with time. How long have you two been together?"

"Just over four years."

"Mmm. Not really long enough for the seven-year itch. How does Lydia feel?"

"I don't know," I said. "I haven't talked to her about it."

"Then you must."

"How can I? She wants to get married and have children."

"So you do know how she feels," Faye said. "Does she love you?"

"Yes, I suppose. She says she does." I stood up and walked around the kitchen, taking deep breaths to hold back tears. "Faye, I don't know what to do." More deep breaths. "Maybe it's just a phase I'm going through. Something about turning thirty. Or perhaps I'm expecting too much from a relationship. We almost never argue or anything, and the sex between us is good. But the thought of marriage frightens me. It's too permanent."

I sat down again on the stool. I could feel my eyes beginning to well up.

"How about children?" Faye asked.

"What about them?"

"Don't you want any?"

"Yes, of course I do."

"Why 'of course'? Not everyone wants children."

"Well, I do." I sighed. "That's part of the problem. I feel I can't be responsible for bringing a child into the world if I'm not completely certain that Lydia and I will last together. It wouldn't be fair on any of us. And I'm not one of those idiots who think that having a baby will save their relationship. It never does."

"No," Faye agreed. "Having a baby puts more strain on a marriage, not less."

"So what do I do?" I asked. "I don't want to hurt Lydia, but I'm not the happiest of bunnies at the moment."

I was very close to crying, and Faye came around the breakfast bar and put a comforting arm across my shoulders.

"I can't tell you what to do, little bro, that has to be for you to decide. All I will say is don't do anything until you're certain it's the right thing. Lydia is a lovely girl, and they don't come along like that very often. Make absolutely sure she's not what you want before you cast her adrift."

14

I caught the train from Waterloo to Ascot at eleven-forty on Saturday morning.

I had meant to be much earlier, but both Lydia and I had overslept and that was because we'd had a really good time on Friday evening. The best in ages.

I had arrived home from Richmond the previous afternoon with Faye's wise words playing over and over again in my head: *Lydia is a lovely girl, and they don't come along like that very often. Make absolutely sure she's not what you want before you cast her adrift.*

It was time to make some real effort on my side.

"Let's go out tonight," I'd said to Lydia when she came home from work. "I'm fed up with staying at home and watching television and minding what we eat and drink."

"Where do you want to go?" She hadn't sounded very enthusiastic, but I was not to be deterred.

"To the West End. How about a show? Then dinner afterwards."

"Will we get any tickets this late on a Friday?"

"Maybe we will or maybe we won't," I'd said. "But we could at least give it a go. Come on, let's try our luck."

And so we had, acquiring the very last two seats in the peanut gallery for *Les Misérables.* We'd both seen the show before, but not together, and we adored the music. Lydia laughed loudly at the inn-keeping Thénardiers, clung tightly to my hand when Éponine was killed, sobbed when little Gavroche was shot and wept openly when Jean Valjean died at the end, only to stand up and shout for more during the curtain calls.

We bounded down the stairs to the street warbling the lyrics of "Do You Hear the People Sing?" at the tops of our voices, and then laughing as other people looked at us as if we were crazy. And we were.

"God, what fun," Lydia cried, hugging me outside the theater.

I hugged her back.

"How about the Dover Street Wine Bar?"

"I thought you didn't like jazz."

"I do tonight."

We had eaten dinner, then danced until they threw us out at three o'clock in the morning.

We hadn't actually made love on the backseat of the taxi on the way home, but it wasn't due to a lack of intent on either of our parts. We just had an annoyingly talkative taxi driver who also wouldn't stop looking at us in his rearview mirror as we giggled uncontrollably behind him.

But we had made up for it when we'd arrived home, not finally succumbing to sleep until nearly five.

Hence, we had overslept.

Now I dragged myself, bleary-eyed and rather hungover, out of the train at Ascot and up the hill to the racetrack.

Thanks to Crispin's little ploy with the parking spaces request, Ascot was brimming with security personnel. And, no doubt, the BHA Integrity Department would also be out in force, even if they were largely unaware of the true reason.

Consequently, I decided not to use my official credentials to get into the racetrack but paid my money at the turnstiles like everybody else.

I wasn't really sure why I was there. It was not as if I could actually do much, not without blowing my undercover status. But I knew I'd be happier being present at the track rather than sitting at home watching anything suspicious unfold on television.

The day was bright and sunny, but it had turned bitterly cold, with a strong northerly wind blowing freezing air straight down off the polar ice cap. Hence, everyone was in thick overcoats with gloves, scarves and warm hats, that greatly helped me to blend in.

I wore the brown woolen beanie that I'd last used at

Cheltenham with the collar-length dark wig beneath. And the goatee was also making a repeat appearance, along with a pair of sunglasses. I had decided to come in disguise as I was concerned most about being recognized by one of my BHA colleagues, something which may have resulted in some awkward questions, rather than to remain incognito for any particular villains.

It did, however, have its other advantages.

I literally ran into Nick Ledder, the banned jockey I'd seen at Cheltenham—or, more accurately, he ran into me on the concourse of the enormous grandstand. Again, he had a tweed cap pulled down over his forehead and the collar of his coat turned up against the wind. I knew him instantly, but, fortunately, he didn't recognize me even though he should know me quite well. I'd been the investigator who had testified against him at the disciplinary panel about his attempts to bribe another jockey.

Why, I thought, is Nick Ledder jeopardizing his future riding career by being seen at a racetrack?

Having nothing else better to do, I followed him.

The main grandstand at Ascot was designed primarily for the Royal Ascot meeting, five days each June, when crowds of up to eighty thousand would descend on this southeastern corner of Berkshire for the annual flat-racing festival of horses, hospitality, and hats.

A jumps meeting in freezing weather at the end of March, even on a Saturday, couldn't muster a crowd hardly a tenth that size, and, despite a large part of the grandstand being closed off completely, the place seemed cavernous and echoey.

And it didn't make following a target particularly easy, not that tailing Nick Ledder was very revealing.

He meandered around with seemingly no real purpose. He spoke to no one of interest and interacted only with the man behind the counter at one of the food stalls, where he bought a large Cornish pasty that he proceeded to inject with copious quantities of tomato ketchup from a pump.

That, I thought, wouldn't do his riding weight any favors.

I used my cell phone to take a picture of him tucking into his high-calorie lunch with the crown logo of the Ascot racetrack clearly visible in the background, but I became bored with that particular game and was thankful when the runners for the first race started to arrive in the pre-parade ring and I was able to switch my attention to the horses.

I leaned on a rail and watched as the ten runners for the two-mile novice hurdle were being saddled, the trainers constantly checking that everything was in order and nothing had been forgotten. Duncan Johnson was one of them. I glanced down to my program and was interested to note that the horse he was preparing was Paperclip, one of those owned by Ian Tulloch.

I looked around for the owner and, sure enough, he was standing to one side, laughing and joking with a group of admiring ladies, all of them protected from the biting wind by thick fur coats and hats.

Paperclip, now saddled and wearing a thick rug against the cold, was led by his groom towards the main parade ring. Ian Tulloch and friends, together with Duncan Johnson, followed behind, all of them in excited good humor.

There was no sign of Duncan's young mistress nor his wife.

I looked up the record of Paperclip in the program. This was only his third-ever run and his first since before Christmas. He'd previously finished only fourth and sixth, but something about Ian Tulloch's demeanor made me think that the horse had improved considerably over the intervening months and clearly much was expected of him today.

I reckoned a minor betting coup was in progress, and it was all aboveboard and legal.

An owner and trainer were not under any obligation to tell everyone else if they thought their horse would run rather better than its past record might suggest just as long as the previous poor record hadn't been manufactured on purpose.

I stood by the rail, watching, until all the other runners had been saddled and had departed the pre-parade area. No unauthorized person attempted to get near any of them, not that I'd really expected them to. I had to assume that the drinking-water truck was in place at the stables, and I could see no other way that Leonardo would be able to drug all the horses running.

I wandered over to the main parade ring.

Thanks to Crispin's personal assistant, there were security guards everywhere, with twenty or more of them standing inside the rail, all facing outwards towards the crowd, to spot any miscreant who might attempt to approach the horses.

I even spotted Crispin himself, standing at the top of the viewing area, keeping watch.

He really must be worried, I thought. I couldn't remember when Crispin had last actually been to the races. The racetracks were the domain of the investigators, not the analysts, and I'd certainly never seen him anywhere but in the London office. I ambled over to stand next to him. He ignored me, keeping his eyes firmly fixed on the horses.

"Anything to report, Crispin?" I asked quietly.

Crispin glanced at me, then took a closer look.

"Jeff?" he said with uncertainty.

"I didn't want any of our own guys to recognize me," I said.

"They certainly won't," he said, laughing.

"Is there, in fact, anything to report?"

"Nothing at all. No one is getting anywhere near any of the horses unless they've been authorized to do so. Even the trainers are complaining because they have to produce their pass cards every time they go to the stables."

"And the drinking water?"

"Clean as a whistle."

"Good," I said. "I see we have one of our esteemed Board members as an owner in the first."

"Mr. Tulloch," Crispin said without warmth. "I never did like accountants."

"Meet you here after the third?"

"Fine."

I drifted away and went through the grandstand to the viewing area beyond to watch the first race, stopping off briefly at a Tote counter to place a crisp twenty-pound note on Paperclip to win.

The hurdle track at Ascot is just over a mile and a half around in a clockwise loop so the runners lined up for the two-mile start some ways to our right. They jumped two hurdles in front of the grandstand and then swung right-handedly down the hill for another complete circuit of the track.

The jockey kept Paperclip closely in touch with the leaders as they raced over the three hurdles on the run down to Swinley Bottom, and then he started pushing Paperclip forward so that he had pulled clear of the others as they climbed the hill to the turn into the straight with just two more to jump.

Paperclip appeared every inch the winner as he flew over the second last, gaining two or three lengths on his pursuers while in the air.

But he didn't win. He finished second.

In the end, it was a close finish, but only because Paperclip's jockey badly misjudged things going to the last flight of hurdles, by which point they were ten lengths in front and bound for victory.

For some inexplicable reason, the jockey asked Paperclip to put in an extra stride before jumping when even the spectators in the grandstand could see that there wasn't room for one and, consequently, the horse was far too close to the obstacle when he took off.

He hit the hurdle hard with his front legs and almost came to a complete stop, landing on all four feet at once. Even then, the wretched jockey very nearly redeemed himself by getting the horse going again, but their momentum had gone and the favorite came sailing past in the last few strides to win by a neck.

Many in the crowd cheered and jumped up and down with excitement, slapping one another on the back, not least to try to keep themselves warm against the icy wind that was blowing straight into our faces. Even I was getting cold and I usually didn't worry about the weather conditions.

I went back through the grandstand mostly to get out of the wind but also to watch the horses come back into the unsaddling enclosure.

Ian Tulloch stood with Duncan Johnson, waiting for Paperclip to appear from the tunnel under the grandstand. Gone was Ian's pre-race bonhomie. Now he didn't look at all happy. In fact, quite the opposite. He stood, stiff-lipped, with his hands clenched into fists inside his brown leather gloves.

I wasn't exactly pleased to have lost my twenty pounds, but I wondered just how many tens of thousands, or even hundreds of thousands, Ian Tulloch had just seen washed down the toilet. He had a well-deserved reputation as a big gambler, and, apart from the debacle at the last hurdle, Paperclip had indeed run a much better race than his starting price of fifteen-to-one might have suggested. Next time out he certainly wouldn't start at such favorable odds.

Mr. Tulloch's little betting coup had failed miserably and any future opportunities had likely vanished with it.

No wonder he was angry.

The horses arrived, the much-backed winner receiving a small cheer from his supporters as his breath made great clouds of mist in the cold air and steam rose from his hindquarters.

Meanwhile, Tulloch glared angrily at Paperclip's jockey. I could just imagine what he was thinking. I was thinking it too.

As with every other racetrack in the country, Ascot provided buckets full of water for the horses to drink or for them to be washed down after their exertions. During the race, the buckets had been left in lines, completely unattended, awaiting the horses' return. Could they have been the source of the doping at Cheltenham? I watched as the water was now given to the horses, the winner gulping down half a bucketful in just a few seconds.

No, I thought, the buckets couldn't have been the cause. If a horse had consumed the methylphenidate only after the race was run, there surely wouldn't have been enough time for the drug to pass through its system and into the urine before it was tested.

Those horses selected for testing were taken directly from the unsaddling enclosure to the secure testing unit, where they had to remain until a sample was given. That could take some time, but most horses would pee within an hour, and many much sooner than that, especially if they were walked around and given more water to drink.

The veterinary technicians became experts at knowing

if and when a horse was about to stale and invariably produced the cup on a stick right on cue to catch the urine for the sample.

And, in the unlikely event that a horse refused to perform within a couple of hours, blood would be taken instead. Either way, no horse was permitted to leave the unit until after suitable samples for testing had been obtained.

The second race ran without incident, and the third also. Only four races to go.

"Any problems?" I asked Crispin as we met again at the spot overlooking the parade ring.

"None," he said. "Everything seems to be going like clockwork."

No sooner had he said it than the racetrack klaxon sounded through the public address system. The klaxon was normally only used to announce a stewards' inquiry. Everyone went quiet to listen.

"Ladies and gentlemen," said the announcer. "It is with regret that the stewards have abandoned the remaining races today due to a severe outbreak of food poisoning in the jockeys' changing room."

Our extra security had concentrated only on the horses.

We'd all been looking the wrong way.

15

"It was the ginger cake."

We were in another specially convened BHA Board meeting held at Scrutton's Club on Monday afternoon, and I was taking considerable flak for having suggested we ignore the previous demand.

"What bloody ginger cake?" Ian Tulloch asked.

"The ginger cake that many of the jockeys ate in the changing room at lunchtime on Saturday," I said. "It was placed in the changing room sometime in the morning before anyone arrived. The caterers are adamant that they didn't provide it. They told me they only put out the usual sandwiches and the cake must have already been there."

"Have we had this cake analyzed?" asked Roger Vincent.

"It was all eaten," I said. "It was apparently very popular."

"I thought jockeys didn't eat cake," said Piers Pottinger. "Too fattening."

"Apparently, they do," I said. "Nearly all of the jockeys had some except a few who were doing really light weights. That's how we know it's the cake that was the cause. Those who didn't eat it didn't get ill."

"Have we any idea what was in it?" asked Bill Ripley.

"No," I said. "But it was something that made people very ill very quickly. Some sort of poison. A few of the jockeys were vomiting within half an hour. Others took longer. But everyone who ate the cake was ill eventually. The stewards had no alternative but to cancel racing as the weighing-room plumbing couldn't keep up with the need."

Roger Vincent pulled a face.

And well he might. Such was the state of the jockeys' area that racing at Ascot had also been abandoned on Sunday due to health concerns.

"How can we be sure that the same man is responsible for both the horse doping and this?" asked Howard Lever. "The food poisoning could have been an accident."

I looked around the table.

It was obvious that no one else believed the food poisoning was an accident. Howard Lever was clutching at straws. And thin straws at that.

"So what the bloody hell do we do now?" Ian Tulloch asked angrily. He'd been in a foul temper ever since he'd arrived five minutes late for the meeting. Indeed, I suspected he'd been in a continuous foul temper ever since Paperclip had failed to win the first race at Ascot on Saturday. "How much do we have to pay this bloody man to leave us alone?"

"Can't we just increase security for both the horses and the jockeys?" said Stephen Kohli. "Surely it's better to stop it happening again rather than giving in to this monster and paying him money."

"It might end up costing us less to pay him than to shell out for the extra security," said Bill Ripley. "He's now shown that when we protect the horses, he attacks the jockeys. If we protect them too, he'll attack somewhere else. Next it may be the racegoing public who become ill or the fabric of our racetracks that's damaged or destroyed. Can we afford that? Can we also afford to turn our racetracks into fortresses? And do we really want to have airport-style security checks everywhere?"

Heads shook around the table and discussion followed for some while, with recriminations flying to and fro. The united front was beginning to crumble.

"I think it's high time we called in the police," said Neil Wallinger.

Howard Lever didn't agree. "We will lose all authority over racing if the public finds out and calling in the police is tantamount to shouting it from the rooftops. If the police themselves don't tell the newspapers, the man behind all of this will."

"So what *do* we do?" Neil asked with irritation. "We are losing our authority over racing anyway because it's this man, not us, who is dictating what happens. We should inform the police before they discover it for themselves because then we will be the ones under investigation simply for staying silent."

"It surely must be illegal to poison people," said Bill Ripley. "I'm surprised the police aren't investigating the matter."

"I doubt it," I said. "No long-term harm was done. The jockeys recovered overnight. And no one else had been there, asking questions about the cake, when I went to see the racetrack caterers this morning. They said they knew nothing about it. I only heard about it from the jockeys. I spoke to some of them yesterday."

"Which jockeys?" Stephen Kohli asked me directly.

"I spoke to half a dozen of them, but Brian Rice was the most helpful." Brian Rice was one of the country's most successful jump jockeys, a naturally thin man who had no trouble with his weight. "He told me he'd never thrown up so badly in his life. He thought he was dying, he felt so ill."

"How much of the cake did he eat?" asked Bill Ripley.

"Quite a lot, it seems, certainly more than the others, because he said it tasted so nice. Very gingery. It was a great big square cake that had been cut up into bite-sized pieces, no doubt to encourage all of the jockeys to have at least one. Brian Rice told me that he'd had the last two bits and then he'd thrown away the foil the cake had been wrapped in. No doubt the ginger was used to mask the taste of the poison."

"It's all well and good talking about the bloody cake,"

said Ian Tulloch angrily, "but what are we going to do about this man?"

"We'll just have to wait to see what he wants," said Roger Vincent. "He's bound to send us another demand. We must all stand firm and stick together over this. Gentlemen, do I have your support?"

He looked around the table and received nods from everyone, even those who didn't really approve of the do-nothing policy. The uneasy alliance had survived for at least one more meeting.

And that was how it was left.

Other than continuing with the water trucks at all racetracks and ensuring that no food was allowed into any jockeys' changing rooms without its source being known and checked, we would do nothing else but wait for the demand.

Crispin called it another first-class example of collective head-in-the-sand behavior.

Could anyone see the juggernaut coming?

WE DIDN'T have to wait long for the next demand to arrive.

Crispin Larson called me at home at eleven o'clock on Tuesday morning. "We've received another missive from our friend Leonardo in this morning's mail. And Howard wants you, dear boy, to do the negotiating under my supervision."

"And what did Leonardo demand?"

"The usual. Five million quid. Acceptance in tomorrow's *Times*—or else. And this time no one is saying we shouldn't reply."

"Who knows about it?"

"Howard's been phoning the other Board members since soon after eight. Roger Vincent arrived at the office at nine and the two of them called in Stephen Kohli and me. They are pretty worried, I can tell you. Five million is a lot of dough and they have no idea where to get it from."

"I'm sure it won't be as much as five million," I said. "Not in the end."

"That's what they are hoping too. That's why they suggested that you should do the negotiating."

"Oh, thanks," I said sarcastically. "What are they putting in *The Times*?"

"That's for us to decide. We have until noon today to get something into tomorrow's paper."

I looked at the clock in my study. Noon was in less than an hour.

"So what's the brief?" I asked.

"Get him down to as low a figure as we can without causing him to do any more disruption to racing."

"Really easy, then," I said with a laugh. "Do we have an upper limit?"

"Roger Vincent remembers that you said at the first meeting that our friend wants about half a million."

"I said that he might expect half a million. He would want more."

"Well, half a million's the absolute limit, though how we're going to find that from the BHA's budget is anyone's guess."

"How about if we start by offering him fifty thousand?"

"Is that enough?" Crispin was concerned. "Might he not do something else to hurt us? Remember what happened last time when we offered him only twenty."

"It's a risk we have to take. If we offer him the half million straightaway, he won't accept it. He'll reckon he could get at least two and the BHA will end up paying much more. Fifty thousand shows that we are interested in real-money negotiations, but also that we're not prepared to go anywhere near his five million figure."

"I still think we should go a bit higher. How about seventy-five thousand?" he said. "You are aware that you really will get sacked if this goes wrong, and probably me too?"

"You and I will be the fall guys," I agreed. "That's why Howard is keen for us to do the negotiating. He can then stand back and say it was nothing to do with him if it all goes wrong. He's watching his own back."

"I reckon we'll be more than just a pair of fall guys, dear boy, if this goes wrong," Crispin said with a hollow laugh. "We'll be put up against a wall and shot and the BHA Board will be acting as the firing squad."

I wished he wouldn't keep using metaphors that involved such finality.

We discussed the matter for another half hour or so before agreeing on a figure of seventy-five thousand pounds as our next offer.

He hung up and I dialed the number for *The Times* newspaper.

"Van Gogh accepts Leonardo's proposal of marriage and now offers seventy-five thousand as dowry." I repeated it twice over the telephone for the young woman in classified ads.

"Are you sure that's right?" she asked. "It seems a very strange item to me. Shouldn't it be in the forthcoming marriages section?"

"No," I said. "Please place it in the personal announcements column."

"OK," she said. "You're paying."

We certainly were.

I HAD only just put the phone down from speaking to *The Times* when it rang again.

"Mr. Jefferson Hinkley?" said a male voice when I answered.

"Yes."

"This is Detective Sergeant Galley from the Gloucestershire Police. You may recall I interviewed you following a fatal attack at Cheltenham races three weeks ago."

"Yes," I said, "I remember. How can I help you?"

"We would like to interview you again concerning the killing of Jordan Furness."

I thought he was being very formal.

"What about it, exactly?" I asked.

"Some information has come to our attention that we wish to speak to you about."

"What information?"

"We will tell you that at the interview."

Now, I thought, he's also being evasive.

"Can't we do the interview over the telephone? It's a long way from Willesden to Cheltenham and I'm very busy."

"That's all right, sir," said the detective sergeant, "we will come to you. Could you please report to West End Central Police Station in Savile Row at eleven o'clock tomorrow morning?"

There was something in his voice that made me believe that I wasn't really being given any choice.

"Am I being arrested or something?" I asked with some concern.

"No, of course not, sir," D.S. Galley replied with a slight laugh that did very little to set my mind at ease.

"Then why can't the interview be done at my home?"

"We would prefer it to be done at a police station in order to use the recording equipment available. I'll see you at West End Central tomorrow morning at eleven. Go to the main entrance and ask for me."

"OK," I said. "See you tomorrow."

At least I'd been invited to attend for an interview rather than having a posse of police in riot gear appearing before dawn to break down my front door. But, even so, I hadn't been completely reassured that I wasn't in some sort of trouble.

There had been something about his tone of voice that I hadn't liked.

16

On Wednesday morning I took the bus along Harrow Road from Willesden Junction and presented myself at the front desk of West End Central Police Station in Savile Row at precisely eleven o'clock.

D.S. Galley came out to meet me.

"Mr. Hinkley?" he said looking at me closely. "You look very different than when I last spoke to you."

I'd forgotten that I'd been wearing my brown-wig-and-goatee disguise for our previous interview at Cheltenham.

"Same man inside," I said, smiling. "Is this going to take long?"

There was something about being in police stations that made me nervous.

I could recall being in a police station at Nad-e Ali in Helmand Province when a rogue Afghan policeman had turned his gun on my section, killing two of my comrades and only narrowly missing my right ear. Even now, thinking about it many years later, my palms began to sweat slightly and my heart beat a little faster in my chest.

Calm down, I told myself, taking some deep breaths. Don't be so silly. But I couldn't help it.

"It shouldn't take too long," said D.S. Galley, leading me down a corridor and into an interview room.

It was much the same as the room I had used to interview Taliban detainees except that here the table and chairs were not screwed to the floor and there were no bars on the frosted window. But it had the same grayness about the decoration and the same smell, a combination of sweet pine disinfectant and fear.

I sat down on one side of the table while D.S. Galley and a second man sat on the other.

"This is Detective Constable Rendle, also from Gloucestershire," said D.S. Galley as he fiddled with the recording machine, sliding tapes into the slots. He pushed a button and a long beep emitted from the machine. "Interview with Jefferson Roosevelt Hinkley at West End Central," he said. He gave the date and time. "Present are Mr. Hinkley, D.C. Rendle and D.S. Galley. This interview is also being recorded on video." We all automatically looked up at the camera mounted on the side wall above the window.

"Now, Mr. Hinkley," said the sergeant formally, "can you give us your full recollection of the events leading up to the fatal stabbing of Jordon Furness and also those that led to the arrest of Matthew Unwin at Cheltenham racetrack."

"Aren't you meant to say to me first that anything I say will be taken down and used in evidence?"

"Mr. Hinkley, I told you, you are not under arrest. You're not even being interviewed under caution. We just want to check on your story."

"It's not a story," I said, "it's the truth. And I told you everything when I saw you immediately after the event. Why do I need to tell you it all again?"

"We want to ensure that what you said before was correct and to find out if you have anything else to add that you may have missed the first time."

"I would have thought this was an open-and-shut case," I said. "Hundreds of witnesses must have seen Matthew Unwin cut that bookmaker's throat. Don't tell me that he's now denying it."

"Mr. Unwin is claiming that he killed Mr. Furness while the balance of his mind was disturbed. As such, he maintains he is innocent of murder and will plead guilty only to a charge of manslaughter."

"So?" I said. "Surely that's enough, isn't it? I thought the maximum penalty for manslaughter was life imprisonment? Same as murder. I can't see the problem."

"Mr. Unwin also claims that he was being harassed by the British Horseracing Authority in general, and by you in particular, and that such harassment was instrumental in his mental state at the time of the attack."

"That's completely ridiculous," I said, leaning back in the chair. "He didn't even know I was following him until after the event, so how could it have had an effect on him? The man is simply making excuses."

"Maybe, but we have to investigate everything so that we don't get any surprises in court. Please, can you describe to us the sequence of events on that day as you remember them?"

I spent the next forty minutes going over everything again in chronological order. As far as I could tell, it was exactly what I'd said to the detective the last time. Witnessing a murder at such close quarters tended to fix events rather firmly in one's memory.

"And are you certain that Mr. Unwin didn't know you were following him after his arrival at the racetrack?" D.S. Galley asked.

"Absolutely," I said. I remembered back to when he had suddenly stopped and looked around. "If he had known me, he would have reacted when I walked past him and he didn't. It was only five minutes between him coming through the north turnstiles and the killing of Mr. Furness. Ten minutes at most. In my opinion, he definitely arrived at the racetrack with his mind made up that he had come to kill. Why else would he bring a knife?"

"He claims that you had been harassing him for several months."

"That's nonsense," I said. "Unless you call a disciplinary hearing harassment. He was found guilty in January of administering an illegal substance to his horses and was disqualified from racing for eight years for doping."

"What was the substance?"

"I believe it was Dexedrine. It's a stimulant."

"Mr. Unwin claims that he knew nothing about any

doping, and he further believes that someone else must therefore be responsible. In fact, he claims that it was you, Mr. Hinkley, who gave the horses the drugs and that's why you knew when to send in a drug testing team to find a positive result. That's what he meant by the harassment."

"The man's a fantasist," I said. "Why, then, did he kill Jordan Furness and not me?"

"He says that you were working with Mr. Furness to destroy his reputation and career."

"Then he's a nutcase," I said. "I've never met Jordan Furness in my life. The first time I even took note of his existence was when blood was pouring from his neck."

"Mr. Unwin claims that you covertly visited his racing stable and planted evidence. Is that true?"

Once again there was something in his tone of voice that I didn't like.

"Are you accusing me of something?" I asked. "Because, if so, I believe I should have been asked if I wanted a lawyer."

"Mr. Hinkley," D.S. Galley said in a condescending tone, "I am sure there is no need for that."

I didn't altogether believe him.

"I'd like to go home now," I said, standing up.

I could tell that D.S. Galley wasn't at all keen on that idea. "But I haven't finished asking my questions yet."

"Maybe not, but I've finished answering them. I have work to do."

"And what work would that be?" he asked.

"My work for the British Horseracing Authority."

D.S. Galley sat quite still, looking up at me.

"My information is," he said, "that you no longer work for the BHA."

"Well, your information is wrong, like pretty much everything else you've said this morning."

He opened his notebook and flipped through the pages. He found the place he was looking for. "Mr. Paul Maldini, head of integrity operations, told me only yesterday that you were no longer employed by the British Horseracing Authority. He further informed me that you were dismissed for gross misconduct."

Paul Maldini always was an idiot. That was why I'd insisted he should not be aware of my true position. In hindsight, that had obviously been a big mistake.

"What was that gross misconduct, Mr. Hinkley?" he asked. "And did it have anything to do with Matthew Unwin and the doping of his horses?"

This could be awkward, I thought. How was I going to explain my change in status from regular to undercover employee without informing the police of the demands being made on the BHA? Maybe it would be better if I did, but I had been specifically instructed by the Board to keep everything confidential, and especially from the police.

"I would like to go home now," I repeated, still standing.

The detective sergeant didn't move. He simply looked up at me.

"Mr. Hinkley, have you something to hide?"

"Absolutely not," I said, "but I've had enough of these stupid questions. You keep implying something that is ridiculous and I've told you I had nothing to do with the doping of Matthew Unwin's horses and I have not been harassing him as you say he's claimed. It's not my fault that you don't believe me. I don't think either of us have anything to gain by you repeatedly asking the same questions to which I give the same answers."

"Why were you dismissed from the racing authority?" he asked again.

"I wasn't," I replied. "I am now working undercover. Undercover even from my colleagues at the BHA. Paul Maldini is unaware of that fact because he doesn't need to know. And the fewer people who know, the more undercover I can remain. You, for one, should understand that. Please call Howard Lever and ask him. He's the BHA chief executive. Or Roger Vincent. He's the chairman. Both of them will vouch for my true position. You can then apologize to me for your insinuations. And after that, maybe we will talk again."

I moved towards the door.

"Interview terminated at twelve twenty-two."

I DIDN'T take the bus home. Instead, I took the Tube from Piccadilly Circus to Richmond and went to see my sister. Somehow, I wanted to spend as much time with her as I could, just in case.

She looked worried as she opened the door.

"Is everything all right?"

"Absolutely fine," I said. "And, before you ask, I haven't come here to move in." I smiled at her, but her worried brow remained firmly in place. "In fact, things have been much better between Lydia and me since I spoke to you last. We went out on Friday to see a show and had our best night out for ages. It was just like old times."

"Oh, good, I'm so pleased."

And it had been better over the weekend as well. In spite of the disaster at Ascot, Lydia had been understanding, comforting and loving, just as she had always been in the past. So was it me that had changed while she had been constant throughout?

I was confused, with my emotions in a twist.

"I think it must be me," I said to Faye as we went through into the kitchen, "rather than Lydia."

"It takes two to make a marriage."

Indeed it did. And if the worst were to happen, how would Quentin ever fare without Faye? She was the only person I knew who could tame him.

"How's Quentin?" I asked.

"Oh, the usual."

"Did he go with you to the Royal Marsden yesterday?"

"You must be joking," she said with a laugh. "Quentin hates hospitals more than I do. Daisy, our neighbor's daughter, she drove me. She's in a gap year and could do with the pocket money."

"How was it?"

"Pretty awful. I can feel the damn stuff going into my

arm like red-hot burning wires running through my veins." She shivered.

"Don't you want to rant and rave at the situation? I certainly do."

"Not really. What good would it do? I'd be the first to scream and shout if it would make me well again." She smiled. "I rather think it's better just to take the medication and save my energy. Not that I have much of that anymore, thanks to the wretched drugs. They'd better be bloody working, that's all I can say. They make me feel so sick all the time, especially at night. And it's not particularly conducive to restful sleep, I can tell you."

I gave her a hug. "If you ever need me, or Lydia, to go with you to the hospital, please just ask. We'll come at once."

"Thank you, my darling, but I'll be fine with Daisy. Tough times require tough medicine, literally, so I've not got much choice, have I? Other than to lay down and die, of course, and I have no intention of doing that. Not for a while anyway."

"That's my girl," I said and gave her another hug.

"So, how's the sleuthing going?" she asked. "Arrested any villains since Friday?"

"I'm not a policeman, you know."

"Same as," she said. "You're a horseracing policeman."

I suppose she was right, but I'd never thought of myself as such.

Maybe D.S. Galley and I had more in common than we both realized.

THE REPLY from Leonardo came in the early mail to the BHA offices on Thursday morning addressed to Roger Vincent. Crispin Larson called me at a quarter to eight, when I was still in bed.

Leonardo thanks Van Gogh for his interest but your sum is way too low. Three million minimum. Perhaps you need persuading. Watch out for the fireworks.

"What do you think it means?" Crispin asked.

"At least he's moved away from five million, which is a big step forward. It shows he's prepared to negotiate. But I don't like the sound of his fireworks nor the fact he thinks we still need persuading. It means he's not going to stop the disruption just because we are offering to pay."

"Oh God!"

"What?" I asked.

"The National. It's this coming Saturday."

Oh God indeed! Grand National Day—the one day in the year when horseracing displaces all other sport from the back pages of every newspaper. In Australia they advertise the Melbourne Cup as "The Race That Stops the Nation." In England the equivalent was the Grand National, when every man, woman and their dog placed a bet and every office in the land ran a sweepstakes.

But the history of the Grand National showed that it was not immune to disruption.

In 1993 the race was voided after most of the field

failed to stop after a second false start. Prior to the race, there had been a demonstration on the track by animal rights activists, who had delayed proceedings by some ten minutes. That had caused the horses to become stressed and agitated, which had largely contributed to the two false starts in the first place. When the second one unfolded, all but nine of the runners failed to respond to the instruction to stop and they went on to jump the first fence. Seven of them completed the whole four-and-a-half-mile race, jumping all thirty fences, while others, realizing something was amiss, pulled up at various points around the track.

One of the key reasons the nine horses didn't stop when people tried to flag them down was that the jockeys thought the officials were simply more protesters trying to disrupt the race.

And in 1997 the race had to be restaged two days late after an Irish terrorist–coded phone call to police stated that a bomb had been planted in the grandstands.

In the run-up to the day, there had been severe disruption due to explosive devices being left under several freeway bridges, so the police had no alternative but to order the evacuation of the racetrack just as the jockeys were preparing to mount the horses for the Grand National.

Sixty thousand people had to leave the enclosures and go to the center of the track or the surrounding streets. The jockeys were still in their silks, and people in the restaurants and hospitality boxes were directed to leave immediately without even having time to collect their coats from the cloakrooms. Cars in the parking lots were impounded overnight as the police and army conducted a thorough search, while the cold and frustrated racegoers had to somehow make their way home or find lodgings in the city's hotels that were already full to bursting. And to make things worse, the police shut down the cell phone networks to prevent them being used to detonate the bomb.

To say there was confusion would be a major understatement, with some people trying to get away from the potential danger as quickly as possible while others initially refused to budge an inch. In the end, of course, everyone had to depart. There were some officials who never recovered from the experience in spite of it all being a hoax call.

There had been no bomb, but, since that day, Aintree is still the only racetrack in England where each car is searched as it arrives at the parking lots, and everyone has their bags X-rayed before they enter through a metal detector.

Could the Grand National afford another scene of such chaos?

"I think we need to get another notice in tomorrow's *Times*," I said, "increasing our offer to a hundred grand, but only on condition there is no further disruption."

"I agree," said Crispin. "Will you deal with it?"

"Yes," I said. "I'll also go up to Liverpool today and go racing tomorrow and Saturday."

"Right," he said. "But let's not take our eyes off the other meetings. Our friend might expect us to be ultravigilant for the National, but there's racing elsewhere."

"I still reckon the National's the most likely," I said.

"You're probably right."

"And, Crispin," I said, "there's an added complication. The police questioned me yesterday about the murder of Jordan Furness. They think I'm somehow involved because Matthew Unwin is claiming that he was being harassed by the BHA in general, and me in particular, and that Furness was working with us."

"That's ridiculous."

"I know," I said, "and I told them so, but that idiot Paul Maldini informed them that I've been dismissed from the BHA for gross misconduct and they now think it had something to do with the harassment or the murder."

"But they didn't arrest you or anything?" He sounded quite worried.

"No, not quite, but at one point I thought they were going to. I told them to check with Howard or Roger Vincent."

"I hope you didn't tell them anything about our friend."

"No," I said, "of course I didn't."

"I'd better warn Howard so that he doesn't have a fit if they call him."

"Good idea," I said. "I think that's all for now. Let's speak soon."

I hung up and lay back on the pillow with a sigh.

"Why didn't you tell me you'd been questioned by the police?" Lydia asked.

I'd forgotten she was still lying next to me.

"I didn't want to worry you."

"But now I am worried."

"Don't be," I said. "Everything's fine."

"Are you in some sort of trouble?" The concern was clearly evident in her voice.

"I promise you, I'm not in any trouble."

"So tell me why the police questioned you. Don't you trust me?"

"Of course I trust you," I said, turning towards her.

"Tell me, then," she said.

"It's all to do with the same problem I told you about before. The man who put the stuff in the water at Cheltenham also put some poison in a ginger cake the jockeys ate at Ascot last Saturday. He's demanding money or he'll keep on disrupting racing."

"A hundred grand? That's what you said to Crispin."

"That's what we are going to offer. He initially demanded five million, but there's no way the BHA will pay that much. He now says he wants three. I'm doing the negotiation and I've been told by the BHA Board that half a million is the absolute limit."

"And what did the police say about that?"

"Ah, well, therein lies the problem. The BHA Board won't tell the police anything."

"That's crazy."

"I agree with you," I said. "I've tried to tell the Board, but they seem to believe that bringing in the police would make the whole thing known by everyone and then the betting public will lose confidence in racing at a time when finances in the sport are pretty shaky."

"But didn't you tell the police all about it when they questioned you yesterday?"

"No, I've been specifically told not to by the BHA Board."

"Then you're all stupid," she said. "Don't you see that this man will never go away? He'll be back for more next year. And then more again the year after that."

"I know," I said. "I've told the Board that, but they think that informing the police doesn't guarantee the man will be caught, and the demands may come again anyway, so what will they have gained?"

"But the police must have a better chance of catching the bastard. Surely that should outweigh any negatives."

She was right.

I knew she was right, and so would almost every other sane person if they were aware of the circumstances. But Howard Lever, Stephen Kohli and Roger Vincent didn't and, so far, they had carried the BHA Board with them. Whether that fragile alliance would survive disruption of the Grand National was another matter.

"So what are you going to do about it?" Lydia asked.

I rolled over and smiled at her.

"I'm going to catch the bastard myself."

17

I sat eating a leisurely Full English without feeling guilty. Two rashers of bacon, a sausage, fried egg, mushrooms, even a portion of black pudding and a slice of fried bread smothered with baked beans—and there was no one around to tell me about how unhealthy it all was.

I smiled to myself.

Lydia always ate only muesli for breakfast, together with some fruit-and-yogurt concoction she made fresh each morning in the blender, which I was also forced to consume whenever I was at home. I knew she did it for my own good, because she loved me, but hotel breakfasts when I was away alone could be so liberating.

I opened *The Times* to the personals page and checked our notice in the announcements:

Van Gogh wants speedy marriage with Leonardo. Proposed dowry of 100K. Conditional on no fur-

ther persuasion. Down payment offered to demonstrate good faith.

"Do you think it will work, dear boy?" Crispin had asked when he'd called me at eight o'clock.

"No," I said. "Do you?"

"I fear not, but we have to try. Perhaps we should have offered more or even given him what he wants."

Crispin and I had discussed the amount at considerable length the previous day. I was sure that if we went up in too large a step, we would end up paying far more than our half-a-million limit.

I had added the offer of a down payment as a bit of an afterthought to try to flush Leonardo out into the open.

I knew from my Afghanistan experiences that a kidnapper was at his most vulnerable when collecting the ransom. That was the moment to identify him, although an actual arrest might place the victim at greater risk. Better to leave alone and covertly follow him in the hope that he would lead you back to where the victim was being held.

Freeing the victim would then become the priority as, all too often, they were in more danger after the ransom was paid than before. In nearly half the cases I had dealt with, the victims were kept alive only long enough to make heart-wrenching phone calls to their families imploring them to pay up. After the payment was received, they would be shot and their bodies dumped from a speeding car in the dead of night.

Here there was no victim, other than racing, and that

was in great danger only while Leonardo was free. There would be absolutely no reason not to detain him at the drop, provided he was careless enough to show himself.

I popped the last piece of sausage into my mouth and washed it down with the dregs of my second cup of coffee.

I was staying in a very modest motel in a service area just off the M6 freeway near Wigan. It wasn't particularly close to Aintree, but this was the only place I'd been able to find a room after two and a half hours of trying by telephone. A combination of the Grand National meeting at Liverpool and the quarter final of a European football competition in Manchester had filled almost every available bed within a hundred miles.

It also meant that I'd been forced to hire a car to drive north rather than using the train as I preferred.

I had discovered from experience that it was almost impossible to follow someone away from a racetrack in a car unless you happened to be parked right next to him. By the time you went to collect your own vehicle the target had long gone. And, if you followed someone away on a bus or by train, you had the major inconvenience of having to return later to collect your own car or have it towed away.

And parking at the Grand National meeting was a particular nightmare.

Poor financial circumstances at the racetrack in the 1980s and '90s had resulted in the sell-off of much of the surrounding space for retail and industrial use as the city of Liverpool swelled to embrace its famous racing suburb. Now the racetrack had to hire back the local retail center's parking lots on race days, but even that did not satisfy the recent demand for parking as the popularity of the race grew year by year.

Of course, I always had my BHA parking pass in my pocket, but I was loath to use it. Crispin had told me that as far as he knew, three other members of the integrity team would be present at Aintree on Friday, including my friend Nigel Green, and I didn't especially want to bump into any of them in the parking lot reserved for the officials. It would take too much explaining.

In the end, I decided to drive to the town of Ormskirk and catch the local train to Liverpool that stopped conveniently just across the road from the racetrack. And, to be on the safe side, I would go in disguise.

AINTREE on the Friday of the Grand National meeting was when the people of Liverpool came in their tens of thousands to have a flutter at the races, the women in particular dressing in their best outfits and outrageous hats for the occasion.

And, for a change, the weather was kind to them.

Instead of freezing half to death in their short skirts and sleeveless dresses as was normal in early April, the problem this year would be sunburn, with acres of bare flesh reddening under the cloudless sky.

The menfolk, meanwhile, came in shiny suits and skinny ties, and the heat of the day would drive them early to the bars for iced champagne or a cooling beer.

The day was going to be bonanza time for both the booze and the ice-cream salesmen.

I waited patiently in the line to pass through the turnstiles and rather hoped that the two security personnel were being more vigilant than their devil-may-care manner would tend to suggest.

They weren't.

Both of them laughed and joked with the racegoers as they passed through the metal detectors and seemed unconcerned that I had loose change, the rental-car keys and a pair of metal-rimmed reading glasses in my pockets, all of which together caused the machine to bleep loudly.

I showed the man the keys from my right-hand pant pocket and he waved me in without checking that I wasn't carrying anything more sinister in my left.

I would have to have words with Stephen Kohli.

I drifted around the enclosures, watching but not knowing what I was actually looking for. Crispin Larson had assured me that the security at both the racetrack stables and in the weighing room would be extreme, but if the security at the entrances was anything to go by, *extreme* was a relative term.

The racetrack stables had been extensively searched before the horses started arriving and no one had been allowed to enter since unless cleared by two different people. Much the same was true of the weighing room, where there were now two officials standing guard with strict instructions that no food or drink was to be provided to the jockeys other than produced under supervision by a specified chef.

I was sure it was all necessary and I was glad it was in place, but I was also acutely aware that Leonardo was far from stupid and he would know exactly what we would do. If he had plans to disrupt the meeting, I predicted it wouldn't involve either the stables or the weighing room. So, where else?

I walked around, looking at the grandstands and other buildings in a fresh light. What would I do if I wanted to disrupt everything? *Fireworks*—that was what he'd said. Setting fire to the grandstands would certainly produce some fireworks. It would also likely cause the National to be cancelled.

Back in 1985, the whole of Arlington Park racetrack, situated in the northern suburbs of Chicago, burned to the ground, but they still held the Arlington Millions race, albeit twenty-five days later, where thirty-five thousand people watched from tents and temporary scaffold-built bleachers.

There would be no time to do the same here. Not with the race due to be run the following afternoon.

I called Crispin, getting a signal on my fourth attempt.

"How about a fire in one or more of the grandstands?"

"What about it, dear boy?"

"Do we organize a fire watch?"

"There is a security presence overnight. They would spot any fire."

"Not until it was far too late if they are anything like those at the entrance gates."

"I will get on to the racetrack management and ensure that adequate security is made available. But, of course, without specifically alarming anyone to an explicit risk."

I reckoned they probably needed alarming.

"That's a start," I said. "But make sure they do continuous patrols especially in the kitchens. And also ensure they check for boilers set to explode."

"Very funny," Crispin said. There was still plenty of racing folklore surrounding a sabotage attempt at Seabury racetrack, where a heating boiler nearly blew up after someone had inserted a dead mouse as a plug into a pipe of the safety system.

"Check the stable fire precautions. We can't afford to lose some of the best racehorses in the country due to arson. The BHA would never recover."

"I'll remind everyone about the need for vigilance against fire at all times."

"And how about round the track?" I said. "Will that be patrolled? We don't want any of the fences set on fire."

"I'll get on to that too," said Crispin. "I'm sure precautions are already in place due to any bloody antis who might turn up. And I know that there will be police on duty at some of the fences tomorrow."

"And check for wire," I said.

"Wire?"

"Stretched across and above the fences to bring down the horses. It's been done before."

"I'll make sure it's checked."

I walked past a long line of food outlets, each doing a roaring trade, with a choice of roast-pork baps, fish-

and-chips, meat pies, bangers and mash, assorted curries, Asian noodles or huge slices of pepperoni pizza.

"I hope he doesn't try poisoning members of the public. There is no way we could check every restaurant and food stall."

Crispin laughed. "Some of those stalls are likely candidates for food poisoning without any help from our friend."

"Yeah, you could be right." I watched as a large man loaded bright yellow mustard onto an enormous portion of sausages, balancing the whole lot on a cardboard plate that was not really big enough for the purpose.

"Check the VIP lunch," I said. Each year the chairman of the racetrack company entertained a couple hundred guests for lunch. "Make sure no one gets into that particular kitchen without proper authorization and double-check the wines are not tampered with."

"Right," said Crispin in a tone that suggested I was becoming rather extreme. "Anything else?"

"Plenty," I said with a laugh. "I just haven't thought about it yet."

It would be so much easier, I thought, if the police knew we had a potential saboteur on the loose. Then there would be far more eyes looking, although they should be looking anyway.

I watched the seven races from various vantage points, but nothing unexpected occurred other than the red-hot favorite for the Melling Chase was beaten by a short head by a twenty-to-one outsider in a photo finish.

I hadn't really expected anything to happen.

If our friend Leonardo was planning any disruption, it would surely be on the following day when the whole world would be watching.

And, sure enough, even though we were looking and did not have our heads in the sand, the juggernaut arrived right on cue at four twenty-five on Saturday afternoon and mowed us all down.

18

Grand National Day started inauspiciously with a call from Crispin at a quarter to nine on my cell. I looked at the number readout on the screen.

"What are you doing in the office on a Saturday?"

"Checking Roger Vincent's mail. And a good job I did too. There's a note from our friend."

It was brief, and to the point.

Too little, too late. Enjoy your day.

"Not much doubt, then," I said.

"No," Crispin agreed. "What do we do?"

A trip to Outer Mongolia seemed like a good idea. Or maybe to the Moon.

"There's nothing that we aren't already doing," I said. "I suppose you could phone the racetrack and say you've had a credible threat to the Grand National, but it will mean calling in the police."

"I could say it was from the antibrigade."

"That would still bring in the cops," I said.

"And we aren't certain that the disruption will be at Aintree. It could be at one of the other meetings."

"We could cope with disruption anywhere else. No, it has to be here."

And it was.

AINTREE on the Saturday of the meeting had been sold out for weeks. Hence, my first problem was to gain entry to the racetrack.

On Friday, I had simply paid my money at the turnstiles, but that was now not an option. Entrance on Grand National Day was by tickets purchased in advance only.

I made my way from the railway station around to the horse trailer parking area to find the special reception set up in a temporary cabin for the owners and trainers.

Aintree, in common with most other racetracks, looked after the horse owners pretty well, allocating up to six entrance tickets per runner, as well as providing free food vouchers and complimentary race programs, all of which had to be collected from reception.

I stood in the line of expectant clusters, many of them no doubt dreaming of winning "the big one," while the three women behind the counter did their best to keep up with the demand.

When it was my turn, I simply passed my BHA pass

across the counter to one of the young women and asked her for an owner's cardboard badge. She looked up at me and then down at the pass and then back up at me again.

"I'm working undercover," I whispered so that those collecting tickets alongside me wouldn't hear. "That's what I look like under this lot." I smiled at her.

The photograph on the pass showed a clean-shaven man with short, spiky blond hair. I was currently wearing a full dark beard with matching curls, together with some thick-rimmed eyeglasses.

She hesitated, turned to the older woman standing next to her and showed her my ID.

"He says he's working undercover," she said rather too loudly for my liking. "He wants an owner's badge."

I smiled at the man standing next to me, who had turned to look my way.

The older woman waved for me to go around to the side door of the cabin.

"Why don't you wear your BHA pass? That's why it has a lanyard."

"I could," I said, "but not without broadcasting to everyone that I'm a BHA investigator. That wouldn't exactly help, now would it?"

"I'll have to call the office." She turned to go.

"I would much rather you didn't do that," I said in my best authoritative voice. "You might just blow my cover altogether. Look at my eyes." I removed the spectacles. "They are the same eyes as in the photo."

She had a close look and then studied the picture.

"All right, Mr. Hinkley," she said, "I agree that you

are who you say you are. But it's most irregular. Wait here."

She went back inside and then reappeared with an owner's badge, a white cardboard rectangle with a big red O5 printed large across the middle.

"The five means you have access to the parade ring for the Grand National. It's the fifth race. Would you like a race program as well?"

"Yes, please," I said.

She disappeared back inside and re-emerged with one.

"Thank you," I said, taking it. "And please don't mention my name to anyone."

"Who are you looking for?" she asked.

"The winner of the National, of course," I said with a smile. "The same as everyone else."

THE GATEMAN raised no objection as he scanned my owner's badge at the turnstile, and even the security personnel seemed to have picked up their game as I was properly searched on my way in.

Once inside, I wandered around with my eyes and ears open, trying to notice something out of the ordinary.

There was nothing. At least nothing I could spot.

I spied Nigel Green standing on the viewing steps outside the weighing room, but he didn't give me so much as a second glance as he chatted to another member of the BHA office staff enjoying a day out at the races.

The excitement of the crowd was palpable and there were many activities put on to keep them busy in the time before the races started. A Dixieland jazz band played a never-ending melody and a troupe of theatrical performers dressed as famous film stars entertained a circle of admirers behind the Princess Royal stand.

Not one of them was conveniently dressed in a mask and striped T-shirt.

I walked through the lines of bookmakers in the betting ring and watched the parade of former Grand National winners as they were walked up the track, past the scene of their greatest achievement, to the nostalgic cheers of the crowd.

I stood with my back to the running rail, scouring the scene with my eyes, looking for any telltale smoke that might indicate a fire.

Nothing.

As the races started I became more and more anxious. It was like sitting in an air-raid shelter during a raid—certain that a bomb would drop but not knowing exactly where or when.

As the time approached for the Grand National itself, I wanted to be everywhere, checking everything.

I went down to the parade ring to be close by in case someone made an attempt to attack a horse, or an owner, or one of the many high-profile guests gathered on the grass as the forty horses for the big race circled around them.

The great and the good were out in force, as one would expect on one of the most celebrated racing days of the year. The five days of Royal Ascot, Derby Day, Guineas weekend at Newmarket in May, the Cheltenham

Festival and maybe the Sussex Stakes at Glorious Goodwood or British Champions Day at Ascot in October—these were the rare days of British racing, those not to be missed, and Grand National Day at Aintree was, for me, top of the list.

It was a day I usually enjoyed from dawn to dusk, and then some.

But not this year.

Roger Vincent, as chairman of the BHA, was holding court in the center of the parade ring, with Ian Tulloch, Bill Ripley and Neil Wallinger in close attendance. I wondered if they were as nervous as I was, but they didn't appear to be as they laughed and joked with their guests.

Piers Pottinger was there too, together with his lovely wife Carolyn. They were deep in conversation with the trainer Duncan Johnson and another man I recognized as Tim Bell, a fellow PR executive of Piers's.

I looked down at my program. Duncan Johnson had two runners in the big race and one was owned by the firm of Bell Pottinger. Last-minute instructions were clearly being passed on by the owners to their trainer.

Graham Perry was also in the parade ring, chatting to a middle-aged couple that I took to be other owners. According to the notes in the program, this was Graham's first runner in the Grand National and his nervousness was clearly visible as he shifted his weight from foot to foot, unable to remain still for more than a few seconds. I hoped, for his sake, that the methylphenidate had long passed out of his horse's system.

The jockeys appeared from the weighing room, bringing a burst of color to the scene.

I was getting pretty frantic as I searched around with my eyes, trying to spot the very first sign of any trouble. But I knew there was nothing I could really do to stop it.

I was reminded of an Afghan tribal leader who had asked his bodyguards if they could prevent him from being killed. "No," they had replied, "but be comforted by the knowledge that we will be there to kill the assassin."

There was no way I could prevent Leonardo from carrying out an act of malicious damage, but maybe I'd be close enough to catch him afterwards.

I watched as the jockeys mounted, their silks shining brightly in the sunshine. Another turn around the parade ring and then they were filing out through the tunnel under the grandstand and onto the track.

I walked through the tunnel behind them, my adrenaline level climbing to stratospheric levels.

The horses circled, forming themselves into race-program order for the traditional parade in front of the stands. The crowd was in position, with every vantage point taken, the buzz of excitement building towards a crescendo.

Now, I thought. Now it will happen.

My heart was beating quickly, and I could even hear the rush of blood in my ears above the sound of the crowd.

But nothing untoward occurred.

The horses continued serenely on with the parade

and the fever pitch of the expectant throng grew ever higher.

The horses broke from the formal parade, their jockeys turning them to canter down to have a look at the first fence while the crowd took a collective breath in preparation for the race itself, and still nothing happened.

The horses cantered or trotted back towards the grandstand in preparation for the start that would take place in the corner of the track right in front of us. Here the horses circled again as their girths were tightened and last-minute checks made of their saddles and bridles. Some of the jockeys stood up on their stirrups to try to release the nervous tension in their legs.

I leaned against the rail and looked back at the sea of faces staring back at me from the stands. I searched along the rooftops, trying to spot something that shouldn't have been there— maybe a marksman taking aim at the starter who was climbing his rostrum.

Nothing.

"They're under Starter's Orders," came the call over the public address system, and the noise level of the crowd was turned up a few more notches.

"They're off!"

The crowd cheered even louder still as the horses swept away from them towards the line of six fences down to Becher's Brook.

As the runners crossed the Melling Road, I could see all the heads move as the attention of the crowd switched from the horses to the giant TV screens, which gave a much better view of the horses jumping the first fence.

The race had started without incident and I began to breathe slightly more easily.

Had I got it wrong?

Maybe something was going to occur at one of the other tracks and not here.

There was a groan from the crowd and my heart rate jumped, but it was due to one of the favorites having fallen at the third fence, the first open ditch.

I chanced a look at the screens and watched as the horses streamed over Becher's, then on towards the Canal Turn for the first time. Here, at the farthest point of the circuit, they turned the famous ninety-degree corner and started back towards the grandstands.

There were a few fallers at the next six fences, but nearly thirty of the original forty runners were still standing and racing in a big group as they sped towards The Chair, a big open ditch in front of the enclosures. The leading horse stumbled on landing, pitched forward and went down to the turf, spilling his rider out in front of him, and there were gasps from the crowd as some of the following horses kicked the jockey around as if he was a football.

But the real disaster occurred at the next fence, the smallest on the track, the fence situated right in front of the main grandstands in full sight of the seventy thousand people present, plus the hundreds of millions viewing worldwide on television.

Watch out for the fireworks.

As they raced towards the water jump the horses were confronted by a wall of fire as multiple fireworks ignited at either side, sending a thick curtain of bright, burning stars ten feet high across the whole width of the fence.

It was like a scene from some pyrotechnic horror movie playing out in slow motion before our eyes.

The cheering of the crowd instantly changed to screams of terror as the horses and jockeys tried to stop or veer to either side to avoid the flames.

Several of the leading horses were too close to the fence to pull up. Three of them clattered through the plastic running rails towards the grandstands, kicking the race sponsors' advertising boards aside, while two others tried to jump the eight-foot-high fence wings on the far side, only to crash to the ground in a flurry of horses' legs, jockey silks and rigid white-plastic spars.

The remainder managed to stop in time, but those closest to the fence reared up in fear of the fire. One toppled right back over, trapping the poor jockey under its bulk as it tried to regain its feet, before running off loose, the whites of its eyes showing in fear and panic.

Even those jockeys who were able to remain in the saddle looked shocked and bemused as to what to do next.

As the fireworks finally died away, one or two of the jockeys set their mounts to jump the fence, to continue with the race, but the horses were having none of it, refusing to move into a trot, let alone a gallop, despite some frantic urging and kicking.

The crowd had initially gone eerily quiet as the mayhem unfolded in front of them, but now there were shouts of anger and frustration, followed by boos of displeasure and condemnation.

My worst fears had been fulfilled.

But why?

The fences should have been searched.

Someone's head would roll for this. And I was all too aware that it would probably be mine.

19

Twenty minutes after the fireworks were set off, the Grand National was officially declared null and void, and the remaining two races of the day were abandoned.

The great race had been murdered and I hadn't even been close enough to kill the assassin.

In truth, I'd been a pretty useless bodyguard.

I walked down to the viewing areas in front of the County Stand and watched as several police officers isolated the area around the water jump with blue-and-white *Police—Do Not Cross* tape. It had become a crime scene.

Not only had the race been disrupted but one of the horses that had tried to jump the fence wing had broken a leg and had been put down in full view of the grandstands. And two of the jockeys had left the scene, flat-out, in ambulances, one with his neck immobilized in a cervical collar.

There was a sort of numbness about the crowd.

All the excitement of the day had vanished in that instant and there had been nothing to fill the vacuum. No winner to applaud, no trophy presentation to watch and nothing to discuss, other than the obvious, and even that was not really being spoken of. There wasn't much to say. People just shook their heads in disbelief and resignedly set off for the parking lots and home.

I remained while all those around me departed, my legs somehow refusing to take me away. Perhaps I would soon wake up and find it had only been a nightmare after all and all was fine.

Of course, I didn't. And the reality of the situation slowly began to sink in.

Now what should I do?

"Our friend" Leonardo had horseracing by the short and curlies.

I stood and watched as Roger Vincent, Piers Pottinger, Howard Lever and Stephen Kohli were escorted down the track to the water jump by two policemen in uniform with silver braid on their peaked caps. The top brass.

They stood near the point where the runners should have landed and were clearly having something explained to them by one of the policemen, who kept pointing at either side of the fence.

I looked closely at the jump itself. It was only about

three feet high but had a nine-foot-wide pool of water on the landing side. Consequently, the horses had to extend as they jumped to clear the water. Many years ago the pool had been two or three feet deep, but safety concerns now meant that the water depth was only six inches so that horses that dropped their hind legs in the water didn't injure their backs.

The Grand National fences are unique in British racing insofar as they are bright green rather than the usual dark brown of birch. That is because they are dressed each year with a thick coat of fresh spruce foliage laid over an inner core. Until recently the cores were constructed of solid, unyielding timber but are now more horse-friendly flexible plastic.

All of them, that is, except the water jump, the center of which is a live, growing yew hedge. On either end, where the wings met the fence, the hedge had been allowed to grow taller so that there were pillars of yew that extended above the normal height of the fence by a couple of feet. From the manner in which the policeman was pointing, I surmised that the fireworks had been hidden in these pillars, facing inwards.

I continued to watch as the group went around the fence to the takeoff side.

The six men stood there for a while, talking and pointing, before finally walking back up the track, past the winning post and on towards the tunnel between the Earl of Derby and the Lord Sefton stands.

I stayed where I was for a little longer, not knowing exactly what to do.

My mission to Aintree had been an unmitigated disaster. Not only had my negotiation plan proved to be an abject failure in preventing the disruption of the great race but I was no nearer in determining who was responsible.

Far from my boast to Lydia that *I'm going to catch the bastard myself*, I felt personally humiliated and broken.

I was also angry.

Angry with myself for my own failings. But also with our *non*-friend, Leonardo.

I won't forget this feeling, I thought, as I drove home.

And I would use my anger in revenge when I determined to whom I should direct it.

MY PHONE rang at half past six on Sunday morning, but I wasn't asleep.

"Do you have any body armor?" Crispin asked without even saying hello. "If you do, wear it. We have been summonsed to appear before the Board at the BHA offices at eleven this morning."

"On a Sunday?" I asked.

"On a Sunday. Have you seen today's papers? They're not good."

"I'm still in bed."

"Tut-tut, dear boy," Crispin said. "The condemned man should be up early on the morning of his execution."

"Shut up, will you. You'll be in the same shit as me."

"Maybe," he said. "But everyone knows it was your idea to ignore him before Ascot. And also your idea to offer such a low sum."

"You agreed to it."

"Only under sufferance. I told you Howard wanted to offer a quarter of a million."

He was right, but I'd been hoping for a touch more loyalty. I could see that contrary to what he'd told me before about us both being in this together, Crispin was going to ensure that I took all the blame.

"What do the papers say?"

"*Incompetence* is the word they like to use most. Applied about equally to the BHA, Aintree management and the Merseyside Police. And the *Racing Post* reminds everyone this is not the first time this month that racing has been disrupted and abandoned. They mention the food poisoning incident at Ascot as a further example of the BHA's inability to run racing properly."

"Do they actually link the events?" I asked.

"Not specifically, but I'd have thought it was only a matter of time. I'll see you at eleven. Have a hearty breakfast, dear boy, and wear two vests."

"Two vests?"

"So as not to shiver."

"What are you on about?"

"History, man, history," Crispin replied. "Don't you know your history?"

With that, he hung up.

"Trouble?" Lydia asked.

"Yeah," I said. "I reckon I may well be sacked properly this time."

"But it wasn't your fault!"

"Maybe not. But I'll still get the blame, you wait and see. Crispin said to wear two vests."

"Two vests?"

"Something about history and not shivering."

"Charles the First," Lydia said. "He wore two vests at his execution so the crowds wouldn't see him shiver from cold and assume he was afraid of the ax."

"Oh, great," I said. "That's all I need. Either I have to come up with something pretty amazing by eleven o'clock this morning or it will be a one-way trip to the scaffold. Or to the Job Center."

"Well, get up, then," she said, pushing me out of bed with her feet. "Get to your desk immediately and think of something pretty amazing. We have a bloody mortgage to pay and I don't earn enough." She didn't say it with a smile and a laugh. She was deadly serious.

I'd been anticipating a bit of nooky to cheer me up, but that was obviously a fruitless hope. I put on my dressing gown and walked down to my study.

I woke up my computer from its slumbers.

You have 4 new messages, I was informed by my e-mail server.

Three of them were junk mail, but the other was from Roger Vincent and had been sent late the previous evening. It wasn't particularly friendly.

For a start, he addressed me as Hinkley, rather than Jeff or Jefferson.

I wondered if it was because he was angry with me. Or maybe it was a class thing. Roger Vincent had always believed that as chairman, he was somehow superior in class to the average BHA staff member.

"Hinkley," it read. "Be at the BHA offices at eleven o'clock tomorrow morning (Sunday) for a meeting with the Board. Don't be late."

No *please*, no salutation, not even his name at the end. It was a command, not a request.

I looked at my watch. It was five to seven. I had just four hours to come up with something amazing.

ACCESS. That was the key.

Who had access to the water supply tanks at Cheltenham and Newbury, someone who also had access to the jockeys' changing room at Ascot before racing, and also to the water jump at Aintree?

The water tank at Cheltenham was not exactly secure. Anyone with a stepladder would have been able to gain access, although doing so without being seen would be more difficult.

I'd called Fergus Hunter, the stables manager, and he'd said that he hadn't seen anyone climbing through the hatch, but that didn't mean that it hadn't occurred. He wasn't there all the time, and hardly ever in the evenings.

The Cheltenham stables had opened on the Friday before the racing started on the following Tuesday, with some of the Irish runners arriving early in order to get over the journey. So from Friday onwards there had been security staff at the stable entrance, which was right next to the manager's office.

But the security was for the stable area itself, not the space above the office. Anyone dressed as a water company employee, carrying a ladder over his shoulder, wouldn't have been stopped from climbing up to the tank even if he'd had a large bag of Ritalin tablets dangling from his belt.

Similarly, access to the water jump at Aintree would have been easy. Whereas the grandstands may have been lit up at night, the track itself would have been in darkness, and it was impossible to patrol the whole perimeter to prevent someone climbing in.

However, access to the weighing room and jockeys' area at Ascot would not have been available to all, even early in the day before racing had started.

The gates of Ascot racetrack, those that allowed the public to enter, had been opened on that particular Saturday at ten-thirty, by which time the Clerk of the Scales in the weighing room had arrived.

Anyone out of place would have surely been challenged.

No one other than jockeys, their valets and those persons authorized by the BHA were officially allowed into the changing room, except that in recent years TV crews and all sorts of others in the media also had access, especially on big race days, but only with the permission of the Clerk of the Scales.

And why had our friend used Ritalin in the water at Cheltenham?

In the Unwin case the drug had been Dexedrine.

I looked up Dexedrine on the Internet. Dexedrine

was a trade name of the drug dextroamphetamine sulfate. According to the various websites I visited, Dexedrine was one of the medications widely used in the treatment of hyperactivity—just as Ritalin was.

Was that a coincidence? Maybe not.

Two very different drugs, two very different chemical formulae, but both treatments for the same disorder.

Was the perpetrator himself hyperactive? Or did he have hyperactive children?

I WAS still researching the drugs when Quentin called me at nine o'clock. That was all I needed when time was short.

"How's Faye?" I asked.

Quentin ignored such niceties. "Have you spoken to the friend about withdrawing his statement?"

"No," I said, "not yet."

"Why not?" he demanded.

"Quentin, I've been busy. Didn't you see what happened at Aintree yesterday?"

"No."

I believed him, despite the disruption of the Grand National being the lead story on every TV and radio news bulletin and the topic of every newspaper headline. Quentin had less interest in sport than anyone else I knew. He was probably the only man in England who didn't know that Manchester United was a soccer team.

"I will try to get round to speaking with him later this week."

"I suppose that will have to do," replied Quentin in a tone that left me under no illusion that I had not, in his eyes, fulfilled my obligations.

"I may be able to convince him to withdraw his statement without there being any payment made. That way, we do not open ourselves up so much to a charge of perverting the course of justice."

"Just do what it takes," he said. "And the sooner, the better. Kenneth is getting very depressed at the prospect of a trial."

Kenneth is getting depressed, I thought, not by the prospect of a trial but at the certainty that his father would then discover that he was gay.

20

I walked into the BHA offices at five minutes to eleven, but it was clear the Board meeting had been going on for some time before I arrived. I could see through the glass wall that even Crispin Larson was in the meeting ahead of me.

Not good news for my mortgage, I thought.

"Ah, Hinkley," said Roger Vincent as I knocked on and opened the boardroom door. "Come in and sit down." He indicated towards one of the empty chairs to his left.

I sat down and looked around the table. I could almost feel the hostility. They were after a scapegoat and I was firmly in their rifle sights.

"Now," Roger Vincent said, turning to me, "we think this Grand National business is all a bit of a mess."

"It's more than 'a bit of a mess,'" said Ian Tulloch loudly from the far end. "It's a fucking disaster."

"Now, now, Ian," said Roger Vincent rather pompously. "There's no need for that sort of language."

"Yes, there is," said Piers Pottinger, leaning forward and banging the table with his fist. "Ian is absolutely right. It *is* a fucking disaster. One of my horses was in that race and he's been completely traumatized. He was still sweating in the stables over an hour after the incident and it will take us ages to get him back on a racetrack, never mind the fact that he was going so well at the time, and that might be my only chance to win a Grand National. But, on top of that, this Board is being ridiculed by the racing press. You've all read today's *Racing Post*. Their front page is tantamount to a call for our collective resignation. They even advocate a return to the Jockey Club as the authority for racing."

"It's not us that should resign," muttered Ian Tulloch, "it's young Mr. Hinkley there."

I looked at the other directors, but I couldn't spot much support. Even Neil Wallinger was looking down at his hands rather than catching my eye.

"We feel humiliated," said Bill Ripley. "Perhaps it's time for a change in policy and a change in personnel."

I was not going to walk calmly up the steps to my execution. If they thought I was going to resign, they were much mistaken.

"You make it sound as if I was responsible for the fireworks," I said loudly. "Let me remind you that I was in favor of bringing in the police right from the start."

There were nods from some, including Crispin Larson and Howard Lever.

"But it was also you who suggested that we should ignore this man and now this has happened." Bill Ripley was going in for the kill. "If we had paid what he wanted in the first place, we wouldn't be in this mess."

"You really think so?" I said sarcastically. "You'd be in a much worse mess if you'd paid the man the five million he originally demanded. The BHA would then not only be bankrupt but you'd still have had no guarantee that he wouldn't disrupt the Grand National." I paused and took a deep breath. "In fact, I think it highly likely that it would have made no difference what course of action we took, he would have carried through his disruption of the Grand National anyway just to make a point."

"That's nonsense," said Ian Tulloch. "How can you possibly believe that?"

"Because I'm starting to understand the way this man acts. There is no way he could expect the negotiations between him and the BHA to have been over by the time the National was run, and obtaining those fireworks would have taken quite a time. They were more like theatrical pyrotechnics than regular fireworks. They are certainly not the sort you can simply go into a High Street shop and buy; they have to be obtained through a special supplier. He must have been planning to disrupt the race for weeks, if not for months. Certainly long before he sent us the first demand."

More sets of eyes were looking me in the face, but no

one was saying anything, so I went on. "I think we are looking for a racing insider rather than a random member of the public."

"Why?" asked Howard Lever.

"Mostly because of Ascot," I said. "Someone had to have access to the changing room before the Clerk of the Scales arrived. And the gates didn't open for the public until ten-thirty, by which time he was already there. Either that or it was someone who was entitled to enter the changing room after ten-thirty, so the Clerk wouldn't challenge them. Maybe a jockey or a valet."

"The Clerk of the Scales wouldn't have been there watching every minute of the time," said Stephen Kohli. "He has other duties. He doesn't have to be at his desk until about an hour before the first race. Anyone could have slipped into the changing room unnoticed before that."

"Maybe," I said. "But would you take the chance of being stopped with a poisoned ginger cake? I don't believe this man leaves much to chance."

"Do we have CCTV at Ascot?" Neil Wallinger asked.

"Yes, we have," I said.

"Well? What does it show?"

"Nothing," I said. "It is only used as a record of what happens in the jockeys' changing areas and in the weighing room with regards to the rules restricting the use of cell phones by jockeys during the period that begins half an hour before the first race and ends when the last race starts. Hence, the CCTV system wasn't switched on until half past one, by which time the cake was in position."

There were a few mutterings of disbelief.

"Who would know that?" asked Howard Lever.

"It's general knowledge, especially among the lady jockeys," I said. "They have reluctantly accepted that CCTV is necessary in their changing rooms for the enforcement of the cell phone rules, but only on condition that it does not operate outside the restriction period. Otherwise, they rightly claim that it's an excessive breach of their privacy."

"So what do we know?" asked Roger Vincent.

"Not much," I said. "But I believe it must be someone involved in racing who knows their way round a racetrack. And it's possibly someone with a hyperactive child."

Did I sense a slight quiver somewhere in the room?

"Why do you say that?" asked Howard Lever.

"Two different stimulant drugs have been used to dope horses, both of which are usually prescribed for hyperactivity. I know it's a long shot, but maybe we're looking for someone who has experience of the condition either directly or through a family member."

"How many people suffer from hyperactivity?" asked Ian Tulloch.

"It's difficult to say," I replied. "It can be diagnosed in different ways, but even the smallest estimate is between one and two percent of the population, mostly children. However, up to half of those affected carry the condition into adulthood. That's about a million people."

There was a collective drooping of shoulders around the table.

"What did the police say about the fireworks?" I

asked. "I saw you four with them after the event down at the water jump." I looked, in turn, at Roger Vincent, Howard Lever, Piers Pottinger and Stephen Kohli.

"They are investigating the matter," Roger Vincent replied. "Initial indications are that the fireworks were activated by a remote signal, possibly from a cell phone or by a special transmitter. The Merseyside Police's forensic labs have yet to report."

"It must have been done by someone actually watching the race," I said. "It was not by chance that the fireworks went off at the very moment that would cause the maximum disruption."

"So anyone watching at home on television could have done it," said Howard.

"That's most unlikely," I said. "I doubt he would take the chance on getting a cell phone signal at Aintree at precisely the right time with all those people there. Far too risky. I had trouble getting a signal to make a call on Friday and there were only half as many people present as on Saturday. So it had to be done by a special transmitter and that means the perpetrator was close by. He had to have been at Aintree watching the race."

"Are these special transmitters easy to obtain?" asked Roger Vincent.

"Have you an electric gate or an automatic garage door?" I asked. "That's all you need. Push a button on a remote to connect an electric circuit with a battery and, presto, you have a firework display. I'm sure that is what the police will find. Maybe they will be able to trace who has bought such a device, but I wouldn't hold your breath. Anyone can go into a hardware store and buy one over the counter for a few pounds, and there'd be no record of the purchaser's identity if it was paid for with cash."

The shoulders drooped again.

"What did the police say about the extortion?" I asked.

"They don't know about that," Roger Vincent replied. "We didn't tell them."

"What! You can't be serious."

"That is what the Board have been discussing this morning."

"Then you surely must tell them. It will be hugely relevant to their inquiries into the fireworks."

I looked around the table and there were some definite nods of agreement, but also some shaking of heads. Both Roger Vincent and Howard Lever were in the second category, and I suspected Ian Tulloch was as well.

"I am of the same opinion," said Neil Wallinger. "It is well past time the police were involved. I insist we call them in straightaway."

"But what guarantee do we have that the situation will remain confidential?" said Bill Ripley.

Neil Wallinger was ready with his reply. "Setting off fireworks in the middle of the Grand National in front of seventy thousand spectators, and with millions more watching on television, is hardly keeping things confidential."

"Most of the media," I said, "seem to be claiming that

the disruption on Saturday was most likely caused by protesters opposed to the Grand National on animal-welfare grounds, although goodness knows why since one of the horses had to be destroyed and the others were so obviously distressed."

"That is the assumption the police have made," said Howard Lever.

"Then they are not going to be very happy when they find out you didn't tell them the true reason," said Neil Wallinger cuttingly. "That's what we're really discussing here, isn't it? It's not whether we should now call in the police over the extortion, it's whether this Board can survive the embarrassment and shame of not having done so previously." He paused and looked around the table at the faces. "I am the member of this Board charged with the responsibility of maintaining the integrity of British racing. I see no integrity at all in refusing to call in the proper authorities. Failure to do so today will result in my resignation from the Board."

There was silence in the room while everyone took in the implications. Neil Wallinger was one of the most respected sports administrators in the country. His departure from the BHA Board would be a major blow to racing and would certainly not go unnoticed by the media. In addition, he would then be set free from any collective obligation to remain silent. Either way, it seemed, the police would get to know about the extortion.

But Roger Vincent was not giving up so easily.

"Neil," he said in his most charming manner, "I

am sure we don't need to talk about resignations. We all have the best interests of racing at heart, and some of us believe that keeping this matter confidential and attempting to resolve the problem from within is the best way for racing in the long term."

"I cannot agree," Neil replied. "The best interest in racing is served by the capture and imprisonment of whoever is responsible. To that end, we should be inviting the police to intervene, especially as we have not made any significant progress without them." He looked directly at me.

"I have to agree with Neil," I said. "I simply do not have the resources to investigate this matter alone. We need police help, but we must be careful not to let them take over everything. This Board still runs British racing and that needs to be made clear to the police. All too often they can ride roughshod over the whole shebang in their size-twelve boots and to hell with the consequences."

"Do any of us have a direct contact with any senior policemen?" asked Roger Vincent.

"I have friends still serving in the Met," said Stephen Kohli. "I used to be an officer there myself. The best man at my wedding is now in charge of the Homicide and Serious Crime Command."

"Ideal," said Roger Vincent. "May I suggest that we instruct Stephen to contact his friend in a semiformal approach, requesting a meeting between him and this Board at the earliest opportunity." He smiled and looked around the room but particularly at Neil. Had he done enough to defuse the unexploded bomb?

"Today?" said Neil.

"I said at the earliest opportunity," Roger Vincent replied with a smile. "If that can be today, then so be it. However, I think we need to be realistic. Today is Sunday. Tomorrow or Tuesday would seem to be more reasonable."

Neil had little option but to agree, and Stephen Kohli was officially asked to set up the meeting between the police commander and the Board "at the earliest opportunity."

The meeting broke up.

I hadn't been executed. I hadn't even been sacked. In fact, I'd been instructed to carry on as best I could until the meeting with Stephen's police friend.

"Jeff," said Howard Lever, putting his arm over my shoulder and steering me into a quiet corner, "I had a Cheltenham policeman on the phone last week."

"I asked him to call you to verify my employment status."

"Yes. It gave me rather a fright, I can tell you."

"Didn't Crispin warn you?"

"Not until after the call."

"I'm sorry."

"I am concerned, however, about these claims of harassment from Matthew Unwin. Not good for our public image. Is there any truth in them?"

"None at all. At least not as far as I'm concerned. I

can't speak for the rest of the BHA, not unless Unwin considers that his disciplinary hearing and subsequent disqualification were harassment."

"Hmm," he said. "You may be right." He didn't sound overly convinced, but he said nothing more to me.

As the other Board members packed up their papers and put on their coats, I looked around at them. Had I felt a slight frisson earlier in the meeting? From whom had it emanated? And what had been said to cause it? I tried to remember but nothing surfaced.

It must have been my imagination.

21

It was not just another note that arrived from Leonardo at the BHA office early on Monday morning in the mail, there was a cell phone in the packet as well.

Crispin Larson called me at home just before eight o'clock and suggested we meet at El Vino for breakfast at eight-thirty.

"Make it nine," I said. "I'm not dressed yet."

"Idle tyke," he said. "You need to get up in the morning. All this working-from-home nonsense is making you lazy."

Maybe he was right, but, on this occasion, laziness had nothing to do with it. Lydia and I had been out for a late night and we'd been up until well past two in the morning.

I had been rather down when I'd returned home to Willesden from the Board meeting. Even though I'd not been sacked, I did feel that I'd achieved little or nothing and that hurt my pride. I'd been so sure I would be able to find the person, or at least get some way towards it but I had learned absolutely nothing about him. Nothing more than a few guesses.

Lydia had done her best all afternoon to cheer me up without any great success, but she had finally convinced me that we should go into central London to see a new high-tech spy movie that had opened in Leicester Square. She was desperate to see it before her friends at the realtors.

"It will cheer you up," she said, "and you can tell me all the things that are wrong in it."

We laughed. I was always saying to her that no real secret agent would ever dress like James Bond or drive an Aston Martin. He would stand out too much. And as for the drinking—well, 007 wouldn't have been able to see straight, let alone shoot accurately, and all that lovemaking to gorgeous birds just made us real secret agents laugh with incredulity, and perhaps a bit of jealousy.

The film had all the usual mistakes and many new ones as well, with science-fiction killer-ray guns and the ability to scream and be heard across the vacuum of space. It was, however, very entertaining, And, of course, the hero saved the world by defeating the bad guys, cheating death in the final scene by floating down from orbital speed at the edge of space with nothing more than a Union Jack parachute and a pair of fancy plastic goggles. It conveniently ignored the fact that, in reality, he would have been burned to a crisp by the heat generated or asphyxiated by the lack of oxygen at such a height. Probably both.

We came out of the cinema laughing and joking.

"So ridiculous," I said.

"But wonderful fun," Lydia said. "And no more ridiculous than Hugh Grant playing the Prime Minister."

"That's true." We laughed again. "I'm hungry. Fancy a meal?"

We went to Balans restaurant in Old Compton Street and quite simply stayed until one o'clock in the morning, eating and drinking, but mostly just talking, and then we caught the night bus home for more wine and sex before sleep.

Things between us had been really good since our night out at *Les Misérables*, and we seemed to have rediscovered the art of communication. It was just like old times, and, thankfully, not a word from either of us about marriage.

"Who was on the phone?" Lydia asked as I went along to the kitchen.

"Crispin Larson," I said. "I have to go and meet him. I'll have breakfast there."

"Trouble?"

"No more than yesterday."

"Good luck," she called as I went out the front door.

CRISPIN WAS at El Vino ahead of me, with coffee and buttered toast in front of him.

"What does he say?" I asked, sitting opposite him and helping myself to a piece of his toast.

"He wants the down payment."

"Does he indeed? How much?"

"He wants two hundred thousand down on two million."

"He's beginning to think he'll get nothing. He's trying to cover his costs and make a bit of profit straight off."

"You think so?" asked Crispin.

"Otherwise, why would he ask? He must know the most dangerous time for him is the drop. Why have two drops when one would do? He's getting twitchy. What do Howard and Roger Vincent say?"

"They're keen to pay. And so, apparently, are most of the Board. Anything to prevent another incident like Saturday's."

"So what are the instructions for the drop?"

"Our friend's letter said to get the money ready in a secure brightly colored canvas bag and await instructions. He'll text them to this phone." Crispin handed me a basic black Nokia cell. "It came with the letter."

I had a good look at the phone. It looked innocuous enough. I removed the back. Someone had scratched off the serial numbers from both the phone itself and from the plain yellow SIM card it contained.

"Does it have a phone number?" I asked.

"It must have, but how do you find it? The settings are password-protected. You can't make a call out—it simply says it's *Out of time*—and you can't add time without the number."

The pay-as-you-go phone. The bane of policemen and security services worldwide. Bought for cash with a false name, there was no means of identifying the owner. It is the communication device of choice among villains and terrorists alike.

"Did the letter say when we are to pay?" I asked.

"This afternoon."

"That's ridiculous," I said. "How can we get two hundred grand in cash by this afternoon?"

"And all in used fifty-pound notes. Roger Vincent is working on it. Apparently, he has a very accommodating bank manager."

"We could always use flash money," I said.

"'Flash money'?" Crispin asked.

"Police slang for *dummy money*—you know, newspaper cut into bundles made to look like cash with a genuine banknote at either end."

"Would that be wise?"

"Probably not."

"You are to make the drop," Crispin said, "with me in close proximity."

No doubt to make sure it wasn't him or me who ran off with the money.

"We need to mark the cash in some way," I said, "so that it can be traced. And also we ought to have a tracker device with it."

"The letter says that the cash should be placed in the bag with nothing else."

"Well, it would, wouldn't it? But it doesn't mean we are going to comply with his wishes. I think I'll go and see an old friend of mine from the army. He now runs one of those spy gadget shops in Kensington High Street. I'll deal with that, you just get the cash." I looked at my watch. It was twenty to ten. "Meet you back here at two with the money?"

"I'll try."

"THIS ONE should do well," said my ex–army mate. He produced a small black box about two inches by one inch and half an inch deep. "Best tracking device on the market. Range of about four miles."

"Don't you have anything smaller?" I asked. That black box was going to be far too visible in a bag of used fifty-pound notes. "Something small enough that you wouldn't notice?"

"Hide it," he said. "Best in a car. It's got a magnet on one side so that it will stick in a wheel well."

"I need something flat that no one would see."

"Sorry, mate, no can do. The electronics are pretty small, but you need a decent battery for the range. Those little watch-sized batteries aren't up to it. This little beauty will go on working for thirty-six hours before the battery needs replacing. What do you want it for anyway?"

He held up the receiver, a silver box the size of a TV remote, with a loop aerial attached at one end and a lead to an earpiece at the other. It made a reassuringly continuous electronic beeping sound in the earpiece when the loop faced towards the little box. It was, however, not as sophisticated as a James Bond tracker, which would almost certainly have had a moving-map display as the receiver and would have worked from outer space for a whole month using a self-charging battery hidden inside a playing card.

"Checking up on the little lady, are we?" He grinned.

"Something like that." I could hardly tell him that it was to hide with a stash of ransom money. The ransom for racing.

"Then put it inside something that won't raise her suspicions, like in an empty cigarette pack or a chocolate candy wrapper."

Lydia didn't smoke, and chocolate was definitely not on her current diet's allowable food list. Both items would have been instantly suspicious if I really had been "checking up on the little lady."

"Or just hide it in her handbag. Women's handbags are so full of stuff, she'll never notice it at the bottom."

"I'll take it," I said. "And the receiver."

He switched them both off and put them back in their boxes.

"Do you have any pens that write with ink that only shows up under ultraviolet light?"

"Security pens," he said. "For marking your property with a zip code. Loads of them. Thin ones or thick ones?"

"Thick," I said. "I'll take a couple."

My friend placed the tracking device, the receiver and

the pens in a bag before relieving my credit card of an extortionate amount of money.

I hoped the BHA was still paying my expenses.

I WAS back at El Vino just before two o'clock and there was no sign of Crispin.

I checked once again that the Nokia phone was properly switched on and I placed it on the table in front of me. The icons on the screen showed me that it had full power and a five-bar signal. All I had to do was wait for the instruction text to arrive.

Crispin appeared with a small battered grip in his hand and stood by the bar, looking around.

I waved at him, but, at first, he took no notice.

Eventually, after more waving on my part, he came over.

"Jeff?" he asked.

When one wears a disguise, you are the only person who doesn't see it. Everything looks normal from within.

"Yes, Crispin," I said. "Stop staring and sit down."

"Why the masquerade?"

"I think it would be better if it's you who makes the drop while I shadow you. If Leonardo is a racing insider and if he knows what we normally look like, I thought it might be to our advantage if one of us became anonymous, that's all. There was nothing to lose and everything to gain."

"I suppose you might be right."

"Have you got the money?"

He removed a bright orange canvas bag from the grip.

"It's a tent-peg bag," Crispin said. "I bought it at a camping shop."

"But is that it?" I asked, surprised. "I thought two hundred thousand pounds would be bigger."

"It's only one hundred thousand," Crispin said. "That was all the banks would provide. Bloody money-laundering regulations. What a nightmare. As it is, we had to get it from three different banks, and, even then, they weren't at all keen about it. Roger Vincent has been pulling in favors from his banker friends all morning to bankroll even this amount."

"At least it's not two million," I said. "Or five. A hundred thousand will have to be enough."

"It's only a down payment."

"Not if we manage to catch the bastard as he collects it."

"What's with the rugby ball?" Crispin asked, pointing at the ball beside me on the table next to the Nokia phone.

"I'm not really sure," I said with exasperation. "I had a crazy idea but now it seems totally mad. I tried to get an electronic tracker we could hide amid the money, but that's impossible as they're all so big and would be seen far too easily. So I've spent much of the past hour putting a tracking device into this." I held up the old, battered, deflated rugby ball. "I found it in a bush in Kensington Gardens and I had the thought that if we could somehow put it with the money, he might just take them both." I held up my hands as if surrendering. "I know it's stupid, but we have to try something."

"It's no more stupid, dear boy, than giving someone a hundred grand with nothing to show for it. Our friend could go and do the same thing next Saturday. And the Saturday after that, for all we know. We need to catch him."

"Did Stephen Kohli call his police friend?"

"He's apparently been in court all day. Stephen's left him a message, but I wouldn't hold your breath."

"Why didn't he go to the court and see him when they broke for lunch?"

"He's giving evidence at the High Court of Justiciary in Edinburgh. It's mostly a Scottish case, but there was a constituent murder in London."

"Then we must find somebody else in the police to contact," I said. "We could really do with their help this afternoon."

"You're not going to get it. Howard and Roger Vincent have decided to wait another day in the hope that Stephen can make contact with his friend this evening."

"What did Neil Wallinger say about that?"

"He doesn't know."

"Madness," I said. "Now, grab one of these and let's get marking."

I gave him one of the invisible-ink pens and together we sat in a secluded corner booth writing *BHA* in big invisible letters on one side of the fifty-pound notes and the office phone number on the other. It was a very long shot, but just maybe someone in a bank somewhere would be curious enough to call.

There were two thousand fifties in the bag, ten bundles each of two hundred notes wrapped in a paper sleeve. We had marked about half the notes when the Nokia phone emitted a beep-beep. A text had arrived.

Both of us looked at it.

Go to Trafalgar Square and wait.

"He's going to give us the runaround," said Crispin, "in case we're being followed by the police."

"I wish we were," I said. "This could be a long afternoon."

22

We took separate taxis to Trafalgar Square and waited patiently among the never-ending groups of foreign tourists.

Crispin was holding the bright orange bag full of cash tightly in his right hand with the Nokia phone in his left hand, while I stood about twenty yards away from him on the other side of a fountain, doing my best to look inconspicuous holding Crispin's battered grip containing the old rugby ball and the tracker receiver.

I had wired us both with microphones inside our shirts and earpieces, mine hidden by my brown woolen beanie, while Crispin's was under his scarf.

We went on waiting. And waiting. And waiting.

It was not until almost two hours later, at a quarter past four, that I clearly heard the Nokia phone beep-beep again through my earpiece.

"Our friend must be watching us," Crispin said into my ear courtesy of the electronics.

"Why, what does it say?"

"Only one person. The others must leave."

"He must be guessing," I said. "He says 'others,' plural, when there's only one of me."

"He may have spotted you and then assumed there are others."

I looked around at the familiar sights of Trafalgar Square and the buildings surrounding it. Could Leonardo be standing on the steps of the National Gallery? Or under the portico of St. Martin-in-the-Fields? Perhaps he was situated behind one of the hundreds of windows facing the square, from the Greek Revival splendor of Canada House on the west side to the Portland stone South Africa House on the east.

I glanced up at Nelson atop his column and wondered if the view was better from there?

"Maybe Leonardo is watching," I said. "Shrug your shoulders or something as if you don't know what he's on about."

I glanced across as Crispin placed the canvas bag on the rim of a fountain and not only shrugged his shoulders but spread his hands open and flat in the universal gesture of not understanding.

"That's enough," I said with a laugh. "Don't let go of that money. Someone will steal it."

Crispin quickly grabbed back hold of the bag.

"Now what?" he said.

"We wait. He will text again. I'm staying right here."

I offered to take a photo of a Japanese couple against one of the fountains using their own camera. They smiled for the picture and then smiled again and bowed. And then bowed some more. OK, OK, I thought, don't make a scene. The couple went on smiling and bowing as I moved away.

The text arrived after another half an hour. I could hear the beep-beep via Crispin's microphone.

"It says I should walk to Oxford Circus. I have fifteen minutes."

"Go on, then," I said. "I'll be watching."

Crispin walked off briskly in the direction of the Haymarket, carrying the bag. I let him go. I didn't need to keep him in view so much as to look out for someone else who might be following him.

If there was anybody, he was very good indeed.

I was almost a hundred yards behind Crispin, as he walked up the hill past the statue of Eros at Piccadilly Circus and on up Regent Street, and I couldn't spot anyone following.

"Stop a moment and look in a shopwindow," I said.

Crispin did as I asked.

No one else varied their stride in response—nobody slowed to light a cigarette or moved past him, only then to wait. As far as I could tell from across the street, no one other than me took the slightest notice of Crispin.

"OK, carry on," I said. "You have no tail."

"You sound disappointed."

"I am, rather. I was looking forward to twisting somebody's arm. I was a soldier once, you know. I like a bit of action. And don't talk, just listen. Just in case someone is watching your lips."

Crispin stopped when he arrived at Oxford Circus and he leaned heavily on the railing around the steps down to the tube station.

"I'm far too old for this bloody lark," he said, putting a hand over his mouth and breathing fast into the microphone.

The phone beep-beeped again almost immediately.

"Now where?" I asked.

I watched from across the road as Crispin pulled out a handkerchief from his pocket and covered his nose and mouth. "Bakerloo Line to Paddington," he said quickly, still panting. "Thank God, I'm not walking there. But why didn't he put me on a train at Charing Cross? It's on the same bloody line and was much nearer."

"Maybe Leonardo doesn't know London as well as you do," I said. Or maybe he was enjoying just giving us the runaround.

I went down to the tube station using a different entrance from street level but ended up on the same train as Crispin.

I still couldn't spot a tail and I was now sure there wasn't one.

"You're clean," I said quietly into the microphone. "I'm in the car behind you."

I could see Crispin through the interconnecting door and I watched as he glanced in my direction and nodded.

My examiner in the Intelligence Corps would have had a fit.

I was six people behind Crispin as he ascended the escalator from the Tube into Paddington Station carrying the bright orange bag with its precious cargo.

"Go and take a seat in front of the departure boards," I said. "It will be easy to keep an eye on you there."

Crispin went straight over to where I had suggested and found himself space in the second row of red metal seats. I, meanwhile, sat down outside a café, with my back to the wall, from where I had an uninterrupted one-hundred-and-eighty-degree view of the station concourse.

We waited.

And waited some more, while all of those seated around Crispin went off to catch their trains and others arrived to fill their seats. At one point, I took a complete turn around the station to check if there was anyone else watching and waiting longer than might be expected. There wasn't.

At a few minutes after six o'clock, the Nokia phone beep-beeped again as another text arrived.

"Bloody hell," Crispin said covering his mouth with his handkerchief. "This is ridiculous."

"What is?"

"I have to buy a first-class ticket to Plymouth."

"Plymouth!"

"That's what it says."

"You'd better do it, then. I'll get one too."

"Do I get a one-way or a round-trip?" he asked.

"Depends if you want to come back or not," I said with a nervous laugh.

"Our friend could make me catch a ferry to France from Plymouth."

"Or to Spain," I said and heard him groan. "Get a round-trip. The BHA will pay."

"Not if they're made bankrupt, they won't."

He walked over towards the ticket office and I followed, keeping him in sight all the time. I wondered if Leonardo had made the buy-a-ticket request just to get Crispin to a certain point in the station where he would then grab the money, so I kept fairly close and alert.

But there was no dash for the cash as Crispin uneventfully bought an open-ended first-class round-trip to Plymouth.

"Have you any idea how much that cost?" Crispin said into his microphone as he turned away from the counter. "Almost four hundred quid. It's scandalous. I could get a chauffeur-driven limo to Plymouth and back for less than that."

"Wait where you are," I said, "while I buy mine."

I used a self-service ticket machine, but it charged the same unbelievable price. Add to that the cost of the tracking device, plus the receiver, and it had been an expensive afternoon for my credit card. I sincerely hoped the BHA wouldn't go bankrupt before my expenses were due.

"Now what?" Crispin asked, again covering his mouth with his handkerchief.

"We wait."

I could hear Crispin sigh. He was clearly getting fed up with this game. But I thought it might go on for quite a while longer yet.

I remembered one particular ransom drop in Afghanistan that had taken three days to complete, with me and the cash having gone on a tour of most of the southern half of the country before being "dropped" only a few miles from where we'd started.

It was all to do with confidence. Only when Leonardo was confident that he would be able to collect the cash securely and anonymously would he give the final instruction to leave it somewhere.

At precisely seven o'clock by the station clock, I clearly heard the beep-beep of the phone once more through my earpiece.

"It says to get on the 19.03 train to Plymouth."

I looked up at the departure boards.

"Platform six," I said, "Go, now. Run. We've only got a couple of minutes."

I ran ahead of him, through the ticket barrier and along the platform. The guard had already walked the length of the train, slamming the doors shut, as I made it to the nearest one and reopened it.

Crispin followed, struggling a bit, but he made it onto the train just before the door was slammed shut again and the guard blew his whistle for the train to depart.

We both sat down wearily in the first-class car, albeit in different sections, as the train pulled out from Paddington Station, gathering speed as it rushed westwards through the London suburbs towards the first stop at Reading.

The phone received no further texts until the train had just left Newbury Station almost fifty minutes later, at ten to eight.

"It says I should go to the rearmost door lobby and prepare to throw the bag of money out the window on the left-hand side of the train as soon as I get the next text."

Bloody hell.

The next scheduled stop for the train after Newbury was at Taunton, nearly a hundred miles away. It would take hours for me to get there and back, by which time Leonardo would have long gone together with the money. He had pulled a fast one. He wasn't on the train at all. He was waiting somewhere beside the line to collect his loot.

"Do we still throw the money out or not?" I asked. "The whole point of offering a down payment was to try and catch him at the drop and that won't now happen. I reckon we should hang on to it."

"I think we have to throw it," Crispin said. "In a strange way, we need to develop some trust with our friend."

Trust? I wouldn't trust him further than I could throw this train.

We went out together into the lobby at the back of the car.

Unlike most of the British railway companies, which

had progressed to installing automatic doors, Great Western trains still used the slam-door system, with a handle only on the outside. The doors were locked shut while the train was moving, but to open a door at a station a passenger had to pull down the window in the door, lean out, and use the external handle.

Crispin pulled down the left-hand window as far as it would go and looked out. I similarly pulled down the one on the right.

The daylight was beginning to fade, but there was just enough of it remaining to see the houses of Newbury give way to the trees and fields of the countryside.

We stood and waited, cold, and with the noise of the train loud in our ears.

My crazy plan of somehow getting Leonardo to take the rugby ball with the cash had gone out the window—literally. Throwing them out together while moving at such a high speed would result in them separating wildly.

"OK," I said. "Throw the bag out, but give it a good firm chuck or else it will be drawn back under the wheels."

We stood in readiness, with Crispin holding the phone up to his ear so as not to miss the sound of the text's arrival.

The phone went *beep-beep* and Crispin immediately threw the bright orange canvas bag containing the hundred thousand pounds out the train window.

At the same time, I tossed the battered old rugby ball out my window, hoping that it wouldn't be seen by someone waiting on the other side.

Both of us stood for a moment looking out into the gathering darkness.

"Now what, dear boy?" asked Crispin, pulling up his window.

"Enjoy the journey and get off at Taunton. You then take a train back to London and I'll find a room for the night. There's absolutely nothing we can do in the dark. I'll rent a car and try to find the rugby ball in the morning. It might tell us exactly where we were when you threw the money out."

"Right," Crispin said gloomily. "I'd better call Roger Vincent and Howard Lever. They'll be wondering what has happened. I can't think that either of them will be pleased."

Rather him than me, I thought.

I looked out the train window into the night that had now completely enveloped us. "Our friend Leonardo has been very shrewd," I said. "He knew exactly what time of day to stage this stunt so there would be just enough light left for him to find the money but would be pitch-black long before anyone else could get there."

"He's a clever bastard," Crispin said, "that's for sure."

Yeah, I thought, but I could be a clever bastard too.

That was also for sure.

23

I stayed the night at the Royal Albion, the first hotel I encountered just a few minutes' walk from the station on the northern edge of Taunton, while Crispin took the nine-fifteen train back to London, muttering about how much money had been wasted in having to get tickets all the way to Plymouth.

"Why didn't he just say Taunton? It would have been half the price."

I reminded him that he had just thrown a hundred thousand pounds in readies out a train window. That was surely far more important than the four-hundred-pound cost of his train ticket, but it didn't seem to stop him grumbling about it as he hurried off through the tunnel under the tracks to catch the eastbound express with his now-empty grip bashing against his legs.

I was still smiling about it when I checked in to the

hotel, declining the receptionist's offer to help me with my nonexistent luggage.

I called Lydia, using the phone in my room. "I'm in Taunton."

"That was very sudden," she said. "Any particular reason?"

"I was desperate for some cider," I said with a laugh.

"Interesting choice. When will you be back?"

"Sometime tomorrow, I expect. Sorry."

Lydia was used to me suddenly disappearing for a night—or more. Most of the time, I couldn't even ring her to say where I was. It came with working undercover.

"That policeman from Cheltenham, Sergeant Galley, he called the house phone round seven this evening," Lydia said. "Apparently, he couldn't get you on your cell. He wants you to phone him. He said it was quite urgent."

I wondered what he wanted.

I looked at my watch. "It's probably too late now. I'll call him in the morning."

"OK," Lydia said. "Take care. Love you."

"Love you more."

We hung up and I lay back on the bed, contemplating my future.

Lydia and I had used the *Love you. Love you more* salutation for years, almost since we met, and I wondered if it had now become a habit more than a true expression of our affection.

Did she love me?

Did I love her more?

What did love actually mean?

Did it mean I was comfortable in my life with Lydia, because, if it did, then that was fine. I *was* comfortable. And mostly content.

Or did it require a level of steamy passion that should have forced me home tonight because I just couldn't bear to sleep away from her?

I mulled such questions around in my head without coming to an agreeable conclusion. Maybe I was making far too much of the whole thing. After all, we'd had a couple of great nights out recently. But, then again, it took more than that to make a successful marriage.

I snapped myself out of such thoughts, stood up and went in search of some refreshment.

Apart from being the county town of Somerset, Taunton was famous for its Scrumpy, and I went down to the hotel bar to sample a pint of their best, together with a sandwich made from local Cheddar cheese and West Country apple chutney.

I had to admit that the cloudy, strong cider was very tasty, but hardly worth the two-hour train journey from London.

I went back up to my room.

The reason D.S. Galley hadn't been able to get me earlier was that my phone was switched off. It would have been too much of a distraction if it had rung during the drop, and also the cell signal tended to interfere with the communication system I'd rigged between Crispin and myself.

I switched it on and connected to the hotel's Wi-Fi.

The train had left Newbury Station at seven-fifty precisely and Crispin had thrown the bag out the window exactly eighteen minutes later at eight past eight.

Even though our particular train hadn't stopped there, the Wiltshire village of Pewsey had a railway station and, according to the timetable on the Internet, nonstop trains took about twenty minutes to get there from Newbury.

I calculated that the point I was looking for should be just east of Pewsey village. That was where I would start looking in the morning.

I DROVE a rental car from Taunton along the A303 to Amesbury before turning north to Pewsey.

I stopped in the market square beneath the imposing stone statue of King Alfred the Great, the revered Anglo-Saxon king who, in the ninth century, had liberated the English from both the Vikings and the Danes. He is still the only English monarch to have been called *the Great*, even if the epithet was added some seven hundred years after his death rather than by his contemporaries.

I switched on the tracker receiver and held it up, rotating through a full three hundred and sixty degrees. Nothing.

I took Milton Road eastwards out of the village for about a mile and tried again.

This time there was a faint beeping sound from the receiver earpiece when facing to the north. Excitedly, I took the next turn and drove north to a bridge over the railway line, stopping in a small parking lot reserved, according to the sign, for the *Jones's Mill Nature Reserve*. From that point, there was no mistaking the electronic beep. It was at its clearest when I stood on the bridge and pointed the receiver loop along the railway line back towards Newbury.

In the end, it was relatively easy to find the rugby ball with the tracker inside, although I would have to have words with my army friend in the spy gadget shop. The detection range was considerably less than the four miles he had claimed, more like a mile at best. But it was enough.

The bag of money had been thrown off the train as it had passed just south of New Mill, a small hamlet some two miles northeast of Pewsey village situated between the River Avon and the Kennet and Avon Canal.

The railway ran at this point along an embankment, with the rails themselves some twenty feet or so above the surrounding farmland. There was a good stretch of a couple of hundred yards on the south side with no trees, just a grassy bank. Ideal, I thought, for locating a bag of cash thrown from a train.

In addition, next to the bridge where the railway crossed a country road, there was a cell phone mast festooned with aerials. I looked at my iPhone—five bars of signal.

Remote, but with easy access, and a good cell signal to boot, this place had been well chosen by Leonardo. It was absolutely ideal for the purpose.

I parked in front of a farm gate, clambered over a

small, padlocked gate and climbed up the steep slope from the road to the railway tracks, still holding the receiver, which was by this stage beeping away very loudly indeed in my ear.

The battered old rugby ball had ended up between the rails of the London-bound line. As I walked alongside the tracks towards it, I could see it clearly lying up against the far rail. Retrieving it might be another matter altogether.

Trains traveled along this part of the line at very high speeds, in excess of a hundred miles per hour, and they would arrive almost without warning, the noise of the engines somehow appearing to follow on after, rather than precede their arrival.

A high-pitched ringing from the rails themselves gave the first warning that a train was imminent and then suddenly it was upon you, clattering past in a cacophony, before disappearing just as swiftly with the abrupt return to rural tranquility.

An express traveling towards London came sweeping around the curve at full speed, and I could see the look of horror on the driver's face when he saw me standing alongside the track. I waved and smiled reassuringly, but I saw him reach instinctively for the brake lever as he swept past. I couldn't tell if the train was slowing or not as it disappeared from view around the next curve, still moving at high speed.

There would have been no chance of the driver stopping the train in time, and suicides on the railways were an all too regular occurrence. However, he would most likely be speaking to the police about me via his in-cab telephone system.

As soon as the train had passed by, I nipped onto the track to retrieve the rugby ball, then I ran back towards the bridge and down the steep slope to the waiting rental car.

I spent a few moments looking around to see if I could spot anything that might give me a clue about who had waited here the previous evening to collect a bag of cash. Perhaps if there had been a full police crime scene team available, then plaster casts of footprints or tire tracks in the soft verges may have been an option, but there was nothing useful I could ascertain with just my eyes.

I used my iPhone to take a few quick photographs of the spot, but they were mostly to make sure I could find it again rather than to provide any helpful evidence.

Then I drove away, silently apologizing to all the rail passengers who would suffer delays on their trains over the next hour or so as the Transport Police searched for a member of the public seen wandering on the tracks.

"DID YOU find it?" Crispin asked me when he called that afternoon.

"Yes," I said. "It was outside a village called Pewsey, where the railway line crosses a country lane. There's no doubt that's where Leonardo collected his bag of loot."

"How about the Nokia phone?"

"Not a dicky bird," I said. The phone had remained by

my bedside during the night in Taunton and in my pocket ever since. There had been no further texts or any calls. "He must know by now that he's been shortchanged."

"Perhaps he doesn't want to use that phone again in case we've found a way of setting up a trace on it."

"Maybe," I agreed. "He probably bought two of those anonymous pay-as-you-go phones, the one he mailed to us and the other one that he used himself to send the texts. His one is probably at the bottom of the Kennet and Avon Canal by now."

"So what do we do?"

"Wait," I said. "He will be in touch, you can bet on it. Has Stephen spoken to his policeman friend yet?"

"Yes, he has. And he will be at the meeting of the Board tomorrow morning at nine o'clock sharp at Scrutton's Club. Howard asked me to tell you that your presence is required."

"Right," I said. "I'll be there. But why is it still at Scrutton's?"

"Howard is obsessed with secrecy."

I thought that rather rich, coming from Crispin.

"What's your wife's name?" I asked.

"I beg your pardon. What did you say?"

"I asked what your wife's name is?"

"What has that got to do with all this?"

"Nothing," I said with a laugh. "But you're the one who's obsessed with secrecy. I don't even know if you have a wife, let alone her name. You never say anything about yourself."

"Don't I? No, I suppose not."

"Definitely not. I only learned that you used to be in MI5 or MI6 due to a slip of the tongue by Neil Wallinger."

"I'll have to have words with him," he said quietly.

"So what is Howard so secretive about?"

There was a pause from the other end of the line. I could almost hear the cogs going around in his brain. Did I need to know?

"He, and Roger Vincent, they're both absolutely paranoid about the newspapers finding out and criticizing them or the BHA. They take everything so personally. I think they now wish they had called in the police on the very first day and they're worried they will be thought of as fools for not doing so."

I reckoned they had good reason to be worried.

"So what did the friendly policeman say when he was told?"

"Oh, he hasn't been told. Not until tomorrow. That's what the meeting is about."

So it would be yet another day before the police became involved. And, all the while, the trail of the Grand National fireworks would be getting colder and more distant in people's memories.

24

Daniel Jubowski came out of the offices of Hawthorn Pearce at five-twenty on Tuesday afternoon and I was waiting for him, dressed as Tony Jefferson, my gay alter ego.

He saw me immediately and came over.

"Hi, Tony," he said. "What brings you here?"

"Daniel, I desperately need some help."

"What's the matter?"

"I need a place to stay for a night or two," I said quickly, "until I can find somewhere of my own."

"I thought you lived with your mother."

"I did." I said it almost in a sob. "My stepfather has found out that I'm gay and he has thrown me out. He owns the house, so there is nothing my mom can do about it. I didn't know where else to go."

He put his arm around my shoulders.

"Come on, Tony, cheer up. I'm sure we can find you a bed. You'd better come home with me."

"Thank you," I said with a wan smile, "that's what I hoped you might say." And I'd made sure I hadn't tried this on a Wednesday evening. I had no desire to go home with him via the Fit Man gym in Soho.

We took the Northern Line from Bank to King's Cross and then walked from there to number 17 New Wharf Road.

As I had thought when I'd first followed him here, this flat was anything but cheap.

"Wow!" I said, going out onto the second-floor balcony overlooking Regent's Canal. "What a place."

"I'm very lucky," Daniel replied.

"Rented?" I asked, coming back in to face him.

He shook his head. "I bought it two months ago."

"Wow!" I said. "Do you share?"

"I used to but not anymore."

"That's good," I said, changing my tone of voice completely. "Then we won't be disturbed. Tell me, Daniel, are Hawthorn Pearce aware that you offer strangers crystal meth at just a tenner for their first wrap?"

He was completely taken aback and just stood there with his mouth hanging open.

"Are they aware of that, Daniel?" I asked again. "And do they also know that your colleague at Hawthorn Pearce, John McClure, solicits sex from men in pubs by groping their bottoms? Do they know that, Daniel?"

"Who are you?" he said finally.

"A friend of Ken Calderfield."

I could see from his body language that he wanted to run. He bunched the muscles in his arms and he began to look around him. The last thing I wanted was for him to disappear again.

"Daniel," I said to him firmly, "sit down. Sit down now."

I pointed at the deep leather sofa and, slowly, he did as he was told.

"What do you want?"

"I want to know why you are accusing Ken of supplying drugs when both you and I know he'd never do such a thing."

"He took them."

"Maybe he did, but he didn't supply them, did he, Daniel?" I stood over him and did my best to make my five-foot-ten-inch frame as imposing as possible. "You do all the supplying, don't you, Daniel? That's how you can afford to buy this flat. You supply crystal meth to your gay friends at parties, don't you, Daniel? I'm sure your elders and betters at Hawthorn Pearce would love to hear all about those, now wouldn't they, Daniel?"

He sat staring at me.

"You can't prove anything."

"I don't need to prove it," I said. "I just need to send an anonymous file to the chief executive of Hawthorn Pearce. I assure you I have plenty of photographic evidence. For a start, I have a video of you trying to sell me drugs at the William Ball pub and of your chum John trying to seduce me into going with him to the Fit Man gym for sex. And I have another video of the two of you going into the same gym later that night together with Mike Kennedy, dragging with you a reluctant teenager." I paused to let everything sink in. "Oh, no, Daniel, I don't need to prove anything. I am sure the directors of Hawthorn Pearce are pretty old-school, with traditional values. Trust me, they will believe enough of it. You may not go to jail, but you would never work in the City again."

"What do you want?" he asked once more.

"Just the truth," I said. "You will withdraw your statement to the police that Ken Calderfield supplied drugs to you or to anyone else. You will also tell the police that the drugs found in Ken's flat did not belong to him and that he had no knowledge of them being there. That's all. Just the truth. Then I will go away and leave you and John McClure in peace."

"How can I be sure of that?"

"You can't," I said. "But what choice do you have?"

"The police might accuse me of wasting their time."

"That's your problem, Daniel, because you have indeed been wasting their time. But it's better than telling lies in court and being convicted of perjury."

He sat slumped into the leather sofa.

"Oh, yes," I said, "there's one more thing. I want to know why you set out to destroy Ken Calderfield. What did he do to deserve it?"

"I won't tell you."

"Oh, yes, Daniel," I said, "I think you will. It's part of the deal to keep me quiet."

"You didn't say that."

"Well, I'm saying it now."

He sat silently for what seemed like a long time but was probably only about thirty seconds or so. Once or twice he appeared as if to start saying something but then didn't.

"Come on, Daniel," I said encouragingly, "you can tell me."

"I was jealous." He said it quietly, without looking up at me.

"Jealous?" I could hardly believe it. "You have a great job and this fabulous flat. How can you be jealous of anyone?"

"I am jealous of Ken," he said. "He is so young and so gorgeous. The others at the gym swoon over him, they won't leave him alone." He swallowed. "That's what they used to do with me."

"Ken also dumped you, didn't he, Daniel, in favor of other men from the gym? So you decided to get your revenge by setting him up, isn't that right?"

He nodded. "It was stupid, I see that now. It was me that called the police on the night of the party. I went into the bathroom to phone them. I claimed to be an angry disturbed neighbor."

"Ken said you had to convince him to have the party in the first place. Was the whole thing a setup?"

He nodded again, then he sobbed. "I'm sorry."

I had wondered if it had been someone trying to get at Quentin, but it was nothing more than a lovers' tiff that had spiraled out of control.

Such was the power of love and jealousy.

25

I arrived at Scrutton's Club more than half an hour early for the meeting on Wednesday morning, but Crispin Larson was there ahead of me.

"Any news?" I asked.

"Our friend has been in touch again in the mail this morning and he's pretty angry."

"I don't care," I said. "It's us who should be angry, not him. He has a hundred thousand pounds of our money."

"He says it's not enough."

"Tough shit," I said. "If it was up to me, he'd get nothing more. In fact, he'd have had nothing in the first place. What else can he do to us that's worse than disrupting the Grand National?"

The others started arriving, and we were taking our places around the table when Howard Lever came into the room, ashen-faced and visibly shaking.

"What on earth is the matter?" Stephen Kohli said, standing up and offering Howard a steadying hand.

"I've just had a call from the Press Association," Howard said in a slightly quavering voice. "They want to know if there is any truth in the tip-off they have received that the winner of the Gold Cup has failed a dope test."

CHIEF SUPERINTENDENT Dominic Allenby of the Metropolitan Police Homicide and Serious Crime Command sat impassively at the head of the table as Roger Vincent and Howard Lever, on either side of him, outlined the sequence of events that had occurred during the preceding three weeks, from the murder of Jordan Furness on Champion Hurdle Day right up to the payment of the hundred thousand pounds.

On several occasions, Stephen Kohli, Crispin Larson and I were invited to add some details, while Ian Tulloch, Bill Ripley, Neil Wallinger and Piers Pottinger were not shy in coming forward with their opinions. The other two directors, Charles Payne and George Searle, both chose to sit quietly, listening intently.

All the directors appeared rather uneasy at having had everything laid out bare in front of the chief superintendent.

I was also feeling slightly anxious, but for a different reason.

I kept remembering back to the meeting at the BHA office on the day after the Grand National. Something then had made me feel uncomfortable and I'd had the same feeling today, although I couldn't put my finger on exactly why.

The chief superintendent was particularly interested in the payment of the money.

"You said this was thrown from a moving train?"

"Yes," I said. "The seven-oh-three express from Paddington to Plymouth."

"And where exactly did this take place?" he asked.

"Between Newbury and Taunton stations," I said. "It was getting dark, so we are not quite sure where. We believe it may have been about halfway between the two, perhaps somewhere near the town of Westbury."

Crispin was sitting next to me and he glanced across, a quizzical look on his face. He was just opening his mouth to speak when I gently kicked his leg under the table. He shut his mouth again and stayed silent.

"A hundred thousand pounds, you say?" said the policeman.

"Yes," I said, "in used fifty-pound notes."

"For what?"

"Sorry?" said Roger Vincent.

"It is normal to pay a ransom in return for something or somebody. You appear to have paid one for nothing."

He made it sound as if we had all been rather stupid.

Perhaps we had.

Some members of the Board squirmed in their seats from embarrassment. It was all too much like having our dirty laundry washed in public.

"And what exactly do you expect of me?" the chief superintendent asked when we had finished.

There was a moment of silence, then Ian Tulloch said what we were all thinking.

"Why, Chief Superintendent, we expect you to catch this man, of course. Then put him in jail and throw away the key."

"Yes," said Howard Lever, "and quickly. Before he totally destroys the integrity of the British Horseracing Authority. As I've previously said, the BHA governs racing in this country by consensus, not by statute. If that consensus is not self-evident, then . . . there could be anarchy."

I personally thought Howard was slightly overdramatizing the situation, but who knew what the outcome could be? I don't suppose the then Football League had anticipated that the English Premier League would be formed in 1992 and siphon off nearly all the TV and sponsorship money.

Could British racing afford half a dozen or so of the larger tracks to break away and run their own Premier League of Racing, retaining all the television proceeds for themselves? Most of the minor tracks, which presently received a share of such revenues, would go out of business overnight.

We might end up with a situation similar to that in the United States, where Thoroughbred racing was administered on a state-by-state basis, with wide variations in the rules, especially with respect to which drugs were allowed and which weren't, and each racetrack separately sold off its media rights to the highest bidder.

Twenty-three of the fifty states have no Thoroughbred racing at all, and a further fifteen have only one track each. Only the mighty state of California has more than three racetracks, but even it has only six to serve a population of almost forty million people, and each track declares its own champion jockey.

It could be argued that the BHA was more than just horseracing's authority, it was also the glue that held the diversity of British racing together as a single entity.

"Catching this man may not be as easy as you think," said the chief superintendent. "I have been involved in several extortion cases before and none of them have been straightforward. I assume here that we are dealing with something you would like to remain confidential until such time as the perpetrator may be apprehended."

"Absolutely," Roger Vincent said. "The whole future of racing depends on the confidence and trust of the betting public."

"That very confidentiality makes detection so much more difficult," said the chief superintendent. "If one can't even explain to people why they are being asked questions, then they are far less likely to answer them. And the very questions themselves have to be circumspect."

Tell me about it, I thought. That had been my trouble all along.

I could sense a degree of disappointment from some

members of the Board who had clearly thought that informing the police would hasten the end of the problem.

But I could tell from his manner that a touch of extortion against the BHA didn't appear that brightly on Chief Superintendent Allenby's radar.

The murder at Cheltenham was being investigated by the Gloucestershire Police, who undoubtedly had the killer in custody, and the disruption of the Grand National was being looked into by those in Liverpool.

There had been no murders or any violence committed on the Met's patch, and I could tell from the policeman's body language that he didn't consider the loss of reputation of the BHA a sufficient reason to mobilize his troops. In fact, he showed all the signs of believing that we'd been fools to pay the man anything at all and therefore probably deserved to lose our good standing.

It was all a bit of a mess.

"If you have certain information that is pertinent to the investigation being carried out by my Merseyside colleagues," the chief superintendent went on, "I would advise you to make it known to the investigating officer at the earliest opportunity. Otherwise, you might be accused of hindering the investigation and hence obstructing the police in the execution of their duty. That is an offense under Section 89 of the Police Act of 1996."

I wondered if there was a special school somewhere that taught policemen to speak in such a haughty and roundabout manner.

"But what about this man?" said Roger Vincent with

a degree of desperation in his voice. "How will he be caught?"

"The Merseyside Police will be continuing their investigation into the events at the Grand National. I would suggest that might present the best opportunity."

"So you will do nothing?" Ian Tulloch's tone was contemptuous. "I thought that extortion was a serious crime."

"And so it is," said the policeman looking straight down the table at Tulloch, "in particular when it follows a kidnap or if it is backed by threats of violence against the person. But this situation surely has more to do with animal welfare than criminality. It is not a case for the Homicide and Serious Crimes Command."

He simply hadn't grasped the enormity of the possible consequences for one of the largest employment sectors in the United Kingdom. Horseracing and bloodstock were not just sport, they were major industries.

"Animal welfare?" Roger Vincent said in disbelief. "This isn't about animal welfare. It's about the whole future of racing in this country."

But he was on a road to nowhere if he thought he could convince the chief superintendent, who stood up and made his excuses, expressing the wish to be elsewhere chasing more important criminals like murderers and rapists.

There was a stunned silence in the room after the door closed behind him.

"Well, that was an utter waste of time," said Bill Ripley.

I had to agree with him. Far from my fear that the

police would move in and try to take over, they had left us completely to our own devices.

"So what do we do now?" Ian Tulloch asked.

"We have to deal with the damn Press Association," Howard Lever said. "It must be the same bloody man who told them. Who else would have leaked information about Electrode's positive test?"

"Could it have come from the labs?" asked Roger Vincent.

"Most unlikely," Stephen Kohli said. "All samples are coded with a number rather than by the name of the horse."

"Who has access to the codes?" I asked.

"No one at the labs. They are kept locked in the Integrity Department's safe."

"So who else knows that Electrode tested positive?" I asked. "Apart from the people in this room."

"Only the man who doped him," said Ian Tulloch. "And now that policeman."

I looked around the table. Could someone here have leaked the information to the Press Association?

It was not the sort of thing one could do accidentally.

THE MEETING broke up without any firm decisions about what to do next.

We would neither confirm nor deny the Press Association's tip-off, although, despite his earlier reservations, Piers Pottinger was now concerned about the PR implications of saying nothing.

"The PR would surely be worse if we confirmed it," said Roger Vincent. "Or if we denied it and then the truth came out later."

"We could declare the Gold Cup void," said George Searle.

"After doing the same to the Grand National only last week?" Howard Lever said sharply. "Our two most prestigious jump races of the year both void?" He shook his head. "We'd be a laughingstock."

I feared that we may be a laughingstock already.

At Neil Wallinger's insistence, it was agreed that Howard should speak to the Merseyside investigating officer to provide him, in confidence, with the information concerning the threats we had received, so as to avoid being accused of knowingly obstructing the police.

Howard, however, wasn't at all keen on the plan. "We have no actual proof that the man responsible for the disruption of the Grand National is the same person who has been sending us the demands for money. His use of the word *fireworks* might have been just coincidental. Isn't it possible that they were set off by someone completely different? For all we know, the police may be right in thinking that it was done by animal rights activists."

More sticking-head-in-sand behavior by the chief executive.

I was sure that no one else around the table believed it.

26

"So what was all that about?" Crispin asked as we walked out of Scrutton's together.

"All what?" I said.

"All that 'somewhere near Westbury' nonsense. And you kicking me under the table."

I glanced over my shoulder at some of the Board members who were leaving at the same time.

"Do you fancy coffee?" I asked.

Crispin and I walked up St. James's Street to Piccadilly and went around the corner into The Wolseley.

"I can give you a table for an hour," said the maître d', "but I must have it back by twelve-thirty."

He showed us to a small table in a far right-hand corner, under the balcony. The Wolseley, with its Italianate architecture, high-domed ceilings and marble floors, was always noisy and hence, strangely, it provided the ideal surroundings to talk privately even though we had to speak quite loudly to make each other heard.

"So, dear boy, what is the reason why you didn't tell the chief superintendent that we knew exactly to the inch where the drop was made?" Crispin asked after our coffee had been poured.

"I just thought it may be prudent to keep that piece of information to ourselves, at least for the time being."

"And why is that, exactly?"

I was silent for a moment wondering if I was crazy. In the end, I decided that I wasn't.

"How well do you know the individual members of the BHA Board?"

He looked at me in astonishment.

"Do you know something that I don't?" he asked.

"No," I said. "Not really. I just felt uncomfortable at the meeting we had last Sunday in the office. I can't explain what, but something happened there that has made me wonder. That's all."

"Dear boy, surely you can't think that the person doing all this is a member of the BHA Board?"

"No, of course not," I said. Or did I? "But I know that if we really want to keep something secret we shouldn't tell anyone at all. Who do you think leaked the information about Electrode?"

"Our friend Leonardo, obviously."

"But why would he?" I said. "What did he have to gain?"

"It adds pressure onto us to pay up."

"Does it? Why? One of the reasons for us paying

would be to keep him quiet, so why is he blabbing about it? Surely that makes us *less* likely to pay, not more."

"But who else would have done it?" Crispin asked.

"If Stephen is correct in saying that someone at the labs couldn't have, then it must have been either Leonardo or one of the people who was in that meeting this morning. We are the only people who knew."

"But what would any of the Board members have to gain by leaking the information to the press?"

"I don't know," I said. "And I also don't know if we are dealing with one person or two. Leonardo is clearly after money, but is he the same person who leaked the story about the doping?"

"He must be," Crispin said with confidence.

"Why?" I said.

"Please don't tell me we have two maniacs out to destroy the BHA."

"I CAN'T thank you enough," QC,QC said effusively, the relief clearly visible on his face and in his eyes.

It was half past six and we were once again sitting in the small café in Brewers Lane, around the corner from his and Faye's house, this time with glasses of wine rather than cups of coffee.

I had just shown him the video that I'd recorded the previous evening.

It showed Daniel Jubowski sitting on the leather sofa in his flat. He was facing the camera and he spoke clearly and precisely. "I withdraw any allegation that I may have made to police that Kenneth Calderfield was in possession of, or had ever supplied, any illegal drugs of any kind. I do this of my own free will and I deeply regret any hurt that I may have caused by my misguided actions in making such a false accusation."

"How much did you have to pay him?" Quentin asked.

"Nothing," I said. "Kenneth never did supply any drugs. Daniel Jubowski did that himself. I simply persuaded Daniel that he needed to tell me the truth."

Quentin looked at me sideways.

"And no violence was involved?" he said.

"Not even a threat of it," I assured him.

"Then why?" he asked.

"There are some things you don't need to know about," I replied.

"But why did he make such an allegation in the first place?"

"That's another thing you don't need to know. Just be grateful that he has seen the light and will withdraw it."

"Do I need to do anything?" Quentin asked.

"If Daniel does what he has promised, then he will have been to the police today to withdraw his statement. I'm sure Kenneth will find out soon enough."

"At this stage, the CPS may still decide to go ahead with the trial," Quentin said. "Only there and then may they offer no evidence, at which point the case would collapse and Kenneth would be discharged, but there is a slim chance that they may still use the original statement and present it to the jury together with the search evidence."

"But surely the jury wouldn't believe the statement if Daniel were to stand up in court and say that it was untrue?"

"We could certainly call Daniel for the defense, even if his statement is presented as evidence for the Crown. There is no property in a witness. But can we be sure that he will keep to his new story any more than he kept to the previous one?"

"I think he could be persuaded," I said.

"But can we be certain that the jury won't believe the prior statement over his verbal evidence. Juries can do such funny things. I'd be so much happier if this case never gets to a jury."

"I'm afraid I can't help you in that department. You only asked me to find the friend and prove that he was lying. I've done that. The rest is up to you and Kenneth."

"Yes," said Quentin, "you've been marvelous."

He even smiled.

"How is Faye?" I asked.

"Bearing up, poor dear. This chemo stuff is a real bugger. Makes her so tired. But I suppose it's worth it if it works."

"I'm sure it will," I said reassuringly.

"Yeah, I hope so. I'd really hate to lose the old girl."

I was surprised. It was the first time I could ever recall Quentin having said anything that could be remotely described as loving about his wife, in spite of the fact that the "old girl" in question was some ten years younger than him.

"I plan to go round to see her," I said.

"Yes, I thought you might. I'll pay the check here and be home shortly. Not good form for us to turn up together. Far too conspiratorial."

I was still smiling at his eccentric ways when I rang the doorbell of his house.

Faye, as always, was delighted to see me and ushered me into the kitchen.

"Coffee or wine?" she asked.

"Wine," I replied, smiling, "as long as that's all right."

"Of course it's all right."

She didn't need to ask if it should be red or white, she knew me too well. She poured me a generous glass of deep-red Rioja.

"Are you not having one?" I asked as she replaced the top.

"No," she said. "It's not because I can't, but the drugs I take make some things taste nasty and alcohol is one of them. I haven't had any for ages and it's doing wonders for my weight."

She did a twirl.

"I can tell."

I hadn't said anything before because I was afraid it was due to the cancer.

"So how are you?" Faye asked. "And how's Lydia?"

What she was really asking was *How's your relationship?*

"Everything is fine," I said, smiling at her. "We are very well, thank you, although we've hardly seen each other this past week, we've both been so busy."

"You should make time," she said. "Wasn't it Arnold

Bennett who said that time is our most precious of possessions? I've certainly found that out during these last few weeks."

Something about her tone of voice worried me.

"You are going to be OK, aren't you?"

"It depends on how you define *OK*." She took a deep breath. "Am I going to die this week? No. This year? Maybe not. Next year? Possibly. Within the next five years? Probably. Cancer hardly ever goes away completely, not when you've got to my age, especially when it's somewhere deep down inside you. I know it will come back sometime and then it will be too late to do the things I still want to do. All they ever talk about at the Marsden is giving people more time, not about curing them completely."

"Everyone dies eventually," I said. "All we should really expect is enough time to watch our children grow up and maybe our grandchildren too, if we're lucky."

"Well, in that case, hurry up and have your children, that's what I say. You never know how long you've got left. Now I understand why all my friends who've survived cancer suddenly start becoming manic about seeing their families all the time and going off to visit far-flung places. They never know exactly when the ax will fall."

Why did everyone keep talking about executions?

At that point, Quentin arrived and I thankfully changed the subject.

"Tell me, Quentin," I said, "you know the law. How serious a crime is extortion?"

"What sort of extortion?" he asked, looking worried.

"Demanding money from an organization in return for not doing something that might embarrass it."

He relaxed a little and I realized he had been worrying that I was talking about Daniel Jubowski possibly extorting money from him.

"It depends on the threats," he said. "Violence or threatened violence is serious. The law takes a dim view of that."

"How about violence towards an animal?"

"Hmm, not as serious. Prosecutions in animal cases are almost always at the request of the RSPCA. The police tend to steer clear of them if they possibly can."

As I now knew all too well.

"So if I say to someone, 'Give me a grand in cash or I'll kill your horse,' the police wouldn't really be interested?"

"They might be, the violence might be considered as being directed against the person by an implied threat. But, in the eyes of the law, horses are just possessions, like a car or a bicycle. If the horse is maliciously killed, then it's possible that a charge of criminal damage could be brought, but there is no such offense as horseslaughter like there is manslaughter. And the RSPCA would get involved only if the killing was done with cruelty. A quick shot to the head—no problem."

"Even if the horse was very valuable?"

"The value in such a case would make little or no difference in the criminal law. You get the same sentence for stealing a Mini as a Rolls-Royce. However, the horse owner would be able to sue for damages based on the value."

"So spiking a supermarket's dog food with pieces of glass would not get you as long in jail as putting the same glass into their baby food?"

"Absolutely not, although the police would definitely investigate both, but there would likely be more manpower assigned to the baby food."

"Did you read about the events at this year's Grand National?" I asked.

He nodded. "There was something in yesterday's paper."

"I watched it live on television," Faye said. "All those poor horses."

"What about the jockeys?" I said. "One of them broke two vertebrae in his neck."

"But they didn't shoot him like they did that poor horse, right in front of the stands. They didn't need to show *that*." She shivered at the memory.

It never ceased to amaze me how much more the British public cared more for the horses than they did for the riders. Sure, I like horses, but they aren't people.

"Is that what this is all about?" Quentin asked. "Did someone disrupt the Grand National because the racing authorities wouldn't pay to prevent it?"

Quentin wasn't one of the country's top legal brains for nothing.

"Pretty much," I said. "And we don't seem to be able to get the police to realize how important it is."

"But is it really important, in the long term?" Quentin asked. "Sure, it was an inconvenience at the time and no doubt lots of people were very cross. And it was obviously very serious for the jockey who was injured and for the owner of the horse that was killed. But, in the context of most people's lives, it was an irrelevant blip."

"It didn't feel like that to me," I said. "I was there."

"I'm sure it didn't, but that is still what the law would say. The perpetrator might even successfully argue that since he had no intention of causing injury to any horse or rider, he couldn't be held criminally responsible. He might also argue that, statistically, there was far more likelihood of injury occurring to horses and riders if they had raced for the second time around the Aintree circuit rather than being stopped after the first."

I was beginning to realize why Quentin was such a good defense lawyer.

"Do you remember the University Boat Race one year," he said, "when an Australian disrupted everything by swimming across the Thames in front of the crews? The race had to be stopped."

"Of course."

"The man was sentenced to a few months in prison for causing a public nuisance. The Boat Race organizers would have happily drowned him in the river, but most of the public thought that sending him to jail was far too harsh. There was even a petition signed by hundreds of Oxford and Cambridge students demanding his release. The man became a bit of a hero in the media and he didn't get deported back to Australia when he was released, as many had expected. It shows that the law generally takes a moderate, even tolerant view of such actions."

Far from Ian Tulloch's desire that the man responsible would be put in jail and the key thrown away, it seemed that even if the police bothered to try to catch our friend Leonardo, he would likely be hailed as a hero by the left-wing press and carried shoulder-high by the "protest brigade."

It was clearly up to the BHA to sort out its own problem.

27

"And about time too," said Detective Sergeant Galley. "I left a message for you to call me back on Monday afternoon."

It was now eight-thirty on Thursday morning and I'd only just called him.

"Yes, I know," I said. "I did get it. But I reckoned that if it were something important, you'd call me again."

"So why are you calling me now?"

"I need to talk to Matthew Unwin."

"That's impossible," he said bluntly. "He's on remand in Long Lartin Prison."

"Can't I visit him?"

"That wouldn't be proper. You are a witness for the prosecution in his case."

"Is there a law against it?"

"Not as such, but you would need permission from the court for an official interview. And I can tell you now you won't get it."

"I thought the police were interested in solving crime."

"We are, and this one is already solved. Matthew Unwin murdered Jordan Furness. There is no doubt about that. There were far too many witnesses."

"If there are so many witnesses, then why do you need me specifically?"

"You are a witness both to the crime and to the subsequent capture of Mr. Unwin."

"But last week you questioned me as if I was somehow involved. You can't have it both ways. I'm either a prosecution witness or I'm a suspect."

"What do you want to speak to him about anyway?"

Was that a movement in the right direction?

"About his claim that he knew nothing about his horses being doped and that he was being harassed by the BHA. I now have reason to believe he might be right about the doping bit, even if I don't accept the harassment claim. Other racehorse trainers have since come forward to say that they were threatened with the same thing. I'm trying to investigate the matter for the British Horseracing Authority, and I could really do with interviewing him."

"It still won't be possible."

"Why not?" I said in a frustrated tone. "Any testimony I would give about what happened at Cheltenham races surely won't be contentious. Have you given my statement to the defense lawyers yet? They will almost certainly accept it without question, so why do I have to appear as a witness?"

"Whether or not you appear as a witness, I can tell you now, Mr. Hinkley, you won't be getting me to arrange it so that you can talk to Matthew Unwin. It's more than my job's worth."

"Who are his lawyers?" I asked.

"Why do you want to know?"

"Because if *you* won't help me speak with him, then I will have to contact his lawyers and ask them if I can visit their client. It might help the defense for them to know that I now believe Unwin's claim about the doping. Do you want me to say *that* in court?"

He was silent for some time and I wondered if he'd hung up, but I could still hear him breathing.

"The law states that the police are not allowed to question a prisoner on remand," he said formally. "Not unless there is fresh evidence in the case, which there isn't."

"I'm not asking the police to question him, I'm asking if I can."

"He may not want to see you."

"I think he might."

"Then why don't you ask for a normal prison visit? Prisoners on remand seem to have as many visits as they like." It didn't sound as if he approved.

"So I just apply to the prison to visit him?"

"I don't see why not. If he were out on bail, mind, there would be conditions that would almost certainly include not having any contact with the witnesses. But if he's inside . . . I don't suppose that applies. But don't tell anyone I told you so. I don't want to know anything about it, either before or after. He probably won't see you, in any case."

"Do I need Unwin's permission?"

"Yeah, I think so. You have to get a VO."

"What's that?" I asked.

"A visitation order. The prisoner applies for one from the prison warden's office and gives your name as someone he would like to see. You can't visit a prisoner if he doesn't want to see you."

"So how do I get a VO?"

"I don't know. Why don't you write to Unwin and ask him to apply, but don't mention to anyone that it was my idea."

"OK," I said. "Thanks. I'll write to him today. Now, what was it that you rang me about on Monday?"

"Only to tell you I'd been in touch with Mr. Lever, the BHA chief executive, and he had confirmed what you'd said about your position. It really wasn't important."

"I thought you might be calling to apologize for doubting what I'd said." I knew I was pushing my luck.

"No, Mr. Hinkley, I was not calling to apologize. The police never apologize for anything. Not unless we are instructed to do so by a court."

I actually thought I could hear him laughing down the line.

NO SOONER had I put my phone down from speaking with D.S. Galley than it rang again.

"Hello," I said, picking it up.

"Jeff, it's Ken Calderfield. I hear from my father that I need to thank you for getting Daniel to change his statement."

"I haven't heard from the police that he's done so yet, but, yes, that is what he promised."

"That's great, thank you."

"You're welcome," I said. "Perhaps I will see you again soon under better circumstances."

"Yes," he said as if distracted. "Jeff . . . there is one other thing."

Oh no, I thought. Now what?

"Does it mean that my father won't now need to find out . . . you know . . . about me being gay? You didn't tell him, did you?"

"No, Ken," I said, "I didn't tell him. But I still think you should."

"You don't understand what he's like."

Perhaps I didn't, but it seemed to me to be very sad that a grown son had to conceal his sexuality from his father through fear of what he'd say.

"I still think it would be better in the long term."

"The *long term*," he repeated with a sigh. "That's what I'm afraid of."

"Afraid?" I said. "In what way?

"I don't want to be a barrister. In fact, I don't want to be a lawyer at all. If these last few weeks have taught me anything, it's that the law and I don't have any rapport. I dread having to go back to it. Half of me was even relieved that if I was convicted of drug dealing, I wouldn't be able to go back. But that hope is now gone."

I could tell that he was near to tears.

"You told me that you enjoyed the law."

"I've tried to," he said. "God, I've tried to. But I don't. I hate it."

"Ken, you can't go on living your life in the way your father wants you to if it makes you so unhappy."

"He even calls me KC,KC. Has done so since I was a kid."

"He'll get over it," I said.

"But how do I tell him?"

"You'll find a way."

"Jeff, would you tell him for me? Tell him everything . . . You know, about me being gay and such. And also about not wanting to be a barrister. Everything."

"No, Ken, I won't. That is something you have to do for yourself."

"Oh God."

He didn't sound very happy and I wondered if he would ever get around to it.

"Perhaps you could practice by telling Faye," I said. "I'm sure she would be understanding."

"Faye?" he said.

"Yes, Faye. Remember her? The wicked stepmother."

He laughed.

"But be careful. She knows nothing about you having been arrested and I think it might be better if it stayed that way."

"She's surely got enough trouble on her plate at the moment."

"I'm sure she'd have a little room left for some of your problems as well. But her health situation does tend to put everything else into perspective."

"Yes," he said, "I suppose it does."

I SAT at my desk and made a list of the BHA Board members and tried to remember what had made me feel uncomfortable in the last two meetings.

The Board consisted of seven nonexecutives, including Roger Vincent as chairman, plus Howard Lever, the chief executive.

Stephen Kohli, director of Integrity, Legal and Risk, had also been present at the meetings, along with Crispin Larson and myself, so I added our three names to my list.

Eleven of us total.

Why would Leonardo, our extortionist, tip off the Press Association about Electrode?

He would surely have had nothing to gain.

So, if he didn't, then one of those at the Board meetings must have.

But why? And was it done accidentally or on purpose?

The *Racing Post* had run with the story on its front page in spite of there being no official confirmation from the BHA. The report was full of *ifs*, *maybes* and *allegedlys* to avoid the paper being sued if the story was incorrect.

The main thrust of the report was that, whether the story was true or not, the lack of response by the BHA was yet another example of the manifest inability of the authority to effectively govern horseracing.

I visited the websites of the national daily newspapers. All of them reported on the story and all were negative and highly critical of the BHA, several with leading articles bemoaning the lack of response from racing's regulator.

So much for our control of the PR.

Piers Pottinger had been right—saying nothing had been a disaster.

There were printed quotes calling for the Jockey Club to take back the mantle of authority, some of them from very influential members of the racing community including the trainers Duncan Johnson and Graham Perry.

That was rich, I thought. Graham Perry was lucky still to have his license after what I'd found at his Cheshire stable. The old Jockey Club would have whisked it away faster than you could say methylphenidate.

Crispin called me at ten minutes to ten from the BHA offices.

"Roger Vincent has resigned."

I wasn't particularly surprised.

"Who's taken over as chairman?" I asked.

"Ian Tulloch, but he claims it's a temporary measure."

Crispin sounded as if he didn't believe it and nor did I. It was common knowledge that Ian Tulloch had been angling to be the next chairman ever since he'd arrived on the Board and now, it appeared, he had seized his chance.

"It might turn out to be a poisoned chalice," I said.

"I reckon there will be more resignations before this lot blows over. What has Howard said?"

"Nothing, at the moment. But what's new? He shut himself away in his office as soon as he arrived this morning and, since then, he has refused to speak to anyone, either directly or on the telephone. I'm actually quite worried about him."

"I hope he hasn't got his service revolver with him," I said with a smile. "And jumping out the window of his first-floor office wouldn't kill him."

Crispin tried to laugh at my poor-taste joke, but it was really not a laughing matter. Roger Vincent had taken one honorable way out. No one would want Howard Lever to take an alternative route.

"Do you know of anyone else who's thinking of resigning?" I asked.

"Apparently, Neil Wallinger has been mumbling about it."

"He's probably the one who should be made chairman—that is, if they want to regain any public confidence. He's the only one of the current Board with a proven track record as a sports administrator, not that I think he's been much good at it. He's become rather dithering as he's got older."

"You are so right, dear boy," Crispin said.

"I reckon the whole Board might have to go. Especially if the press discover they authorized a payment of a hundred thousand pounds from BHA funds for nothing in return."

"There's a real sense of panic here," Crispin said.

"There are rumors flying round like confetti. Everyone is suddenly worried they may lose their jobs if the authority is closed down."

"Surely that couldn't happen."

"You say that, but no one thought the GLC could be abolished."

"The GLC?" I asked.

"Greater London Council. Closed almost overnight in the mid-eighties by Maggie Thatcher, who claimed it was an unnecessary tier of government and a huge waste of public money. People said she couldn't do it, but she did."

"Before my time," I said.

"You young whippersnapper."

"Yes, all right, Granddad."

I wasn't sure how old Crispin actually was, somewhere in his early sixties maybe. It was one of those bits of information that he would divulge only on a need-to-know basis and I didn't need to know.

"But who would control racing?" I said.

"Well, all the administration would continue as now. No one is suggesting that Weatherbys should go."

Weatherbys was the private firm that had been responsible since 1770 for both the administration of British horseracing and the keeping of the *Thoroughbred Breeding Registry*, more commonly known as the "General Stud Book."

"It is just the regulation and disciplinary functions that would change. There seems to be a growing campaign in the press to reinstate the Jockey Club in that role."

"But that's ridiculous," I said.

The Jockey Club had lost its position as the sport's regulatory authority back in 2006 owing to criticism of its self-electing policy and also because of a general desire to increase the transparency and independence of racing's governance.

"Is it?" said Crispin. "The system had worked pretty well for over two hundred and fifty years and now some people are asking why it was changed."

"But you know why it was changed. Racing was seen as being run by the toffs. It was a throwback to a gentlemen's club of the eighteenth century."

"Maybe," he said. "But at least the toffs had some gravitas. Racing is steeped in their aristocratic blue blood and they always had the sport's best interests at heart, even above their own."

"Are you saying the BHA doesn't have racing's best interests at heart?"

"No, of course not. But the BHA is more of a commercial enterprise and it recruits from outside the racing family."

"But surely that's a good thing," I said.

"Not in everyone's eyes. You probably don't remember the uproar when Howard Lever was appointed chief executive. His father had been a coal miner and he was seen as a complete outsider. He was accused by some of being nothing more than an insurance salesman who didn't know one end of a horse from the other."

Crispin was being somewhat unkind. Howard Lever had risen rapidly from his humble start to become the chief operating officer of a highly successful shipping insurance company in the City of London. And prior to his appointment with the BHA, he'd owned shares in a couple of racehorses, albeit within commercial syndicates.

"Are you telling me," I said, "that you agree with the press?"

"I don't know," he said, "but I feel we shouldn't dismiss the notion out of hand."

In other words, he did agree with the press.

"So how does the BHA regain the confidence of the racing public?" I asked. But I already knew the answer.

We had to catch Leonardo. And quickly.

I SPENT much of Thursday afternoon watching the racing from Fontwell Park on television as well as going over in my head everything that I knew about our friend Leonardo.

There was precious little.

I'd said at one of the Board meetings that I thought he was a racing insider, someone who knew his way around a racetrack. That was because he had been able to deliver a poisoned ginger cake to the jockeys' changing room at Ascot without being intercepted or questioned. He must, therefore, have had a right to be there or at least a reasonable excuse.

Ritalin and Dexedrine.

Only Matthew Unwin's horses tested positive for Dexedrine. All the others had Ritalin's methylphenidate in their systems.

Methylphenidate hydrochloride and dextroamphetamine sulfate.

I looked them both up once more on the Internet just in case I'd missed something the first time.

Both drugs were used as treatment for narcolepsy, a sleep disorder, and also for ADHD, attention-deficit/hyperactivity disorder, especially in children.

That was it! That's what had caused the quiver in the room.

My comment about Leonardo possibly being a person with hyperactivity in their family had struck a chord with someone in that meeting.

I was sure that's why I'd felt uncomfortable.

I went back to the list I'd made of the eleven people who had been present at that meeting.

Could one of the eleven have anything to do with doping the horses? Or did one of them know the person who had? And did that person have hyperactivity in their family?

One of the eleven was me and I knew for certain that I hadn't been involved, so that left ten. And Crispin Larson could hardly have both thrown the money off the train and have been standing beside the track to collect it unless, of course, he'd had an accomplice.

But what about the other nine?

I stared at the list of familiar names.

There was Roger Vincent, the six remaining nonexecutive directors, plus Howard Lever and Stephen Kohli.

How many of them had been at Aintree for the Grand National and hence able to set off the fireworks remotely?

All of them, I expect.

As the controlling elite of British racing, why wouldn't they be present at one of the greatest days in the horseracing calendar? They had probably all been invited to have lunch with the chairman of the racetrack.

I'd actually seen Roger Vincent, Piers Pottinger, Howard Lever and Stephen Kohli with my own eyes as they had stood with the policemen at the water jump after the incident, and I'd also seen Bill Ripley, Ian Tulloch and Neil Wallinger in the parade ring prior to the big race. I imagine that the other two directors, George Searle and Charles Payne, would have been there as well, enjoying the hospitality that would have readily been on offer to BHA Board members.

Perhaps I would get Crispin to ask the racetrack chairman to send the guest list for his Grand National Day lunch.

I watched on the television as Duncan Johnson's runner won the three-mile chase at Fontwell, the horse storming up the hill to triumph by three lengths at a price of five-to-one. The cameras then showed the smiling trainer as he greeted his winner in the unsaddling enclosure.

Racehorse trainers were definitely racing insiders and they certainly knew their way around the weighing room and the changing rooms, especially if, like Duncan Johnson, they had once been jockeys themselves.

"There has just been an unusual announcement from the stewards' room," said the TV announcer, looking straight into the camera. "The remainder of today's racing here at Fontwell has been abandoned due to a serious bout of food poisoning among the officiating stewards, two of whom have been taken to the hospital by ambulance."

I stared at the screen for a few seconds in disbelief, then called Crispin.

"I've just heard from the Clerk of the Course at Fontwell," he said.

"It has to be Leonardo again," I said. "How the hell can we be so short of stewards that the racing has to be abandoned because a couple are taken ill? Surely they could have recruited temporary stewards from the great and the good among the Fontwell crowd."

"It seems that the most seriously ill are the two stipes," said Crispin.

Stipes—or stipendiary stewards, as they are officially known—are full-time employees of the BHA who, along with approved and trained amateur stewards appointed by each racetrack, are responsible for policing the Rules of Racing at all the thirteen hundred–plus race meetings that take place each year in Great Britain.

Without either of the assigned stipendiary stewards being fit to act, or even present at the racetrack, the remaining amateur stewards had little choice but to abandon the meeting.

"Who do we have there?" I asked.

"Investigators?"

"Anyone. Get someone to find out what the stewards had for lunch and tell them to collect some samples of the food."

"I'll see what I can do."

"And one more thing," I said. "Who were the trainers who complained to you that someone was trying to extort money from them?"

There was a lengthy pause down the line.

"Other than Matthew Unwin?"

"Yes," I said with some impatience, "other than Matthew Unwin."

There was another long pause as Crispin's brain worked out whether I needed to know. In the end, it decided that I did.

"Richard Young and Duncan Johnson."

"When did they talk to you?"

"Richard approached me in January and Duncan at the beginning of March, a couple of weeks before the Cheltenham Festival."

"What did they say, exactly?" I asked.

"They told me they'd received anonymous letters stating that unless they paid an insurance premium, their horses might end up testing positive for banned stimulants."

"The same for each?"

"Pretty much. I can't remember the exact words. Duncan was telling me unofficially, but he still wanted it on record just in case any of his horses subsequently proved positive. He was covering his back. Both of them claim they didn't respond to the letter. Do you think the same man is responsible?"

"It would be rather a coincidence if he's not," I said. "But I wonder why he switched his attention from individual trainers to the BHA as a whole."

"Maybe he was getting no joy from any of the trainers," Crispin said. "Or perhaps he was trying out his doping technique before he did it wholesale at Cheltenham. I just wish we knew what he'd do next."

"How about running live wires under the grass to kill the horses? If I didn't know better, I'd say that Leonardo did that too."

Two horses had been electrocuted in the parade ring before the first race at Newbury in 2011. The stewards had abandoned racing that day as well.

"I hate to think what the press will say about this latest incident," Crispin said. "Talk about fanning the flames as the BHA burns."

28

If things had been bad for the BHA in the newspapers on Thursday morning, by Friday they were even more disastrous than even Crispin had imagined.

Not only was there extensive criticism of the previous afternoon's abandonment of racing at Fontwell Park but the *London Telegraph* proclaimed a "World Exclusive!" with a banner headline stating that ALL CHELTENHAM WINNERS WERE DOPED, a theme that was soon picked up by all the other newspaper websites and also by the television news channels.

Ian Tulloch was shown on the BBC making a statement on the sidewalk outside the BHA offices in High Holborn.

Without exactly confirming the reports, he stated that the British Horseracing Authority was investigating the possibility that the drinking-water supply to the Cheltenham racetrack stables had somehow become contaminated. Against a tirade of hostile questions from the assembled journalists, he asserted robustly that the BHA remained in full control of the sport and there was nothing for racing's stakeholders to concern themselves about.

Business as usual, was the official message.

He reminded me somewhat of the *Titanic* stewards who initially told worried passengers, who had been awakened by the impact with the iceberg, that everything was fine and they should go back to bed, quoting the flawed acceptance that the ship was "unsinkable."

Was the BHA about to plunge headlong into the abyss?

The *Racing Post* clearly thought so, with a drawing of a grave with BHA RIP chiseled in the headstone adorning the full title page of its online edition.

The attached article called for a return to proper stability within the sport, something that it claimed the Jockey Club had provided for over a quarter of a millennium. It didn't outright call for the Jockey Club to be reinstated as horseracing's regulator, but it left the reader in little doubt that that was exactly what they wanted.

And there were more quotes from leading figures in the sport lending support to the notion.

I thought it was strange how people's attitudes could reverse so quickly. Some of those who only a few years ago had argued passionately for a change to a more transparent and democratic system of governance were now being equally vociferous in their encouragement for a return to how things had been before.

At ten o'clock, I called Crispin Larson.

"You're well out of it here," he said. "Half the staff are suicidal and the other half are just bloody furious. I've had Paul Maldini in here, demanding to know if I was aware that all the Cheltenham winners had been doped. What could I say?"

"So now everyone knows it's true?"

"I suppose so. Paul also now knows that you weren't really sacked and that you've continued to work for us undercover. He's bloody furious about that as well. Says he should have been told."

Perhaps he should have been.

"How did he find out?"

"Howard Lever told him when he accused the Board of sitting on their fat arses and doing nothing about it. Howard told him that they had been doing something. I think Howard's in line for a nervous breakdown. And Ian Tulloch is on the warpath too."

"I saw him on the TV news."

"He's called another emergency Board meeting for later today."

"Where and when?" I asked.

"Here in the office boardroom at two, but you and I are specifically not invited."

"Do you think they're going to resign en masse and hand the whole thing back to the Jockey Club?"

"I've no idea about that, but I do fear for Howard's position. I'm not sure that Stephen Kohli is safe either. And if I read the vibes correctly, dear boy, you and I might be up for the boot as well."

Crispin was a master at reading the vibes, so it didn't bode particularly well for my mortgage.

"That's hardly fair," I said, "not when it was the Board as a whole who took the decision to say nothing. It's just like those government ministers who say they take full responsibility for something and then they fire their junior aides."

"'Theirs not to reason why, / Theirs but to do and die.'"

"I have no intention of doing and dying," I said. "I intend on finding out who's really responsible for this mess. What exactly did Leonardo say in his letter that arrived on Wednesday morning? You said that he was angry because the payment hadn't been enough. Was that all?"

"He said he'd teach us a lesson."

"Well, we now know what he meant by that. Did he say anything about getting some more money?"

"He said he wants a million pounds or there would be more disruption, but he surely must know he won't get it. Especially now."

"At least he's come down from two million," I said. "How about if we offer to pay him?"

"With what? Monopoly money?"

"We need him to arrange another drop. That would give us another chance to catch him."

"But we didn't get even close to catching him last time. We just threw away a hundred grand by chucking it out the window of a fast-moving train."

"But what if he used the same drop point again? I could just wait there for him to walk into a trap."

"But that's hardly likely, is it? It would be far too risky."

"Why?" I said. "Leonardo has doped racetrack water supplies twice and he's used poisoned food twice. Perhaps he's a man of habit."

"I think it's a bit of a long shot."

"Maybe," I said, "but the spot he chose was ideal for the purpose. There can't be many stretches on that line with a nice long, isolated grassy embankment and no trees to get in the way."

"But he could use a different line."

"Not if he wants opening windows to chuck things out of. Almost every other line now has sealed trains with automatic doors."

"I still think it's a huge risk," Crispin said.

"We always have the option of not throwing out the money if it's at a different spot. And we have to do something. I'm fed up with us just waiting for him to disrupt things again. But we do need to be at that Board meeting this afternoon. Tell Howard that we have to be there."

"How, dear boy?" Crispin asked.

"Say we'll be there to help divert some of the flak away from him. I'm sure he'll agree."

"It might get us fired even faster."

"Do and die," I said. "If we're going to die, I'd rather die doing something positive."

"OK. I'll ask him. But don't be surprised if Ian Tulloch vetoes it."

"Don't let Howard tell him," I said. "At least not until

we're already in the boardroom. And, Crispin, don't be surprised at what I say at the meeting. Go along with it. Don't question anything. I promise you, I've not lost my marbles."

He laughed. "Now, why would I think that, dear boy?"

I ARRIVED at the BHA offices in High Holborn at a quarter to one just as many of the shell-shocked staff were going out to find some lunch.

I was confronted by Nigel Green in the lobby.

"You could have told me," he said angrily. "You made a fool of me. I've been going round telling everyone that it was a scandal that you'd been fired and, all along, you hadn't been."

"Thank you," I said smiling at him. "You're a good friend."

"Better than you," he said.

That hurt.

"I'm sorry."

He looked at me for a moment, nodded, then walked past me to the door.

Paul Maldini was not so forgiving when I met him in the corridor outside Crispin Larson's office.

"You're a bloody disgrace," he said. "I'm your damn boss, for God's sake." He pursed his lips and shook his head. "Don't you trust me?"

"It isn't a matter of trust." Although I suppose it was.

"It certainly feels like it to me," he said. He pointed his right index finger straight towards my face. "I've got my eye on you, young man. In the future, you'd better watch your step."

He turned on his heel and marched away stiffly down the corridor.

In the future, Paul had said.

He was assuming that the BHA had a future and that I would still be in it.

Governance by consensus, not by statute. That's what Howard Lever had said. The way things were going, the British Horseracing Authority was rapidly losing the confidence of the racing industry and hence would soon lose its consensus as well.

The Jockey Club, under the terms of its Royal Charter, has overall responsibility for governance of racing but had delegated that remit initially to the Horseracing Regulatory Authority in April 2006 and subsequently to the BHA a year later.

I wondered what the reaction in racing would be if the one hundred and thirty-four self-electing members of the Jockey Club now decided to take back the regulatory control of the sport for themselves.

In the past there would have been uproar, but now I was not so sure.

I knocked on Crispin's office door.

"Come in," shouted a voice from inside. So I did.

"Ah, my brother-in-arms," said Crispin, rising briefly from behind his desk. "Come on in and sit down. You look very smart. We don't often see you in a suit and tie."

"I thought I should dress properly for my execution. I'm also wearing two vests so I don't shiver."

He laughed out loud and banged his desk in approval.

"Did you manage to speak to Howard Lever about us being at the meeting?" I asked, taking the chair opposite him.

"Yes, I did." Crispin hesitated, which I took as not such a good sign. "But he's very worried about his own position and he doesn't want to upset the new chairman."

"Did you explain that we might be able take some of the flak away from him?"

"Yes, but he wasn't convinced."

"We really need to be in that meeting," I said.

"Why exactly?" Crispin asked.

"We just do."

"Come on, dear boy, I can hardly say to Howard that we really need to be there just because we do. You'll have to give me a more definite reason."

I sat and looked at him for a moment.

"Crispin, can I trust you?"

"What a strange thing to say," he said. "Of course you can trust me."

I paused again, wondering if I was crazy.

"I believe that someone who attends those Board meetings knows more about what is going on than they are saying."

"Go on," he said, sitting quietly—and not reaching for a telephone to fetch the men from the lunatic asylum to come and take me away.

"I'm not saying that one of them is our friend Leonardo, although he might be, I'm just sure that someone on that Board reacted to something I said."

"What?"

"Do you remember the meeting we had here on the Sunday after the Grand National?"

"Of course."

"I said at that meeting that I believed the person responsible was a racing insider and that because of the drugs used to dope the horses he might have a hyperactive child."

"I remember."

"Well," I said, "something happened in that meeting and I now think it was a reaction from someone when I said that."

"What sort of reaction?"

"I'm not sure. Some sort of frisson of excitement. Or maybe it was fear. Either way, it made me feel uncomfortable."

"It's not much to go on," he said.

"I know. I only remembered it yesterday afternoon and I've spent most of the night thinking about it. But I'm sure I'm right."

"So why does that mean you need to be at the meeting today?"

"Partly because I want to say it again to see if there's another similar reaction and this time I'd be ready for it."

"And?" he encouraged.

"I want to argue in favor of paying our friend some more money so that I can set a trap for him at the drop."

"Assuming it will be at the same place?"

"Yes," I said. "We made it quite clear at the last meeting that we didn't know where the first drop had been, so there's no reason for him to change it. We just have to make sure we don't let on that we are planning a trap."

"But what if you're wrong, dear boy?"

"Then we don't throw out the money and nothing will have been lost other than my time and energy."

IAN TULLOCH was far from happy when Crispin and I entered the boardroom with Howard Lever, upon whom Crispin had spent the past half an hour applying undue pressure to get us in.

"This is a meeting of just the Board," he said. "We do not need any supernumeraries."

"I think they should be here," said Howard. "And Stephen Kohli as well. They have been present at all the other emergency meetings and their contributions may be relevant."

Ian Tulloch didn't like it. I could see in his eyes that he felt his authority as the new chairman was being undermined. He looked around for support but didn't find any.

"Seems sensible to me," said Neil Wallinger, and there were nods of agreement from Charles Payne and George Searle.

"Very well," said Ian Tulloch reluctantly. "But I may ask them to leave when we get on to questions of accountability."

Howard raised his eyebrows in apparent surprise at the remark, but he must have known what was coming.

We waited while Stephen Kohli was located and took his place at the table.

"Gentlemen," Ian Tulloch said loudly to bring the meeting to order. "We face the most difficult period in our short history, but we must be strong and resolute. The BHA *is* the authority for racing in this country and we should not shy away from our responsibilities.

"I know that the departure of Roger Vincent is seen by some of you as a major blow to our credibility, but I see it as an opportunity, a chance to put the past behind us and to move forward with aplomb.

"This Board has my total confidence, and we must strive to regain the trust of those in our industry who rely on us every day of their lives. It is not the time to shirk our duty or to quit. That would plunge racing into disrepute and greater chaos. Now is the time to stand up and be counted, the time to demonstrate that the BHA is up to the challenge and ready to perform its task with integrity and sureness."

He finished with a flourish and looked up and down the table as if seeking approval or even some applause.

"Bravo," said Neil Wallinger. "Well said."

There were also murmurings of approval from the others.

"But what about the press?" Bill Ripley said, pointing down the table at the chairman with the arm of his tortoiseshell glasses. "They seem to be out for our blood."

"We must remain firm," Ian Tulloch responded.

"And we absolutely must give some explanation of the events at the Cheltenham Festival and what we propose to do about the results," Piers Pottinger said. "To continue to say nothing is greatly harming our image."

"But what *are* we going to say about the results?" Neil Wallinger asked. "We can hardly make the whole meeting void. The betting public would be in meltdown, to say nothing of the owners, trainers and jockeys."

Crispin was ready with an answer. "We can simply announce that the levels of methylphenidate found in the tested samples were too small to have made any difference how the horses ran and, consequently, all the results stand."

"And was it too small?" Neil asked.

"Yes," said Crispin confidently. "It was only slightly above the no-effect threshold. Hardly enough to make any significant difference."

"How close were the races?" I asked. "If a horse that tested positive won by a nose, are we then open to a legal challenge from the one that finished second."

"But it would also have had methylphenidate in its system."

"Can we be sure of that? Most of the horses that finished second weren't tested. And we know that at least three were clear of the drug."

Stephen Kohli was dispatched to get a record of all the Cheltenham results.

"Now," said the chairman, "while we wait for Stephen, can we have a report on yesterday's events at Fontwell Park?"

"Ten people total were made ill," Howard said. "Two of those were the stipendiary stewards appointed for the day and both were taken to the hospital with severe dehydration."

Nobody liked to ask for the finer details of why they had become dehydrated.

"What was the source?" Ian Tulloch asked.

"We don't have the results back yet, but it would appear that it was something in one of the salads that was served for lunch in the stewards' dining room. Remains of the lunch are currently being tested by the Food Standards Agency."

"Was it the same stuff as in the cake at Ascot?" asked Neil Wallinger.

"There wasn't any of the cake left to analyze, but I wouldn't be surprised. The symptoms were the same."

"You think it was the same man?" asked George Searle.

"We can't be sure," Howard replied, "but I think it would be too much of a coincidence if it wasn't."

There were more nods of agreement from all around the table.

"How easy is it to get poison?" Neil Wallinger asked. "Don't you have to sign a register or something?"

"Maybe you do for arsenic, or something like that, but lots of other things are poisonous," I said. "Everyone knows that eating just a couple of deadly nightshade berries can be fatal, but there are many more readily available poisons. Red kidney beans are highly toxic if eaten raw, and elderberries can kill you as well, to say nothing of toadstools and other fungi, most of which are lethal. The army instructs soldiers in survival techniques and part of the training is given over to foraging for food, in particular what you can eat safely and what you can't."

"Are you suggesting that this man has been a soldier?" asked Bill Ripley.

"No, not necessarily," I said. "Anyone can find out about poisons easily enough on the Internet. All I really suspect is he's a racing insider and that maybe there is hyperactivity in his family."

I was ready for any reaction, but there was none. Not even a flicker. Was I wrong? Or had the person been ready for it and been able to control his emotions? Perhaps it was only on the first occasion, when the individual was unprepared, that it had produced such an effect.

"And I reckon it is the same man who has been doping horses in their home stables as well," I said. "You may recall that the trainer Matthew Unwin was disqualified for eight years in January after some of the horses in his care tested positive for a banned stimulant. Crispin Larson and I are now of the opinion that his claim that someone else drugged the horses was probably true. Of course you also know that Unwin killed Jordan Furness at Cheltenham on Champion Hurdle Day. He is currently in Long Lartin Prison awaiting trial for murder and I'm trying to arrange to visit him."

"For what purpose?" asked Neil Wallinger.

"I want to ask him why he thinks Jordan Furness had something to do with the doping. That's what he's apparently told the police. I know it's a long shot but we seem to be up against a brick wall at the moment."

"Yes," said Ian Tulloch. "And what are we going to do about it? We simply can't afford for this man to go on disrupting race meetings."

"We should pay him," I said.

All the eyes in the room swiveled around in my direction.

"You've changed your tune," Piers Pottinger remarked. "Why the sudden conversion?"

"This has been going on now for a month," I said, "and we're no nearer finding out who's responsible. He's always been one step ahead of us. He poisons the drinking water so we introduce the trucks, so instead he poisons the jockeys. We put systems in place to stop that, but he then sabotages the track. And now he's got at the stewards. He's been leading us in a right merry dance and, as a result, the BHA is imploding round us. Perhaps it is time for a different approach before it's too late."

"But can we afford to pay?" Howard said. "And there's no guarantee that doing so will make him stop. That policeman made it quite clear that he thought we were fools for paying anything."

"Exactly," said Ian Tulloch. "And raising that amount of cash is not that easy. Could we even do it again?"

"You originally said that the upper limit was half a million," Crispin said. "So far, we have paid only a fifth of that."

"I agree that we should try something," said Bill Ripley. "Maybe paying him is the right thing to do."

"What I can't understand," said Charles Payne, "is how this man could make use of such a large amount of cash anyway. Money-laundering regulations are so tight these days that it's almost impossible to pay for anything with readies." He sounded as if he had tried.

"Casinos," I said. "Or a dodgy Indian diamond dealer."

"What about them?" he asked.

"Many casinos will take cash and ask no questions. Just buy fifty or a hundred thousand quid's worth of chips, sit at a table and play with only a fraction of that, then cash out at the end for a check or direct payment into his bank account. Easy. And even if you can't do it in this country anymore, you certainly can in Egypt or Lebanon where the high rollers and superrich Arabs go to gamble and where fifty or a hundred thousand is regarded as mere small change."

"And the diamond dealers?" asked Charles Payne.

"It doesn't have to be diamonds," I said. "Any commodity will do. And it's the purchase contract that's important, not the actual stones. You pay cash to an Indian broker in Wembley for a contract to buy diamonds and then those contracts are 'sold' in India. The diamonds never actually exist. It's just a ruse to get money out of India because the Indian government has tight control of the movement of their currency. You pay a hundred thousand in cash to the guy in Wembley and end up with a transfer of ninety thousand into your bank account from India as a legitimate diamond trader and, presto, the dirty money is now clean, minus the broker's commission. They are always desperate for sterling cash to pay out to the Indian community living here in exchange for rupees received back home. No questions would be asked."

Nine sets of eyes were staring at me.

"How on earth do you know all this?" Charles Payne asked.

"It's my job," I said. "Finding the villains and cheats is dead easy if you can find their money. Some of them will even pay tax on the profit from their so-called diamond dealing. But it's all a scheme to launder hot cash, and ending up with fifty or sixty percent of it as clean money is worth it."

Stephen Kohli came back into the boardroom.

"Of the twenty-seven races at this year's Festival," he said, "remarkably only one had a photo finish to decide the winner. That was the last race on the Wednesday, the bumper, where the winner won by a head. There were a few other photos to determine minor placings and a dead heat for third in the Kim Muir."

"Could this methyl stuff have affected the result in the bumper?" Ian asked.

"It's unlikely," said Crispin, "but we can't be sure."

"We'll have to take a chance on that," Ian said. "Howard, issue a press release stating the facts and announcing that no action will be taken concerning the results at Cheltenham, all of which will stand. But there is no need to mention that the contamination of the water supply was deliberate."

"Why not?" Neil Wallinger said. "Why not give them the whole truth? Why not tell the public what is really going on? If the police won't help us, then maybe the public will."

That interjection, while sensible, was not particularly helpful for my cunning plan.

"Won't that undermine our authority?" said Bill Ripley.

"I agree," said Charles Payne. "What we need to do is

to catch this man. Simply telling the press everything will make the clamor for the demise of the BHA and a return to the Jockey Club even louder. I'm all for telling the press as little as possible. Horrible people. Treat them like mushrooms, that's what I always say."

"'Mushrooms'?" said Howard.

"Keep them in the dark and feed them shit."

Nobody laughed, and Charles Payne blushed slightly in embarrassment.

"We all agree that we have to stop this man," I said. "And, to that end, we must reestablish a two-way dialogue. The alternative is to just sit and wait for him to disrupt things again. Do we really want the Guineas meeting abandoned next month? Then it will be the Derby and Royal Ascot the month after." I looked around at the glum faces. "Is anyone checking the mail now that Roger Vincent is no longer round to receive it?"

"Yes," said Crispin, "I am. The last letter to arrive was on Wednesday. He demanded another million pounds to stop his activities."

"Ridiculous," said Ian Tulloch dismissively. "The man's a fool."

"I fear he is far from a fool," said Howard Lever. "Otherwise, we wouldn't be in this mess."

"Do I have your authority to place another announcement in *The Times*?" I asked.

"Saying what?" asked Ian Tulloch.

"Maybe offering another payment in return for an assurance to stop his disruption."

"I can't think that would do any good," said Neil Wallinger. "Any assurance given by this man wouldn't be worth a tinker's damn."

"But we have to do *something*," I said. "What else do you suggest?"

Neil Wallinger looked at me for a moment, then shrugged his shoulders.

"How much?" asked Ian Tulloch.

"Enough to stop the disruption," I said, "even if it's not all he wants."

"Can we raise another hundred thousand in cash?" Ian Tulloch asked of no one in particular.

"I'm sure it could be done," Howard Lever replied, "provided we have a few days' notice."

"I'm not saying that I'll agree to pay it," Ian Tulloch said, "but let's make the contact and the necessary preparations just in case."

And so it was left, with no questions of accountability raised, at least not while I was in the boardroom, although the chairman had individual meetings with Howard Lever and the other Board members for the rest of the afternoon.

"Did you get what you wanted?" Crispin asked when we returned to his office.

"Partially," I said. "There was no reaction I could see to my comment concerning hyperactivity, but there is the possibility of another drop."

"I also watched the others when you mentioned it, but I couldn't see or feel any reaction either."

"Stephen Kohli wasn't there when I said it."

"You can't think that Stephen is involved," Crispin said. "I've known him for years."

"Has he got a hyperactive child?"

"Not that I'm aware of," said Crispin. "I don't know much about his private life."

I wasn't surprised. Both Crispin and Stephen were incredibly secretive about anything that was not to do with work, not that they were particularly forthcoming about work matters either.

"Where does he live?" I asked.

"Somewhere in north London. Finchley, I think."

"Perhaps I should pay him a visit."

Crispin shook his head. "I'm sure you're wrong there. I may not get on especially well with him, but I can't think he has anything to do with this."

"Then who on the Board would you say has?"

He thought for a moment. "None of them. You must be wrong. What have they got to gain?"

"The money, for a start," I said.

"But the press have been pretty unkind about all them. Why would anyone want to damage his own reputation like that?"

It was a good question.

"Perhaps the money is the incentive," I said.

"But all of them have mountains of money already."

Did they? Perhaps I would look at that too.

29

I spent half an hour on the phone trying to convince a woman at *The Times* that it was imperative that I place an announcement into their Saturday edition.

"I told you, you're too late," she said. "It will have to now be Monday."

"This is an emergency," I said. "Is there not a late-entry fee? You won't have gone to press yet."

"But the editor has made up the page," she said.

"Surely you can squeeze one more in," I pleaded.

"I'll try," she said, "but I'll not promise anything. What is the announcement?"

"Van Gogh offers Leonardo a further payment in exchange for a quiet life."

"That doesn't sound much like an emergency to me," said the woman.

I used my most sincere tone of voice. "Trust me, it is."

She wasn't very keen but she agreed to try to get it in the Saturday paper if she could and took what I thought to be an excessive fee from my credit card for the privilege. Even so, I didn't hold out much hope that it would appear before Monday.

AFTER LEAVING the BHA offices, I took the Tube to Kensington to see my ex–army friend at the spy-gadget shop.

"Night vision goggles?" he said. "Sure, I've got those, although they're not really goggles as such. And they're not cheap."

"Nothing here is cheap," I said with a smile.

But a hundred thousand pounds wasn't cheap either.

He showed me a top-of-the-range night vision monocular. It looked like half of the pair of small binoculars and it attached to a harness that held it in place, hands-free, over the right eye.

"You need only one eye covered. Your brain sorts out the image. The other eye is then clear in case you get a bright light coming on."

"Would that harm the eye looking through the sight?"

"Not at all. The image intensifier shuts down instantly if it's in bright light. I tell you, this is the best night vision available. Made by the same people who make night vision equipment for army helicopter pilots. There's usually enough ambient light from stars and stuff if you're outside, but this has also got an infrared illuminator for when it's completely dark."

He pushed a switch and a tiny red light came on next to the eyepiece.

"Come and check it out in my storeroom."

We went into his storeroom, which had no windows. He closed the door and switched off the light, plunging the room into total darkness. I placed the monocular against my eye and was amazed that I could see everything, albeit in black and white, overlaid with a slightly green tinge.

"Good, isn't it?" said my friend.

"Amazing. I'll take it."

We went back into the shop and I waited while my friend turned the device off and put everything back in the box.

"Still checking on the little lady, then, are we?" he said. "On her nighttime excursions?"

"Something like that."

He laughed as he too charged an exorbitant amount to my credit card.

"It's guaranteed for a year," he said, handing me a plastic bag containing the box.

So it should be, at that price.

I STOOD in the tube station ticket hall debating with myself whether I should take the train north towards home or south to Richmond.

It was four-thirty on a Friday afternoon. Lydia always worked late on Fridays, something about more people wanting to view apartments after work on a Friday than on any other day. She wouldn't be home before seven at the earliest.

Richmond won. Easily.

"Hello, little bro," Faye said, opening her front door. She didn't express the enthusiasm that usually greeted my arrival, and there was something about her manner that worried me.

"Are you OK?" I asked with concern.

"Ha!" she said with a hollow laugh. "Am I OK? No, I'm not OK. I've got cancer, so I'm not bloody OK." She began to cry.

I was rather shocked. I had assumed she was coping well.

"Come on," I said, stepping inside the house and putting my arm around her shoulders, "let's get you a drink."

"Good idea," she said. "I could really do with a drink."

I'd meant a cup of tea or coffee, but Faye went to the fridge and poured herself a large glass of white wine.

"White OK? It's all I have."

"White is fine," I said.

She poured a second glass and handed it to me. I took a small sip while Faye gulped down a mouthful.

"Have you had some bad news?" I asked carefully. "About the cancer?"

She took a Kleenex from the box on the counter and blew her nose.

"No, nothing like that. No bad news. Everything's fine. I'm sorry." She dabbed at her eyes with another tissue.

"There's no need for you to be sorry," I said. "Everything is clearly not fine. So talk to me."

She took some deep breaths.

"I am fine," she said, smiling. "Really I am. I just sometimes have minor bouts of depression about my own mortality, that's all. You caught me in the middle of one. I'll be OK now."

"Are you sure?"

"Absolutely," she said. "Especially after this."

She held up her glass and took another generous swig of her wine.

"Do you want to talk about it?" I asked.

"There's nothing to talk about. I don't want to die and the prospect depresses me. It's silly, I know. The operation was a success, and the damn chemo should do the rest, but . . . suddenly you realize that your life won't go on forever and it's quite a shock."

There was nothing to say so I gave her a hug instead.

"Thank you," she said, "I needed that. Now, how are you and Lydia?"

"We're fine," I said. "Busy as always."

"You need to make more time for each other."

"I know. You told me on Wednesday."

"Are things any better?"

"Things were never really that bad," I said. "It was more my state of mind rather than anything tangible about our relationship. And, yes, things are better in that department. Let's just say I might be coming through my midlife crisis."

"Midlife crisis! Don't make me laugh. You're only thirty. Your midlife crisis is still a long way off. That only occurs when you buy a sports car or you start wearing designer jeans and funny hats."

She clearly hadn't seen my brown woolen beanie.

"How's Quentin?" I asked.

"Same as ever," she said, "although he seems slightly less stressed this week. He even came home from chambers early yesterday afternoon. He's not normally home until eight or nine at the earliest. He damn near caught me."

"Doing what? Sleeping with the garden boy?"

"Chance would be a fine thing," she said, laughing. "Our garden boy is pushing eighty. No, nothing like that. Kenneth had been here to see me."

"Ah," I said.

There must have been something in my tone.

"You *knew*!" she said suddenly.

"I knew that he might come to see you," I said. "I suggested it."

"Do you also know that he's gay?"

"Yes," I said.

"Poor boy is terrified at what Quentin will say and with good reason. Quentin is not wholly enamored of gays."

"According to Ken, that's an understatement. He says that Quentin would happily castrate them all."

"Quentin will just have to learn to live with it," Faye

said. "But I think it's Kenneth not wanting to be a lawyer that he will hate more. He's been set on it for so long."

"So Ken told you that as well."

"He told me everything—about the party, the drugs, the police raid on his flat—everything. It was quite an eye-opener, I can tell you. The poor boy was in tears for most of the day. It all just spilled out of him."

I wondered if he'd also told her about his visit to the Soho gym, but I decided not to ask.

"Did he tell you that he'll probably not now have to face trial?"

"Yes. And also that it was all because of you." She held up her hands. "I don't want to know how you managed it, but thank you anyway."

"Does Quentin know?"

"That Kenneth's gay? No, not yet. I'll have to choose the right time to tell him. I'll also have to pick my moment to give him the news that Kenneth intends leaving the law. That could be trickier."

"He asked me if I would tell his father for him, but I said no. I told him he'd have to do that for himself."

"But it might be better if I did it," Faye said seriously. "Quentin can sometimes overreact and say things he'll later regret."

"Rather you than me. He'll go nuts."

"Quentin will do exactly as he's told," she said firmly. "He always does in the end."

I was surprised. I hadn't realized that it was my sister Faye who really wore the pants in this house.

I TOOK an Overground train from Richmond to Willesden Junction and then walked the last hundred yards or so towards the flat in Spezia Road. The sky had turned very dark and large raindrops were beginning to bounce off the sidewalk around me. I turned the collar of my suit jacket up to stop the water running down my neck and hurried on.

I had spent rather longer with Faye than I had expected, talking about nothing in particular but trying to avoid the topics of mortality and sexuality.

"Hadn't you better get home?" Faye had said as she'd emptied the last few drops from our second bottle of sauvignon blanc. "You don't want to upset Lydia now that your midlife crisis is over." She had giggled and then drained her glass.

"You're drunk," I'd said accusingly.

"So are you." She'd giggled again. "And it's so much more enjoyable than being dead."

I turned into Spezia Road as the rain began to fall harder and I started to hurry even more. I should have taken my raincoat, I thought, or an umbrella. This wouldn't be doing my best suit any good at all.

In fact, it was probably the rain that saved me because it made me run.

I darted out between two parked vehicles, crossing the road directly towards my front door.

I didn't notice the car until it was almost upon me, by which time it was too late to avoid being hit. It raced up

Spezia Road at high speed and caught my hip with a glancing blow from its right front fender, sending me cartwheeling across the sidewalk and into the red-brick garden wall topped with an iron railing that belonged to my neighbor.

I ended up lying flat on my back on the cold ground, trying to catch my breath, as the rain continued to hammer down both on and around me.

My breath quickly returned, but excruciating pain tagged along for the ride.

I thought it was my left shoulder that was the worst, but the whole of my body seemed to hurt.

Come on, I said to myself, you can't lie here all night in the rain. Move.

But moving was agony. Every muscle contraction hurt, with all nerves seemingly leading to my shoulder. Even breathing was painful.

I gritted my teeth and sat up, cradling my left wrist in my right hand.

It was not a great improvement.

I looked down. My left hand was wet from the rain, but there was something else about it that worried me more. My whole lower arm was in a strange position, with my palm turned out and the thumb pointing down at an unnatural angle.

Damn it, I thought, it's broken.

I tried shouting.

"Help! Help!"

Nothing happened. No one came.

I tried to shout again, but it hurt so much that my

cries were little more than a whisper. The rain drumming on the garbage cans in my neighbor's front garden was making more noise.

I sat very still, and gradually the pain subsided from a totally debilitating 10 to a merely agonizing 9.

Meanwhile, I was getting cold.

The rain had completely soaked my clothes right down to the skin. Jumping fully clothed into a swimming pool could not have made me more wet.

April was not the coldest month of the year, but, at half past eight in the evening, it was proving to be quite cold enough and I had begun to shiver uncontrollably. It may have been due to the cold, or maybe to the shock, or probably a bit of both, but it certainly did nothing to ease the severe ache that had gripped me right across my upper body.

Still no one came. Anyone sensible was sheltering from the weather, not sitting in an ever-deepening puddle on a suburban street becoming hypothermic while waiting for nonexistent rescuers to arrive.

The very last trace of daylight faded away into total darkness, with only the streetlight down the road providing any useful illumination. I looked at the plastic bag lying beside me that still contained the night vision monocular and wished it was a hot-water bottle.

I needed to do something or else I would die here of the cold just ten small steps from my own front door.

I decided to stand up, using my right hand to pull on my neighbor's railing. The plan seemed to be fine in principle but not so good in execution. It required me to let go of my left wrist, which gravity then caused to hang down unsupported as I rose.

I screamed and swayed precariously as a wave of nausea and dizziness swept over me. I steadied myself and again took my left hand in my right, which improved the situation slightly.

Those ten small steps took me a good five minutes, but I made it.

Finally, I leaned my head against the doorbell and kept it there.

Lydia opened the door with thunder in her eyes that turned to instant shock and concern.

"Oh my God!" she said. "What happened?"

"I was hit by a car," I croaked, removing my forehead from the bell.

She steered me in through the front door and into our front room, where I perched on the arm of the sofa.

"I'm calling an ambulance," she said, running off to find her phone in the kitchen.

I didn't complain. An ambulance sounded just fine to me.

"It's on the way," she said, coming back. "Just a few minutes."

I was still shaking with cold, so Lydia went to fetch the duvet from our bed and draped it around me. The weight of it on my left shoulder sent more spasms of pain shooting up into my neck, but the shivering diminished.

"What happened?" she asked again. "Where's the car?"

That was a good question.

The car hadn't stopped. And, thinking back, I was

sure that it hadn't had any lights on despite the heavy rain and the gloom of a wet April evening in northwest London.

The more I thought about it, the more certain I became.

Someone had just tried to kill me.

30

According to one of the green-uniformed paramedics who arrived with the ambulance, my left arm wasn't broken. It was my shoulder that had dislocated.

"It's more painful than a break," he said.

Tell me about it.

The ambulance took me to the Emergency Room at Northwick Park Hospital, where I was forced to sit in a wheelchair and wait for over an hour while the trauma team dealt with a motorcyclist and his passenger who had come off their bike and used their heads as brakes.

Lydia had come with me in the ambulance and she now sat next to me on a metal chair, muttering about how disgraceful it was that I had to wait so long.

"How much longer?" I asked one of the passing nurses. "It bloody hurts."

"But it won't kill you," she replied. "I'm sorry, but there are others who need us more at the moment."

There was no arguing with that, so we waited in silence along with a whole host of other sick and injured members of humanity. Nine-thirty on a Friday evening was a busy time in the E.R.

A uniformed policeman came into the unit and went over to the reception before making a beeline to me.

"Mr. Hinkley?" he asked.

"Yes," I said.

"The paramedics called me. They told me you claim to have been injured in a road traffic accident. Is that correct?"

"Yes," I said. "I was hit by a car on the road outside my house."

The policeman removed a notebook from his pocket and sat down on the chair next to me.

"Did you speak to the driver?" he asked.

"No," I said. "The driver didn't stop. In fact, I believe the driver tried to run me down on purpose."

That grabbed his interest. And Lydia's as well.

"Why do you think that?"

"Well, for a start, because he didn't stop. And I don't remember the car having any lights even though it was quite dark. The driver just drove straight at me without slowing. In fact, he was still accelerating as he hit me."

The policeman leaned towards me slightly and sniffed.

"Mr. Hinkley," he said, "have you been drinking?"

EVENTUALLY someone came and wheeled me to a treatment room, but not before my notion of being an attempted murder victim had been completely trashed by the policeman.

"Perhaps the driver just didn't see you in the rain as you ran straight out in front of him."

He made it sound as if it were my fault.

I suspected that he didn't even believe I'd been hit by a car in the first place. I could tell from his attitude—he thought I'd had too much to drink and had simply fallen over in the street, dislocating my shoulder.

Maybe he was right about the first bit—I probably had drunk too much—but I still knew exactly what had happened. And I was convinced that it had been deliberate.

I had a developing bruise on my hip to prove it.

I SCREAMED a bit more, but, eventually, a doctor managed to get the ball at the top end of my humerus to slide back into its socket. It did with an audible clunk and, magically, it switched off the pain.

From being in agony one moment, I was almost completely free of pain in the next. The relief was amazing and made me feel quite light-headed, although that might have had something to do with the bottle of sauvignon blanc that was still sloshing around in my system somewhere.

"You'll have to keep that arm in a sling for a while," the doctor said. "The joint will be loose and the tendons need time to recover or it will be out again. And it will ache a bit for the next few days. Take some painkillers."

An ache I could cope with, and I'd happily keep it in a sling—anything to prevent it dislocating again.

"Do you really think someone ran you down on purpose?" Lydia asked as we were in the taxi on our way home from the hospital.

"Yes," I said.

"That policeman didn't really believe you."

"He didn't believe me at all," I said. "But it's true nevertheless."

"But why would anyone do that deliberately?"

Why indeed?

Was it just some maniac intent on hitting any random pedestrian or had I, Jeff Hinkley, been specifically targeted?

If it were the latter, then who would want me dead?

Leonardo?

How could he have known where I lived? He clearly hadn't followed me today as I'd come home by train and he'd been in a car, but it didn't mean he hadn't followed me on another day.

Lydia and I were not in the phone book and we had chosen not to include our address in the public register of voters.

Sure, the BHA knew where I lived, it would be on file in the personnel department and also in finance, but I didn't think it was general knowledge among the staff.

Not that finding someone's address was really that difficult, I knew. I'd obtained lots of people's addresses without their knowledge or permission.

These days, one's address is part of one's identity. You

are required to provide it to get anything from a credit card to a driver's license, an income tax form to a drug prescription. Any form of insurance requires a home address, to say nothing of vehicle registration, online purchases or almost any other financial transaction.

One is constantly being asked to provide a utility bill for everything from opening a bank account to obtaining a library card. Solely for someone to record your address.

New money-laundering regulations have, bizarrely, made it easier for the unscrupulous few to gain previously private information about the law-abiding many, placing them at greater, not less, risk of identity theft, deception and fraud.

And it wasn't as if Jefferson Roosevelt Hinkley was a common name like John Smith or Harry Jones with which one could hide among the throng.

Anyone who was capable of disrupting racing as effectively as Leonardo would have been able to find out where I lived in a heartbeat.

But why take the risk of being spotted? As it was, I hadn't seen the make or color of the car, but I could have, especially if it hadn't been raining. Surely the risks involved outweighed any potential gain.

And what did he have to gain by having me dead?

Only that I would stop investigating. So what was it that I was doing that made it important enough to kill me?

I was still pondering those questions when we arrived back in Spezia Road and I insisted on having a good look around before getting out of the taxi.

Lydia and I made it safely to our front door and I checked it was properly locked behind us, rattling the door just to make sure. My sudden security concerns were making Lydia nervous.

"Do you really think someone hit you on purpose?" she asked again.

"Yes."

"But they'd have hit anyone, right? You just happened to be in the wrong place at the wrong time."

"I'm not sure, but I don't think so, no."

The implications of what I'd just said slowly registered and Lydia's eyes widened with fear.

"Are you telling me that someone tried explicitly to murder *you*?"

"Yes."

"Why?"

Such a short question with such a long answer.

"I don't know. Obviously, I am doing something they don't like."

"What?"

"I wish I knew. Then I'd do more of it."

"You're mad," Lydia said without any humor. "You must go to the police."

"You saw what that achieved at the hospital. That policeman didn't believe a single word I said."

"Then go and see someone more senior."

Would it make any difference? I couldn't describe the car, not even its color, so what would the police have to go on? A car with a slight dent or scratch on its right front fender? There must be thousands of those, if not tens of thousands. And would they provide me with a twenty-four-hour bodyguard? Not a chance. They didn't have the resources.

"I'll be careful," I said. "No dark alleys or lonely parking lots."

I smiled at her, but it didn't appear to reassure, not that I didn't appreciate her concern.

"Come on," I said, "it's late. Let's go to bed."

Going to bed was one thing. Going to sleep was quite another.

My aching left shoulder, together with my arm in the sling, prevented me from lying on my left side or on my tummy, as I normally did, and, in spite of the painkillers, the bruise on my hip ruled out lying on my right side. The most comfortable position, I discovered, was lying on my back, almost sitting up, with my head and shoulders supported by a stack of pillows.

Between snatches of uneasy dozing, I thought back to exactly what had happened earlier, trying to recall any minor detail I might have missed.

I remembered running down the sidewalk and then out between two cars parked on the far side of the road, opposite our front door. I must have instinctively glanced each way up and down the road to check it was clear, even though I couldn't recall actually doing so. But I would never forget the total shock and disbelief that had accompanied my last-second awareness of the speeding car.

I tried hard to think what had made me realize it was there. I knew that I had been aware of it fractionally before it hit me, long enough for me to register that a collision was inevitable. Perhaps it was the roaring noise of the engine. Or maybe some slight movement in my peripheral vision.

Try as I might, I couldn't recall anything about the car other than it hadn't slowed down and seemed to be accelerating. That must have been due to the constantly rising note of the engine.

However, I could vividly remember being tossed to one side by the impact, my legs being thrown up while my head went down.

In that moment, as I'd hurtled face-first towards the concrete, I had thought undeniably that I was going to die.

It is said that one's whole life flashes before your eyes in that moment of realization of imminent death.

But that didn't happen to me.

Far from being from the past, it was images of the future, and what I would be missing, that had materialized in my head: my wedding day, with Lydia walking down the aisle dressed exquisitely in white; the birth of a son; living in the country with a houseful of dogs and children playing in the garden.

They had seemed so real, so clear.

Was my subconscious trying to tell me something?

I reached out with my right hand and touched the delightfully naked form of Lydia lying fast asleep beside me. I softly stroked her arm and shoulder with my fingertips and thanked my lucky stars that I hadn't died.

Yes indeed, it was high time I made an honest woman of her.

THE VISITATION ORDER arrived from Long Lartin Prison in the mail on Saturday morning as Lydia and I were having breakfast in our kitchen.

Wow! I thought. That was quick.

I had only sent in the request on Thursday and had imagined it would take several weeks to be processed.

I immediately called the visitor's booking number on the VO and was told that due to a cancellation, there was an available slot at two o'clock on the following afternoon. I took it.

"What was all that about?" Lydia asked.

"I have to go to prison tomorrow."

"Permanently?"

"On a visit."

"Who to see? Should I bake a file into a cake for you to take with you?"

"I'm going to see a man called Matthew Unwin. He killed that bookmaker at Cheltenham last month."

The humor drained out of her face.

"Is that wise?" she said. "Please do be careful."

"I'm sure it will be quite safe. He has agreed to see me."

"Maybe only because he wants to kill you too."

It wasn't him that I was worried about.

31

The lady at *The Times* had failed me dismally, as the announcement in the personal column failed to appear in the Saturday edition. I wasn't particularly surprised. And, the way I felt, I didn't particularly care.

I spent the afternoon drugged up with painkillers, lying on the sofa in my front room, watching the racing on the television and wondering how I was going to get to Long Lartin in Worcestershire the following afternoon.

My shoulder ached badly and I certainly didn't fancy driving, even though, theoretically, I could have done it if I'd rented a car with an automatic gearbox. But I was too sore for that.

I thought of asking Lydia to drive me there, but she

had a long-standing commitment to go with her parents to visit her grandmother in Kent.

In the end, I decided to take the train from Paddington to Evesham and get a taxi from there.

I watched on the TV as a horse trained by Duncan Johnson won the second race at Ayr, the Future Champions Novices' Chase.

Duncan Johnson. He was someone else I needed to talk to.

What connected Matthew Unwin, Duncan Johnson and Richard Young, other than they had all claimed that someone had demanded money not to dope their horses? And how about Graham Perry? Where did he fit into this jigsaw puzzle?

Ian Tulloch had horses in training with both Duncan Johnson and Richard Young. I wondered if he had any connection to Matthew Unwin. If he had, it was something I'd not come across when I'd carried out the background check before Ian Tulloch had joined the BHA Board. Not that it would have been a problem—Matthew Unwin had been considered a respectable member of the racing family prior to his horses testing positive for Dexedrine, in spite of his previous warning for administering Lasix.

But had Tulloch had any dealings with Unwin since his appointment to the BHA Board?

Next I speculated as to whether either of Ian Tulloch's two teenage daughters had ever been treated for hyperactivity.

How could I find out? Medical records were notoriously difficult to obtain legally, although I had a journalist friend who had claimed in the past that he could get them—for a hefty fee, mind, as bribery was involved.

I was tempted to telephone the Tulloch family home and claim to be from a hyperactive support group to see if there was any reaction, but even I balked at such an invasion of their privacy. After all, Ian Tulloch was now chairman of the BHA, head of the organization for which I worked.

I watched the big event of the afternoon, the Scottish Grand National from Ayr, more in dread that there would be another disruptive episode rather than in interest at which horse would win, but the race passed off without incident.

Duncan Johnson's fancied runner finished second to a horse owned and trained by a very happy-looking farmer from the Scottish Highlands who could hardly talk due to his excitement.

And at a price of fifty-to-one!

I smiled at the farmer's ruddy-faced image shown on the television, his huge grin stretching almost from one side of the screen to the other.

It was such moments that were essential elements to the success and popularity of jump racing. The fact that a part-time Scottish farmer could do it gave others hope that they too might one day own the winner of a great race. The anticipation of such a victory kept many racehorse owners paying out hefty training fees for years in its pursuit.

After the trophy presentation to the still-grinning farmer, there followed a part of the program addressing the future of British racing.

One of horseracing's most respected reporters pulled no punches in his criticism of the current system, citing the recent disruptions to racing as evidence of "the rife ineptitude and incompetence of those individuals at the top." He went on to imply that a return to stability could only be achieved by the sweeping away altogether of the BHA and the reestablishment of the Jockey Club in its rightful place.

I felt that the whole world must have gone mad.

Only ten years previously, the same reporter had used identical rhetoric in his argument for the demise of the Jockey Club as the sport's regulator and for the creation of a new, independent authority.

But he was only echoing what had already been written elsewhere in the press, in what seemed to me to be coordinated manipulation of the media.

Where was this story coming from? And why?

The very name *Jockey Club* was a misnomer, as not a single current or former professional jockey had ever been admitted to its ranks as a member. Professional jockeys were simply not considered to be from the right class. Sir Gordon Richards, the greatest British flat jockey of all time, was eventually made an honorary, but nonvoting, member, and then only after he'd been champion jockey twenty-three times and had been knighted by the Queen.

Did racing really want to go back to a system that had

garnered so much criticism for being elitist and self-serving?

I simply couldn't believe it.

IT WAS difficult to imagine that over six hundred of the most evil and dangerous criminals in the country were housed behind the high walls of Long Lartin Prison, set as it was in the glorious open countryside of the Vale of Evesham, an area of outstanding natural beauty where much of the country's fruit and vegetables were grown in the fertile soils of the River Avon floodplain.

However, the natural beauty ended at the prison walls. Even for the visitors.

There were about thirty of us waiting in the visitors' center. Most of the others were women, some of them with small children in tow. I'd seen some of them on the train from London but hadn't realized they were going to the same place.

I had my driver's license closely checked against the name on the visitation order and was then required to leave my phone, most of my money, my watch and even my belt in a locker before passing through a metal detector, being patted down in a body search and then sniffed at by a drug dog.

Only when all the visitors were finally declared clear of contraband were we taken through to the visiting area, a bleak, gray-painted room with three rows of gray metal tables and chairs that were all bolted to a sky blue vinyl floor. Even though there were two small heavily barred windows at one end, the room was mainly lit by banks of overhead fluorescent tubes that gave everything a rather stark and cold appearance.

There was a small table on one side that provided tea and coffee in plastic cups and there were two vending machines for sodas and snacks in the far corner.

I allowed the other visitors to choose first in case I took one of their "usual" places and then selected an empty table close to the tea and coffee.

A door opened at the far end and the prisoners came streaming through, some in gray T-shirts and gray track-suit-style pants, one or two in green-and-yellow coveralls and the rest, including Matthew Unwin, in jeans with various colored tops. Two burly prison officers accompanied them into the room, one standing at either end, as the men made their way to the tables to greet their friends and relatives.

Matthew Unwin had the look of a broken man. His eyes seemed deep set in their sockets and there were dark bags under them as if he hadn't slept for a week.

He spotted me and ambled over, his body language shouting his lack of enthusiasm.

"Hi," he said.

I stood up and offered my hand. "I thought you might not know me." I had been in disguise at Cheltenham on the day of his arrest.

"I know you," he said without taking my hand. "You were at my inquiry."

He sat down on the metal chair opposite. I sat back down as well.

"How are things?" I asked, leaning forward and speaking quietly, conscious of the others around us.

"How would you expect them to be? I survive."

"Tea?" I asked. "Or coffee?"

"Tea," he said.

I went over to the table and collected a plastic cupful of hot brown liquid in exchange for fifty pence.

Unwin lifted the cup and sipped at its contents, never taking his eyes off me.

"What do you want?" he said.

"To know why you attacked Jordan Furness."

"Have the police sent you?"

"No," I said.

"Then why are you here?"

"You said at the inquiry that someone else gave your horses drugs because you wouldn't pay them." He nodded. "I now believe you."

He stared at me without saying anything.

"Was it Jordan Furness?" I asked.

"What difference would it make if it was?"

It was like trying to get blood from a stone. Every one of my questions was answered with another question.

"I'm trying to help you," I said.

"Why?"

"I'm trying to find out who doped your horses."

"Why?"

"Because I believe that the same man is behind all the disruption currently going on in racing. You must have heard about it even in here."

He nodded. I hadn't intended telling him that so openly, but I was getting nowhere otherwise.

"When did you last see Graham Perry?" I asked.

"Why do you want to know?"

"Wasn't he once your assistant trainer?"

"He was. Then he took off and left me in the lurch." There was no affection whatsoever in his voice. "I never see him now away from the races."

Two young children began running around and around the room between the tables, shouting and screaming. They had obviously quickly become bored with visiting their father, who was one of those wearing green-and-yellow coveralls. No one made any move to stop or quiet the children until their father suddenly bellowed loudly at them to shut up and sit down, raising his hand as he did. They immediately sat down on the floor, gripping their knees tightly to their chests and with their heads down. I thought it was an action born out of fear, but it didn't keep them sitting still for very long. They soon returned to their game of chase, albeit without the shouting and screaming.

Meanwhile, everyone else went back to talking, but more quietly.

"Was it Furness who doped your horses?" I asked.

Matthew Unwin stared at me again.

"Why should I help you?" he said. "What has the BHA ever done for me other than taking away my life?"

"Why did you agree to see me, then?" I asked.

"Anything to alleviate the boredom," he said miserably.

I began to think I'd wasted my time coming here. I felt a bit like these wretched children—running around in circles and getting nowhere.

"It wasn't the BHA that murdered Jordon Furness, you know," I said, "it was you."

"Little shit had it coming to him." He said it with real venom in his voice.

"Why?" I asked.

"Because he was greedy," Unwin said.

"Did you owe him money?"

He shook his head. "It was him that owed *me* money. Refused to pay his training fees, didn't he?"

"I hadn't realized that Jordan Furness was one of your owners."

"Not officially," he said. "Wouldn't have passed your lot's fit-and-proper-person test, now would he? Not that one. Far too many skeletons to find in his closet."

"So who was the registered owner?"

"I was. But the horse ran on Furness's orders."

"Winning or losing?"

"Losing, I reckon—but I knew nothing about it. All I know is, the horse never won a race when I thought it could have."

"What was the horse's name?" I asked.

He laughed. "Criminal Intent. I'm not kidding. It was called that when we bought it. Furness thought it was a huge joke."

"How often did it run?"

"Loads of times. Mostly up north."

"And you're sure Furness arranged that it didn't win?"

"I reckon," he said again. "He must have fixed it with the jock. Or got his bloody son to dope it."

"Lee Furness is his son?"

"Yeah. He worked for me—at least he was meant to. Idle toad. I only took him on because his father insisted and then he didn't pay up. Old Man Furness deserved what he got, if you ask me."

I wasn't sure that I would ask him. Murder seemed rather an extreme measure to settle a training debt. Any sympathy I might have had for Matthew Unwin's situation was rapidly fading away.

"So Furness had nothing to do with the drugs found in your horses?"

He laughed again. "Is that what you think? I suppose he might have done it. I wouldn't put anything past the rat."

I clearly had been barking up the wrong tree. The killing of Jordan Furness had been unrelated to the reason Matthew Unwin had lost his trainer's license.

One of the two noisy children, a girl, age about five, ran over to our table and stopped, staring at me from about two feet away. I stared back at her and she pulled a face. I smiled at her, but there was no smile in return, just a scowl. How sad, I thought. She turned and ran off.

"Have you ever trained horses for Ian Tulloch?" I asked Unwin.

"You must be joking. Tulloch would have never come to me. He's far too much of a snob."

Another dead end.

My left shoulder had started to ache again and the

painkillers I needed were shut away in the locker outside with my other things.

I glanced up at the clock on the wall. It was ten minutes to three and my taxi wasn't booked until half past.

I'd obviously wasted my Sunday afternoon coming here and I was suddenly eager to get out of the oppressive atmosphere in the prison, with its heady bouquet of stale sweat and cheap disinfectant.

I decided to wait for the taxi out in the fresh air.

"I think that will be enough," I said. "I'll be on my way."

"Suit yourself."

I stood up and turned for the door, but I was almost knocked down by the little girl, who was weaving in and out of the tables at high speed in pursuit of her brother.

"Just one last thing," I said, turning back. "Do you happen to know any hyperactive kids, other than these two?"

"Yes," Unwin said. "As a matter of fact, I do."

32

I spent most of Sunday evening and much of the night doing some one-handed research on my computer, logging in remotely to the BHA files and following up on what Matthew Unwin had told me at Long Lartin.

By Monday morning I had obtained just a few snippets of information, most of it conjecture, and nothing much of any real interest.

At nine-thirty, I called my journalist friend at the *London Telegraph*.

"Tim," I said. "I need some medical records."

"No way," he said.

"But you've always boasted you could get them."

"It's become far too dangerous. These days, there are too many high-profile prosecutions for misconduct in a public office. People now go to jail just for passing on a bit of innocent info. Bloody data protection. I could be in deep doo-doo just for asking. Who do you want the records for anyway?"

I told him.

"I thought you meant for some A-list celebrity, an actress or something. You know, like Joss Carder and her bulimia."

There had been a huge outcry the previous year over the release of that particular secret. Even Oscar-nominated stars were entitled to their privacy.

"Was that you?" I asked.

"I couldn't possibly say. But I'm not doing it again."

"So how do I get them?"

"Do you know the doctor?"

"No."

"Then I can't help you, mate. Sorry."

Frustration.

"Perhaps you could help me with something else."

"Is it legal?" he asked.

"Perfectly," I said. "Ask your racing correspondent if he believes there's been any orchestration in the campaign to get rid of the BHA."

"And has there?" he asked.

"I don't know. That's why I'm asking. But it does tend to feel like it."

"I'll get him to give you a call."

"Thanks."

He called me ten minutes later.

"Hi, Jeff, Gordon Tuttle here. How can I help?"

"I know this might sound crazy, but are you aware of

any organized campaign to oust the BHA as the racing regulator?"

He was quiet for a few moments.

"In what way?" he asked.

"Maybe I'm wrong," I said, "but it seemed too much of a coincidence that every one of the national dailies ran the story last Thursday and each expressed exactly the same opinions about the BHA when the rumor broke that Electrode had failed a dope test."

"It was more than just a rumor," Gordon said. "The official BHA press release of Friday afternoon made it clear that what we printed was true. The BHA only issued its press release as a direct result of our story."

"As may be," I said. "You know it's true now, but, at the time, you didn't. But what I'm more interested in is the opinion pieces. They were all extreme and all identical. Don't you think that's rather surprising? You guys hardly ever agree on anything."

"What are you looking for, exactly?" he asked.

"The original factual report about Electrode came from the Press Association. I know that. But are you aware if there was any concerted effort to mold the *Telegraph*'s editorial comment?"

There was another quiet pause at his end.

"Did you write the piece?" I asked.

Another pause.

"Come on, Gordon," I said, "tell me. Off the record, if you like."

"The paper received a document. It had 'Press Briefing' printed across the top."

"Who from?"

"I don't know. It was handed in at the paper's reception desk last Wednesday afternoon. Initially, I thought it was an official release from the BHA, but it obviously wasn't. It had some of the facts, but it was very critical of racing's governance. And it was very convincing."

"Do you still have it?" I asked. "Can I come and have a look?"

"Sure," he said, "anytime. And there was more than one. We received a second release late on Thursday afternoon, telling us that not only Electrode but all the Cheltenham winners had been doped. We were confident enough in the story to run it as an exclusive in Friday's paper."

"I read it," I said. "Do you know where these documents came from?"

"I don't know for sure but I'd guess they're from a whistle-blower within the BHA."

"Why do you say that?"

"Well, for a start, the facts have turned out to be very accurate. But also they named names—references to Roger Vincent as the chairman and Howard Lever as chief executive. People don't do that unless they are insiders."

"What sort of references?"

"Nothing specific. Just questions mostly, like 'When are Vincent and Lever going to own up to their failings?' Stuff like that. Lots of leading questions that invited negative answers." He paused. "Whoever sent it knew exactly what he was doing and I reckon he got the answers he wanted."

"BHA bashing has certainly become the sport of choice among the media. There was a very damning segment shown on television on Saturday afternoon."

"I saw it," Gordon said. "It was repeated on the *Inside Racing Show* on Sunday morning."

"Do people really want a return to governance of racing by the Jockey Club?"

"Maybe it's more a feeling that the BHA experiment has failed."

"It's not an experiment," I said angrily. "And it hasn't failed. You have all been hoodwinked by someone who is controlling the agenda. Wake up, will you? Before racing is damaged beyond repair."

"Can I quote you?" Gordon said, always the journalist.

"Yes," I said. "Loudly and often."

CRISPIN CALLED my cell at eleven o'clock.

"Ian Tulloch has raised the money," he said. "I think he saw it as a test of his chairmanship." He laughed. "If Roger Vincent could raise a hundred grand in a morning, then so would Ian Tulloch. But quicker. Although I suspect he had to give some personal guarantees to the banks."

"Yes—but will he agree to paying it?"

"Ah, dear boy, that's the hundred-thousand-pound question. We'll just have to wait and see what our friend Leonardo has to say. There was nothing in today's mail."

"The announcement didn't make it into the paper on Saturday. It's in today's so let's hope it does the trick."

"We've had the results back from the labs about Fontwell," Crispin said. "Apparently, someone grated up the skin of something called cassava and mixed it in with one of the salads. That was what made the stewards ill."

"Cassava," I repeated. "It's a type of sweet potato, a major source of carbohydrate in much of the tropical world. But it also contains dangerous toxins unless it's cooked properly."

"You seem to know a lot about it," Crispin said.

"I once did a peacekeeping tour with the UN in Rwanda. Cassava was the staple for most of the population. They grew tons of the stuff, and often it was all *we* had to eat as well. We had to learn how to cook it properly or we'd have starved or died of the poison."

"Well, that's what made the stewards ill at Fontwell and I expect it was the same stuff used in the ginger cake at Ascot. Apparently, the ginger would have covered the slightly bitter taste of the cassava skin, as the vinaigrette dressing did in the salad. How easy is it to get hold of this cassava stuff in the UK?"

"I suspect most supermarkets sell it," I said, "especially where there's a sizable African community. And there will be plenty of specialist food shops in London that will stock it. It's what comes of having such a multicultural city."

"So not much chance of finding out where it came from."

"No," I agreed. "But I might have another lead worth following."

"Oh yes?"

"Can we meet later? It's something I'd rather talk to you about face-to-face."

"Sure," he said. "I'll be in the office all day."

"I'd rather not meet you in the office, if you don't mind. How about at El Vino at one o'clock."

"Fine," he said. "I'll be there."

He hung up. But before I had a chance to put the phone down, it rang again. However, it wasn't Crispin ringing back, it was Quentin Calderfield.

"I've just heard from the CPS," he said. "They are going to offer no evidence in Kenneth's case."

"So he'll be acquitted?"

"Absolutely." I could clearly hear the relief in his voice.

"Good," I said. "Thank you for letting me know."

"Kenneth's a very lucky boy," Quentin said.

"Perhaps he can now get his life back on track."

There was a lengthy pause on the other end of the line. "Yes. Maybe he can."

I reckoned that Faye must have found the right moment over the weekend to tell Quentin that Kenneth didn't want to be a lawyer.

"So will he be going back into chambers?" I asked. It was a leading question, but I had to know for sure.

"No," Quentin said firmly. "We've decided he should take a break from the law for a while. Until people have forgotten about this little episode. Kenneth is going traveling round the world. Taking a gap year, I think they call it."

"Good idea," I said.

There was another pause from his end.

"Right," I said. "Anything else?"

"No," he said. "Well, yes, actually, there is. Did you know about Kenneth?"

"What about him?" I asked. It was not that I was particularly trying to be vague. I just didn't want to give away any secrets if Quentin didn't know them already.

"That he's queer."

"Quentin," I said forcefully, "that is not a word you should ever use. I find it offensive and so would many others. You'd never dare use it in court, now would you?"

"No," he said, "I suppose you're right. But did you know?"

"Yes," I said, "I knew that Ken was gay."

"When did you find out?"

"Does it matter?" I asked.

"Why didn't you tell me?"

"Ken's sexuality is his own affair. It was not my place to tell you. But I did say to him that he should stop living a lie and tell you himself."

I could tell from the lengthy pause that QC,QC wasn't very pleased with his brother-in-law. He clearly thought that I should have been more loyal to him than I had been to his son.

He obviously didn't know me very well.

Was our uneasy companionship of the last few weeks about to revert to the frostier relationship of the previous ten years?

Probably.

CRISPIN WAS at the El Vino wine bar ahead of me.

"What's with the sling?" Crispin said as I walked over to him.

"Dislocated shoulder," I said. "A car hit me."

"That was careless." He smiled.

"Very," I agreed. "But I don't think it was an accident."

"Explain."

"Someone tried to kill me."

Crispin looked suitably shocked. "Are you serious?"

"Perfectly. Someone tried to run me down in the road outside my house on Friday evening and they very nearly succeeded."

"Have you been to the police?"

"They didn't believe me. I'd had quite a few drinks and they clearly thought I was drunk and making up a story to cover the fact that I hadn't seen the car coming and had simply wandered out in front of it. But, I'm telling you, it was a deliberate act."

"I assume that the car didn't stop."

"You assume correctly."

"That's dreadful."

"Indeed it is. And, ever since, I've been very careful to keep my eyes open and watch my back in case of another attempt."

"Why would anyone want to kill you?"

"I think it was to stop me talking to Matthew Unwin."

Crispin sat in silence, staring at me, waiting for me to go on.

"I went to see him yesterday in Long Lartin Prison. I

was initially looking for some sort of link between him, Graham Perry, Richard Young and Duncan Johnson."

"Other than they had horses doped or had been threatened with it?"

"Exactly," I said. "Graham Perry was once Matthew Unwin's assistant trainer, but the two haven't remained friends. It seems it was an acrimonious parting. As for the other two, there seems to be no common factor with either of them."

"So why would someone want to stop you speaking to Unwin?"

"I now know it wasn't any link between the trainers that was important, it was something else entirely."

"What?"

"Hyperactive children."

"What about them?"

"Matthew Unwin's fifteen-year-old son is hyperactive. The poor boy had meningitis as a baby and he subsequently developed ADHD."

"So?"

"Unwin's wife is a leading light in an ADHD support group. She knows the parents of almost every severely hyperactive child in southeast England."

"And?"

"One of those parents is a member of the BHA Board."

I told Crispin everything Matthew Unwin had told me and also the limited amount I'd since been able to discover on the Internet.

"Do you think we should go to the police?" he asked.

"How can we?" I said. "We have absolutely no proof.

It's all circumstantial and guesswork. Lots of people have hyperactive kids. We'll need far more than that or the police will just laugh at us again and send us on our way."

"Then maybe we should confront him."

"What good will that do? He'll only deny it. And we can't prove anything. No, what we really need to do is catch him in the act of collecting his loot."

"That could be risky, dear boy," Crispin said, "especially as he's tried to kill you once before."

"All the more reason why we should nail the bastard before he tries again and succeeds."

33

I took a taxi from El Vino to the offices of the *London Telegraph* to see Gordon Tuttle. He came down to meet me in the lobby.

"What did you do?" he asked, looking at my arm in the sling.

"Fell off a horse," I said.

I could tell that he didn't believe me. "You don't ride."

"That's why I fell off," I said. "What about those briefing documents?"

"I've made you copies," he said, handing over two sheets of paper. "Just don't tell my editor I gave them to you. He's very protective of our sources, even the anonymous ones."

"Thanks," I said, looking down at the sheets. As Gordon had said, each of them had "Press Briefing" printed large across the top and one major fact underneath, in capital letters and underlined, followed by a series of leading questions concerning the suitability of the BHA to govern racing. I read through them all and I could understand how they had molded press opinion. Whoever had written this had been very clever.

"Why do you think you had an exclusive with the second briefing? The first clearly went to all the papers because they all ran the same story."

"I've no idea," Gordon said. "Maybe because we printed quite a large spread for the first one. And perhaps we were more critical of the BHA than the other papers."

There was no *perhaps* about it.

"I read your follow-up piece this morning," I said. "Not quite as bad, but you were hardly complimentary either."

"Maybe not," he said, "but at least I wasn't calling for a return of the Jockey Club."

"It will take more than that to stop the media bandwagon against the BHA."

"I did take notice of what you said, you know, and I agree with you."

"Then bloody well say so in your paper. Start a campaign to keep things as they are. You know I'm right."

He didn't reply and I feared that my pleadings were falling on deaf ears.

"Will you do me a favor, then?" I said. "Off the record."

He was careful. "What favor?"

"Ask your financial fellows if there are any City rumors flying round about someone."

"What sort of rumors?"

"Anything to do with personal financial difficulties or irregularity."

"Of whom?"

I told him and his eyebrows lifted almost to his hairline.

"Is there a story here, Jeff?" he asked seriously, his journalistic antennae twitching madly.

"No. Not yet. But if there is, you'll have it."

"An exclusive?"

"It depends on what you find out." I gave him one of my business cards. "Call me this evening round seven on my cell."

ON MY WAY back to Willesden I called in at my usual car-rental office and picked an inconspicuous silver Ford Fiesta with no sporty stripes painted on the bodywork. It had to be an automatic, I told the agent behind the desk without telling him exactly why. Meanwhile, the sling was carefully hidden out of sight in my coat pocket.

I found a free parking spot at the far end of Spezia Road and cautiously made my way to my front door without being attacked or molested.

"Good day?" Lydia asked as I walked into the kitchen.

"Pretty good," I said. "And you?"

"Contracts were exchanged on two of my sales today," she said, beaming with excitement. "One of them was a one-bedroom flat that has sold for over half a million. That's fifty-five grand over the asking price!"

"Well done," I said, giving her a hug and a kiss.

She smiled. "And the other was an unremarkable house in Kilburn that went for one-point-two. It's crazy out there. London prices are going through the roof. How do people have the money?"

"God knows," I said. "It must be hell for first-time buyers."

Our little two-bedroom flat seemed to be an ever-improving investment. Perhaps we might just be able to afford that house in the country with a garden for our kids to play in.

"What's for supper?" I asked.

"Spaghetti bolognese," she said. "I'm getting it now."

"Great. I'm starving."

Gordon Tuttle from the *London Telegraph* called.

"Bingo," Gordon said into my ear. "You were absolutely right."

"How so?"

"According to a mate of mine at the City desk, your man is indeed thought to be in a spot of financial hot water. He's absolutely loaded, as we know, but his money is all tied up in a trust created by his grandfather and the word is that the family trustees are being bloody-minded about doling it out. It seems they don't approve of his gambling habits and are refusing to bankroll his debts."

"A cash flow crisis," I said.

"Absolutely. Asset-rich but cash-poor. Not an uncommon problem."

"But are his difficulties widely known?"

"Possibly they are among the City editors, but certainly not by the general public. No one is sure enough of the facts to publish, for fear of being sued. But my mate tells me he's certain it's true, he just can't prove it."

"That's really helpful," I said. "Thank you."

"Come on, Jeff, what's the story?"

"Sorry, Gordon, I don't want to be sued either," I replied. "If and when there's a story, you will get it first. I promise."

I hung up.

"Don't want to be sued about what?" Lydia asked, standing at the sink, draining the pasta from a saucepan.

"It's nothing important," I said.

Lydia turned around and slammed the pan down onto the counter with a crash.

"Why won't you ever tell me things?" she said loudly and crossly. "You won't even tell me why someone tried to kill you and now I feel that you're keeping me in the dark over something else." She put her hands on her hips. "Jeff, I need to know what's going on in your life. It matters to me."

"I didn't want to trouble you," I said, rather taken aback by the strength of her reaction.

"But don't you understand, you silly man, I want to be troubled. I need to be able to support you. I know that you've been really worried these last few days because you've been so quiet, but I don't know how to help because you won't talk to me."

WE HAD our spaghetti bolognese sitting at the kitchen table and I told her it all—everything from the events at Cheltenham, when Matthew Unwin killed Jordan Furness, right up to the financial information just given to me an hour previously by Gordon Tuttle.

I went through the whole story in chronological order, including the disruption of racing at Ascot, Aintree and Fontwell Park, the doping of horses at Cheltenham and at Graham Perry's yard, the notes from Leonardo, the replies in *The Times*, the first drop of money, my visit to Matthew Unwin. Everything.

"But if you know who this Leonardo really is," she said, "why don't you and Crispin just go to the police and tell them?"

"Because we have no proof. I'm not even sure it's the right man. The only evidence I have is that he has a hyperactive child and he's in a spot of trouble with his cash flow. That would hardly convince a jury, now would it? The police would probably tell me to get lost."

"But isn't it worth a try?"

"No," I said. "All that would happen is the police would interview him and that would alert the target to our suspicions. He would simply go to ground and we would never prove anything. We need to catch him in the act. To get him as he collects the next drop."

"Target?"

"Surveillance-speak," I said. "It's how I now think of him."

"So what will you do next?"

"It would be simple if I could be certain that he'd use the same place for the next drop. Then I could just wait for him to fall into a trap. But I can't be sure of that, so I'm going to follow him."

"Do you know where he is?"

"I assume he's at his home."

"Hadn't you better make sure? You have to find him in order to follow him."

I smiled. "You sound like my old army instructor. And you're right. That's why I rented a car."

"I'll come with you," Lydia said.

"No," I said, "you don't have to get involved."

"I want to get involved," Lydia said. "You know that you could do with some help driving, especially if you have to follow him on foot."

She was right. It was difficult, if not impossible, to follow someone properly on your own if they first used a private vehicle and then, say, a bus or a train. By the time you had found somewhere to leave your own car, the target would be long gone.

"How about work?"

"They can survive for a day without me. I'll call in sick."

"OK," I said. "That would be wonderful. But I was intending to get up really early."

"How early?"

"About three-thirty."

"Then we had better go to bed now," she said, pushing away her empty plate.

I smiled at her. "What a great plan."

THE TRAFFIC was very light in the middle of the night and we were outside the target's house in Weybridge, Surrey, well before five o'clock, a good hour or more before sunrise, with only the occasional streetlamp lighting the darkness.

Lydia had giggled most of the way there.

"What are you laughing about?" I'd asked her as we'd got into the car.

"You," she'd said, wiping tears from her eyes. "I can't get used to what you look like."

The brown woolen beanie plus wig and the goatee were making a further appearance, together with the black roll-neck sweater, dark-blue jeans and my brown leather bomber jacket. In addition, I had placed small cotton balls in my mouth between my teeth and cheeks to alter the shape of my face.

I was going to follow someone who knew what I looked like so I needed to change my appearance. A pair of thick-rimmed glasses completed the disguise.

"What's in the bag?" Lydia had asked as I'd placed it on the backseat.

"Camera with telephoto lens and night vision equipment," I'd replied. "Just in case."

"And what about your sling?" she had asked disapprovingly.

"I'll do without it. My shoulder is not so sore today, and wearing a sling would be far too memorable. I've got lots of painkillers." I had tapped my pant pocket.

I stopped the car on the tree-lined suburban street, with its multimillion-pound mansions set back away from the road, mostly hidden behind high hedges or fences, electronic wrought-iron security gates shut tight across their driveways.

"Why are we here so early?" Lydia asked.

"First, to ensure we get here before the target goes out. And, second, because today is garbage pickup day in these parts."

"Garbage pickup day?"

"Yes," I said. "Look." I pointed at the line of wheeled garbage cans standing outside the houses, all of them placed outside the gates. "The council website states that the cans have to be outside before seven a.m. I correctly assumed that people would put them out the night before."

"But what about them?" Lydia asked.

"Watch," I said.

I got out of the car, being careful not to slam the door shut, lifted two black garbage bags out of the car trunk and walked straight across to the can standing outside the target's house.

I lifted the lid, removed the bags from within and replaced them with those I had brought from home full of our own trash. I then calmly walked back and placed the target's trash in the trunk.

"What was that for?" Lydia asked when I'd got back in the car.

"I want to find out about our target's life and rummaging through his garbage may reveal more than just what he had for dinner last night. We should have at least an hour before there's any movement from within."

I drove the few miles to the Cobham freeway service area. Even at this early hour, the freeway was busy, with lines of heavy-goods vehicles trying to beat the traffic before the usual morning rush. However, the service area's parking lot was sparsely occupied, with only about twenty cars, all of them parked close to the buildings. I opted for an empty space some distance away from any other vehicle, one conveniently situated right beneath one of the high-powered floodlights that lit up the area almost like daylight.

I donned a pair of latex gloves, laid out a waterproof sheet in the car trunk and then emptied the target's garbage bags onto it.

One at a time, I picked up each item and returned it to one of the bags.

"What are you looking for in particular?" Lydia asked as she stood and watched me, shivering slightly in the cool of the April morning.

"I'm not really sure," I said vaguely, "but I'll know if I find it."

There were all sorts of things, including plastic food wrappers, several soup cartons, used Kleenex, about a dozen eye makeup–removal pads, some potato peelings, wet coffee grounds, an old toothbrush, a broken lightbulb and some rather smelly fish skins.

The recycle police would have had a field day, as there

were also three empty Coca-Cola cans, an instant coffee jar, numerous glossy magazines and various other papers that all should have been sent for recycling rather than for landfill.

There were, however, among the mass of true rubbish, a couple of items of great interest to me.

One was an empty plastic bubble strip of the drug Ritalin. *Methylphenidate hydrochloride* was clearly printed on its underside.

The second was a letter from a major bookmaking firm.

I nearly missed it, as the letter had been ripped into small pieces, and I noticed the torn-off top corner only because of the bookmaker's distinctive red logo printed on it. I dug around among the other detritus until I had the majority of the letter, albeit in about fifteen separate bits, some of them rather badly stained with coffee.

As I found the pieces, Lydia laid them out on the backseat of the car like a jigsaw puzzle.

Although some of the letter was missing, the two central paragraphs were easily readable.

Thank you for the recent payment into your account, which has gone some way towards clearing the outstanding debt. Under normal circumstances, we would be unable to accept such a large payment in cash, but, in this instance, we are prepared to make an exception in order to reduce the substantial balance of the account.

However, we should make it clear that this recent payment is in no way an end of the matter. The rest of the debt remains overdue, and, unless we receive a similar further sum before the end of this current month, we will have no option but to seek alternative methods to recover the unpaid amount.

I wondered what the "alternative methods" might be. All gambling used to be considered as a simple wager between friends, freely offered and accepted, viewed by the law as a "gentleman's agreement" or as a "debt of honor," and hence any debts accruing were unenforceable by a court.

"Alternative methods," then, would often involve large men with baseball bats turning up on one's doorstep and demanding to be paid or else.

However, since the passing of the 2005 Gambling Act, a bet made with a licensed bookmaker was now deemed to be a binding contract and any debt arising from it could therefore be recovered by legal means, although the baseball bats were still usually quicker and cheaper in the long run.

I looked again at the fragments of the letter.

Was the recent payment, made in cash, a result of the hundred thousand pounds thrown from the train?

There was nothing else of any significance to be found, but what I had was enough to confirm my suspicions. I was now certain we had the right man.

I kept the pieces of the letter and the Ritalin bubble

strip but returned the rest of the trash to the bags, which I then placed in a dumpster situated behind the service area's hamburger outlet, while Lydia went in to buy some protein bars to dispel her hunger pains.

"We'd better get moving," I said to Lydia. "I don't want the target to leave home before we get back."

34

We were back on the road at Weybridge by a quarter to six, by which time the sky in the east was lightening with the coming of the day.

It certainly wasn't the best place to sit and watch.

I would have preferred a nice urban street with lots of parked cars to hide among, not this wide-open space where a waiting car tended to stand out like a sore thumb. The only mitigating factor was that, as I couldn't see through the high hedges to look into the house windows, the occupants couldn't see out to spot me either.

I parked the car so that we were on the opposite side of the road, about thirty yards away and facing the target's gateway. There was just one other vehicle parked, a white van on the same side as us but much farther down towards the junction at the end.

"Exciting, isn't it?" Lydia said sarcastically after we

had been there for half an hour without seeing any movement in the road whatsoever, either in a car or on foot.

"Stunning," I agreed. "Relax. We could be here for hours, maybe even for days. It depends on when the target calls the drop."

Lydia looked at me. "You're joking?"

"No, I'm not."

"What about when I need to pee?"

"Do you?"

"Not now, but I may in a couple of hours."

"Didn't you go before we left?"

"Yes, but I also had a cup of tea and some orange juice while you were in the shower."

"That was careless," I said, smiling.

"Seriously, what *do* we do when we need to pee?"

"Personally, I've always used a plastic drink bottle."

"Oh, great," Lydia said. "Do you have a funnel as well?"

It was, however, a serious problem for anyone carrying out surveillance.

The mistaken police shooting of an innocent Brazilian man, Jean Charles de Menezes, at a London tube station in July 2005, was largely as a result of misidentification caused by one of the observation team being away from his post answering a call of nature. That gave rise to rushed and incorrect assumptions, and ultimately to de Menezes being shot seven times in the head with dum-dum bullets. Unsurprisingly, he died at the scene.

"We'll just have to hope that the target moves before it becomes necessary for you to."

At about half past six, a man appeared through the gates of the house two down from the target. He had a lively young black Labrador on a lead, and the pair turned away from us and walked off down the road. Someone else farther down appeared with a garbage can, clearly having failed to roll it out the night before, and a second dog walker emerged from a house behind us.

The road was slowly waking up, and a few cars moved up and down.

Lydia and I sat chatting in the front seats, looking for all the world as if sitting and talking in a car in residential Weybridge at six-thirty in the morning was the most natural of pastimes. But I never let my eyes wander for more than a few seconds from the wrought-iron gates across the target's drive.

I had parked the car facing west for two reasons. First, so that we were not looking straight into the rising sun, and, second, because I reckoned that if the target left home by car, he would probably turn west towards either the railway station or to the main road to the freeway. The added bonus was that anyone looking at us from the target's driveway would be staring into the light, which meant that our faces would be in shadow.

The man and his black Lab returned after about twenty minutes and went back into their house without either of them appearing to give us a second glance. The last thing I wanted was the police turning up and asking us awkward questions.

Traffic slowly built up as some of the local residents left home for work. Even though the road could never be classified as busy, other traffic made it easier for us to remain inconspicuous, as drivers turning out of driveways were more on the lookout for moving vehicles than for stationary ones.

At seven-thirty, the council garbage pickup team arrived, making their way up the road behind us, stopping at every driveway to maneuver the garbage cans into the hoist that emptied them automatically into the truck. The three men came slowly past, ignoring us, and I watched as our trash was tipped from the target's can into the truck's compression jaws.

They continued slowly along the road and eventually disappeared around the corner. And still there was no movement of the target's gates.

"I spy with my little eye something beginning with *H*."

Lydia was getting bored.

"Hedge," I said.

"That's not fair!"

"What's not fair about it?" I whined in mock annoyance. "You chose it."

"Yes," she said, "but it was too easy."

"Have another go, then."

"I spy with my little eye something beginning with . . ." She paused and looked around.

"T," I said. *"Target."*

The gates were opening, and we watched as the target walked out through them to the edge of the road, collected his empty garbage can and retreated back inside. After a few moments, the gates closed again.

It all happened so fast that I barely had time to lift the camera from my lap and snap a couple of shots.

"At least we know he's here," I said. "That's a good start."

"He doesn't look much like a villain," Lydia said.

"Appearances can be misleading," I said. "I read somewhere that Al Capone looked very dapper in his handmade three-piece suit as he personally beat a man's brains out."

"But it's still difficult to believe," Lydia said. "He looks so normal."

"Don't be fooled. That normal-looking man tried to kill me, and he's also been disrupting racing for weeks. To say nothing of extorting money by threats and orchestrating a determined campaign in the media to discredit the BHA."

For some time I'd been wondering why he did that. He was a member of the BHA Board, so, by extension, some of the discredit would also fall on him.

It didn't really make any sense.

Suddenly I began to doubt myself.

Was I actually correct? Was this indeed the right man? Or were the bookmaker's letter, the methylphenidate tablets and the hyperactive children all mere coincidences?

I would soon find out.

CRISPIN CALLED my cell at ten past eight as Lydia and I were still waiting outside the target's house.

A note had arrived in the BHA mail from Leonardo, along with another cheap Nokia cell phone.

"Same as before?" I asked excitedly. This is what I'd been hoping for.

"Exactly the same. Another Nokia pay-as-you-go phone with no time and password-protected settings. Incoming calls and texts only."

"And the note? What does that say?"

"'Put the money in a brightly colored canvas bag and await instructions.' Identical to last time."

"So the target has taken the bait," I said. "Now we need to convince Ian Tulloch to give us the green light for the drop."

"I don't suppose he'd have raised the cash if he wasn't prepared to go through with it, but surely the Board will have to be asked first?"

"You might be right," I said, "although I'd much rather the rest of the Board weren't involved. It will only cause a delay. Try and convince Ian Tulloch and Howard Lever to make the decision themselves rather than calling another meeting. Tell them it's really urgent and the decision needs to be made now."

"I doubt if they will make it without at least consulting the others."

"I'm not so sure," I said. "Ian Tulloch has finally secured the role of BHA chairman, something he has coveted for years. I suspect he now believes that he is in total charge and he can do exactly as he likes, and Howard will do as Ian tells him. Play on his vanity and praise his courage in being decisive."

"The Board won't like it if it goes wrong."

"Maybe not," I said. "And they'll like it even less if we throw away another hundred grand of their money for nothing. However, this time I'm sure we'll catch him. But don't say that to Howard or to Ian Tulloch. I don't want either of them knowing we are setting a trap. The fewer people who know, the better. We can't afford a leak."

"I sincerely hope we're doing the right thing, dear boy," Crispin said. "I could really do with not getting sacked. I'm too old to start looking for another job."

I worried that he was wavering.

"Crispin," I said. "If this does go wrong, the BHA will be ancient history and we will all be looking for another job."

"Then it had better not go wrong," Crispin said decisively. "I'll go and see Howard and ask him to call the chairman straightaway, although, to be honest, I'm quite surprised Howard hasn't resigned or been fired by now."

"I suspect that Ian Tulloch may think it's better for Howard to stay until this is all over and then to let him go. That way, all the stories of incompetence may depart with him."

"You're a cynic," Crispin said.

"No, I'm a realist," I replied, laughing. "Now, please go and see Howard. I will wait for the drop instructions. Did the note say anything about when they might come?"

"No," Crispin said. "But last time it was in the afternoon of the same day that the phone arrived."

"You'd better get moving, then, and brief Nigel Green."

We hung up.

"Trouble?" Lydia asked.

"Not at all," I said. "All good. It seems likely that the drop may be on for today."

TEN MINUTES LATER the gates opened again and a woman drove out in a light blue Mini with two children sitting in the back.

"School run," I said.

"Do we follow?" Lydia asked.

"No," I said. "It's him I'm interested in, not his wife or kids."

We waited some more and, after about twenty minutes, the Mini returned minus the children. The gates closed automatically behind it.

"That was exciting—not," said Lydia. "I think I'd rather be at work."

"Hadn't you better call them to say you're not coming in?"

She called her office, doing a fine impression of sickness, even adding a few convincing coughs at the end.

"I'll never believe you again when you say you've got a headache," I said, laughing.

"Maybe not," she said, smiling. "But you'll have to believe me when I say that I do now need to pee."

"There's a filling station down there," I said, pointing ahead and to the right. "I saw it when we arrived. You'll have to walk there for a pee. I'm not leaving. And if the target moves, I'll have to go without you."

Lydia wasn't very happy, but she got out of the Fiesta and hurried off without a word.

Slowly the sun climbed higher in the sky, but still nothing moved in the target's driveway.

Lydia was back in fifteen minutes and she had bought some chocolate bars and two bottles of water.

"Well done," I said, smiling at her.

We sat and waited.

"This is so boring," Lydia said after a while. "Is it always like this?"

"Just be thankful you're dry and comfortable," I said, "and not lying half submerged in a drainage ditch that doubles as an open sewer."

I shivered at the memory. I'd been in that god-awful Afghan ditch for thirty-six hours, baking hot during the day and freezing cold at night.

Thankfully, my thoughts were interrupted by the ringing of my cell.

It was Crispin.

"Howard has spoken to Ian Tulloch and he's given us the OK for the drop."

"Did he consult any of the other Board members?" I asked.

"It seems he called them last night to discuss paying. Howard is absolutely desperate to prevent any trouble at the Guineas meeting. He's staking his whole reputation on that passing off without any problems and he seems positively keen to pay up in order to achieve it."

"He's crazy," I said, although I'd argued for it to happen. "We'll just have to ensure that we catch our friend red-handed. That's the only thing that will guarantee a stop to the disruption."

"How about if we were to confront him with what we already know?" Crispin said. "That would surely be just as good."

"Maybe," I said. "But not so satisfying as getting hard evidence that it was him collecting the loot at the drop."

He laughed. "It's not a game, you know, dear boy."

"Isn't it?" I laughed back.

35

By two o'clock in the afternoon we had eaten all the chocolate bars, Lydia had drunk most of the water and we had exhausted almost every single letter of the alphabet in a marathon game of *I spy.*

Finally, at twenty past two, as I was trying desperately to spy something beginning with *X*, the wrought-iron gates opened and the target drove out in a black BMW, turning west.

I started the rental Fiesta and pulled out behind him.

"He's on his own," I said. "That's good. He's not being dropped off at the station."

I had feared he might take the train, which would have meant leaving Lydia alone with the rental car.

At the end of the road, the target turned away from the railway station towards the M25, the London orbital freeway, which he joined traveling clockwise towards

Heathrow Airport. I settled in behind him with two cars between us.

He left the M25 at Exit 16, taking the entrance ramp to the M4 westbound. Was he going towards the previous drop spot near Pewsey? He had certainly turned in the right direction.

We tailed him past Windsor and the three Slough exits, on towards Reading, where he pulled off the freeway into the service area. I followed.

The BMW stopped close to the parking lot entrance, so I went past and into a space between two cars, from where I could see the target in the rearview mirror.

"Get out and stretch," I said to Lydia.

"Why?"

"Because people who arrive at service areas and then just sit in their cars are suspicious. Like the man in the BMW."

She did as I asked while I went on watching behind. However, the target clearly wasn't interested in us. He had his head down as if looking at something in his lap. I twisted around between the seats and took another photo through the rear window.

After about five minutes, he set off again, rejoining the freeway towards the west, driving conservatively within the speed limit, with Lydia and me three cars behind.

Crispin called my phone and Lydia answered, which surprised him somewhat.

"Put it on speaker," I said.

"I've just had a text on the Nokia phone," Crispin said. "It says to go to Trafalgar Square just like last time."

"The text was sent from the Reading service area on the M4."

"Are you sure?" Crispin said.

"Pretty much."

"So do I need to go to Trafalgar Square?"

"No," I said. "Don't bother."

"You don't think anyone will be watching out for me there?"

"No," I said. "I think Leonardo works alone, and he's driving the car three in front of me westwards down the M4 as we speak."

"Right," Crispin said. "I'll get moving as we planned."

"If it's like last time, you should have plenty of time. The train we caught before left Paddington at three minutes after seven."

"Do you think he'll use the same train?"

"I've no idea," I said. "But everything else has been the same as before."

It was over a week since the last drop and, consequently, sunset was about fifteen minutes later. But the next train from Paddington on that line, after the 7:03 p.m., didn't arrive at the drop site until well past half past eight, by which time it would be completely dark.

"I reckon he'll go for the same train," I said, "unless he has a different drop point in mind. One nearer to London."

THE TARGET turned off the freeway again and into the next service area at Exit 13 near Newbury. Again we followed. And, as before, he stopped the black BMW near the parking lot entrance.

I drove around to a point where I could see him through the gap between two other parked cars.

Once more he was looking down. Texting, I presumed.

After a few minutes, he got out of his car and walked towards the service buildings while I snapped several more shots that clearly showed his face.

"Wait here," I said to Lydia, giving her the camera.

Being careful to see that the target had gone through the doors into the building, I ran over to his BMW. Sure enough, there was a dent in the fender above the right front tire, together with a couple of scratches in the paintwork.

I would bet my shirt that this was the car that had hit me last Friday.

I leaned down and attached the magnetic tracker, which I had recovered from the old rugby ball, to the inside of the wheel well. Just in case we lost sight of him.

I then hurried after the target and followed him past the newsstand and the burger bar into the gents. He went over to one bank of urinals while I went to another, keeping an eye on him via the mirror above the washbasins. As he turned to wash his hands, I moved away and waited for him on the general concourse.

He went straight back out to his car and I rejoined Lydia.

"Crispin called," she said. "He received another text telling him to go to Victoria Station."

"Victoria?" I repeated in some alarm. "There are no

trains from Victoria that go down the right line. I hope we haven't got things wrong."

The target didn't move. He just sat in his car and appeared to recline his seat and take a nap.

"Why did you go over to his car before following him?" Lydia asked.

"To see if there is a dent in the right front fender."

"And is there?"

"Yes," I said. "One consistent with hitting me in Spezia Road last Friday."

Lydia was angry on my behalf. It was almost all I could do to stop her from going over to the BMW to demand why the target had tried to kill me.

"Can't we call the police?" she asked. "Get them to arrest him for attempted murder."

"We know what the police think," I said. "Much better to wait and catch him red-handed with the cash. I also took the opportunity to place a tracking device in his wheel well."

I lifted the receiver from the backseat and it made a reassuring beeping noise in the earpiece when the aerial loop faced towards the BMW.

We went on watching and waiting. I swallowed another painkiller and I took a few more photos, but there was nothing new to see.

After about half an hour, the target sat up and appeared to send another text.

Crispin called almost immediately.

"It says take the Circle Line to Paddington Station and wait."

I breathed a small sigh of relief. We hadn't got it wrong.

I looked at my watch—just coming up to five o'clock.

"OK," I said. "Where are you now?"

"In traffic on Cromwell Road," Crispin said.

"How about Nigel Green?"

"He's at Paddington waiting for my call. Anything to report your end?"

"The target is simply sitting in his car at Chieveley Services off Exit 13. I'll let you know if he moves."

The target had appeared to go back to his nap and Lydia and I went on waiting and watching.

And we waited some more and still we watched.

Time dragged.

"Where do you want to get married?" I asked.

Lydia turned sharply to look at me.

"Is that a proposal?" she asked.

"Maybe," I said.

"Oh."

"You sound disappointed," I said.

"I was rather hoping for the down-on-one-knee treatment."

"Not my style," I said.

"But you *do* mean it?"

"Yes," I said, smiling at her, "I do."

She squealed with delight and I leaned over to kiss her.

"Forget it, sunshine," she said, pulling a face and turning her head away. "I'm not kissing you with all that stuff stuck on your face."

It was not a particularly romantic start to our engagement.

WE REMAINED in the Chieveley Service Area parking lot until after six o'clock, by which time the sunshine of earlier had been replaced by the gloom of low gray clouds and a persistent drizzle as a weather front moved in from the west.

I had been worried that the target might notice that our rented Ford Fiesta had been sitting in the parking lot without moving for rather a long time, so just before five I'd driven it around to the BP filling station and parked in front of the payment kiosk.

It meant that we couldn't actually see the man anymore sitting in his BMW, but we would still see if the car moved. And the one-way traffic in the service area would bring him past us anyway, whichever way he went after that.

Crispin called my phone again.

"*'Buy a first-class ticket to Plymouth,'*" he said. "The text arrived a couple of minutes ago."

"Have you told Nigel?"

"I told him to buy a standard-class ticket to Taunton and wait to be told which train to catch."

Crispin had always been rather miserly with his departmental budget.

"Where are you?" I asked.

"Just turning in to the service area now. Where are you parked?"

"Near the filling station."

"Where's the target?"

"In the main parking lot next to the main service building," I said. "You go into the motel lot near the entrance and wait there."

I didn't want Crispin driving right past the target and being recognized. That would be sure to put a premature end to our plan.

"Right you are," he said. "Just turning in now."

"Good. It's twenty-five miles from here to the drop point that he used last time. If he's using the same place again, then it will take a good forty to forty-five minutes to get there from here. If he also uses the same train. And if it's on time, then it should pass the spot at eight minutes after eight."

There were far too many *if*s for my liking.

"So he should leave here soon," said Crispin. "He'll surely want to be in position in good time."

"If he's using exactly the same routine as before," I said, "he will have to send the board-the-train text at seven o'clock. There's good cell signal here but can he be sure of it en route?"

"How about at the drop point?" Crispin said. "Is there a good signal there?"

"Full signal," I said. "There's an aerial mast right there where the rails cross the bridge. He'd need to be sure of a good signal in order for the Nokia phones to send and receive the text, and quickly. He couldn't afford a delay."

Lydia and I had sent each other several texts to find

out how long they took to arrive. Three to four seconds was average. If the train was moving at a speed of a hundred miles per hour, I had calculated that it traveled almost one hundred and fifty feet every second.

Services from Paddington to Plymouth used a standard Great Western InterCity train, eight cars long, with a diesel-electric engine on either end, a total length of seven hundred and fifty feet.

Hence, the train took about five seconds to pass any given point.

The first-class section was always at the back of the train on the journey away from London.

If Leonardo sent the text exactly when the front of the train passed over the bridge, and allowing for transmission and response times, he might expect the loot to be thrown out a little over five seconds later, into the perfect spot on the treeless grassy bank of the railway embankment.

"Does Nigel know he has to be at the back of the train when he throws out the bag?"

"Yes," replied Crispin, "I've given him a full briefing."

I looked at my watch. Six-thirty.

"I think the target may be staying here to send the board-the-train text," I said. "Crispin, I'll drive round to the motel to pick you up. One car will be easier. You leave yours there. See you in a mo."

I hung up and started the car's engine.

It was a bit of a risk. I would lose sight of the BMW for the few minutes I would need to drive around to the motel and get back, but it was much less of a risk than

Crispin walking through the main parking lot and being spotted by the target.

"You stay here," I said to Lydia. "Go into the filling station shop and keep watch. Call me immediately if the target moves. I'll be back in a couple of minutes."

"I'm sorry but I desperately need another pee," she said. "I didn't want to tell you but now I must. I'm really bursting."

Great, I thought, all that bloody water. I bit my tongue and said nothing. I didn't want to have our first row as an engaged couple so soon after my proposal.

I looked at my watch again. If the target was going to send the board-the-train text from here, we should have a good twenty minutes before he moved.

"OK," I said. "You go to the ladies while I fetch Crispin."

It was a risk, but we needed to be ready to move off as quickly as possible after the text.

Lydia climbed out of the car and went running off towards the main building, holding her knees together in a classic I'm-trying-not-to-pee-in-my-pants mode.

I smiled and drove off around to the motel parking lot to collect Crispin.

"Come on!" I shouted at a slowpoke driver in a flat cap who dawdled at the traffic circle and then crawled along at ten miles per hour. "Come on, I'm in a hurry!" Not that he could hear me. And, of course, it made no difference to his speed or the lack of it.

"Get in the back and lie flat," I said to Crispin when I finally arrived.

He did.

"Where's Lydia?" he asked without batting an eyelid about my appearance. He had seen me in disguise before.

"She's gone to the ladies room," I said. "Stay down."

I drove quickly back towards the main parking lot.

The black BMW had vanished.

36

Bugger!"

"What?" said Crispin from his prone position on the backseat.

"The target's gone."

"He can't have," Crispin said, sitting up.

"But he has," I said. "He must have driven off as I was coming round for you. He can't have been gone for more than a couple of minutes at most."

I screeched to a halt outside the main building and Lydia climbed back into the car.

"He's gone," I said. "We missed him."

"Oh my God," she said. "I'm so sorry."

"It's not your fault," I said, giving her a smile.

No, it had been mine. Stupid, stupid.

I swung the car sharply to the right out of the parking lot, putting the accelerator pedal to the floor, which brought a few stern glances from other motorists.

I drove up to the traffic circle and braked sharply.

"Which way?" I said, mostly to myself.

There were two ways the target could have gone to get to the drop point, assuming it was the same as last time. Either west along the freeway to the next exit and then south or south first, down the A34, and then west. Both routes went via Hungerford and both were equidistant.

I grabbed the tracker receiver and pointed it south down the A34. There was no beeping in the earpiece. I pointed it west. Still nothing.

Panicking, I turned it through a full three hundred and sixty degrees, but there was no sound from it in any direction.

Damn it, I thought.

How I wished the tracker really did have a range of four miles, as my ex–army mate had claimed. The target was already out of range.

But which way had he gone?

I'd been careless—bloody careless.

A car came up behind me and hooted. I was blocking the road.

I took the freeway westwards, racing up the entrance ramp at breakneck speed and causing a large truck to take evasive action to avoid a collision.

"Steady, tiger," said Lydia. "Better to get there late than not at all."

"Sorry," I said, but I still pulled sharply into the outside lane and put my foot down.

Flat out, the Ford Fiesta would have been no match for the target's high-powered BMW. But if he continued as before within the speed limit, I should be catching up to him soon. Provided, of course, that he was on this road.

Lydia held the tracker receiver so that the loop aerial scanned the road ahead.

"Anything?" I asked.

She shook her head and I pressed even harder with my right foot.

"Don't get stopped, dear boy," Crispin said from behind me. "It would be highly ironic if it were the police that prevented us getting to the drop and solving the case."

I glanced down at the speedometer. The little Fiesta was doing well over ninety, so I eased up a little and allowed the needle to slide back to eighty-five. Even that should be fifteen miles per hour faster than the black BMW and we should be catching him hand over fist.

I left the freeway at the next exit, but there was still no sign of the target either visually or on the receiver.

Damn it, I said to myself again.

He must have gone the other way.

"What time is it?" I asked.

"Quarter to seven," Lydia said.

"He'll surely need to stop to compose the text," said Crispin.

"Not if he's previously typed it into the phone," I said. "All he'd have to do then is push the send button."

I turned south and went as fast as I could on the winding road, heading for the town of Hungerford. Lydia went on holding the receiver up towards the windshield.

"I can hear something," she said as I drove into the outskirts of the town. "It's faint, but there's a definite beep."

She rotated the receiver.

"Getting stronger," she said, moving the loop from side to side.

We were the second car in the line at the junction with the A4 when we saw the black BMW pass by from left to right in front of us.

There was a collective sigh of relief from the three of us inside the Fiesta.

The target had indeed gone the other way, but we were now back with him. I pulled out behind and followed as the BMW turned left at the Bear Hotel into Hungerford High Street.

He pulled over halfway up the hill and I went past, stopping a little farther up, from where I could keep watch on him via the rearview mirror. However, as before, he was concentrating not on his surroundings but on something in his lap.

The Nokia phone in Crispin's hand went *beep-beep* as another text arrived.

"Catch the seven-oh-three to Plymouth," Crispin read, but he was on his regular phone to Nigel Green at Paddington Station. "Nigel, get on the seven-oh-three to Plymouth." There was a lengthy pause. "Good. Well done. Speak to you soon." He hung up. "Nigel's safely on the train."

The drop was definitely on and my adrenaline level had started to rise.

THE TARGET remained exactly where he'd stopped in Hungerford for a good ten minutes, seemingly doing nothing but waiting.

"Stay down," I said to Crispin. "We don't want him seeing you."

"What are we going to do when we get to the drop?" Lydia asked. "He'll surely see you then."

"Maybe not," I said. "What I plan to do is to photograph him collecting the loot. That alone will be sufficient to nail him. We don't need a physical confrontation."

"But will it still be light enough to get a picture?" Lydia asked.

"It should be," I said. "Sunset tonight is at eight-oh-seven. That's just a minute before the train is due at the drop."

"If we could see the sun," Lydia said, staring out into the gloom that had seemingly settled in for the night.

"There should still be enough light," I said.

Crispin's phone rang and he answered.

"It's Nigel," he said. "The train's delayed leaving London. Some problem with the signaling."

"How long?" I asked.

Crispin spoke to Nigel.

"They say about five minutes."

I thought that probably meant ten at best.

I checked the *Train Times* app on my iPhone. *Delayed seven minutes,* it said. I was concerned that the light might have faded too much at the drop point.

It was not that I wouldn't be able to see him in the dark that worried me, I had the image-intensifying night vision monocular, but photographs might be a problem. And would the target chance not being able to find the bag of cash if it became too dark? Maybe he had night vision goggles as well, but it would still be a risk.

What would he do? Did he have a backup plan? Would he choose to carry on or abort for today and have another go at it tomorrow?

Did he even know that the train would be late? He must surely have the same information on a smartphone as I did.

Bloody trains, I thought. Never on time when you really needed them.

"So what do we do?" Crispin said.

"Wait for the target to move. He's running this show. Either he goes on to the drop or else he goes back to London. It's his choice."

The black BMW pulled out and came up the hill towards us.

"Keep down," I said. "He's going on."

The target swept past and I waited until he was out of sight around the bend before I followed.

"Don't lose him," Crispin said, concerned that he was getting away.

"I'd rather let him go a bit than allow him to spot us.

The roads are too empty now to follow closely. And we do know where he's going."

"Are you sure?"

"Yes," I said with confidence. "The grassy embankment at New Mill is the perfect spot. Everything he's done has indicated that he's using the same drop point."

"I hope you're right," Crispin said.

So did I.

We took Salisbury Road out of Hungerford, through the village of East Grafton and on towards Pewsey.

"He's still there in front," Lydia said, holding up the tracker receiver with the loop pointing forward through the Fiesta's windshield. "I can hear the beeping in my ear, but it's very faint."

"OK," I said and speeded up, chancing us getting a little closer.

Crispin's phone went again.

"The train is on the move," he said. "Nine minutes late leaving Paddington."

It was going to be a toss-up, I thought.

Even if the train lost no more time, it would be pretty dark by the time it arrived at New Mill. It was currently nearly an hour before the expected drop time and, thanks to the low cloud, it was already beginning to get quite murky.

As if to emphasize the fact, I was flashed by an oncoming car for not having my headlights on.

I could see the brake lights of the car in front as he slowed to take the numerous bends. Close enough, I thought.

"Still there?" I asked Lydia.

She nodded. "Slightly stronger."

We continued on towards the drop point, taking a right turn down the country road to the hamlet of New Mill. Here I slowed right down. I wanted to make absolutely sure that the target couldn't think he had been followed, so I was giving him plenty of time to park his car before we drove past.

"We'll go right through," I said. "Crispin, you stay down. Lydia and I will try and see where the target has stopped his car."

The road curved to the left through the hamlet, passing under the railway twice, once at either end, with the drop point next to the second bridge.

Now I switched the headlights on full. It would be more difficult for someone to look through the windshield into the car against the bright light.

I almost missed the black BMW, hidden as it was in a field just beyond the second bridge. I caught a fleeting glance of it at the last moment through an open gateway as I drove past and, only then, because the loud beeping of the tracker receiver told us that we were right next to it.

"Good," I said. "He's on the south side of the railway as expected. I'll go round to the north and stop there."

Rather than turning the Fiesta around and having to pass him again, I drove the three sides of a sizable triangle to return to the hamlet of New Mill from the far end, pulling into another farm gateway about a hundred and fifty yards north of the bridge.

"Time?" I asked.

"Seven-fifty," Crispin said. "The train should be at Newbury."

I again checked the *Train Times* app on my phone.

"According to this, it's still nine minutes late. We will wait here until after the next text."

"Then what?" Lydia asked.

"I'll creep forward to get some photos. You and Crispin remain here in the car."

"You must be joking, dear boy," Crispin said from behind me. "I haven't come all the way from London just to sit in the car and miss all the action."

"Nor have I," said Lydia. "We're coming with you."

I didn't like it. One person, especially one trained in surveillance techniques, could move so much more stealthily than three.

Crispin was an intelligence analyst more used to sitting at a desk than operating in the field as a covert agent. And Lydia was hardly turned out for scrabbling around in the dark, dressed as she was in a skirt and heels.

"You may blow the whole thing," I said, but I could tell I was fighting a losing battle. They desperately wanted to see the bag of cash thrown off the train.

"OK," I said eventually. "But you'll both have to stay well back near the bridge. I will go on ahead alone."

They reluctantly agreed.

The Nokia phone went *beep-beep.*

"'Go to the rearmost door lobby and throw the bag out the window on the left-hand side of the train as soon as you get the next text,'" Crispin read off the screen, and he was calling Nigel using the other phone. "You throw the bag out the window on the left-hand side from the rearmost door. Do it immediately when I text you. Got that? Good."

He hung up.

"Exactly the same pattern as last time," I said.

"It worked before," said Crispin, "and our friend clearly expects that it will do so again. But if he thinks he's going to get away with it a second time, he's in for quite a shock."

"But I *do* intend to let him get away with it," I said. "At least for now. We just watch from afar, take photographs and stay well hidden. We will have all we need to confront him later with the police."

Departed Newbury seven minutes late.

"The train has caught up a couple of minutes," I said. I removed my brown leather bomber jacket and replaced the wig and brown beanie with a black balaclava that showed my eyes peeping through two small holes, with another small hole for my mouth.

"That's really scary," Lydia said as she watched me put it on. "It makes you look like a rapist."

"Maybe," I said, smiling at her in reassurance. "But a white face in the dark can so easily give you away. Come on, it's time to go."

37

The three of us climbed out of the Fiesta without slamming any of the doors.

"Stay under the bridge until the very last moment and then just go far enough forward to see the train as it passes along the embankment," I said. "The target should be well down the track from the bridge, but don't take any chances. When you've seen the drop, go straight back to the car and wait for me there."

They both nodded.

I still didn't like it. I would have much preferred them to stay in the vehicle the whole time.

"And, Crispin, don't forget, in all the excitement, to send the text to Nigel."

"Already set, dear boy," he said. "All I have to do is push the button."

It was another risk. The text from the target to the

Nokia phone would take three to four seconds. That from Crispin to Nigel would take the same. Adding the response times could result in a full ten-second delay between the first text being sent and the bag being thrown out the window. The train would move some fifteen hundred feet in ten seconds. Twice as far as the target was expecting. That would probably put the drop point close to the far end of the grassy embankment.

"You will almost have to anticipate the text arriving," I whispered to Crispin. "As soon as you hear the train be ready, and keep the Nokia close to your ear. The trains are loud."

"OK," he whispered back. "Will do."

We moved forward along the road until we were under the brick arch of the bridge. I had the night vision monocular fixed over my right eye with the harness and I held my long-lens camera at the ready.

A train suddenly rattled noisily over our heads and, for a moment, I panicked that we were not yet in position. It took me a few seconds to realize that the train was going the other way.

I took some deep breaths and allowed my heart rate to return to normal.

Stupid, I thought. Keep calm. It would be at least another ten minutes before the correct train arrived. But keeping calm was easier said than done. My blood adrenaline concentration was again up to stratospheric levels.

"You two stay here," I whispered to Crispin and Lydia. Even though it was still quite light in the open air, it was almost completely dark under the bridge. However,

I could see their faces clearly using night vision. Lydia's eyes were wide open in excitement.

I left the two of them there and walked forward alone, silently, scanning the ground in front of me to ensure I didn't inadvertently trip or snap a twig.

I moved out from under the bridge and kept to the road for ten or fifteen yards before moving to my right. There were a few bushes in the field to the side of the grassy bank and I worked my way forward to them, crawling across the wet ground on my stomach at one point so as not to be seen.

I took up position lying in a narrow gap between two of the bushes. From here I could observe the full length of the embankment but hoped that I was invisible to anyone looking the other way.

I lay very still and searched with my eyes for any movement. Movement was always easy to spot and could be detected even by one's peripheral vision. Movement was a dead giveaway.

And there it was.

My adrenaline level rose another notch.

A shadowy figure was changing his position away to my left, close to the base of the embankment.

I carefully lifted the camera. By now it was getting quite dark, but there was still plenty of light remaining for the camera's sensitive digital-imaging system.

I took a couple of shots, but even at maximum zoom there was nothing much to see. The figure appeared merely as a dark splodge against a slightly lighter ground.

I could hear a train approaching in the distance. This must be it.

I changed the camera to video mode, widened the view slightly and switched it on record.

THE ORANGE canvas bag of cash was clearly visible through the camera viewfinder as it was thrown out the train window, and I captured the whole thing as it arced forward and landed at a point about halfway up the grassy bank towards the far end.

I continued to film and zoomed in as the shadowy figure climbed rapidly up to the spot to retrieve the bag.

It was all over in less than a minute and seemed so quick and easy.

I stayed exactly where I was between the bushes.

The target would have to come back close to my hiding point in order to get back to his car. I was confident that he wouldn't spot me in the shadows and I would use the chance to get some close-up shots as he passed by.

I watched as he hurried along the base of the embankment back towards the bridge.

He came within ten yards of where I lay in the field, almost running, but not moving so fast that I didn't have plenty of time to take a couple of photos of him holding the distinctive orange bag in his gloved left hand.

But I couldn't see his face. It was covered.

He too was wearing a balaclava, with just his two eyes and mouth visible.

I recognized the eyes, but I had hoped to get some full-facial shots to provide positive, undeniable identification. I snapped a third picture as he hurried past.

I smiled to myself.

Gotcha!

The photos may not be ideal, but they were enough. Especially if I could get a shot of him getting into his car with its distinctive personalized number plate.

I waited a few moments and then stood up and started quickly back towards the road.

THE FIRST indication that things had not gone entirely to plan was a woman's scream emanating from under the bridge. In fact, it was not so much a scream as a primeval screech of sheer terror.

I felt a distinct chill run down my spine.

I recognized that scream. It was Lydia.

Oh my God!

I sprinted back to the road and turned left towards the bridge, shouting out at the top of my voice. "Leave her alone! Leave her alone!"

There was a body lying facedown in the road at the far end of the bridge, I could see clearly with night vision.

Oh my God, no! Please, no!

I rushed forward and bent down, my heart beating away at twenty to the dozen in my chest.

But it wasn't Lydia, it was Crispin and he was groaning slightly.

"Jeff, is that you?" said a frightened voice away to my right.

I turned my head and saw Lydia cowering near the wall at the side of the bridge.

"Yes," I said. "What happened?"

"We thought it was you," she said. "It looked like you." She was crying.

"What happened?" I asked again.

"We saw someone in a balaclava and Crispin said it was you. We called out and came back." She sobbed. "But it wasn't you."

I turned Crispin over so he was lying on his back. He groaned again as I moved him. I looked at his face. His eyes were wide with fear and he was trying to speak, but no sound was coming out, just a trickle of blood ran from the side of his mouth. I opened his coat. The whole of the front of his shirt was wet with blood.

"Call the police," I shouted at Lydia. "Quickly. And an ambulance. He's been stabbed."

She was already dialing on her cell.

What an absolute mess.

Why hadn't they gone back to the car and stayed there like I'd asked them to?

"Which way did the man go?" I asked when she'd finished the call.

She pointed at the small metal gate that I'd climbed over last time, when I'd collected the rugby ball. "Over there."

Towards the path up the slope to the tracks. I reckoned he would be trying to get back to his car by going up and over the railway lines rather than past me through the bridge.

"Look after Crispin," I said to Lydia, but I was afraid that he might be beyond help. The blood from his mouth had increased from a trickle to a flood and his eyes had started to roll back into his head. I'd seen that look before in Afghanistan. In fact, I'd seen it all too often.

It's not a game, you know, dear boy, Crispin had said to me only that morning.

No, it wasn't.

Oh, Crispin, my colleague and my friend, why hadn't you remained in the car?

The anger rose in my throat—the anger that I had vowed to remember on the day of the void Grand National.

I leaped over the metal gate and ran up the slope to the tracks.

THE TARGET was standing there at the top of the slope facing me, a bloodied knife in his right hand and the bag of cash in his left, as if somehow waiting for me to appear.

I stood slightly below, facing him.

I reached up and took off my balaclava, then I peeled away the stuck-on facial hair and removed the cotton balls from inside my mouth.

If he was surprised to see me, he didn't look it. But, then, it was difficult to tell as I could only see his eyes and mouth.

"Hello, Bill," I said.

That focused his attention, but still he said nothing.

"I know it's you," I said.

He switched the knife into his left hand, together with the bag, and lifted his hand to his head and pulled off his balaclava. Then he took the familiar tortoiseshell spectacles from his pant pocket and put them on his face.

Bill Ripley. Member of the BHA Board. Grandson of a Scottish Earl.

Leonardo. Our friend. One and the same.

"How did you know it was me?" he said.

"I just did," I replied. "I followed you here from Weybridge."

"Unwin," he said, nodding. "Bloody Matthew Unwin. I knew that if you visited him it would be a problem. I should have killed you when I had the chance."

"You nearly did," I said, instinctively rubbing my shoulder.

"How's your colleague?" He waved the knife.

"I think he's dead."

It didn't seem to surprise him or particularly to worry him. He just pursed his lips and nodded once as if accepting that it was all over.

"Just for a couple of hundred thousand quid," I said. "Was it worth it?"

"It wasn't really about the money," he said, "although the first lot was useful."

"To pay off some of the debt with your bookmaker?"

He was clearly shocked that I knew, but he slowly nodded.

"Was it also about the press briefing documents you sent to the newspapers?"

He nodded again.

Just the one man—extortionist and whistle-blower.

"Why?"

"They took away my birthright." He said it almost casually.

"Who did?"

"The bloody BHA." He lifted his chin. "Ripleys have been senior stewards of the Jockey Club for over two hundred years. *We* should be in charge of British racing, not some bloody insurance salesman who doesn't know his withers from his fetlocks. It is my right. And it should be my son's right."

"Your hyperactive son?"

He stared at me with contempt in his eyes.

In the distance I could hear the sirens of approaching authority. Bill Ripley clearly heard them too.

I took a step towards him and he retreated. I took a second step and he backed away some more.

There was a high-pitched ringing sound in my ears.

Bill turned his head slightly to the left.

I couldn't tell if he saw it coming or not.

Either way, he turned his head back to look directly at me and didn't move a muscle.

The evening express from Plymouth to London struck Bill Ripley full on at over a hundred miles per hour.

One moment, he was standing there just a few feet away from me, and, the next, the train was thundering by in his place.

As suddenly as it arrived, the train was gone and so was Bill, with nothing to show that he had ever been standing there other than a shower of fifty-pound notes fluttering down around me like confetti.

I reached into my pocket, removed my phone and called Gordon Tuttle at the *London Telegraph*.

"Gordon?" I said. "I've got you a story."